"You know I wouldn't force your hand, Georgiana."

Barrett took a seat on the chaise longue, facing her. "But think of your aunt," he continued. "You must see that she'll feel much more comfortable if she can introduce her English niece as my betrothed."

Once more, resentment flared in Georgie. What ruthless, scoundrelly methods he employed.

"I don't need you to remind me of my duty to my Aunt Letty," she said stiffly. "By all means, let's be 'betrothed.'"

He leaned forward, clasping her hands in his. His touch set her skin atingle. "Let us first complete all the formalities of a 'betrothal,'" he said.

Then suddenly Barrett was down on one knee before her. He let go of her hands, cupped her face instead, and pressed his mouth against hers...

"A stolen kiss," he murmured. "But then you might say it is a fiancé's prerogative."

A Daring Alliance

Also by Karla Hocker

A Bid for Independence
A Madcap Scheme
*An Honorable Affair**

Published by
WARNER BOOKS

*forthcoming

A Daring Alliance

KARLA HOCKER

WARNER BOOKS

A Warner Communications Company

WARNER BOOKS EDITION

Warner Books, Inc.
666 Fifth Avenue
New York, N.Y. 10103

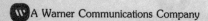 A Warner Communications Company

Printed in the United States of America

First Printing: August, 1988

10 9 8 7 6 5 4 3 2 1

To Esther and Judy

One

She knew she was behaving badly, yet she did not stop. She'd rather be apostrophized a shockingly fast girl than spend another moment in Lady Sparling's stuffy drawing room.

"Georgie!"

Pursued by the exasperated yet decorously subdued call, Lady Georgiana Rutledge whisked through the half-open glass doors and onto the moon-bathed terrace of her hostess's elegant Kensington home. She was too late. Her niece, the Honorable Fenella Codrington, stepped out after her, foiling Georgie's plan of escape.

"Don't try to hide," Fenella said sharply. The agitated motion of her fan stirred tendrils of ash-blond hair against her plump cheeks. "Mama has had her eye on you for the past fifteen minutes. She's well aware that you're again trying to slip away."

Georgie suppressed a sigh. No matter what she did, or wished to do, either her half sister Lady Charlotte Codrington or Fenella was on hand to tell her nay. It was enough to give the most compliant girl the dismals! And compliance was not one of Georgie's virtues.

She leaned against the spiky trunk of a potted rattan palm. The night was cool, as befitting the first week of May, and she had wrapped her shawl around her shoulders. Yet the rough bark pierced the soft layer of casimir as Fenella's voice cut through the sweet notes played by the string quartet in the large chamber next to the drawing room.

"Do you hear, Georgie? You must come inside this instant!"

Georgie's eyes narrowed as she looked at her niece. "Why won't your mama leave me alone? I've told her more than once that I find no pleasure in being dragged from ball to rout to soiree."

"How can Mama find a husband for you if you don't show yourself?"

"She had better concentrate her matchmaking on you, Fenella. *I* am not about to let myself be sold off to the highest bidder!"

Fenella closed her fan with a snap. Her hazel eyes, so commonplace when compared to Georgiana's wide, deep-brown orbs, glittered angrily. She was very much aware that her dark-haired, willowy Aunt Georgie, despite the "Rutledge nose," completely cast her into the shade. It was also indisputable that Fenella was two years older than Georgie, and had yet to receive her first offer. Some spiteful tongues were starting to wag that Fenella, at two-and-twenty, gave promise of becoming an ape leader.

If only Uncle William had not insisted that Georgie put off her black gloves quite six months earlier than etiquette dictated! If only Georgie were still immured at Wolversham Court in Sussex! Or if she were to be married soon....

Fenella tried for a conciliatory tone. "Please come, Georgie. Mama wishes to introduce you to Sir Perceval Hargrave."

Georgiana pushed away from the palm but did not move toward the drawing room. She strolled into the dark shadows cast by giant chestnut trees bordering the flagged terrace. Only her silvery white gown of gossamer silk was still visible to Fenella.

"Come back!" Fenella peered into the darkness. Her voice rose. "Mama will be so cross if you misbehave again! It is not at all the thing for a young lady to walk off alone."

"I've no objection to your company, Fenella."

"Oh!" Fenella gritted her teeth against the anger boiling in her. Of course Georgie did not object to her company;

Georgie was not the one who'd look dumpy and plain next to Fenella. "You're impossible! You were always wild and irresponsible, but now you are a veritable shrew, Georgiana Rutledge!"

With her fingers laced tightly through the ends of her crochet shawl, Georgie spun to face her niece. "I have never been a simpering miss, Fenella. And I shan't turn into one now—especially not for the gratification of any London fop or dandy!"

"There's no need to get on your high ropes." Hesitantly, as though hidden dangers were lurking in the shadows, Fenella stepped closer to Georgiana. "I only meant to point out that your tongue has turned into a double-edged sword since Aubrey's death."

"Don't!" Georgie tried to block out Fenella's voice. Any mention of her brother's death at *Fuentes de Oñoro* in the previous year was bearable only when it came from Charles and James, or from Blakeney and Lewis, for they understood their sister's hurt and loneliness. At times it seemed to her that William, too, sensed her loss, perhaps experienced similar feelings; but her older half brother did not permit himself a show of emotion.

"You can't deny it!" Fenella, arms akimbo, came to a halt before Georgie. Her high-pitched voice defeated every effort to ignore it. "In the fortnight that you've spent in town you have driven away the most eligible men who paid attention to you, and alienated some of my suitors as well with your cutting remarks."

"Cowardly fribbles!" said Georgie. "Useless weaklings, padded and stuffed by their tailors to show the semblance of a man. Too lily-livered to fight in the Peninsula! Hiding instead behind the skirts of London hostesses."

Fenella drew herself up. Still, her eyes were level only with Georgiana's chin. "And what would you say, pray tell, if *all* the young gentlemen were to join Wellington in his campaign? Who, I ask you, would dance with us?"

Georgie didn't give a button if none of the fops ever asked her to dance, but she swallowed the biting rejoinder. Fenella would not believe her. "It is not Wellington's campaign," she pointed out instead. "The fight against Napoleon is—or should be—the topmost concern of every Englishman."

"That kind of speech, *dear Aunt*, is exactly what will turn the gentlemen against you. A female should not concern herself with politics. She should—" Fenella broke off and whirled around guiltily as the drawing room doors behind her opened wide, spilling a path of bright light across the terrace.

Georgie, quite untroubled by guilt and only thinking fleetingly that now she'd be in the suds once again, watched as her half sister swept out. Flanked by two lackeys carrying lanterns, and followed by a score of heated ladies and gentlemen, Lady Charlotte Codrington was a force to be reckoned with.

Charlotte smiled brightly at Georgiana. "A stroke of genius, my love! I'm so glad you asked me to come outside, but you should have waited until I arranged for the lights, you naughty puss." She turned to her daughter. "And you, Fenella, without your shawl!"

Meekly Fenella accepted the lacy confection her mama held out to her and draped it across her plump shoulders. She was given no opportunity to apologize, for Charlotte, her silken robes trailing across the flagstones, sailed determinedly toward Georgiana.

"But I shan't scold you girls," Charlotte said, still with that forced smile on her face. "After all, I was young once—and not too long ago I should say!" She tittered. "I perfectly understand your impatience to escape from that stuffy room."

Georgie felt her elbow clutched in a relentless grip. Silently, reluctantly, she applauded her half sister's masterful performance and accompanied her to join the other guests under the hastily strung lanterns.

She was acquainted with most of the company, but her eyes were drawn to a stranger. He stood in the background, alone. A tall man, his skin deeply tanned as though he had lived in warmer climes. One broad shoulder resting against the window frame behind him, dark brows raised slightly under a shock of black hair, he gave every appearance of a man wishing himself elsewhere.

My feelings exactly, Georgie thought sympathetically.

A sharp pinch on her arm hastened her steps. She tore her gaze away from the tall, dark gentleman and hurried along beside Charlotte.

Barrett Gray had indeed been wishing himself anywhere but at this damnably boring soiree when Lady Charlotte harpooned him to populate the terrace. Or rather, Barrett thought cynically, he had been suffered to tag along since he had been standing beside his uncle when the formidable matron issued her not-to-be-refused invitation to Sir Charles Gray. The lady, to whom Sir Charles had referred as "dreadfully high in the instep," was, no doubt, unaware that Barrett Gray was an American, and engaged in trade.

When Barrett stepped outside and saw the pale shimmer of gowns in the deep shadows beneath the trees, his mouth curved in a wry smile. Undoubtedly, a closer scrutiny of the darkness would also reveal two male truants. Barrett drew back, allowing his uncle Sir Charles Gray and his cousin Robert to step forward and direct the footmen in stringing the colored paper lanterns among them.

Pools of blue, red, yellow, orange, and green rippled, blended, and separated again as the lanterns danced on a soft breeze. The shorter, plumper of the young ladies, after accepting a shawl from Lady Charlotte, scuttled closer. Her face burned as though touched by the Caribbean sun Barrett had left behind a few weeks ago—undoubtedly the result of a rare trimming.

He recognized that truant as Miss Fenella Codrington, Lady Charlotte's daughter, to whom he had been introduced earlier in the evening. A simpering, giggling miss! Barrett averted his eyes, hoping to escape her notice. When he heard her speak to his cousin Robert, boring him with a catalog of events planned for her London season, he breathed a sigh of relief.

Chalking up the evening as an utter waste of his brief time in England, Barrett propped his shoulder against the window frame behind him. His eyes slid past Miss Codrington. He could detect no male companions, but when Lady Charlotte propelled the second young lady into the bright lights he raised his brows, incredulous. Either the gentlemen had taken to their heels when discovery threatened by the arrival of the formidable Lady Charlotte—or else Englishmen were slowtops indeed.

Tall and slender, the girl moved with the grace of a dancer. She seemed to float beside the heavier Lady Charlotte. He saw her glance his way, but before he could straighten to bow, she increased her pace. The soft material of her gown, touched by red and blue, then green and orange, as she walked beneath the lights, hugged her supple curves and flowed against her shapely legs.

Barrett pushed himself away from the window frame. He inhaled sharply as the girl stopped before Miss Codrington and Robert, just beneath a yellow lantern. The light reflected in her dark eyes and spread a netting of soft gold over her deep brown hair. Her voice, rich and melodious, sang in his ears; and her fragrance, fresh and sweet, drifted caressingly about him.

She looked past his cousin Robert, straight at him. Their eyes met and held for one breathless moment. Her mouth curved in a tentative smile as though she wished to greet him.

"Georgiana!" Lady Charlotte's voice, sharp, demanding, broke the tenuous contact between them. The young lady turned and walked away in response to the summons.

Barrett filled his lungs with air. *Georgiana!*

Georgie's smile lingered as she moved toward her half sister. The flutter that had started in her breast when she met the stranger's intent green gaze ceased. Her clamoring thoughts did not still as rapidly.

He's no longer bored! He no longer wishes himself elsewhere! And neither did she.

Georgie knew she hadn't seen him at any of the events she had attended since coming to London. It would have been impossible *not* to notice his height and broad shoulders or the deep bronze of his skin that made his eyes appear the color of newly unfurled birch leaves.

Georgiana had never indulged in dreams of a knight on a white charger carrying her into the sunset. She'd been too busy organizing a school for the village children at Wolversham and teaching them their letters and numbers in an effort to ease her mourning—first for her father, then for her brother Aubrey.

But if, she thought, *if I were inclined to indulge myself— just for the duration of my stay in town, of course—the tall, dark stranger would be just the man to suit my dreams.*

"A penny for your thoughts, Lady Georgiana."

Georgie blinked at the gentleman standing beside Charlotte. He smiled, but his voice had sounded peevish. Sir Perceval Hargrave. Thank goodness, she had at least caught his name when Charlotte introduced him. She really must pull herself together!

"A reckless offer, Sir Perceval. They're foolish fancies, I'm afraid. Not worth a farthing."

"You must let me be the judge of that, dear lady."

She didn't like Sir Perceval, Georgie decided. He might be handsome with his wavy, reddish brown hair and blue eyes. He might be top of the trees in his beautifully tailored evening coat and high shirt points. Aubrey, she felt certain, would have condemned him as a dapper-dog and a gabster. The way Charlotte was beaming at him, it was obvious she looked upon the baronet as a possible suitor for her half sister's hand. But Georgie didn't want a suitor. Only dreams, and a quick return to Wolversham Court.

"If you will excuse me," she murmured. "I promised Sir Charles a game of piquet."

"Alas, I am crushed!" Sir Perceval placed a hand over his heart and bowed. "I had hoped you'd honor me with a dance, Lady Georgiana. In fact, I had counted on it."

"What nonsense is this, Georgie?" Charlotte's carefully darkened brows drew together over the bridge of her proud nose. "Sir Charles knows better than to draw you off to the card room when there's dancing for the young people. Go on, Georgie! With Sir Percy. Unless"—Charlotte smiled a sweetly triumphant smile—"you're promised to one of the other gentlemen?"

Georgie assumed what she hoped was a mortified look. "Surely you noticed, Charlotte, that my dance program remains sadly empty," she said, praying that the eagle-eyed matron was unaware of the methods she had employed to maintain that pristine condition of the gilt-edged card dangling from her wrist. "Sir Perceval could solicit my hand for a dozen dances and not infringe on another's time."

It was Charlotte who looked mortified. Had the girl no pride? Before she could open her mouth to utter a reprimand, Sir Perceval Hargrave spoke up, doubt and chagrin raising his voice to an imprudent level.

"You don't say, Lady Georgiana! A beautiful young lady like you, and not asked to dance! Why, it's unbelievable! There must be a reason . . . ah, I mean . . . only reason I can think of is that every male in London has suddenly been struck blind. That would account for it, I daresay."

"Alas," Georgie said mournfully. "I do not dance at all well, and I have no conversation. I've stepped on more toes, literally and figuratively speaking, during my first ball than another lady would in a lifetime."

Sir Percy looked taken aback, wondering if his pursuit of the Lady Georgiana was worth the embarrassment it might cause him. Lady Charlotte Codrington had hinted at a great fortune, and the gal was not at all bad looking. He studied her furtively. Something *must* be wrong with Lady Georgiana since Lady Charlotte had been most persistent in wishing to introduce him to the heiress. Most chaperons would snatch their charges away if he so much as glanced at them. It was only too well known among the *ton* that his pockets were to let and that he must marry well—and soon—if he wished to save his encumbered estates.

"Let's take a turn on the dance floor," Sir Percy said bravely if without enthusiasm. "I wager you won't do too badly under my guidance."

Conceited fop! Only knowledge that Charlotte would complain to William, Georgie's half brother and much tried guardian, kept the words from being spoken aloud. "I dare not, Sir Perceval. It's a waltz I hear playing."

"Ah, you've not received permission to waltz," Sir Percy said, relieved.

"On the contrary. The Countess Lieven was most gracious when I attended Almack's subscription ball. She introduced me to Lord Ebrington, and I received permission to waltz with him. Only he took the most ignominious tumble, and we didn't get to finish the dance. No one else," Georgie finished on a sigh, "has asked me to waltz since."

"Oh, I say! Ebrington is a most accomplished dancer! A few lessons perhaps . . . or, ah—" Sir Perceval came to a stammering halt. He was not about to give up on Lady Georgiana, but he wished he could extricate himself from this embarrassing situation so that he might think of a better way to pursue the rich young lady.

"Mayhap you'd like to teach me? Now?" Georgiana smiled up at the perspiring baronet. "Shall we waltz, Sir Percy?"

He inserted two fingers under his starched collar and tugged. Words seemed to fail him. He was relieved of the necessity to reply from quite unexpected quarters.

"Seems to me, in England gentlemen are a dying breed."

Georgie whirled when she heard the lazy, deep-voiced drawl. Aubrey's voice had taken on just that tone when he had reminisced about his two-year stay across the Atlantic. She encountered the smiling gaze of the bronzed, green-eyed stranger.

"I'd be more than happy to oblige, Miss Georgiana."

"You're an American!"

"Barrett Gray from Norfolk in Virginia. At your service, Miss Georgiana. And here's my cousin Robert Gray, who promised he'd perform any necessary introductions."

"That was before I realized you'd put me to the blush." Robert, blue-gray eyes alight with laughter beneath his shock of unruly blond hair, bowed gracefully. "Lady Charlotte. Georgie. Pray forgive my boorish relative. Grew up among barbarians, don't y'know."

Charlotte extended two fingers. "How d'ye do, Mr. Gray.

No doubt you've come to England to acquire a bit of polish. Very commendable," she said graciously. "Robert can't rival Sir Percy here in elegance of dress, especially out of uniform, but you won't go wrong if you listen to your cousin's advice. He'll soon show you the ropes, Mr. Gray."

"Aye, that he will," Barrett said equably. Encountering Georgiana's look, a mixture of rueful apology, laughter, and inquiry, he added, "And no doubt he'll also get around to recommending me to Miss Georgiana as a dance partner. In his own good time, of course."

"It's *Lady* Georgiana," Sir Perceval cut in. "And she's promised to *me* for this waltz!"

"That's not the way I see it." Barrett's voice didn't lose its lazy drawl, but his jaw tightened and the hint of a frown shadowed his forehead.

"Mr. Gray. Sir Perceval." Georgiana looked from one to the other. "Perhaps I may be allowed to state my preference?"

"That's the dandy, Georgie," Robert said gleefully. "Give 'em both the set-down they deserve, and then let's you and me show them how to waltz. After all, *I* taught you."

Georgie's mouth curved upward. "Because you lost to Lewis and Blakeney. And you a naval officer! Fie! After seven years at sea, you still haven't a head for cards."

"No one can win against your twin brothers," Robert grumbled. "There's many a time I might have suspected them of Greeking practices if I hadn't known them all my life. But come now, Georgie, before these two hotheads create an international incident."

"The waltz is long finished, Robert. And besides"—she looked at Barrett, a frank, open gaze, free of coquetry and guile—"I'd rather take a turn on the terrace and hear about America."

Barrett offered his arm, wondering whether she, like so many of the English, would ask him if Indians always wore feathers in their hair. "What do you wish to hear, Lady Georgiana? Where shall I start?"

Georgie, placing her fingers lightly on his sleeve, was silent. Now that he was so close to her, Mr. Barrett Gray appeared overpowering. He took her breath away. No weakling he; no useless fribble. Through the material of his sleeve she felt the steel of rippling muscles.

"Well," she said after a moment. "You might tell me of your home. Is it at all like the Sussex coast?"

Barrett looked at her with approving warmth. "You're the first person I met—aside from my uncle and cousin—who knows that Norfolk is a coastal town."

He lunged into a description of Serendip, the spacious home his parents Edward and Sarah Gray had built in 1788; where Barrett had lived since he was four years old, where his young brother Franklin had been born, and where Sarah had died of a fever.

As Barrett spoke of sand dunes and long stretches of beach, of cypress swamps draped in Spanish moss, of Serendip resting peacefully and cool in the center of twenty acres of shady woods, he realized that he could hardly wait to see the place and his father after his latest stay—fifteen long months—at the Gray plantation on St. Croix. Even the knowledge that Franklin would never again return to Serendip could not detract from Barrett's longing.

"Then you were born in England, Mr. Gray?"

The sound of Georgiana's melodious voice broke into his musings. *Damn!* How long had he been silent, staring at the border of white and red peonies? He hadn't even noticed that they had walked the length of the terrace and had stopped, away from the colorful lights and the other guests.

"Pardon me for woolgathering, Lady Georgiana. It's been a long time since I was at Serendip, and describing it to you made me realize that I miss it."

In the dark, Georgiana could not see his face clearly, but a flash of white teeth told her he was smiling.

"But to answer your question," he said. "Yes, I was born in England. As were a great many of my countrymen. Nevertheless, we're all Americans now. Naturalized Americans."

She nodded. "Like my Aunt Letty in Boston. Aubrey told me all about that when he returned from his visit to your country."

Taking her elbow, Barrett guided Georgiana back to the lighted part of the terrace. "I wonder how many ladies named Letty live in Boston. I visit there quite often. My father's business partner Caleb Morris owns a house in Summer Street. One of his neighbors is Mrs. Lyman Bainbridge. Lady Letty as she is called fondly, even by the starchy Bostonians.''

"She is my aunt!"

A smile lurked in his green eyes as he looked down at her. "I should have known when Robert called you Georgie. Two years ago, I met a very enthusiastic young Englishman at one of Lady Letty's dinners. Mr. Rutledge spoke often of his sister Georgie. He planned to bring her to America and to settle in Virginia or in Georgia, just as soon as he whipped Napoleon Bonaparte. Aubrey is your brother, isn't he?''

Barrett saw her eyes take on a dark, shuttered look. "Yes," she said brusquely. After a pause, she added, "Aubrey won't return to America. He was killed in Spain."

"I am sorry, Georgie." Barrett's hands, warm and strong, closed around her upper arms. He said no more, but his silence was more comforting than mere words could have been.

William Rutledge, Fifth Earl of Wolversham, tossed his hat and gloves to Lord Codrington's butler. "No need to announce me, Sellers. I'll find my own way. Is my sister still at luncheon?"

"No, my lord. Her ladyship and Miss Fenella are in the blue salon. I'll send word to Lady Georgiana that you are here."

"Tell her I'm driving my bays. That'll send her scurrying."

Mothers of nubile daughters had been casting out lures to William for the past two decades, while the daughters and many a comely young widow kept exercising their wits for new ways of attracting his attention. Yet, at four-and-forty, he remained staunchly dedicated to bachelor life, a situation he himself attributed to the existence of his numerous younger half siblings. William had always felt more paternal toward them than had their sire. It was William's sense of duty that now carried him into Charlotte's blue salon to fetch Georgie, the youngest of the

Rutledges, and to take her to the House of Commons. Charlotte had refused point-blank to accompany the girl.

Georgiana had always shown an unladylike interest in politics and matters of world affairs. When Aubrey returned from his tour of the United States of America, Georgie's interest had focused in particular on that new, republican country. William could find no fault with Georgie's preoccupation. It was Charlotte who called her a bluestocking.

Without ceremony, the Earl of Wolversham turned the knob and pushed open the door to the blue salon, surprising his sister and his niece as they sat over cups of coffee and tore his character to shreds.

"Your uncle is a fool. He's convinced he knows how to handle Georgiana," Charlotte was saying in a tone of voice that left no doubt of her opinion to the contrary. "Hence he indulges her one moment, and the next he'll forbid her going to tea at the vicar's house! The only sensible decision he ever made was to bring her to me for the season."

"Uncle William is so very brittle-tempered. Thank goodness he's not *my* guardian. I'd—" Fenella broke off when her mother emitted an indignant cry and jumped up as though a hat pin had been driven through the upholstery of her chair.

"William!" Charlotte's high color assumed an even deeper hue. "I didn't know you arrived."

"That is very obvious." William joined the two ladies before the imposing Adams mantel.

"I really must speak to Codrington about the slipshod manners of his servants," Charlotte said angrily. "What can Sellers be thinking of? If he's getting too old to come upstairs and announce my visitors, he must be retired!"

"Don't blame Sellers for your getting caught with your tongue running on like a fiddlestick, Charlotte. I told him he need not announce me." William eased himself onto a short couch which, as he knew from bitter experience, was dashed uncomfortable but more up to his weight than any other piece of furnishing in the salon.

"Tell me why the deuce you can't accompany Georgie to

hear the debates when I'm all but paying you to take her around?'' he said with a scowl.

Gathering the shreds of her dignity, Charlotte resumed her seat beside Fenella. "Because I promised to attend Maria Sefton's tea this afternoon and because, dear brother, Georgiana should accompany me and Fenella. Sir Perceval Hargrave has been very marked in his attentions to Georgiana, and I know for a fact that he plans to be there."

"That basket-scrambler! Don't tell me you've encouraged him to dangle after Georgie!" William's fist smacked against the carved arm of the couch. "I won't have it! Gad, Charlotte! The man's a gazetted fortune hunter."

"Be that as it may, William. You brought her to town to find a husband, did you not?" Charlotte said sharply. "Since Sir Percy's appearance last week Georgiana has finally shown an interest in attending some of the entertainments to which we've been invited. Before that I had to drag the dratted girl by her ears. I had to watch her like a hawk lest she slip away and hide herself in the library or''—Charlotte shuddered in remembered embarrassment— "outside."

Fenella's eyes darted from her mother to her uncle. "I don't believe Georgie likes Sir Percy," she said, demurely lowering her gaze to her folded hands. "She avoids him when she can. I believe she has been so agreeable lately because she's been looking for Robert Gray's American cousin. Only he's never shown himself anywhere except at Lady Sparling's boring soiree in Kensington."

"Rubbish!" Charlotte would have said more, but at that moment Georgie made a tempestuous entrance, still fumbling with the buttons on her soft kid gloves and her hat askew.

"You're an angel to take me, William!" Georgie, oblivious to the strained atmosphere in the salon, planted kisses on her guardian's dark brows. "May I drive the bays? Please, dearest William?"

"Not in town, Georgie." Smiling indulgently, he said, "But since you didn't keep me waiting, we'll drive out to Richmond later on this week and you may handle the ribbons. Now, are you ready to go, Georgie? Don't want to be late. The Prime Minister is expected this afternoon.''

"You can't go out looking as though you've crawled backward through a hedge!'' Eyes snapping angrily, Charlotte rose to fuss over Georgie's clothing.

William would have none of it. "Looks fine as five-pence.'' He glanced at Georgie's deep rose walking dress and matching spencer with black braiding and thought proudly that she looked very well indeed. Her eyes sparkled with excitement, and the soft glow in her cheeks was even more pleasing than the very becoming gown.

"Let's not keep the horses standing,'' he said, pushing Georgiana toward the door.

"Enjoy your tea at Lady Sefton's,'' Georgie called over her shoulder, then, giving her hat a quick shove to the left, whisked out into the corridor.

In perfect charity with each other, Georgie and William drove from Upper Brook Street to Westminster. "You may return for us at six,'' William told his groom as they got down before the Houses of Parliament.

When he and Georgie entered the lobby, William grinned down at his ward. "I have a little surprise for you. I've arranged that you may sit on the balcony overlooking the Tories' side. You'll have a good view, and you'll be able to hear much better than from the Strangers Gallery.''

Georgiana gave a cry of joy, hastily stifled when William scowled. "Thank you, best of brothers! This afternoon will make up for many a dull party I must attend this month.''

His brow smoothed. "Ungrateful chit,'' he said without heat. "If you knew what I had to go through to get you invited to those dull parties! Off you go now. Just up those stairs and you'll be on the balcony. I'd take you, but I must take my seat if I want to speak before the Prime Minister arrives.''

"Will you speak *for* repeal of the Orders in Council, William? And Spencer Perceval? Surely he won't side with those who wish to lay more trade restrictions on American shippers?''

William gave her shoulder a quick pat. "Not many voices

will be heard against repeal of the Orders. After all, none of us wants to fight America; it's Boney we're after."

Georgiana ascended the narrow flight of stairs. The stairwell was dark and she had to feel her way, but by the time she reached the balcony landing, her eyes had adjusted to the gloom. A buzz of voices reached her from below. Someone rapped a gavel. Then one voice, which she recognized as that of William's Whig friend, Henry Brougham, filled the hall below and rose to the balcony.

Quickly she moved to the gallery rail. As she took her seat, a movement on her left caught her attention. Georgie turned and met the smiling green gaze of Mr. Barrett Gray.

Two

Georgiana caught her breath. After watching for him during the past week at such illustrious gatherings as Mrs. Drummond-Burrell's musicale and Countess Lieven's ball, she was unprepared for a meeting on the gallery of the House of Commons. To cover her confusion she inclined her head in a fair imitation of Charlotte's regal nod. "Mr. Gray."

The American rose. His long stride made nothing of the distance of a dozen or so seats separating them. "It's lonely up here," he said with a bow and a disarmingly crooked grin. "May I sit with you, Lady Georgiana?"

Georgie's stiffness melted. "Please do. You see, William cannot be with me since he's planning to speak."

"The Earl of Wolversham?" said Barrett, who had learned quite a bit about Lady Georgiana Rutledge and her various relations from his uncle and his cousin. "So that's why you're here."

"Well, in part." She looked amused as though she

guessed he didn't believe it was interest in politics that brought her. "And you, Mr. Gray? Did Sir Charles drag you to these revered halls?"

"Do you think I can be easily dragged? No, Lady Georgiana. My uncle merely arranged that I need not sit in the Strangers Gallery." Barrett sat forward a little, glancing down into the vast hall below. "Where is your brother? Has he taken his seat yet?"

Georgie pulled an opera glass from her reticule. After a brief scan of the chamber below, she offered the glass to Barrett. "Would you like to take a look, Mr. Gray? William is seated in the fifth row of benches. The very tall, dark-haired man speaking to Mr. Wilberforce."

Barrett leaned over the gallery rail. "Ah, yes. There can be no doubt."

"You noted the resemblance to Aubrey."

Barrett turned, fearing he had caused once again that sharp look of pain that had drained the lovely bloom from her cheeks and had blanched and tightened her mouth when he mentioned Aubrey Rutledge during their last meeting. She was smiling, however, and he thought he detected a twinkle in her velvety brown eyes, but in the dim light of the balcony he could not be certain.

"It's the Rutledge beak," Georgie said. "All of us have it to some extent." She turned her head so that Barrett could judge her nose in profile. "Poor William, though, has been blessed with the unmitigated original."

He studied her for such a long time that Georgie's face grew warm. She tried to see his expression but could not do so without turning. Losing patience, she swiveled on the bench to face him. "My nose is not *that* large! Surely you've seen all of it by now."

"Not too long, not too short. Hmm . . . narrow with sensitive nostrils, and a delicate arch." Tilting his head this way and that, Barrett prolonged the game until the mulish set of her jaw warned him of her rising temper. "Yes, indeed, Lady Georgiana. I've admired aristocratic little noses like yours on the cameos found in Italy."

"What a bouncer!" The firm mouth relaxed, and he

could hear the laughter in her voice. "But you do know how to turn a pretty compliment, Mr. Gray."

Sounds of booing and stamping drew Georgie's attention to the hall below. "Listen," she said. "That is Mr. John Gladstone speaking. He's a shipowner, testifying in favor of the Orders in Council, but as you can hear, the majority of members do not agree with his views."

"I'm indeed glad to hear it, Lady Georgiana. When my father's last letter reached me on St. Croix, President Madison had just signed the bill imposing a ninety-day embargo on all trade with England. I fear our Congress will demand still harsher measures if England does not repeal her Orders."

"Then America should not trade with France!"

"We're a neutral country, Lady Georgiana, and demand to be treated as such. If we import silks and wines from France, and if we carry goods from the French West Indies, we also ship great quantities of grain and flour to the British troops in Portugal and Spain."

Georgiana leaned over the rail, pretending an interest in the proceedings below. "I know," she said after a while. Many a time had she used the same argument when one of her brothers' friends or Charlotte's acquaintances insisted that the trade restrictions imposed on the United States by the English government should be enlarged and severely enforced. Yet she could not bear the American's implied criticism of British protective measures.

"England has been at war with France for almost two decades," she said quietly. "We must win. If we do not, all of Europe will be lost to Napoleon Bonaparte."

"Many Americans feel just as you do, Lady Georgiana. We prove it by supplying the British troops, and," Barrett added in a low voice, "some men fight beside their English cousins in the Peninsula."

Georgie turned to him, a question in her eyes. There was no doubting his sincerity or his seriousness, but before she could speak and assure him that the preposterous Orders in Council were bound to be repealed, Barrett's face had taken on a stern, implacable look. "We are, however, no longer a colony, at the mercy and whim of a capricious king. Mark my words, Lady Georgiana, if matters do not change fast, America will stop *all* trade with England.''

''Nonsense!'' From the corner of her eye, Georgie caught sight of William rising. Resolutely she fixed her full attention on Mr. Barrett Gray. This was much more interesting than William's predictable comments. *Her* debate with Mr. Gray was exciting, stimulating. So he believed the Americans could do without trade, did he? ''What,'' she inquired softly, ''would Ameica do without Birmingham? She could not even shave herself, or catch her mice without Birmingham steel.''

Barrett gave a short bark of laughter, but Georgie did not mistake it for amusement. ''If America cannot shave herself,'' he said harshly, ''she can *shave old England,* as the battles of Bunker Hill and Saratoga so plainly evince. And as to mousing—I ask you, Lady Georgiana, who manufactured the mousetrap in which Cornwallis was taken?''

Georgie raised her hand in the gesture of a fencer acknowledging a hit. ''Touché, Mr. Gray. But surely you're not suggesting there might be war between England and America!''

''I hope not.'' Already Barrett regretted his outburst. She was, after all, only a very young lady. And English. The young ladies of Richmond, New York, and Boston might show an understanding of political matters equal to that of their brothers; a very few days in London had shown him that young English ladies had the understanding of a peahen, seeing only the brilliant feathers and the size of fortune boasted by the sprigs of the English nobility.

Yet Barrett felt compelled to say, ''There's no doubt, however, that there will be trouble if the British navy continues to stop our ships. American merchant vessels are seized and held for no reason whatsoever, our goods are confiscated, and our sailors are impressed into the English navy. I tell you, it's intolerable!''

A spatter of applause marked the end of Lord Wolversham's brief speech. Aware that William would be looking for her, Georgie rose, dutifully clapping her hands. For

William's sake she smiled, but her words, addressed to Barrett, were delivered in freezing accents.

"Mr. Gray! Only English deserters are taken from American ships."

"Thousands of them, Lady Georgiana? That speaks ill of conditions in the British navy, does it not? But believe me, our secretary of state did not exaggerate when he announced that more than six thousand American sailors have been impressed by the British."

Coldly she said, "Thank you for your company. I'm afraid I must leave now. My brother has finished speaking."

"You're not staying to hear the Prime Minister, Lady Georgiana? He should arrive any moment."

Dash it! How could she have forgotten! William would not yet be waiting downstairs, and neither would the carriage be outside!

Barrett handed her the opera glass. "I hope to see you again before I return home."

She had half turned away, but stopped and said, "You're leaving England? I understood you had only just arrived." There was a curiously hollow sensation in the pit of her stomach—a condition caused, of course, by his outrageous statements on the British navy. The sooner he left, the better! He'd only find himself in the suds if he voiced his opinion to others as he had to her!

"I did not come on a visit, Lady Georgiana. There was a small matter of business requiring my personal attention at Whitehall, but it has been taken care of, and I must leave for Bristol very shortly. I'll be sailing as soon as my ship is fully outfitted."

He lightly clasped her elbow and guided her toward the stairs. Impossible now to say that she had not planned to leave until after Mr. Perceval's speech. She'd take a hackney even if it meant a thundering scold from William.

"*Your* ship, Mr. Gray?" she said to break the uncomfortable silence between them. "Are you a sea captain, then?"

"I have my captain's papers, yes. But I traveled as supercargo on the *Boston Belle*. She's jointly owned by my father and his friend Caleb Morris and carried a load of sugar and rum in which I hold several shares.''

''You shipped rum!'' Georgie, glaring at him indignantly, stopped on the half landing of the narrow stairs. ''Rum!'' she repeated. ''When you could have brought grain! Our farmers cannot grow enough wheat to meet the needs at home, let alone those of our troops!''

''Before a battle, Lady Georgiana, every man in the British navy is issued a ration of grog, a potation of rum, sugar, and water. And in the army as well, soldiers are given a measure of rum.''

His stiff, tutorial voice made her cheeks sting. ''No doubt you're right, Mr. Gray. I do not know. Rum was not a topic Aubrey mentioned in his letters from Portugal.''

Slowly Georgie resumed her descent. As she followed the last twist of the stairs, the lobby came into view. She saw Spencer Perceval cross from the street entrance toward the corridor leading to the vast hall where the House of Commons conducted its business.

The sharp crack of a pistol shot in the lobby exploded in her ears. Georgie started and stumbled against Barrett. She choked down the scream rising in her throat. Not ten feet from her, Mr. Perceval lay sprawled on the floor.

Barrett's arms closed around her, protectively drawing her face against his coat—but not before she had seen the blood and the man, still pointing a pistol at the Prime Minister.

Shouts echoed in the lobby. ''A surgeon! Mr. Perceval is shot!''

Footsteps pounded in the corridors as members of the House of Lords and the Commons came running from all directions.

Firmly Georgie pushed against the broad chest that sheltered her. ''We must see if we can help.''

''Better stay here until the Guards have arrested that lunatic.'' Barrett maneuvered his own broad back between Georgiana and the weapon, but even while he did so, several members surrounded the man. He made no effort to evade them and willingly gave up his gun.

''No! We must help!'' Grimly determined, Georgie pulled

free. She hastened down the last steps and approached the still figure of the Prime Minister lying in a pool of blood and surrounded by men shocked into sudden silence.

Barrett noted that with every step Georgiana grew paler, and her eyes took on a glassy look. In a few quick strides he was at her side, supporting and guiding her. Georgiana's weight on his arm grew heavier. Beads of perspiration glistened on her forehead. From the corner of his eye, he saw William Rutledge, the Earl of Wolversham, approaching.

"Georgie! Are you all right?" the earl asked. He frowned when he saw her pale face. "Devil a bit! You can't faint now, my girl!"

"I'm not fainting," Georgie protested weakly.

"No, but you will if you don't get out of here," her knowing older brother said gruffly. "What a damnable mess! I can't leave, and the carriage isn't due for another hour at least."

"I'll be happy to take Lady Georgiana home, Rutledge. I'm Barrett Gray."

William threw a harassed look at his colleagues milling around Spencer Perceval before addressing Barrett. "Much obliged to you, sir. You see, in every other aspect Georgie is game as a pebble, but she *will* faint at the sight of a drop of blood. A cursed nuisance, but there it is. Nothing anyone can do about it."

"I'll see her safely home. If you'll just open the door for me?" Barrett scooped Georgiana into his arms.

"Much obliged to you," William muttered again. He hurried ahead to push the street doors wide. "You're Sir Charles's nephew, I assume? Heard my sister Charlotte speak of you. Daresay you know the direction? Codrington House, Upper Broo—"

The Earl of Wolversham's voice was cut off by the slam of the doors as they closed after Barrett and Georgiana. It made no odds to Barrett. He knew where Lady Georgiana resided.

Fresh air did much to revive Georgie, as did the power and strength emanating from the man who carried her as though she weighed no more than a child. For a moment she gave herself up to the feeling of being protected and looked after, but by the time a hackney cab had pulled up before them in response to Barrett's shout, Georgiana was sufficiently recovered to demand to be set down.

"I can get in by myself," she insisted. "And no matter what William says, I do *not* faint. I am, however, feeling most dreadfully ill."

Barrett pushed her into the musty-smelling carriage. "Let me see your reticule," he said as he draped his coat over her shoulders, then, for good measure, placed an arm around her as well. "A dose of smelling salts will soon put you to rights."

"Don't have any," she murmured, leaning her head gratefully against his conveniently offered shoulder. "Never need the stuff."

"So you say." Barrett reached for her reticule. It took him a moment to undo the drawstring with one hand, but at last the bag opened. After some fumbling, he found a small square of lace-edged lawn, scented with the fragrance he remembered from their first meeting on the lantern-lit terrace. Without further comment, he dabbed her cold, moist forehead.

For a while they sat in silence, but finally Georgie pushed away the handkerchief. She straightened and raised her eyes to Barrett. "He's dead, isn't he?"

"I can't be certain, of course. But yes, I do believe Spencer Perceval is dead, Lady Georgiana."

The American ambassador in London, Jonathan Russell, drummed impatient fingers against his jaw. His troubled eyes met Barrett's across the oak desk, which took up a goodly portion of his cluttered office.

"With the Prime Minister dead, Parliament is in a dither, Barrett. Debates are taking place about a pension for Spencer Perceval's widow and his crowd of children, and about the forming of a new government." Jonathan Russell paused briefly to give more emphasis to his next words. "A repeal of the Orders in Council is completely relegated to the background, damn it!"

"It still seems absolutely incredible," said Barrett. "That crazed man—Bellingham, I believe. James Bellingham— had simply waited in a dark corner until Spencer Perceval arrived. And no one was there, no Guards, no one, to prevent the shot!"

Jonathan Russell nodded, but his mind was on those aspects of the dreadful affair that concerned the United States of America. "If you can afford to stick around for another couple of weeks, Barrett, we'll see how things are shaping up. They'll have to pick someone soon to lead the rest of Perceval's administration, and you can carry word back to Washington."

Barrett thought of King George's Army Gold Medal, posthumously bestowed on his young brother Franklin, and now resting safely wrapped at the bottom of his sea chest on the *Boston Belle*. His father would be waiting impatiently to receive this last memento of his youngest son—his American-born son. Yet Edward Gray would also be the frst to tell Barrett that the opportunity to serve their adopted country must take precedence over personal desires.

"All right, Jonathan." Barrett raised his glass and sniffed the amber liquid the ambassador had poured for him. His dark brows rose. "Cognac, Jon?"

Leaning back in his chair, Jonathan Russell grinned. "A gift, Barrett. From a Devonshire squire. So don't ask me whether the stuff was smuggled." Turning serious again, he said, "Thanks for obliging me. I'm not too happy about this delay of the repeal. In fact, it's a damnable thing! Recent communications from Washington show that the war hawks are shouting louder all the time, and it's so damned difficult to get a message to Washington quickly."

"My pleasure, Jon, but try not to keep me above a month. There's something I'd like to give my father."

"I heard about the medal awarded your brother. Quite an honor."

Barrett nodded. "Won't bring him back to life, of course, but it'll be something to keep the old man's memories warm." His fingers tightened on the delicate stem of his glass. What about his own memories of Franklin? Five years younger than Barrett, Franklin had tagged after his older brother from the day he could stand on his chubby legs until Barrett had been sent to oversee the plantation of St. Croix in 1807.

Barrett tossed off the measure of cognac, then rose. He collected his hat and gloves from a chair by the door. "Shall I see you at my uncle's dinner tomorrw night, Jon?"

"Indeed you will. Can't disappoint the old gentleman. He has always been most gracious to me and my family."

Walking to his uncle's home in Curzon Street, Barrett reflected that undoubtedly he'd also see Lady Georgiana at Sir Charles's table. Surely the baronet would invite his old friends, the Rutledges.

Barrett's steps slowed as he thought of the young lady who had scolded him for bringing sugar and rum to England. Not a peahen at all, was Lady Georgiana Rutledge. She showed a good deal of knowledge about British–American trade policies.

That had been three days ago. Barrett had spent every waking hour of those days at the American embassy, trying to settle the fate of ten sailors from the *Boston Belle*. He had not joined his uncle and cousin at any of their evening engagements and had, therefore, not had an opportunity to look for Lady Georgiana. Barrett wondered how she was faring now. Perhaps a call at Codrington House to inquire after her health would still be in order?

Nonsense! Even a delicately nurtured English girl must have recovered by now from the gruesome sight in the House of Commons.

When, a few moments later, he passed a little girl balancing a large basket filled with white and purple flowers on her head, Barrett came to an abrupt halt. He turned back, staring at the posies with a puzzled frown.

"Flowers, sir?" The child's thin voice sounded pleading. Her gown, much too large and streaked with dust and dirt, was hiked up and belted around her tiny waist with a length of rope. Wide gray eyes looked beseechingly up at Barrett. "Violets, sir? Sweet lilies of the valley?"

Barrett stepped closer, his nose guiding him to a bunch of

tiny, white, bell-like flowers. The fragrance reminded him of Georgiana. "Those," he said firmly. "Can you take the flowers to Upper Brook Street?"

"Yes, sir."

Scribbling a few words on the back of one of his calling cards, Barrett said, "Take the flowers and my card to Lady Georgiana Rutledge at Codrington House."

A brief message conveying his hopes that Lady Georgiana had recovered from her indisposition was a much more sensible act than a personal call, he told himself as he watched the child walk away. Jonathan Russell might detain him in London for three or four weeks, but that didn't mean he must pursue the acquaintance of Lady Georgiana!

And if that were so, he wondered, why did he feel as though he'd just lost a golden opportunity?

Even as Georgiana curtsied before Sir Charles and suffered to have her cheek pinched by her silver-haired, stout friend, she was surveying the dinner guests already assembled in Sir Charles's drawing room. Her gaze skimmed over the ladies and a handful of elderly gentlemen seated comfortably on sofas and chairs, then carefully searched among the younger men standing in tight little clusters all along the window side of the chamber.

"Looking for someone, Georgie?" Robert Gray, his blond good looks set off to perfection by his black evening clothes, grinned down at her.

With an air of innocence, Georgiana widened her eyes at him. "Not anymore, Robert."

Ludicrous to be so disappointed by the absence of a brash, arrogant American, she scolded, when he had told her he'd be sailing soon. In fact, when Barrett hadn't called the day following the shooting of Spencer Perceval, she had assumed that he had left England already. And then the lilies of the valley had arrived.

"He'll be down soon, little one. Barrett's still changing." Laughter bubbled in Robert's voice, and he watched in some amusement as a soft blush stained Georgiana's peach-golden skin. "Barrett spent most of the day at the American embassy. In fact, he stayed so long he brought Jonathan Russell with him.''

''I thought your cousin had sailed already,'' Georgie said with feigned indifference, but she could not fool Robert. He knew her too well, having made her acquaintance when she, a lively six-year-old, had filled his bed with frogs, spiders, and thistles on his first visit to Wolversham Court.

Robert grinned knowingly but was prevented from making a comment by the American ambassador, who joined them. ''Still out of uniform, I see, Lieutenant Gray.''

Robert chuckled. ''If one is careless enough to be caught in, ah, dishabille while attacked by a French gunboat! But a cursed nuisance it is, Mr. Russell. I've been assigned command of a neat little frigate, and my tailor is so dashed slow, I may have to sail next month without a uniform.''

Georgie's fingers tightened on the beaded straps of her reticule. Her brother Blakeney, too, was being fitted for uniforms. It was a thought she must put from her mind.

''I wish you luck, Lieutenant,'' said Jonathan Russell. ''By the by, you'll be glad to hear that Barrett won't need to spend quite so many hours away from you and Sir Charles any longer. Although, as a naval officer, you may not be glad of the reason.''

''Oh, I say!'' Robert held up a hand as thought to ward off an accusation. ''I'm not an advocate of impressment, Mr. Russell! But in truth, I don't know how else the navy could get enough men.'' He raised a brow quizzingly. ''Did you free all of Barrett's sailors, then?''

''I was able to return eight men to the *Boston Belle*. Two, unfortunately, had no proof at all of their American citizenship and must remain in England.''

''Jolly well done, Mr. Russell!''

''Are you saying, Mr. Russell,'' Georgiana interjected incredulously, ''that our navy impressed ten sailors from an American ship?''

The ambassador nodded. ''Yes, indeed, Lady Georgiana. And Barrett's cargo was confiscated, but that matter I was able to clear almost instantly.''

''Braggart!'' Barrett had entered the drawing room

unobserved. Smiling, he bowed to Georgiana. "Don't pay him any attention, and, most importantly, don't ask him any questions, Lady Georgiana. Jonathan will bore you to tears with tales of his diplomatic skills."

"Obviously Mr. Russell *is* very skillful." Georgiana looked up at Barrett. "And quite as obviously I owe you an apology, Mr. Gray."

His bold green eyes rested warmly upon her, approving her high-waisted gown of sheer white muslin with a wide gold border of Greek design. Suddenly she felt beautiful. Beautiful and desirable. If only he didn't have to sail so soon! Her season in London might not be quite a waste of time if the American were here to share it. It was merely wishful thinking, but she could feel her face light up at the thought.

"I am pleased to have this opportunity to thank you personally for the lilies of the valley. They are my favorite flowers, Mr. Gray."

She moved a little to the side as a footman stopped to offer glasses of sherry, and Barrett smelled her fragrance drifting around him. Lilies of the valley.

"It wasn't difficult to guess, Lady Georgiana." He took two glasses from the tray, offering one to her.

Robert interrupted his conversation with Jonathan Russell. "I say, must you two be so formal? Since I regard Georgie in the light of a sister, and you're my cousin, Barrett, surely you can drop the Lady and the Mister!"

Barrett thought, *Damn you, Robert! There's protection in formality.*

Georgiana's eyes met Barrett's. She detected a certain aloofness in his gaze, a subtle withdrawing. "I wouldn't wish to presume," Georgie said stiffly.

A rueful grin curved one corner of Barrett's mouth. "I deserved that. Please accept my apologies for my churlishness, Georgiana."

"Very well, Barrett. Tell me, how does the outfitting of the *Boston Belle* progress?"

She listened to his account of a misunderstanding with the ship's chandler in Bristol, which had resulted in the delivery of five hundred live fowl instead of fifty, and barely noticed that Barrett was guiding her away from Robert and the American ambassador. Sipping sherry and talking, they moved slowly toward the open French doors leading into the tiny walled garden of Sir Charles's town house. In one accord, they set their glasses on a Buhl table near the doors, then stepped out into the clear, moonlit night.

"It certainly sounds as though provisioning of the *Boston Belle* is well under way," said Georgie. "I am almost sorry to hear it, for I'd have liked to learn more about Boston and your home in Virginia. Do you plant tobacco at Serendip, Barrett?"

"No. We don't own a plantation in Virginia, you see, but on St. Croix in the Caribbean where we grow sugar cane." Barrett removed his coat and spread it over the seat of a stone bench. "Would you like to sit out here for a while, Georgiana? Unless—do you find it too cool?"

"Not at all." Georgie sat down, absently arranging the folds of her gown so that only the tips of her soft, golden slippers showed. "You told me, I believe, that Serendip is a white house built atop a wooded knoll, some few miles south of the Chesapeake Bay."

Barrett stood with his back against a sturdy lilac hedge opposite the bench. His gaze went past her, as though he were seeing in the distance the stretch of Virginia coast that was his home.

"It is beautiful in a rough sort of way," he said. "We own several miles of beach, including a hidden cove where Franklin and I used to lie in wait of pirates. They never came, but then we could always go into the swamps south and east of Serendip and pretend we were explorers."

"Franklin? You have a brother, Barrett?"

His bronzed face above the white stock and shirt looked like a chiseled mask. "Franklin is dead." He pushed away from the lilac hedge. "It must be almost time for dinner. Shall we go inside?"

Rising, Georgie picked up his coat and brushed it out as best she could with her hands. "I am sorry," she said softly.

"I understand how you feel, Barrett, and I shan't ask questions unless you would like to talk about Franklin."

Their hands met as she passed him the coat. Her fingers tightened over his in an unspoken message. The moon was brighter than a hundred candles, and in its milky light Georgie saw his face relax.

"You may ask any questions you like, Georgiana. I'd not find it painful at all speaking to you about him."

Georgie felt a kinship of minds with Barrett, a rapport she had not shared with a man since Aubrey was killed. It gave her a warm feeling, a feeling of being welcomed.

"Georgiana!" Charlotte's harsh voice shattered the moment of quiet communication with Barrett. Their hands fell apart, and Barrett shrugged himself into his coat.

Swiftly Charlotte bore down on them. "I should have known! Whenever you disappear from a gathering, I have only to look on the terrace or in the garden. This must stop, Georgiana! It simply is not done! And you, Mr. Gray!" She turned her indignant stare on Barrett. "How could you be so lost to propriety as to follow her outside! But, I daresay, I must excuse your behavior on account of your upbringing."

"You go too far, ma'am." Protectively Barrett offered his arm to Georgiana. He could feel the trembling of her fingers through the material of his coat. "No one," he said in cold, clipped tones, "could possibly regard our behavior as reprehensible. We were in full view of the drawing room."

"Holding hands!"

Barrett stiffened, but when he would have spoken, Georgiana tugged on his sleeve and started to walk toward the house. "That is quite enough, Charlotte," she said, turning her back on her half sister and leaving her to follow them. "You know I dislike scenes, and besides, you're way off the mark!"

Charlotte was denied further opportunity to scold. As they entered the drawing room, Sir Charles approached. "Dinner is served. May I show you to your chair, Charlotte?"

Georgiana entered the dining salon on Barrett's arm but found to her dismay that the seating arrangement prescribed Sir Perceval Hargrave as her dinner partner. To her right sat

Mr. Jonathan Russell, and Barrett was seated across the table from her. No further speech would be possible between them until the gentlemen joined the ladies in the drawing room after the port and cigars.

Despite a huge silver epergne filled with peaches, grapes and pineapples in the center of the table, Barrett enjoyed his view of Georgiana across from him. When, with the removal of the first course, she turned from Sir Perceval Hargrave to Jon Russell, he caught a look of relief on her face. Barrett smiled. Sir Perceval might be dressed to the nines, as Robert would say, but the dandy could not elicit the keen interest that his own tales of America evoked in Georgiana.

With much greater charity than he had believed himself capable of showing, Barrett devoted himself to Lady Charlotte on his left. He had not, however, exchanged more than a dozen words with the formidable matron when the Earl of Wolversham, sitting next to his sister, committed an unprecedented breech of etiquette. He leaned across Lady Charlotte and, ignoring her outraged glare, started to speak to Barrett.

"Never had the chance yet to thank you for taking care of Georgie," William said so loudly that most of the conversation around the table came to a halt.

"My pleasure, Rutledge." Barrett inclined his head in acknowledgment, then turned again to Lady Charlotte.

The Earl of Wolversham, however, had not done yet. "I do appreciate it, Gray, and to show that it's not just empty talk, I want you to be the first to know that Liverpool has agreed, less than an hour ago, to head the government."

The news was welcome. "My felicitations," Barrett said with a smile. "Lord Liverpool will make a competent Prime Minister."

"And you can expect debates on the repeal of the Orders in Council to resume within the week, Gray. There's no doubt in my mind that we'll have trade relations back to normal between our two countries before the month of June is out."

"That is indeed good news. Thank you, Rutledge."

Barrett looked across the table at Georgiana. She smiled at him, pleased on his behalf.

Barrett could think only that he'd be sailing soon.

Three

"Really, William!" Charlotte's voice was a clearly audible whisper. "Must you be so rude? And to talk about Georgiana's visit to Westminster!" Her tone implied that an appearance in the Houses of Parliament was no less scandalous than had Georgiana exhibited herself in a notorious bagnio.

There were some nods from beturbaned and beplumed heads, but, Georgie noted, most of the gentlemen took William's lapse as a signal to start a political debate. More than one lady found herself ignored as her male neighbors struck up a conversation across her or—horror of horrors! —tossed heated arguments back and forth across the table.

Sir Charles surveyed the apparent chaos around his table with white brows raised, and a quizzing glass held to his eye. He decided he enjoyed it. Without regret he abandoned the hard-of-hearing dowager Duchess of Melthorpe to his right and the adoring Miss Simperkins, an aging spinster with more hair than wit seated on his left, and called to his nephew halfway down the table, "Mind you, Barrett, my boy, that you tell your father to keep the guest chamber aired! I'll be over to see him yet. Stap me if I don't!"

"Disgraceful!" Sir Perceval Hargrave saw his opportunity to turn the heiress's attention on himself. "I assure you, my dear Lady Georgiana, that nothing like this would ever happen at a dinner where I was host."

Georgiana had been listening to the American ambassador's conversation with one of Sir Charles's oldest friends,

Admiral Lord Melvin Calcote. Reluctantly she turned to the baronet. "Indeed, Sir Percy. I can well believe it."

Sir Percy looked at her through narrowed, light blue eyes, and she feared she had allowed sarcasm to color her voice. Then he nodded complacently. "I hope to have the pleasure of your company at dinner soon, Lady Georgiana. I've opened Hargrave House but have yet to find the chef to suit my palate. May I instead ask you to take a turn in the park with me tomorrow afternoon?"

Georgiana toyed with a morsel of fricandeau of veal on her plate, the only dish she had accepted while the third course was served. "I'm afraid I must decline your invitation, Sir Percy. I am otherwise engaged."

"I see I must be on my toes if I want to steal a march on the American next time," he said with an attempt at playfulness that did not quite hide his annoyance.

Raising her eyes, Georgiana met Barrett's quizzical look across the table. She felt certain he had overheard the baronet's remarks; yet she said nothing to refute Sir Percy's assumption that her outing was with Barrett. It was none of Sir Percy's business that she'd be driving her half brother's famous bays in Richmond Park.

"I trust I shall see you at Almack's tomorrow night," Sir Percy went on. "May I be so bold and bespeak two of the waltzes?"

"I'm sorry. I cannot grant you waltzes either," Georgie replied with some satisfaction. She had every hope of coaxing William to take dinner at the Star and Garter after their excursion. If her schemes succeeded, they'd be back in town well after Charlotte and Fenella had left for Almack's. If not—Georgie gave a mental shrug. She'd not be the first young lady to plead a headache.

To her right, Georgie heard Admiral Calcote's voice raised in anger. "Castlereagh's message by the *Hornet* should have reached your capital by now," the old seadog said belligerently to the American ambassador. "And if your secretary of state has acquired any sense at all since he was recalled from London, he'll know it's a very good offer and will present it accordingly to President Madison and your Congress."

The ambassador, who had studied his copy of the English foreign secretary's message, raised his glass and swallowed a retort along with a large sip of the wine.

Georgie turned away from Sir Percy. Not bound by restrictions of diplomacy, she said to the admiral, "Did you read the excerpt of Lord Castlereagh's letter in the newspaper, sir? I did. If I were an American, I'd be insulted. The tone of the dispatch was lofty, overbearing, and condescending, as from an elderly relation pontificating on conduct to a young man!"

The admiral's face took on a purplish hue. He opened his mouth for a blistering reply, but before he could speak, Barrett's lazy drawl distracted him from the source of his ire.

"I quite agree. It was maddeningly lofty. Unbearably high-handed."

Georgiana's glance flew to Barrett's face. She met warmth in his gaze but also a glint of amusement as though he found it entertaining that she had spoken up for the United States.

The admiral's thundering reproof, now aimed at Barrett instead of Georgie, filled the dining salon, and it was Georgie's turn to suppress a smile as the American, eyes on his plate, sat meekly through the barrage. She knew Barrett was far from meek and could only admire his control.

Dinner dragged on, as did Sir Percy's efforts to win her acceptance of his manyfold invitations. He was very persistent, and Georgie's ingenuity and inventiveness were taxed severely.

When Lady Calcote, who was Sir Charles's hostess that evening, gave the signal for the ladies' departure from the dining salon, Georgie rose hastily. She had run out of excuses, and Sir Percy's last words to her had been an invitation to ride in Hyde Park before the rest of the fashionable world was astir—a pastime that had become a habit with Georgie and that she did not wish to have spoiled by Sir Percy's unwelcome presence.

When the gentlemen rejoined the ladies in the drawing

room, she spent an interminable hour evading the annoying baronet, with indifferent success.

She wished she had not promised William to watch her tongue after Charlotte complained that she was speaking too bluntly to gentlemen with annoying habits and mannerisms. Sir Percy was spoiling her every effort to converse with Barrett or, for that matter, with any of Sir Charles's guests, and his blatant attempts to monopolize her were trying her patience to the utmost.

During the following days Georgiana was more successful at dodging the baronet's company. She did not attend the many evening engagements Charlotte had accepted. She was "not at home" when Sir Percy called at Codrington House the first time; next morning she was at Hookham's lending library—or rather, slipping out the back door as he entered through the front; she was in Curzon Street, playing piquet with Sir Charles Gray when the baronet personally delivered a bouquet of red and white roses for Georgiana and allowed himself to be invited to tea by Charlotte.

Her evasion tactics held one drawback, though. While she had avoided Sir Percy, she had not seen Barrett Gray either since the night of the dinner. Yet Barrett was never far from her mind.

Thoughts of Aubrey would automatically bring thoughts of Barrett and America. They were pleasant associations. Quite unreal, she admitted. In fact, they were very much the fancies of a romantic schoolroom miss. But she was *not* a schoolroom miss, swooning over a handsome face! She merely wanted to hear more about that vast young country across the ocean. She wanted a dream to sustain her for the duration of the season.

A dream of a young English girl setting out into a brave new world to meet head-on the adventures Aubrey had described, to get to know her Aunt Letty, who had defied parental opposition and had married her American love. . . .

These dreams, however, would bear no fruit. Georgie must banish them from her mind, as, without Aubrey, there could be no journey to America. Fortified with a goodly amount of resolve, she started to make the rounds of museums and exhibitions. The more interesting tales she could take back to the children in Wolversham, the easier it would be to retain their attention during school sessions. Her activities, moreover, provided an excuse for retiring early and avoiding those nightly crushes which were life and blood to her half sister and niece, but which Georgie found tedious and boring. And if she was also too tired to lie awake, thinking of America and one particular American, so much the better!

Descending the wide steps of Somerset House on a bright Tuesday morning, Georgiana saw a curricle pulling to a halt in the Strand, mere yards away. She glared at the driver, a young blood whose driving cloak sported upwards of a dozen capes, but Georgie's annoyance fled quickly. It was not, as she had at first feared, Sir Percy, finally catching up with her. It was Robert Gray.

"Paintings again, Georgie?" Robert called. Tossing the reins to his tiger standing rigidly behind, he alighted from the sporting vehicle. "Dashed if I know what you see in them that you haven't seen last week already."

As Robert fell into step beside her, Georgiana nodded to her maid Rose, indicating that the girl should walk ahead to their carriage around the corner in Savoy Street. "It's a wonderful diversion, Robert. Try it sometime."

A look of horror crossed his face. "I'd rather go see the marbles Lord Elgin carted off from Greece. Although," he added after a brief pause, "I can't see either why everyone is so crazy about a pile of rubble, for that's all it is, you know. Heads missing or bashed in. Arms and legs broken off."

"Indeed," Georgie said, trying to stifle the unseemly giggles rising in her throat. "You're very wise to stick to such pursuits as boxing in Gentleman Jackson's saloon or shooting at wafers in Manton's gallery."

Robert's eye kindled. "I just had a lesson from the great Gentleman Jackson himself. 'Twas the most famous sport I've had in years!" he said enthusiastically, then, sounding disappointed, "I say, Georgie! Is that your landaulet here?"

Life with five brothers had made Georgiana sensitive to

the needs of young gentlemen who liked to boast of their prowess in the manly arts. "Yes, but it is such a lovely day. Shall we walk a little farther?"

Robert agreed, instantly becoming engrossed in a description of various punches and throws he had been taught.

"I'm surprised you did not take your cousin along," Georgie said when Robert paused for breath and looked over his shoulder to make certain his curricle and Georgiana's carriage were following them. "He looks to me like a man who'd share your pleasure in all sorts of, ah, physical exercise."

Robert's face fell. "I did," he said crossly. "Damn him. *He* landed Jackson a flush hit!"

Georgiana laughed, and Robert frowned at her. "Dashed if I know how he did it, Georgie! Jackson must have a weak spot for Americans, and let down his guard on purpose."

Still shaking his head in wonderment, Robert went on to say, "He'll be sailing on the twenty-ninth. My cousin, that is. Not Gentleman Jackson."

Robert's casual announcement hit Georgiana with the force of a pugilist's well-aimed punch. Rendered breathless and speechless, she knew that she must have a soft spot for Americans as well.

After a while she became aware of Robert's eyes on her and the ever increasing noise of traffic as they approached busy Charing Cross. She stopped. "You'll wish to spend your time with Barrett, then," she said in a voice that even in her own ears sounded forced and overbright.

"Daresay I might—if he were around. Barrett's a great gun," Robert said with a grin. "Almost as good company as Blakeney."

Georgie realized that was high praise indeed, for Robert and her brother Blakeney were very close friends.

"Quite an accolade," she said, trying to disguise her interest in the whereabouts of Robert's cousin. "Has he gone to Bristol already?"

"Lord, no! He's rushing around town, taking in all the sights his father bade him see. Uncle Edward, I fear, is secretly still as English as the day he set foot on American soil, and he wants to hear a detailed description of his favorite haunts.''

Robert handed Georgiana into the landaulet that had pulled up beside them. "Quite a man-about-town, was my uncle—if my father is to be believed. It'll take all of Barrett's time to visit half of the places Uncle Edward frequented. 'But not tomorrow night, old fellow!' I told him. 'Tomorrow *I'll* show you a sight!' ''

Accepting her parasol from Rose, Georgiana twirled the handle of the dainty sunshade on her shoulder. "And what's that, Robert?''

"The Marriage Mart, child! You should try the place sometime,'' he mimicked her earlier words.

Her startled gaze flew to his face. Seeing a twinkle in his eyes and a very knowing look, she quickly turned to the young groom on the box. "Drive on Ferdie,'' she said quietly.

Georgiana spent but a few moments wondering if Robert had read romantic motivation into her interest in Barrett. Her thoughts became fixed on the notion to attend Almack's herself and watch Barrett's face as he beheld the awesome sight of London's "Marriage Mart.''

By the time she reached Upper Brook Street and entered the tiled vestibule of Codrington House, she had quite made up her mind to go. He was Sir Charles's nephew, after all. It would be only polite to bid him farewell.

Sellers, the stately butler, greeted Georgiana with a smile. Not so Charlotte, who came sweeping down the wide, curving stairs with Fenella following demurely in her wake.

"Where have you been, Georgiana? I swear you're the most tiresome girl!'' Charlotte, her Junoesque figure encased in a stylish carriage dress of plum-colored silk, stepped closer to her young half sister. "Just look at that!'' she said sharply, pointing to a smudge on the hem of Georgiana's sprigged muslin gown. "You're a hoyden, miss! An ill-mannered, inconsiderate hoyden. And the sooner you're married the better!''

"So that my husband can take me in hand and school me?'' Georgie said sweetly. "What makes you think, dear

Charlotte, that a husband will be more successful where you have failed?''

Charlotte's lips thinned. "William has been overindulgent with you. But this I promise, Georgiana! If you do not come to Almack's with us *this* week, I shall speak to William and open his eyes,'' she pronounced with awful calm.

"I'll come,'' Georgie said airily. "As will Blakeney. He promised his latest flirt to put in an appearance, don't you know.''

Before Charlotte could recover from her astonishment and remember some other grievance that might be remedied with a threat of laying it before William, Georgie added, "I only hope that Madame Bertin will deliver my new gown on time,'' and escaped from her half sister and her niece.

In the small third-floor sitting room she shared with Fenella, Georgiana flopped onto the padded seat before the open window. Wrapping her arms around her knees, she stared down into the street below. If she leaned forward a little, she'd be able to see around the corner into Park Lane thronging with riders and carriages on their way to the park. Five o'clock was the hour when the *ton* turned out for the fashionable promenade. It was where, undoubtedly, Charlotte and Fenella were headed, but Georgie was not interested in mincing sedately along the bridle paths and showing off a dashing new hat or riding costume. She missed her gallops across the wide open fields and green meadows of Sussex.

In the morning, she decided, *at sunrise, I'll be out there in Rotten Row for a good run! And the devil fly away with Sir Perceval! He may have the pleasure of seeing me gallop if he's lying in wait for me, and he may have his dances as well at Almack's tomorrow night.*

The face that came to her mind was not, however, that of Sir Perceval Hargrave. It was a bronzed face with rugged, chiseled features that looked almost harsh when not lit up by a smile. The memory of a pair of glinting green eyes caused an uncomfortably tight feeling inside her. Soon he would be gone!

Georgie, wriggling into a more comfortable position on

the window seat and propping her chin onto her knees, thought about Barrett's departure to that exciting country across the Atlantic Ocean.

Yes, she wanted to see him once more—and bid a secret farewell to her dream.

"If you follow me, John, I'll take young Ferdie next time I ride in the park!" Georgie nudged her mare before the last words had quite left her mouth.

Stardust required no further encouragement. After a bare minimum of exercise during the past two weeks, the long, sandy stretch of Rotten Row before her beckoned irresistibly.

John shook his grizzled head as he watched his young mistress gallop hell for leather toward the west end of Hyde Park, but he made no attempt to follow her. Not that he was afraid she'd make good on her threat. Or that she could! He, John, had set Lady Georgie on her first pony. *He* had taught her to ride and take her fences with steadiness and courage.

A rare pluck 'un, was Lady Georgie! And even though John knew for certain that she wouldn't be content to stay on Rotten Row but would charge across Hyde Park as though she were down in Sussex where her mad gallops were a known and accepted sight, he hadn't the heart to take off after her and put a stop to it, as he well knew he should—and could. He'd only have to say that the earl would turn him off for sure if he got wind of his half sister's exploits.

Lady Georgie needed her moment of freedom. John had watched her fret under Lady Charlotte's restrictions. He had seen the bright glow of her eyes dim since they had come to this gray city where a body could see nothing but soot-darkened houses and filthy, stinking streets. Scratching his chin, John suppressed a longing sigh and turned his gelding toward the park gate where he intended to walk up and down until his mistress rejoined him.

Georgiana, leaning over her mare's neck, tried hard to forget that she was in London. After a quick glance over her shoulder to make certain John was out of sight, she guided Stardust to the right. They flew across the turf in a wonderfully exhilarating neck-or-nothing fashion, closer and closer to the Serpentine.

She felt her small, plumed hat loosen and bounce, felt the tug of wind in her hair and the crisp morning air whip against her cheeks. She felt alive!

After a while Georgie started to rein the mare in until she had slowed to a canter. Far ahead, beyond the keeper's lodge, she noted a horse and rider gallop as she had done moments earlier. She was not alone, after all, in her desire for exhilaration, for untrammeled freedom.

She pulled Stardust to a halt. Squinting into the sunrise, Georgie saw a dark head, hatless, bent low over the horse's glossy black neck and had to fight an impulse to give chase. It was impossible to recognize the rider's features, but, somehow, she felt certain that it was Barrett Gray.

She felt Stardust's powerful muscles flex. The mare tossed her head and rolled her eyes back at Georgie as though to say, "Wake up! They're getting away from us!"

Georgie wavered on the brink of assent. The horse and rider disappearing into a grove of birches ahead seemed to issue a silent challenge.

"No, love." Georgie relaxed in the saddle. She leaned forward, rubbing her hand against Stardust's chestnut mane. "I'll see him tonight. Besides, I've broken enough rules with our gallop. No need to add racing to my sins."

The sound of hooves beating on the turf behind her alerted Georgie. The morning was advancing; it was time to find John and return to Codrington House. Soon the park would be overrun with riders: officers from the Whitehall barracks; those gentlemen who could tear themselves from their soft featherbeds after a long night at their clubs; and even some young ladies, accompanied, of course, by their grooms, would venture out.

Stardust responded instantly to Georgie's gentle nudge but seemed reluctant to stick to a decorous canter, or to obey a tug of the reins directing her east, toward the park gates. The rider approaching from the direction of the Serpentine was fast coming closer. Wishing to be near her groom before she was recognized, Georgiana gave Stardust her head.

Once again they flew across the park, but the pursuing hoofbeats came ever closer.

"Courage, Lady Georgiana! Hold on!"

Sir Percy. And he thinks my horse bolted, the fool!

With a firm hand, Georgie reined in. Stardust gave a great show of rearing, tossing her head, and neighing her protest. Sir Percy's mount came to a skidding halt beside them. The baronet's arm shot out to take Stardust's reins, but Georgie stayed him with a blazing look.

"I know how to handle my horse, Sir Percy! There was no need to ride *ventre à terre* if it was rescue on your mind."

She saw a flash of irritation in his eyes, gone as quickly as it had appeared. He doffed his hat and bowed from the saddle. "Pardon me, Lady Georgiana," he said stiffly, "but I had another reason to ride after you. It's been a week since I invited you to accompany me in the park. I cannot let this opportunity slip by."

Georgiana inclined her head. "Some other time perhaps, Sir Percy. I must find my groom. No doubt he's worried by my prolonged absence."

"No need to be coy, m'dear. I perfectly understand," he said. "You don't want me to think that you came out to meet me, but since I've waited patiently for so long, I find I have no heart to play games now."

Georgie's eyes widened in disbelief. The man was utterly depraved to think—"Good-bye, Sir Percy," she said coldly, nudging her mare to move on.

The baronet grabbed Stardust's reins. He smiled apologetically, but it was a smile that did not reach his eyes. His look touched Georgiana like chips of ice, and despite the sun that now had fully emerged behind the trees she felt cold.

Stardust tossed her head and made a valiant attempt to break free. Sir Percy's fist tightened on the bridle. Without apparent effort he brought the mare under control.

His expression changed. "I say, Lady Georgiana," he

said ruefully. "I seem to be always putting my foot in when all I really want is to get better acquainted with you."

"Holding me captive is not the way to go about it, Sir Percy!"

"Indeed, and I apologize, dear lady. But you know the saying of the bird in hand and all that."

Georgie eyed him with disdain. She never carried a crop. Stardust required no prodding, and any gate that might bar her way in the country Georgie preferred to jump. From now on, however, she'd carry the handy little whip to ward off animals of the two-legged kind!

Sir Percy dismounted. Keeping one hand firmly on Stardust's bridle, he held out the other invitingly. "Come, Lady Georgiana. Let's walk together for a while."

In his riding coat and breeches, without excessively high, starched shirt points and the many foppish falderals he had worn when she encountered him before, Sir Percy was no more the effeminate dandy than was Barrett Gray. Georgie suspected that, despite the handicap of having to hold Stardust as well, he was capable of snatching her from the saddle if she did not comply with his invitation.

Slipping her knee free of the pommel, Georgiana gathered her riding skirt in her left hand. Sir Percy stepped closer to her. She saw his arm crook and snake out to grip her around the waist. His eyes burned her face, moved lower to the fall of lace at her throat, to the tiny mother-of-pearl buttons on her thin lawn shirt and the larger silver buttons of her low-cut riding jacket, as though he were mentally stripping away every layer of her clothing.

Revulsion shook her. Quickly she hooked her knee back over the pommel. Her left heel dug into Stardust's side. Surprised, the mare started forward, but Sir Percy's cruel jerk on the reins was too much. Stardust whickered in pain as the bit cut into the soft inside of her mouth, bringing her head down.

"Stop it!" Unmindful of her precarious position, Georgie leaned over and struck at the baronet with her fists. His hat flew off, one fist connected painfully with his jaw; then

Georgie's blows lost aim and power as she felt herself slipping.

Arms like the bands of a vise clasped around her middle. Ungently she was pulled completely off the horse. Her feet, encased in the soft leather of her riding boots, hit the ground. She swayed when Sir Percy removed his hands from her waist, but he quickly caught her again, this time pinning her arms to her sides in a bruising grip. Before she could gather her wits Sir Percy's mouth came down on hers, crushing her lips against her teeth.

She kicked and struggled against his embrace, but it was like a feather trying to break out of a steel cage. Behind her, Stardust snorted, then took off at a fast clip.

She'll find John!

It was the last coherent thought Georgie had for the next few moments as she renewed her efforts to break free from Sir Percy. Anger churned within her as the pressure of his mouth increased agonizingly. Her head was tilted back at a painful angle, and he held her too close to use her knee as Aubrey had taught her. The reek and taste of spirits emanating from her captor made her stomach heave in protest.

With a suddenness that sent her sprawling backward, she was free. Georgie choked down a cry as her outstretched arms and her backside hit the turf. She blinked, sitting up a little higher. The fumes of gin and brandy about Sir Percy must have made her drunk! She saw *two* men!

Two men of equal height and stature, dressed in tan corduroy riding coats and fawn-colored breeches. One with chestnut hair, the other with a shock of black hair falling onto his tanned forehead.

She forgot her smarting hands, her bruised body and mouth, as she focused on only one of them. Barrett Gray.

His fist shot out, connecting precisely with Sir Percy's jaw. Barrett didn't wait to see if his adversary had been eliminated. He spun on his heel and without a backward glance strode over to Georgie. Only she observed Sir Percy as he seemed to fold over, then slowly crumpled to the ground.

"Georgie!" Barrett's voice was deep and urgent with concern.

"I'm all right, Barrett." A smile tugged at the corners of her mouth as she remembered that she had once likened him to a knight on a white charger. Softly she added, "Thank you for coming to my rescue."

He reached out, pulling her gently to her feet. His eyes searched her face. "*Are* you all right, Georgie? You don't look it."

Suddenly, painfully, he became aware of her disheveled appearance. Her hands were scratched and dirty, her riding habit showed a layer of dust on its once powder blue skirt and jacket, her hat was gone, and her hair tumbled untidily about her shoulders. Georgie felt her cheeks sting hotly. No doubt they, too, were streaked with grime and dust!

Pulling a snowy handkerchief from his pocket, Barrett dabbed at her lower lip. "Blood," he muttered. "The bastard! He'll pay for this!"

"No, Barrett!" Georgiana laid a restraining hand on his arm. She couldn't bear for him to leave her side, even if it meant that Sir Percy came to his just deserts. One punch was hardly that, and the baronet was already stirring. "Please take me to John. To my groom. He'll be somewhere near the Chesterfield Gate."

Barrett hesitated. "All right," he said finally. "I suppose it's more important to get you home than to teach that oaf a lesson."

He sounded so reluctant that Georgie had to smile. "Indeed it is, Barrett. The sooner I'll be on my way, the less chance that I'll be observed in my"—an eloquent gesture with her hand encompassed her whole person—"disreputable state."

Her eyes widened in dismay as she remembered Stardust. "I must find my mare, Barrett! She galloped off. I thought she'd go to John. But he hasn't come!"

"Calm down." Barrett's hands closed around her upper arms. He turned her slightly so that she could observe her chestnut mare and his black stallion grazing side by side a few feet away.

Not a white charger...

"It was your mare who alerted me that something was amiss," said Barrett. "Be sure to give her an extra carrot."

Georgie felt breathless. Barrett still held her arms. It was such a different touch from Sir Percy's bruising grip! Slowly she looked up to meet his eyes. There was warmth in their green depths, and they moved across her face like a gentle caress.

"You tremble," he said. "Are you afraid of me, Georgie?"

Unable to speak, she merely shook her head. She heard a rustling and a groan from where Sir Percy had been felled, but she did not take her eyes off the face that was so close to hers.

Coming ever closer...

It was Barrett who turned to look over his shoulder at the baronet. "We had best get moving. He's coming to."

As in a daze, Georgie followed him to the horses and let him toss her up into the saddle.

She glanced at Barrett as he mounted his stallion and surprised an expression of regret on the strong features that were becoming more and more familiar to her. Her heartbeat quickened. Had he, too, felt the current between them? The magnetic draw?

But he looked back at Sir Percy, and she knew that the regret had been for the missed opportunity to mill the baronet down once more.

"Do you really wish to search for your groom, Georgiana? I could take you home just as well."

So she was Georgiana again. *He called me Georgie. Three times!* "It'll be best if John accompanies me, Barrett. He'll be at the gate, fretting himself into a stew over my long absence."

"As you wish. If there's anything at all I can do for you—"

Again she felt herself warmed by his gaze. "Thank you, Barrett. You've done more already than I could have asked."

He grinned suddenly. "Oh, no. I would have gone back and drawn his cork. Gladly so, had you but asked it."

"You have been too long in Robert's company. I feel sure that drawing someone's cork is not an American expression."

"Perhaps not. Remember, though, that my father grew up in England."

What she remembered, with a pang of regret, was that he'd be sailing in two days.

As though in agreement with Georgie's feelings, the sun hid behind a cloud. A sudden gust of wind stirred the leaves of the tall beech trees meeting above their heads. Stardust, smelling rain, increased her pace as Chesterfield Gate came into view. And John.

"Lady Georgie!" Relief and exasperation blended in her groom's voice. Having waited on tenterhooks for an agonizing half hour, John urged his horse to his mistress's side.

"Took a toss, did ye?" he said with grim satisfaction when he had taken in her soiled and crumpled habit and her disheveled hair. "And pray the lord that it be a lesson to ye! How's the mare?"

Georgiana did her best to look like a stern mistress. "Stardust is unhurt. Ride on ahead, John. I want to get back to the mews before William comes to the stables."

John attached himself firmly to her side. Casting a baleful look at Barrett, he muttered, "Aye, that I can well believe. A rare trimming ye'll get if his lordship lays eyes on ye."

Accepting that the old groom would not let her out of sight or earshot again, Georgiana said, "Thank you, Barrett. You need not accompany me further. John will look after me."

He smiled a lopsided smile. "That I can see. Good-bye, Georgiana."

"*Au revoir*, Barrett," she said softly.

His fingers tightened on the riding crop in his right hand. "It must be good-bye. I'm leaving for Bristol in the morning."

She smiled and shook her head. "May I have it?" She pointed to the crop. "For remembrance?"

Bringing his stallion to a halt close beside her, he handed her the short whip with the braided loop at its tip. A gleam of understanding lit his eyes. "May it serve a dual purpose."

"Oh, it will. I have no doubt about it," Georgie assured

him. She wanted to say more, but John had felt a drop of rain and was urging her homeward.

She was impatient now to see whether Madame Bertin had delivered her new ball gown, a luscious creation of peach-colored silk. Barrett's last view of her must not be that of a disheveled hoyden, of a careless young woman whom he had to rescue from a foolish predicament.

How will it feel when his arm encircles me? When we dance the waltz at Almack's. . . .

Four

Almack's was always crowded at the height of the season. When it became known that the subscription ball on Wednesday, May 27, 1812, would mark the departure of eight noble young gentlemen to the Peninsula, the number of attendees promised to turn the event into a veritable squeeze.

The approach to Almack's was choked with coaches, all waiting to disgorge their passengers before those same imposing portals in King Street. Over Charlotte's strident objections, Georgiana and her brother Blakeney left the Codrington carriage at the top of St. James's Street, and walked.

"Tonight it doesn't matter. No one will be in the clubs," Blakeney said, more to soothe his own conscience, Georgie suspected, then to reassure her.

She saw him dart glances at The Cocoa Tree and at Brooks's, but only the doormen were outside the famed gentlemen's clubs. Even the notorious bow window of White's club was deserted.

With a moue of disappointment, Georgie hastened her steps to keep up with Blakeney. It *would* have been rather fun to ogle back at George Brummell and his cronies who generally occupied the window.

As they approached the corner of King Street, Georgie noted that more elegantly clad ladies and gentlemen were deserting their coaches and walking to Almack's. The ladies looked like butterflies beside their dark-coated male companions. Pale-colored evening capes in hues from white to pink, powder blue, jonquil, and sea green fluttered and billowed as excited young ladies tripped along the sidewalk. Feathers of all shades and lengths nodded majestically in rhythm with the matrons' more sedate steps. The tapping of silver- and gold-topped canes carried by the gentlemen mingled with the jingle of harness as every now and again a horse moved impatiently, and at times, well over a minute apart, the clopping of hooves and the rumble of wheels filled the night as the coaches moved forward, one by one.

"Knew I shouldn't have come," Blakeney muttered in disgust when he could see the throng of people inching up the wide steps to Almack's double doors.

Georgie looked at him sharply. Surely he wouldn't draw back at the last moment and leave her to the mercies of Charlotte and Fenella—when they showed up at last!

Blakeney would, she admitted wryly. He'd rather muck out the large Wolversham stables single-handedly than do the pretty at one of Almack's assemblies.

"You gave your word to Marian Fellingham," Georgie reminded her brother hastily. "You can't just walk out on her after you've been dancing attendance on her for weeks and after promising to be one of her partners tonight!"

"I shan't." Merging into the crowd on the stairs, Blakeney lowered his voice. "I don't understand, though, how the devil she can enjoy these crushes. What does she expect?"

"Marian expects romance, brother dear. And perhaps your ring before you leave."

"Never!"

The exclamation came as no surprise to Georgie. She had long since realized, perhaps before Blakeney himself had done so, that he had become disenchanted with the viva-

cious blonde, who had not a serious thought behind her
pretty face.

On the surface, Blakeney might be as volatile and hey-
go-mad as Marian, but Georgie knew that it was a front he
had learned to put up as protection against Lewis's barbed
tongue. Lewis, a mere half hour older than Blakeney, was a
thoroughly devil-may-care here-and-thereian, who looked
down on anyone admitting to deeper feelings. Only Georgie
had won his grudging respect, expressed through utter
silence, when she had started the village school at Wolversham
because she wanted the children to have a choice: remain, or
leave and find gainful employment in the city if they so
chose.

Georgie stumbled and was recalled to her surroundings
with a jolt. Blakeney's hand tightened on her arm, steadying
her, and a portly gentleman, the cause of her stumble,
muttered apologies for setting his foot on the flounced hem
of her gown as she ascended the last step into the vestibule.

Red-faced, the gentleman moved on, leaving Georgie to
contemplate the smudge of dust on the peach silk of her
gown. Thank goodness for Madame Bertin's craftsmanship!
The deep flounce had not torn.

Cocooned within a rolling sea of voices, some loud and
cheerful, some low and secretive in the conveyance of
scandalous tidbits of gossip, she was carried toward the
ballroom. As she passed through the doors, Georgie craned
her neck for a peek at those already inside.

Although she knew that Robert had the annoying habit of
slipping in mere seconds before eleven o'clock, when the
doors would be closed against latecomers, she caught herself searching for the dark head of Robert's cousin. His
height would make Barrett an easy target. She couldn't miss
him—if he were there.

"Look at that!" Blakeney said crossly, nodding toward a
gathering of young ladies around three of his fellow officers.
"Why is it that females are drawn to a scarlet coat like flies
to a strip of tar paper?"

Georgie chuckled. A typical Blakeney metaphor! And
he'd be even more disgruntled when the ladies discovered

him. "There are birds in the United States that are drawn to every red flower. Hummingbirds, if I remember correctly. Could it be that we females have some of their instincts?"

Blakeney's hand on her elbow propelled her toward the laughing and chattering young people by one of the windows flanking the dance floor. "More than likely," he said dryly. "You females flutter about like a flock of birds surprised by a scarecrow, and the hum of your conversation drowns out the screech of the string quartet, which I remember from previous visits as extremely noisy. Or maybe the fiddlers couldn't come tonight," he added hopefully.

But Georgie saw four men scraping away energetically in the musicians' gallery, and below, on the polished dance floor, couples were performing a contredanse to an almost inaudible tune.

As though drawn, her eyes returned to the three young officers. She knew them all. Peter Farnsworth. George Whitfield. Edward Stanhope. Friends of Aubrey. Friends of Blakeney. All in smart, scarlet dress coats, only the different colors of braiding on collar, facing, and shoulders giving each a distinctive identity.

Tomorrow they'd be posting down to Portsmouth and board the vessel waiting to carry them to Spain. Suddenly, the fears she had suppressed so long for Blakeney's sake came rushing back.

"Ok, Blakeney—" Her voice caught, and to her dismay she felt tears welling up in her eyes. She blinked, trying to hide them, and she could not go on speaking.

"I understand, little one." Gently Blakeney pulled her around to face him. "But I must. You know that, don't you?"

She saw compassion in his steel-gray eyes and something else. Excitement, she thought, perhaps anticipation of the danger that lay ahead of him. Briefly she leaned her cheek against the rough braiding across his chest, and nodded.

Blakeney patted her shoulder awkwardly. "Pluck up, Georgie. The Rutledges have always had one of their men in the army. It is my turn."

"You'll make an excellent officer, Blakeney. It's only—"

Georgie broke off. She simply couldn't tell him that seeing him in his uniform brought back memories of Aubrey's departure eighteen months ago. Aubrey had looked just as handsome and proud, just as vibrantly alive with his glowing eyes and that indefinable air of expectancy. Six months later Aubrey was dead.

"Go on, Blakeney." Straightening, she gave him a little push and smiled. "Find Marian and try to enjoy your last evening among civilized people. Tomorrow is soon enough to start thinking of Spanish beauties and endless gambling sessions in flea-riddled tents."

"Is that what Aubrey wrote?" Blakeney said. "I see that I'll have a most difficult time fitting in."

Georgie laughed. "Off with you, graceless imp, as soon as you take me to Peter Farnsworth. I'm hoping he'll ask me for a quadrille. There's no one to rival him in elegance and grace."

She stood by Lieutenant Lord Peter Farnsworth and watched Blakeney wend his way through the crowds. Gold and red flames danced in his wavy, dark brown hair as he passed under the chandeliers. She saw the proud arch of his nose as he turned his head. And again, in her mind's eye, she saw Aubrey.

In the musicians' gallery, Sir Perceval Hargrave congratulated himself on his foresight. When he arrived he had instantly perceived that it would require a great amount of good fortune to find Lady Georgiana in the great crush of people. Sir Percy had no wish to rely on Dame Fortune; that lady had proven all too fickle at the card tables. Instead, he had made his way to this vantage point.

He had noticed Lady Georgiana the moment he flung aside the velvet curtains at the rear of the little balcony, and for the space of a heartbeat he feared that she had seen him too. Standing beside her brother Blakeney just inside the doors, she was looking up at the musicians' gallery. She turned away smiling, and Sir Percy had realized that he stood too far back, hidden in the folds of the curtain, to be seen from below.

Sir Percy's lips stretched in a thin, mirthless smile when he saw Blakeney escort her to Peter Farnsworth. The Honorable Blakeney Rutledge was shipping out in the morning—as were the other scarlet coats at this illustrious gathering. Lady Georgiana, from the looks of it, was going to "do her duty" by her brother's fellow officers. She'd dance with them and laugh with them and make certain they marched off to the battlefields with pleasant memories.

Slowly Sir Percy descended the narrow stairs. He must apologize to Lady Georgiana, but an apology alone wouldn't get him closer to his goal. If an announcement of his betrothal to a rich heiress was not made soon, his creditors would descend on him like the vultures they were.

A curious weakness attacked his knees. With some difficulty Sir Percy negotiated the last steps. For a moment he leaned against the wall of the small antechamber in which he found himself and closed his eyes. But he could not shut out the dark shadows of the King's Bench Prison creeping inexorably toward him.

With shaking fingers he dabbed a scented handkerchief against his moist brow. Lady Georgiana it must be—and soon!

Bloody hell! Marriage to that young lady might turn out more amusing than he had believed possible. He must watch his step, though. No more slipups like this morning! Especially as long as that American was still around. Gray had set on him like a man ready to do murder.

Instinctively, Sir Percy flexed his right hand. The square of snowy lawn fluttered unheeded to the floor as he imagined the hilt of his sword touching his palm. His fingers curled, gripping tightly. Bending at the knee, Sir Percy put his right leg forward.

"En garde, mon américain!"

The door to the ballroom swung open, admitting a rush of stale, warm air ahead of a giggling young lady and a gentleman, whose wilting shirt points and flushed countenance gave mute witness of the overcrowded conditions in the large main chamber. They drew to a startled halt just as Sir Percy straightened to a more conventional posture.

The young gentleman raised a brow. "What's that, Percy? Always knew you were a hothead, but I've never seen you fence shadows before."

Without a word Sir Percy stalked into the ballroom. He squeezed his way toward the spot by the window where he had seen Lady Georgiana and Peter Farnsworth, just in time to observe them join the couples on the dance floor in a lively quadrille. The gentlemen in Georgiana's set, he noted, were all young officers.

Hell and the devil confound it! Sir Percy gritted his teeth until his jaw ached. He hadn't spent the better part of a month dangling after Lady Georgiana without learning of her penchant for uniforms. A man in a scarlet coat could always count on being received by her with a smile and a friendly word, whereas those who had elected to keep up appearances at home must guard against the sharp edge of her tongue. Lady Georgiana was known to have administered some blistering set-downs.

With narrowed eyes Sir Percy followed the movements of the dancers. Gradually his face relaxed. His foot started tapping in beat with the music drifting—barely audible—from the musicians' gallery.

On the dance floor, Georgie did her best to pay attention to Peter Farnsworth's light-hearted banter. Yet time and again her gaze strayed in search of Barrett Gray. Determinedly looking away from the door, she smiled at Peter.

"How dashed pretty you look, Georgie! Something about this gown, I believe."

"Perhaps you feel it is too daring for a debutante?"

"Fustian! It's that peach color. Yes, it does something to your skin and eyes. Adds a golden tone or something. Makes me realize that Blakeney's hoydenish sister has grown into a beautiful young lady."

The dance was over, and she started to walk back to the window, which some courageous soul had opened slightly. "If I didn't know better I'd suspect the orgeat has been laced with brandy tonight," she said, her eyes alight with teasing laughter. "How can you tell such bouncers, Peter, and not blush?"

"And how can you bear to speak cruelly to me on the eve of my departure to the battlefields!"

Peter Farnsworth looked suitably crushed, but Georgie had known him too long to be misled. Besides, how could she help but feel pleased? If Peter believed she looked well, Barrett might think so, too.

The soft breeze from the window felt good after the furnacelike atmosphere on the dance floor. Georgie turned her face into the cool air and wondered why Barrett and Robert were so late.

"Peter!" A very young lady came to a breathless halt beside them. Her red curls bounced excitedly. "You promised me the next waltz! You know you did, Peter!"

Grabbing his hand, she started to drag him away. "Hurry, can't you? It'll take forever to find one of the patronesses in this crush, and you know I must have permission first!"

Peter grinned. "Duty, you know," he said to Georgie. "My neighbor's youngest. I must have been foxed when I promised to lead her out."

Laughing, Georgie sent him on his way—but her face was beginning to ache from the smiles she had forced to her lips. It wouldn't be so hard to smile if she, too, might dance the next waltz.

"Immodest, scandalous," some called this most daring of dances that had come from the Continent. "Might as well make love in public," others said. Many a hostess had placed a strict taboo on the waltz and would not permit it to be performed in her ballroom. At Almack's, a young lady required the sanction of one of the patronesses before she could venture onto the dance floor to be clasped in her partner's arms; but Georgie had already been granted permission. She'd be able to waltz the moment Barrett solicited her hand.

Georgie's eyes flew to the clock above the door. Its hands moved inexorably toward the eleventh hour. Robert and Barrett had apparently decided not to come.

Her shoulders drooped with disappointment. She let her

gaze wander along the crowded chamber. She felt isolated, alone among hundreds of laughing, chatting merrymakers. She might have stepped up to any of the clusters of ladies with their overbright smiles and overworked fans, and gentlemen with perspiring brows and furtively wielded hand-kerchiefs. She might have joined their conversations; she might have looked for Blakeney, who was leaving on the morrow; she might even have searched for Charlotte and Fenella, who should have arrived sometime these past thirty minutes. Yet she stood there by the window, gently moving her fan and trying not to look toward the door again.

Barrett had tried to tell her that they would not see each other again, but she had relied on Robert's word. Robert had assured her they would be at Almack's.

The buzz of various conversations all around her was distracting. She tried to block it out and at first paid scant attention to the voice raised insistently behind her.

"Eight scarlet coats—but for a foolish mix-up at Whitehall," the man said, "I should have been the ninth to ship out with the transport in the morning. Dear Lady Georgiana, may I beg most sincerely for your forgiveness?"

The last words brought her head around sharply. Her fan closed with a snap. How dare he! How dare Sir Perceval approach her!

Georgie's eyes bored right through him. She started to walk away, pointedly turning her back on him.

"I don't blame you for cutting me, Lady Georgiana. And indeed, I do not ask that you look at me. I could not do so either. My valet had to shave me, for the sight of my countenance in the mirror filled me with loathing. I only ask that you permit me to beg your pardon most humbly."

Sir Percy followed close on her heels while he spoke, and his voice carried sufficiently to be heard by those crowding their path. In the shake of a lamb's tail the *ton* would be abuzz with speculation about her contretemps with Sir Percy if she insisted on ignoring him.

Georgiana spun. Facing him, she said coldly, "I accept your apology, sir. Now pray excuse me. I must find my brother and Charlotte."

She would have turned away then, but he grasped her hand, raising it to his lips. "Most gracious lady, I thank you!" Looking at her with a penitent expression, he added so softly that this time only she could hear, "Believe me, Lady Georgiana, but for the stupidity of a Whitehall clerk I would not have had to drown my disappointment while your brother and his friends celebrated their imminent departure to the field of honor."

She snatched her hand from his unwelcome clasp. Although he gave every appearance of a man smitten by remorse, although he gazed at her most earnestly, there was an air about Sir Percy that denied him Georgiana's true forgiveness and her sympathy. Remembering the reek of brandy about his person, she said coldly, "Are you saying you were too drunk to know what you were about this morning, Sir Percy?"

"Drunk as a brewer's horse, Lady Georgiana," he confessed. "In fact, I was clean raddled. I don't remember much, but I must have behaved with the utmost depravity toward you to have warranted Mr. Gray's, er, treatment of me."

Unconsciously, his hand went to his chin where, beneath a layer of face powder and fairly well hidden behind his high shirt points, Georgiana saw a purplish bruise and repressed a satisfied smile. *Serves him right, the brute. No doubt it hurts like the dickens, but it's no more than he deserves. I, too, ached for hours.*

Still, she did not wish to be unjust, and what he said about Whitehall intrigued her sufficiently to ask, "What about this clerical mistake? Are you trying to tell me, sir, that you hoped to be one of the party of officers sailing for Spain?"

"Yes, indeed, Lady Georgiana." Again lowering his voice, he added, "One doesn't like to sound peevish of course, but I did expect my commission to come through in time for the transport tomorrow. And what must I hear, Lady Georgiana?" Giving her no time to reply, he said with a great show of outrage, "My papers have not been processed yet! And

there's Wellington, asking, nay begging, to be sent competent officers!''

Georgie stared at him, trying to make sense of his
grievance. Blakeney's commission had come through in
February; he had known the date of his departure in March
or April; and Blakeney and his friends had completed their
training.

Sir Percy was lying! He hadn't applied for a commission
at all. If he had, he wouldn't have found out only yesterday
that something went wrong. But why? *Why would he lie to
me?*

"Pardon me, Lady Georgiana," Sir Percy said smoothly.
"I would not wish to add to your discomfiture. You've
suffered more than enough at my hands. But we *are* attracting
an ungoodly amount of attention. Perhaps if we were to
dance? Or will you bestow your hand only on those wearing
a scarlet coat?''

Georgie drew herself up. She measured him with a
haughty stare, then, deciding to leave well enough alone,
turned away. To her dismay, she saw Charlotte coming
toward her. Charlotte, who regarded Sir Percy as an eminently
eligible suitor to Georgie's hand!

As though she swept a broom before her, a path cleared
for Charlotte's regal approach. And William was with her!
William, who abhorred any kind of public attention, and
who would look at Georgie with hurt and disbelief if so
much as a breath of scandal were attached to her name.

It would certainly cause a stir if Charlotte ordered her to
dance with the odious baronet, and she refused! To spare
William's feelings, Georgie would have to smile and accept
Sir Percy as a dance partner.

But, Georgiana thought, *I can deprive Charlotte of the
satisfaction of issuing that command!*

She gave Sir Percy a cool nod. "Very well, sir. We shall
dance.''

There was a disquieting gleam in the baronet's blue eyes,
but his manner was punctilious, even deferential, as he
proffered his arm to lead Georgiana onto the dance floor.
The musicians struck up a tune.

Georgiana's step faltered. *A waltz! I wanted to waltz with Barrett!*

The gleam in Sir Percy's eyes deepened. He placed his right hand on her back, just below her shoulder blade. Georgie knew he was wearing gloves, was not touching her directly. Yet she had to fight a shudder of revulsion.

She must not have succeeded, for his face darkened. He snatched up her cold right hand, saying impatiently, "If you were to smile you'd look less like a lamb being led to the slaughtering block. Or are you worried I'll take a tumble—like the unfortunate Lord Ebrington when he danced with you?"

Georgie lifted her chin. She did not respond, did not even say anything when he pulled her closer to guide her across the crowded dance floor. She stared coldly past his ear to the spot where she knew Charlotte would be standing, watching her.

And then she saw Barrett.

She felt hot and cold at the same time, and she could feel her mouth stretch in a wide, silly smile. She couldn't help it. Barrett had come!

His bronzed face was turned toward her, and as Sir Percy weaved around the dancing couples and guided her closer to the edge of the dance floor, she realized that Barrett was not smiling. On the contrary. He looked angry.

Georgie's heart plummeted. Her smile wavered. Surely Barrett must realize that she could not have avoided Sir Percy! That, had she given him the cut at Almack's, she would have caused just the kind of lurid speculation she had been at pains to prevent that morning!

The next turn brought her even closer to Barrett. Their eyes met briefly, hers asking for understanding, his conveying cold disdain. Then she lost sight of him as Sir Percy whirled her into a reverse.

Georgiana decided she had danced long enough with Sir Percy. Barrett would leave in the morning. She must speak with him! He must be made to see—

"I wish to leave, Sir Percy. I don't feel well."

The baronet looked at her sharply. "You wouldn't wish to

attract undue attention, my lady. I shall place you in Lady Charlotte's care as soon as the dance has ended."

Anger, quick and wild as a sudden summer storm rose in her breast. "*Now*, Sir Percy! Unless you wish to be left standing here?"

He bowed. Grim-faced, he led her around the dancing couples toward the chattering crowd ringing the dance floor. His eyes narrowed when he saw the tall, dark-haired American. He tried to change direction, but Georgie was no will-o'-the-wisp to be borne hither and thither. She stubbornly held her course, and then Barrett had seen her and was making his way toward her.

"My lady." Not a muscle moved in his face, not a shred of feeling warmed his green eyes as he addressed her. "I see I did you a disservice this morning. You must have wished me to the devil."

"Barrett—" she faltered under his cool gaze.

"My lady?" he said in a voice that conveyed to her nothing but ill-concealed boredom.

He should know, she thought angrily, without her telling him yet again, that she had been grateful that morning! How could she explain anything with Sir Percy and a score of gossips latching on to every word she uttered! If only they could have a moment of privacy!

"We should move on, Lady Georgiana," said Sir Percy.

Barrett looked at him as though he had only now noticed the baronet's presence. "Ah, Sir Percy," he drawled. "No doubt I should apologize to you, but somehow I can't bring myself to do it. Strange, wouldn't you say?"

He turned to Georgiana, and she caught an expression in his eyes that belied the coldness of his voice as he took his leave.

"Servant, my lady," he said curtly, spun on his heel, and stalked off.

For a moment she was too numb to move or speak. She couldn't believe that this would mark the end of their brief but, or so she believed, growing friendship. He was walking away! Leaving with the impression that she had played fast and loose with both Sir Percy and with him.

She saw that Barrett was approaching the doors and instantly perceived what she must do. The vestibule would be empty at this time. There they could talk.

"Barrett!"

Heedless of curious stares and sharp whispers, she pushed her way through the crowded chamber toward the door where Barrett had disappeared. Someone in a scarlet coat flung open one of the wings to let her pass through into the vestibule.

It was empty.

She hesitated only briefly before moving toward the street entrance, but that instant was enough to put an end to any plan she might have had to follow Barrett into the streets.

"Georgie! Are you mad?" Blakeney took her arm and drew her into an alcove. "Whatever is the matter with you?"

Before she could pull herself together and formulate a reply, William burst into the vestibule, followed moments later by Charlotte and Fenella.

"Georgie!" he shouted.

She winced at the concern in William's voice and quickly stepped out into the light. "I'm here. With Blakeney."

The earl put his arm around her shoulders. "Are you all right, little one?" Studying her pale face, he said harshly, "If Sir Percy misbehaved—I'll have his hide if that bounder made improper advances to you!"

"Please don't ask questions, William. Just take me home. Please!"

Fenella giggled. "I think you've got it all wrong, Uncle William. It was Georgie who misbehaved again. Shouting the American's name for all the world to—"

"That'll do, Fenella," Charlotte interrupted sharply. "William and I will discuss Georgiana's behavior in the morning. Now we must consider what we can do to scotch any possible scandal. I propose that you go in search of Sir Percy, William, and invite him to leave with us."

"No!" shouted William, while, at the same time, Sir Percy made his presence known with a dry cough.

"There's no need to search for me, dear lady," the baronet said smoothly. "I am at your disposal."

"Dammit, Percy," said Blakeney sharply. "Can't you see you're de trop?"

Charlotte showed her perfect teeth. "So kind of you, Sir Percy," she murmured. "Georgiana is not well, the poor child. It would be best for her to leave immediately."

Sir Percy bowed. "I shall be happy to escort Lady Georgiana home."

"Georgie has two of her brothers in attendance," Blakeney put in. "It would cause less speculation if one of us were to take her home."

Grudgingly, Charlotte ceded the point, but she refused to be defeated in her purpose of throwing Sir Percy and Georgiana together. The sooner the chit was married, the sooner Fenella would be relieved of her beautiful cousin's troublesome presence!

"Blakeney and Sir Percy will take Georgiana home," she said decisively. "William, Fenella, and I shall remain here and try to make light of Georgiana's extraordinary behavior."

Georgie listened to the bickering in stony silence. Even with the threat of Sir Percy's company hanging over her, she did not speak. The moment Blakeney had pulled her to a halt, she had realized that she would not be allowed to follow Barrett that night. And in the morning, by the time it would be deemed proper to make a call, he would be well on his way to Bristol.

Someone put her cloak around her shoulders. Firm hands guided her toward the outer doors. She looked up. William was on one side of her, Blakeney on the other.

"If you find Sir Percy's company so desirable, Charlotte," William said, "you may take him up in your own coach."

Wrapped in misery that was lightened only by a faint stirring of resentment, Georgie passed through the doors she had entered earlier with such expectations. Obviously, Barrett believed that she had only pretended outrage in the park that morning; that she welcomed Sir Percy's embraces.

If it had been William who jumped to these conclusions,

Georgiana would have understood. But it was Barrett, and he should have known that a woman would regard a waltz as an intimate embrace only if she had the fortune to dance it with a man for whom she cared.

Irrepressibly, the question flashed through her mind how she would have felt if she had been waltzing with Barrett.

Sir Perceval directed his most charming smile at Lady Charlotte. "I think it best if you and Miss Fenella were to return to the ballroom, dear lady. I see no reason why your daughter should forego the pleasures of a ball."

Charlotte's eyes flew to his face. "And you, Sir Percy?"

"Trust me. I shall do everything within my power to nip a scandal in the bud."

"Will you call in Upper Brook Street in the morning?" Charlotte probed.

"At ten o'clock, if it is convenient."

"I shall look forward to it, Sir Percy."

Still smiling, Sir Percy took his leave. As he trod down the wide steps into King Street, he let his eyes run over the carriages lined up on either side. Soon, very soon, *his* carriage would outshine them all!

He turned into St. James's Street. Whistling softly, he approached the hackney stand in front of White's club.

"Fleet Street. Offices of the *Gazette*," he told the sleepy driver on the box before pulling open the scratched panel of the door and entering the musty interior.

Five

On the morning following his hasty departure from Almack's a bare ten minutes after he had squeezed into the celebrated assembly room, Barrett Gray faced his cousin and uncle across the breakfast table in their comfortable Curzon Street home.

He raised heavy eyes from his untouched plate of beef-steak and eggs. "Think I'll be off. Thanks for lending me your curricle, Robert. I'll see that your groom has a good night's rest at The Swan in Bristol before turning back."

Robert scrutinized Barrett's haggard face, mute witness, he thought, to a sleepless night. "Wish I could accompany you, but I'm expected at the Admiralty today. I have an inkling I'll be off to Gibraltar before the week's out."

"Don't trust me with your curricle, eh? I assure you, my friend, I didn't drink half enough last night to impair my judgment." Barrett pushed back his chair. He strode to the head of the table where Sir Charles sat, calmly reading his papers and consuming mounds of red beef and succulent ham. "I am ready to leave, Uncle."

"What? Oh, aye. You're off, are you, my boy?" Sir Charles's gaze fell on Barrett's plate. "But surely not without eating! No, no, sit down. You have a long drive ahead of you. Fifteen, mayhap sixteen hours, if conditions are favorable."

"I intend to make it in twelve hours or less, sir."

"Only if you plan to fast all day," Robert interjected dryly.

"What nonsense is this, Robert? Of course Barrett won't fast like some lovelorn schoolboy. Now sit down, both of you, and finish your breakfast." Sir Charles folded and set aside the *Morning Post*, picking up the *Gazette* instead. Without further ado, he immersed himself in his food and his paper.

Barrett darted a look at his uncle as he resumed his seat at the table. Lovelorn be damned! He was furious that he had allowed the Lady Georgiana to make a fool of him. He had sullied his hands on that scalawag Hargrave to rescue the lady from what he had idiotically believed to have been unwanted attentions. She had even thanked him—only to return to the baronet's arms in full view of the *ton*! She had permitted the dirty dog to hold her close. So close, their bodies had touched!

Barrett grew warm. He attacked his steak with vigor, downed a tankard of ale, then thrust his chair back once more. "It's eight-thirty, Uncle Charles. I must be going if I wish to reach Bristol before midnight."

"Great Scot!" Sir Charles's voice rose to a roar, and he angrily stabbed a finger at the *Gazette*. "Georgie betrothed to Sir Perceval!"

A blow from Gentleman Jackson could not have hit Barrett harder than his uncle's announcement.

"What rot! Georgie would never—" Robert reached for the *Gazette* to study the insert. "It's Lady Charlotte's doing," he said finally. "She knows she can't fire off Fenella as long as every eligible bachelor hankers after Georgie."

Barrett's hands clenched. An American, engaged in trade, might not be eligible—but he was a bachelor, and he had hankered all right! In a few brief meetings, Lady Georgiana had turned to dust and ashes his conviction that he was immune to charm, intelligence, and an utterly delightful manner. Qualities that would be wasted on Sir Percy.

But he had suspected as much last night, hadn't he? Bowing to his uncle and cousin, Barrett unceremoniously interrupted their dispute about the announcement in the paper.

"I shall be delighted," he said with a tinge of bitterness in his voice, "to carry the glad tidings to Lady Georgiana's aunt in Boston."

"It's impossible! Preposterous!" Georgie, still in her nightgown and with a shawl flung hastily around her shoulders, faced the Earl of Wolversham in the parlor of Codrington House.

She eyed William warily as he brandished a crumpled copy of the *Gazette* before her face. Purple veins knotted on his temples and forehead, his eyes were bloodshot. It would be no exaggeration to say that he was in a devil of a rage.

"I gave Sir Perceval not the slightest reason to believe his suit would be welcome. On the contrary," Georgie said tartly. "I made it abundantly clear that I wish nothing to do with him whatsoever!"

"I'm still your guardian!" William shouted, punctuating his words by pounding his fist against the marble fireplace mantel. "I'll not tolerate—" He broke off, his dark brows knitting in a frown as Georgie's emphatic denial penetrated the fog of his anger. "Do you mean to tell me he had the unmitigated gall to insert the announcement without your knowledge?"

Her eyes kindled. "Did you really think I'd marry such a one as he?" she countered.

His anger shrank before her outrage. As though weary, he brushed the back of his hand across his forehead. "No. I suppose not," he said with a shrug. "There's nothing for it, then. I'll have to call on the bounder."

"You need not." Charlotte's smug voice startled them. Neither one had heard her enter.

Georgie spun to face her half sister, who closed the parlor door firmly behind her. "What are you saying, Charlotte? That I marry him?"

"There has never been a jilt among the Rutledges." With an air of complacence and utmost satisfaction, Charlotte seated herself in a straight-backed chair. "You have no alternative, Georgie. You would not wish our good name dragged through the mud. But that's not what I meant to say."

Charlotte looked at William, her proud Rutledge nose raised in a mixture of defiance and triumph. "Sir Percy will be calling here in less than half an hour. You need not bother to seek him out."

"If I find you were part and parcel of this . . . this dastardly trick, Charlotte," he said with ominous calm, "I'll see to it that Codrington removes you to the country for the rest of your life."

Charlotte's face flushed an angry red. "You wanted a husband for her, didn't you? Sir Percy is from an ancient and noble line. He—"

"He's a lecher and a cad!" cried Georgie. Her skin

crawled as she remembered his attack on her person in Hyde Park. "I'll emigrate to America before I marry him! William, make him send a retraction to the papers!"

Ignoring her outburst, William addressed Charlotte. "Hargrave is a gambler, a womanizer, and a fortune hunter. I will not have his name mingled with ours." He paused, allowing his words to sink in, then said, "I take it Codrington is still at Newmarket? Very well. In that case I shall see Hargrave in the study."

Georgie breathed a sigh of relief. She had not realized how tense she was. Her temper had boiled when William showed her the announcement, but she had kept a tight rein on her mounting fury. Confronted with one of William's rare but towering rages, she had known she must tread warily lest his pride and his fear of scandal betray him into uttering a command he would later regret but not retract. But now he had told Charlotte he would not accept Sir Perceval into the family. Now she could be easy.

Following his tall, solid form into the corridor, she slipped her hand into his. "Thank you, William," she said softly.

He gave her fingers a comforting squeeze, but his smile was strained. "Get dressed, little one. I'll send for you when I've finished with the cad," he said gruffly before turning toward Lord Codrington's study at the end of the hall.

Georgie hurried to her chamber on the third floor. She scrambled into a gown, dragged a comb through her unruly hair, then paced the floor while the minutes dragged by with unbearable slowness.

Her fingers trailed across the dainty writing desk standing against the wall opposite her bed, drummed a quick tattoo on the top of her dresser between the window casements, brushed along the leather spines of her favorite volumes, which she had carried in her trunk from Wolversham Court and stacked on the narrow mantel ledge above the fireplace.

She stopped in her tracks, staring at a slender book of verse by Philip Freneau and a collection of Benjamin Franklin's pamphlets, *Poor Richard's Almanack*. Aubrey had brought the two volumes from America and had presented them to Georgie, but it was Barrett's face she remembered, his contempt when he watched her waltzing with Sir Percy.

Barrett, who would undoubtedly be on his way to Bristol, for he was to sail on the morrow—Had he, too, read the announcement in the *Gazette* before setting out? It hardly mattered; he could think no worse of her than he had on the previous night.

A tightening in her chest, a sudden problem with her breathing, drove her to the open windows. Pushing aside the lace curtains that filtered the sunlight and dappled her bedcover with shifting, lacy shadow patterns, Georgie sank down on the windowsill and breathed deeply of the soft May breeze.

Where was her summons? William would make short shrift of his interview with Sir Percy. He'd simply order him to send a retraction of the announcement to the papers, and that would be that. Any moment he'd call for her and tell her not to worry any longer.

But the summons did not come.

After a while, Georgie slid down from the windowsill to resume her pacing. She had taken no more than half a turn about the room when impatience and curiosity would no longer be denied. Raising the flounced hem of her gown, Georgie fled the chamber and raced downstairs.

On the second-floor landing she was met by her abigail carrying a tray. "Oh, my lady!" the girl cried when Georgie flew past her. "Lord Wolversham's compliments, but ye're to take a bite to eat in yer chamber."

Georgie stopped, one foot poised to proceed down the next flight of stairs. "Don't bother, Rose. I'm not hungry. Do you know where my brother is? Has Sir Perceval Hargrave left yet?"

"I believe so," Rose said cautiously, then rattled off the rest of Lord Wolversham's message in a great hurry. "An' his lordship's gone out. To gather the family. An' ye're to stay in yer chamber until one o'clock, Lady Georgie."

Unconsciously, Georgiana's hand went to her throat where her pulse raced erratically. If William was summoning the family, something was dreadfully wrong. Nothing short of disaster, or scandal, would induce him to confer with his half brothers Charles, James, and the twins about Sir Percy's false announcement.

But of the twins only Lewis would come, Georgie remembered. Blakeney had left with the break of dawn to join his transport at Portsmouth—Blakeney, who next to Aubrey was closest to her in affection.

Slowly Georgie started to retrace her steps to her chamber. She felt very much alone, but there was no point in disobeying William's order. Downstairs she would find only Charlotte and Fenella.

Waiting was a penance. In desperation, Georgie took down Benjamin Franklin's pamphlets, which Aubrey had had bound in a handsomely embossed leather cover. She had always gotten a chuckle out of some of the sayings; not so this day. "Necessity never made a good bargain" only served to remind her of the fiasco at Almack's. Necessity had driven her to stand and speak to Sir Percy when all she had wanted to do was give him the cut direct. Again, it had been necessity that forced her to dance with him.

And instead of rushing after Barrett, shouting his name for all the world to hear, she should have listened to Mr. Franklin's words of wisdom, "Make haste slowly."

A surge of warmth burned her face. The book closed with a snap. She had, indeed, been thoughtless. She admitted it freely. But, then, she had so looked forward to dancing with Barrett, had wanted to wipe from his memory the disheveled hoyden he rescued in the park that morning and replace her with a picture of a poised, elegant young lady.

When the summons to the salon finally came, Georgiana went down sedately enough, but she was more shaken than she dared admit, even to herself. It did not help that her older brothers Charles and James greeted her with silence. They sat side by side on one of a pair of silk-covered couches and, after one stern glance at her as she entered, resumed their low-voiced conversation.

Lewis, in looks as like Blakeney as he was unlike him in disposition, leaned with inimitable negligence against the fireplace. He raised a mocking, black brow. "In the basket, love?'' he drawled. "And here I prided myself on the distinction of being the only Rutledge to set the town by its ears.''

"Oh, hush!'' Charlotte said angrily. "Your sniping will only set up her back.'' Patting the space between her and Fenella on the second couch, she turned to Georgiana. "Come and sit by me, my dear,'' she said with false cordiality. "William has news for you.''

As she took her seat, William walked over from the credenza where he had been pouring wine. Without a word, he handed Georgie a glass.

"Is it that bad?'' she asked, forcing a smile to her lips as she looked up at her guardian. "Does Sir Percy refuse to retract the announcement?''

"He does,'' William said grimly. "But I've written the retraction myself, and if you're still of the same mind, I'll have it published.''

"But of course I am! I told you I'll not marry that man under any circumstances!''

There was a silence after Georgie's words; only her heartbeat pounded in her ears like the sudden roll of a drum. Her brothers, Charlotte, and Fenella all seemed to have stopped breathing. They stared at her as though she had said something unexpected.

William stood before her, booted feet planted apart, one hand in his coat pocket, his handsome head atop strong shoulders pushed forward as though he had difficulty seeing her properly. "You were observed in the park,'' he said heavily. "In Sir Percy's arms.''

Georgie opened her mouth to protest, to explain, but William forestalled her. "It matters not if you were struggling with him, Georgiana. It is all over town by now that you were trysting with Sir Percy. That you were alone, without a groom.''

"William—''

"Don't deny it, Georgiana! You were seen.''

"I'm not denying anything! I only want to know who saw me.''

"Does it matter?'' William said impatiently.

Georgie shook her head. There was no need for him to give her a name. She knew that only Barrett Gray had seen her struggling in Sir Percy's arms.

"There you have it!" Charlotte said, beaming with satisfaction. "You must marry Sir Percy."

"No!"

"But there's no one else who'd have you, Georgie dear," Fenella interjected sweetly. "You alienated every eligible bachelor."

"Dear me!" Lewis leveled his quizzing glass at Fenella and surveyed her in a manner that drove a blush to her cheeks. "Surely you're not trying to tell us that Georgie's tongue is more waspish than yours, Fenella my sweet?"

"Silence!" William gave Lewis a stern look, then ordered Fenella from the room. "Your mother should never have asked you to attend. This is none of your concern, Fenella."

Lewis grinned. He pushed himself away from the fireplace and rushed across the room to open the door. Sweeping an imaginary hat off his glossy dark hair, he bowed Fenella out with a flourish. "Now," he said, "let's get on with it. I've an appointment at Tattersall's this afternoon."

Charles and James, the oldest sons of the late earl's second marriage, looked at each other, then at William. As always, Charles was the spokesman. "May I ask why it was so necessary for all of us to appear? Seems to me this is something you had best settle yourself, William. After all, you're Georgie's guardian."

"Must I remind you that you, too, bear the Rutledge name?" William said sharply, surveying his family from beneath knitted brows. When his gaze came to rest on Georgie, she thought she detected a deep sadness in his eyes. The jut of his chin, however, and the tight set of his mouth betrayed none of this gentler emotion. They showed only sternness and implacability. They showed her that she was in for more than a scold.

Lewis, pouring himself a generous measure of brandy, shot a cynical look over his shoulder. "My dear William," he said in his low voice that yet held the sharpness of a razor. "I am all ears. I am all eagerness to assist you in this plight. But for heaven's sake, come to the point!"

Nettled, William shot back, "The point is, dear Lewis, that because of Georgie's thoughtlessness, because of her lack of decorum, the Rutledges are involved in a scandal. That is something I will not tolerate!"

"Have to do more than tolerate it," said James mildly. A blush spread upward from the top of his clerical collar when all eyes turned on him in astonishment, but for once he did not allow himself to be intimidated by his more forceful brothers, nor by Charlotte's indignant stare. "Have to accept it. And have to find a way to protect Georgie from all those cats who'll want to sharpen their claws on her."

"Why, thank you, Jamey," said Georgie, touched. "But you mustn't worry about me. I have a very tough hide, you know."

William tapped a boot irritably. "No one's going to hurt Georgie! And that's why I called you all together. We must decide where she should go. With the retraction in all the papers, and with Georgie out of sight for a year or so, even the busiest tongues of the *ton* will have no fuel to keep them wagging."

"Splendid!" said Georgie, her eyes brightening. "I'll return to Wolversham Court."

William shook his head. "I'm not of a mind to reward you, Georgie. It'll have to be Charles's place in Cambria unless someone can think of a better spot. Far removed from London."

Georgie's eyes widened in disbelief. *Banishment from Wolversham Court! My home! My school in Wolversham! The children are expecting me the end of June....*

As from a far distance, she heard Charles's voice. "Sorry, but Cambria is out. Violet's increasing. Wants to stay in London until after her confinement, so I leased the house."

A lively debate followed Charles's announcement, with Charlotte insisting that Georgie must marry Sir Percy, James shyly offering his parsonage in Marylebone where Georgie would not likely meet any member of the *ton*, and Lewis making snide remarks about putting his sister in breeches and sending her after Blakeney to act as his batman.

Georgiana paid them little heed. Her mind was a whirl of confusing emotions. Her heart ached at the thought of losing Wolversham Court. She'd never have believed it possible that William would punish her so severely. There was anger in her as well, resentment that a grown woman of twenty must bow to the edicts of a guardian.

She allowed none of these feelings to overpower her. She knew that somewhere at the center of that whirlpool of her thoughts was lodged a tiny germ, the concept of any idea. If she could catch it, she'd be able to accept her punishment and yet remain mistress of her own fate.

I'll emigrate to America before I marry Sir Percy!

Her words to William earlier that morning! As they echoed through her mind agitation fled, supplanted by growing excitement.

"Aunt Letty in Boston."

Georgie did not realize she had spoken aloud until Charlotte's voice, cheerful in contrast to her earlier, harsh demands, filled the salon. "That's an excellent solution, Georgie dear! And what's more, you'll enjoy it. I remember, when Aubrey returned, you were ready to pack your trunks and set out then and there."

"Balderdash!" said Charles, rising from the couch and starting to pace with his hands clasped behind his back in preparation of the delivery of lengthier arguments.

James forestalled him. "You cannot have considered, Georgie," he said seriously. "The situation between England and America is grave. There's talk of war."

"Talk!" Lewis returned to the brandy decanter for a refill. "My dear James, being in a "talking" profession yourself, I expected better from you. Whether speech is delivered from the pulpit or from the benches of Parliament, it's credited only by the gullible."

James uttered a protest but subsided when Lewis, at his most silky, said, "You can't seriously believe that, with memory of the last war still alive and bitter, England will compound her foolishness by fighting the Americans once more!''

Georgie caught William's eye and held it. Again she saw sadness reflected in his gaze. The decision to banish her had not been an easy one for him. But he had made the decision. It was up to her now to turn her supposed punishment into a pleasurable adventure. Visiting her Aunt Letty in Boston would in part fulfill the dream she and Aubrey had shared.

Unbidden, a harshly handsome face dominated by a pair of bright green eyes intruded upon her thoughts. Barrett Gray had, for a short while, been a part of her own secret dreams. She had thought him a knight, but he had proven himself a knave. She did not fear meeting him in Boston. On the contrary! She'd relish putting him in his place.

"Well, William?" she said, sitting tense and motionless beside Charlotte. His reply seemed a long time in coming, and only Lewis's eyes on her, filled with speculation and lazy amusement, kept her from fidgeting with the folds of her gown.

"Lewis is right," William said finally. "Not in his assumption that England would not have the courage to fight America again, but simply in the fact that there will be no war."

Georgie could sit still no longer. She flew off the couch and into William's arms. "I may go? Please say I may go, dear William!"

His arms closed around her in a brief embrace. Stepping away from her, he said gruffly, "My yacht lies in Milford Haven. I'll send word to Captain Morwell to take her into Bristol for outfitting. Be prepared to leave on Monday."

The hem of her skirts weighted with grapeshot to prevent them from flapping up around her calves and knees, a scarf wrapped around her head and shoulders, Georgie stood in the bow of the *Rutledge Pride*, William's large, frigate-built yacht. Her gaze was fixed on the grayish blue green expanse of choppy ocean.

She had often sailed with William, but it had been mainly

on trips along the English coast or for a brief hop across to Ireland. This was different.

It was the morning of her twenty-seventh day aboard the *Rutledge Pride*, and still there was so much water, so much sky, all blending in the distance with no distinct line of separation. It was awesome.

At times she liked to pretend that the long yardarm with its two billowing spritsails was the horizon, a goal on which her eyes could focus. But it never helped for long. Her gaze would return to the opaque distance, always longing for a sight of solidity, a glimpse of the many islands Captain Morwell had told her lay scattered in the Boston Bay.

A shout from the maintop made her whirl around. "Sail off the starboard catheads!" the lookout bawled, shattering the sensation of isolation that had held Georgie spellbound. She was aware again of the padding of bare feet across the decks, of the constant creaking of timber, the flap of sails.

Putting a hand to her brow to shade her eyes against the early sun's glare, Georgie looked toward the quarterdeck where the first mate was swinging himself over the bulwarks into the mizzen ratlines. Halfway up the mast he stopped, grabbed the glass dangling on a leather strap around his neck, and held it to his eye. Apparently dissatisfied with what he saw, he shook his head and started to climb to the crossbars of the mizzentop.

Adjusting her gait easily to the constant roll of the ship, Georgie hurried aft across the scrubbed planks of the main deck. The stiff northeasterly breeze hit her full in the face. It tugged the scarf off her head and toyed with stray tendrils of her hair, which she had tied at the nape of her neck. Despite her hurry to reach the quarterdeck before the first mate made his report to Captain Morwell, she took time to respond to several seamen in blue-striped shirts and canvas petticoat breeches as they stopped in their tasks to offer her a "good morn'."

Daniel, the tow-headed cabin boy, approached at a run. "My lady," he panted. "Mistress Rose, she be askin' if you're comin' below. Breakfast is gettin' cold."

"In a moment, Daniel. I want to hear what Mr. Selwyn has to say about the vessel they've sighted."

Daniel's urchin face broke into an expression of pleasurable excitement. Trotting alongside Georgiana, he said eagerly, "He's up there a long time. Do you reckon it's a pirate ship?"

"Might be," she said, keeping a straight face. She saw that the first mate was taking the glass from his eye, and increased her pace. At the short ladder leading up to the quarterdeck, Georgie halted. Smiling into Daniel's expectantly upturned eyes, she nodded.

Daniel beamed. His chest swelled with pride and a gallon of air as he inhaled deeply. He yelled at the top of his lungs, "Permission to approach quarterdeck. Sir!"

A white-haired, blue-clad figure appeared at the head of the stairs. Captain Morwell saluted smartly. "Permission granted."

He reached down to help Georgiana up the steps. "Good morning, Lady Georgie. You'll be pleased to know that we averaged five knots again last night. It's a good omen I'd say that your journey is blessed with one of the rare northeast winds."

"Excellent! Then we'll be in Boston in two days. A record crossing!" cried Georgie, stepping onto the quarterdeck just as Mr. Selwyn swung down the ratlines.

"A brig, sir. American," he reported. "Too far off to make out her name, but I'll eat a boom if she isn't the *Boston Belle*. She sailed out of Bristol harbor just as we made fast."

Georgie's eyes widened. "We sailed three days later!"

"Aye, but she's a heavy merchant brig. The *Rutledge Pride* is faster even than His Majesty's frigates."

"That be on account of havin' only three guns 'stead of thirty or forty," piped Daniel, forgetting his disappointment that the other vessel was no pirate ship.

"Will we pass her? There's someone I know aboard the *Boston Belle*," said Georgie, feeling quite breathless all of a sudden. She'd enjoy waving to the traitorous Barrett Gray, then thumbing her nose at him.

"We'll pass the brig all right," the first mate assured her, "but it won't be close enough to be sure it's the *Boston Belle*, let alone recognize anyone aboard. Our present course is more southward than hers."

Georgie went below to eat her breakfast then retired to her luxurious sleeping cabin—her home away from home for almost a month.

The furnishings were of mahogany with hammered brass trim. Soft rugs covered polished teak flooring, and velvet curtains draped over the portholes assured complete privacy. The cabin was like William, Georgie thought with a smile. Handsome and solid.

The smile lingered while she wrote letters to be entrusted to an English vessel once she reached Boston harbor. She read a little, and sorted through her belongings to see what Rose might pack ahead of time.

Only two more days! Then she'd be in the country Aubrey had fallen in love with. Excitement welled up in her. Suddenly she couldn't bear to remain below. Although the deck levels of the yacht had been arranged to provide ample headroom in the main cabins, Georgie felt closed in. Pulling a cloak from her wardrobe, she hurried from the cabin.

On the quarterdeck once again, she looked forward where the sun dipped low like a huge orange red ball, staining water, firmament, the sails and brass rails of the *Rutledge Pride* with a touch of flame. Forward, where America was waiting.

When Captain Morwell asked if she would care to take the helm for a spell, Georgie assented with alacrity. Mr. Selwyn stayed close behind her, ready to take the wheel if she should flounder. But this was not the first time that Georgie had steered her brother's yacht, and after a while, the first mate lit a pipe and relaxed against the bulwarks.

Beneath her hands, Georgie felt the pulse of the *Rutledge Pride*, a tremble and throbbing that responded to the slightest turn of the helm. As the yacht pressed onward into the deepening dusk, Georgie wondered if her eyes held that same gleam she had observed in Aubrey and in Blakeney before they left for the Peninsula. A glint of excitement and anticipation, an air of expectancy. She could understand their emotions now, for she was feeling just as they had.

She was steering her own destiny.

Six

With the gradual disappearance of the sun, the gusting tail wind that had pressed the *Rutledge Pride* westward lost its vigor. No longer did Georgie's cloak slap her legs, no longer did her pinned up hair threaten to escape. The great canvas squares of sail sagged imperceptibly; the ship's pulse faltered.

Instinct guided Georgiana's hands on the wheel; the vessel's course was corrected before Mr. Selwyn had covered the short distance from the bulwarks to the helm. She glanced over her shoulder at Captain Morwell, at ease on a low canvas stool beneath the braces. He was logging the entries of the day.

"Wind's shifting, sir," she said.

"Be a miracle if we make three knots tonight," muttered the first mate.

Captain Morwell closed the log book, swathed it in oilskin wrappings, and placed it in a small chest. "Aye," he said, rising stiffly. "There'll be a change. Have felt it all day."

He put an ink-stained forefinger to his mouth, then, holding the upthrust, moistened finger into the wind, nodded. "Be west-southwest come morning. It'll set us back a day or so."

"Sail to the larboard bow!" yelled the lookout in the maintop.

Georgie squinted into the orange glow to her left, but if another vessel was out there in the vastness of the Atlantic Ocean, it could not yet be seen from the decks. Mr. Selwyn knocked out his pipe and thrust it into a trouser pocket. Once again he scrambled up the ratlines.

"A small brig or a schooner, flying the American ensign," he shouted from the mizzen top.

Georgiana craned her neck, trying to catch a glimpse of the first mate. He did not sound at all convinced, and he remained on his high perch to keep watch on the stranger. If Daniel were here, he'd suspect a pirate vessel, Georgiana thought.

She smiled, but a prickle at the base of her neck made her feel cold all of a sudden. It was the wind, she told herself as she coaxed the wheel to adjust to an unexpected gust and another barely perceptible air shift to the south.

Captain Morwell stamped to larboard. He stared silently in the direction of the sighted craft. The second mate appeared at Georgiana's side. She had not heard him come. Not a word was exchanged between them; but she stepped aside, giving the wheel into his capable hands. And even as she looked into his face, wondering at his tenseness and thinking that it was said of sailors they had a sixth sense for unexpected trouble at sea, Mr. Selwyn called down from the masthead again.

"It's a brigsloop, sir! Sixteen guns! Long pivot gun in the forecastle!"

Georgiana joined Captain Morwell at the railing. A breeze, stiffening rapidly after the unexpected change of direction, tugged at her hair, blowing a few short curls into her face. The sloop was now close enough that Georgie could see her two tall masts, rigged for full speed; yet too far away to disclose her gunports to the naked eye.

"She's signaling!" Mr. Selwyn shouted from his lofty perch. "Signaling to heave to!"

"The devil you say," muttered Captain Morwell. "I'll be damned if I do!"

Georgie darted a look of surprise at him. Never before had he forgotten to mind his tongue in her presence.

The captain stirred. Briskly he strode to take up his position beside the helmsman. "Turn up all hands!"

The boatswain's whistle shrilled, followed almost immediately by the thudding and thumping of eighteen pairs of bare feet as the seamen ran to their stations. Georgie's eyes moved to the yacht's topsails. They were slack. Chanting and sweating, seamen hauled at the heavy yards. The canvas squares bellied; hesitantly at first, then proudly they filled as the prow of the *Rutledge Pride* nosed a few degrees northward.

Georgie went to stand beside Captain Morwell. "Are we trying to get away?" she asked in a low voice.

"Aye." He directed a frowning glance at her. "Mayhap you'd best go below now, Lady Georgie."

"Why? She's an American craft, isn't she? Why should we run?"

She thought he would not answer, but finally he said, "Sixteen guns and a long pivot gun. Could be a sloop-of-war. When we lay in Bristol harbor, there were reports that the Americans are retaliating against impressment by our navy. I owe it to Lord Wolversham that my crew—all of them—return safely to England."

Impressment . . . Georgiana saw herself on the balcony of the House of Commons. How angrily she had refuted Barrett's statement that the English navy was impressing American sailors; but ten seamen had been taken by force from the *Boston Belle*.

"What worries me more, though," said Captain Morwell, "is that she might be a French privateer masquerading as an American craft."

Past the larboard ratlines and out to sea, the interloper drew Georgie's gaze like a magnet. She could see the sloop out there, sails glowing pink as the last rays of the sun hit the squares of canvas, then changing slowly to a grayish white. Coming ever closer.

Mr. Selwyn dropped onto the quarterdeck. He handed his glass to Captain Morwell. "She's too fast, sir. Just look at the hoist to her topsails! Unless we turn more northward, we won't outrun her."

The captain leveled the magnifying lens at the sloop,

whose prow was aimed at the larboard side of *Rutledge Pride*. "Get the yards squared around, Mr. Selwyn. We'll show 'em a clean pair of heels," he said quietly, then turned to Georgiana. "Go below and stay there."

She met his look, clear and compelling, and nodded. As she climbed down the steps from the quarterdeck, she heard him give another order to the first mate.

"Man the guns, Mr. Selwyn."

Georgie's step faltered. She stood on the deck, staring with unseeing eyes at the companionway leading to the cabins. Guns! What had Captain Morwell seen? Was the stranger, indeed, a French privateer?

Mr. Selwyn bellowed commands. High up in the rigging, seamen grunted as they worked to move the heavy yards. There was no chanting this time, only a muttered curse now and again.

Georgiana gave herself a mental shake. She must go below; but she could not resist a last peek to larboard. Her eyes widened. Above the yacht's bulwarks,, the sloop's topgallant and topsails were clearly visible, the American ensign and pennant flying high atop her masts.

So close! Impossible to outrun her!

And just as the slap of sail against mast, the creaking of timber, and the tremor beneath her feet told Georgie that the *Rutledge Pride* was veering into her new course, she saw a plume of smoke rise from the sloop's forecastle.

A thunderclap split her ears; a jolt shook the deck of the *Rutledge Pride*, knocking Georgie to her knees. Acrid fumes burned her nostrils. Screams and curses rent the air. The crackle of splintering wood filled her mind with terror.

Hit! We've been hit!

She scrambled to her feet and, planting them wide apart, looked frantically about her. The masts still stood, thank God! The quarterdeck, as far as she could see, was intact.

A few hundred yards out lay the American sloop, watching, waiting. But her gunports were now silent.

Before she could breathe a sigh of relief, Georgie noted black smoke billowing aft of the *Rutledge Pride*'s quarterdeck, and flames lighting the darkening sky. Briefly, she saw the silken banner bearing the Wolversham coat of arms atop its long pole. Then smoke engulfed it. When next she caught a glimpse of the pennant, it had transformed into a flaming torch at the yacht's stern.

The ship was on fire! Her brother's pride and joy.

The galley, she thought numbly. They hit the galley! Pray God Daniel wasn't there!

Georgie did not know whether fear or anger was upmost in her mind; she knew only that she was trembling and that she had difficulty keeping upright on the swaying deck.

Clinging to a brass ring, she became aware that the seamen had stopped shouting, that the noise she heard now was caused by the roar of flames at the stern of the yacht. With every swell of the sea, the *Rutledge Pride* rolled drunkenly, her prow riding high.

From the quarterdeck drifted Captain Morwell's steady voice. "Man the boats, Mr. Selwyn. Abandon ship."

Georgie started as though waking from a nightmare; but this nightmare was not a dream! Not only was the *Rutledge Pride* on fire, but she was also taking on water!

She must fetch Rose! And Daniel! Must get them into the boats! Georgie reeled into the companionway and started down the narrow iron steps. She had not gone far when she heard her maid wailing, and Daniel's high young voice trying to calm her.

"Come now, Mistress Rose," the boy said shakily but with an effort to sound encouraging. "Only a few more steps an' we're there."

"Rose!" Georgie said imperatively. "I'm in the companionway. Come on up, and I'll take your hand."

Her voice served as a tonic to Rose's frayed nerves. "Praise be!" cried the maid. "It's Lady Georgie! Ye're all right, my lady! Just you stay put now. I'm coming."

The words were followed by a hiccough and hurried footsteps. The ladder jiggled as Rose scooted upward. Her hand clasped first Georgie's foot, her cloak, then her fingers.

"Praise be!" Short blond curls disheveled, her nose and eyes red and puffy, Rose scrambled onto the deck close behind Georgie just as the yacht gave a sickening lurch.

Rose fell headlong onto the planks, pulling Georgie down with her.

A hoarse voice shouted, "Sail to starboard!"

Georgie heard the words but paid little heed as she struggled to her feet. Friend or foe—the arrival of a second vessel would not alter the fate of the *Rutledge Pride*.

The rising wind was heavy with the smell of hot tar and smoldering rope. Smoke, like wisps of fog, swirled on the deck, burning Georgie's nostrils and scratching her throat.

"Hurry, Lady Georgie!" Mr. Selwyn clamped his fingers around her upper arm, holding her up, for she found it impossible to stand. The yacht's prow was riding high. They were taking water fast.

"Hurry!" The first mate half carried, half pushed her to larboard where Rose was already being helped over the side. "The boats have been let down. Can you climb the rope ladder, my lady?"

"Of course!" Georgie coughed as more smoke filled her lungs. She saw Captain Morwell, clutching the chest that contained his log book and his precious new sextant. Leaning against the rail, he was counting the sailors who swung themselves one by one over the side.

"Where is Daniel?" She asked the first mate. "Has he gone down yet?"

"I don't know, Lady Georgie. Over you go now. Hurry!"

"What if he's still below? What if he fell from the companionway when the ship lurched?"

Georgiana tore herself free from the hands that wanted to assist her onto the swinging rope ladder. Sliding and stumbling, she hurried across the slanting deck, back to the open hatch that led below.

"Daniel!" A paroxysm of coughing shook her. She clung to a lanyard the thickness of a man's wrist to keep herself from tumbling headlong into the gaping hole. A quick glance at the quarterdeck showed flames licking greedily at helm and mizzenmast, and she shouted again, desperately, "Daniel!"

"Here, Lady Georgie!" Daniel's voice was husky as

though he'd been crying. "I can't make it! Ship's tiltin' and the steps are too steep."

Without hesitation, Georgie tore off her cloak, then crouched, facing the fore of the yacht, and started down the companionway. It was steep, indeed. In fact, she thought, it was probably leaning backward, and if the steps hadn't been open-ended so her hands could cling, she wouldn't have been able to get down.

Her feet were five or six steps away from the bottom and her hands clenched around the back of the third slat from the top, when the opening of the companionway was suddenly blocked by a solid, dark mass. Georgie broke into a sweat as the acrid, hot air of the yacht's belly closed around her. Below, Daniel gave a frightened cry.

"That you, Daniel?" Mr. Selwyn shouted from above. "Lady Georgie?"

"Yes!" Her voice was high with relief. "Daniel can't get up."

"Move aside," Mr. Selwyn ordered. "I'm coming down."

Hard on his words, a blaze of light and smoke appeared in the opening. The first mate's booted feet scraped past Georgie's arms. She pressed as far to the right as she could while Mr. Selwyn brushed past her, saying, "Go on up now. Lie on your stomach and reach down so you can help me with the boy."

Georgie did as she was told, couldn't have done otherwise, for the smoke on deck was so thick that only by lying flat was she able to breathe. She heard a scream from below, high-pitched in agony. It broke off abruptly, leaving a silence that tore at her nerves.

She felt the heat of the wooden planks through the layer of her clothing, and once a fat drop of liquid tar splattered onto her arm from somewhere above. She gritted her teeth against the pain and concentrated on the two people still below deck.

Finally she heard Mr. Selwyn's ragged breathing, an occasional grunt as he labored up the companionway. She crawled forward as far as she dared, feeling the emptiness below with her fingertips. A thin shoulder pushed against her hands. Daniel's shoulder.

"One more step," panted Mr. Selwyn. "Then—try to grab him. I'll push. Protect his head—he's fainted."

A seaman with a neckcloth tied around his nose and mouth dropped onto the deck beside her, and with his help Daniel was pulled to safety.

Raising herself to her knees, Georgie wrapped her cloak around the unconscious boy. No wonder he hadn't made it up the companionway! His arms and hands were raw and puffy with innumerable burns, oozing blood. She swallowed hard as a wave of nausea turned her stomach upside down.

"Captain says to hurry up," the sailor muttered.

"Aye." A grin on his sweat-drenched face, Mr. Selwyn disappeared into the companionway again. "Tell 'em to hold the boat, Marvin," his cheerful voice came from below. "I'll just fetch one of Lady Georgie's trunks."

"No!" shouted Georgie. "For heaven's sake, leave—" She couldn't go on. Coughing and gasping, she lowered her head to the planks.

"Crazy," muttered Marvin. "He's gone plumb crazy!"

He cradled Daniel in his arms and stood up easily, as though he were standing on perfectly level ground instead of a dangerously tilting deck. The yacht was pitching and rolling, and as Georgie stumbled after Marvin, she could feel the disconcerting tremor of the ship's wooden frame. Like a creature dying.

A strong gust of wind scattered the dense clouds of smoke. Briefly, she saw the mizzenmast, a gigantic torch pointing at the sky.

There was a splintering sound. She heard Captain Morwell's shout, "Cut loose! Cut the boats loose! She's going!"

Then a noisome crack. The giant torch slowly veered starboard, gathered speed, and dropped with the force of a cannonball.

The deck jumped. Georgie fell heavily as the yacht listed to the right. She slid and rolled across the deck until her feet crashed against the starboard bulwarks. Instinctively, she reached for one of the lanyards, winding it around her arms to keep from tumbling over the side.

She saw Marvin, on his knees, his back toward her, struggling with Daniel's limp form. She wanted to help, but her hands refused to let go of the thick rope. Trembling and shaking, she watched when a further heave of the yacht sent the two skittering toward her.

She heard the boy's whimper as his side hit the rail beside her. Marvin said, "Pray God, the boats cut loose in time."

Georgie was too dazed and numb to say anything, but she added her silent prayers to Marvin's. If the two small boats had still been fastened to the larboard of the *Rutledge Pride*, the sudden listing of the yacht must have smashed them against the hull.

"Ho, there!" Mr. Selwyn, clutching an oilskin-wrapped bundle under one arm, came sliding feet first toward them. "What are you waiting for? If we want to jump, we must do it now. Can you swim, Lady Georgie?"

A breaker washed over the side, dousing Georgie with a spray of cold, salty water. She looked at the cut above the first mate's left eye, at his tattered shirt and trousers.

And all for the sake of a few of my gowns! she thought bitterly. Well, she had better see that his efforts were not wasted.

"Yes, I can swim, Mr. Selwyn. Shall we go?"

"I don't hold with swimming," Marvin said quietly. "Never learned how."

"And what about Captain Morwell?" asked Georgie. "I heard him just before the mast toppled."

"He's dead." Mr. Selwyn shoved his bundle at Marvin. "You take this," he ordered. "Might help keep you afloat for a while. Give me the boy."

"Dead!" A lump of pain lodged Georgiana's chest, tears flooded her throat. "How?" she asked hoarsely.

"Broken neck. Must have been knocked across the deck when the ship listed. Found him at the foot of the companionway. I've put his log in with your gowns."

The first mate clasped Daniel to his chest. "You first, Marvin. There's a brig out there. She'll pick you up."

Pale but with his mouth set in lines of grim determination, Marvin clutched at the brass rail, then pulled himself up with a mighty heave, and dropped overboard.

"Now you, my lady."

Captain Morwell's dead, she thought. He'll be going down with the *Rutledge Pride*.

With shaking knees, she pushed up against the side of the dangerously tilting ship. Her breath caught in her throat at the sight of white-crested breakers not three feet below her. She saw Marvin, clutching the oilskin-wrapped bundle and kicking away from the yacht. And she saw a brig faintly illumined by the flames shooting from the quarterdeck of the *Rutledge Pride*.

"Go!"

Closing her eyes, Georgie let herself fall. The coldness of the water came as a shock after the oppressive atmosphere on the burning yacht. She surfaced, gasping and kicking.

Moving her arms in wide circles, she looked back at the *Rutledge Pride*. The yacht was lying on her side, listing at a perilous angle with her bow nosing out of the water. The stern, or what had been left of it after the hit and the fire, had been swallowed by the ocean, Any moment the rest of her brother's proud vessel would disappear forever.

She saw Mr. Selwyn, with Daniel clasped in his arms, jump clear. Heaving a great sigh of relief, Georgiana rolled onto her back and started kicking again.

It was then that the leaded hem of her gown turned into a trap, coiling itself around her ankle and holding them immobile. Fighting the swells of panic that weighted her arms and legs and bubbled into her mouth in hard-to-deny screams, she forced her knees to her chest so she might reach the bonds that tied her feet together.

The sea engulfed her, like arms dragging her down; cold fingers pressing into her ears, her nose. She clawed and tore at the tangled fabric. Her chest started to hurt. Thinking of the brig lying close by, thinking of Captain Morwell's log book among her frivolous gowns, Georgie fought desperately. Her lungs screamed for air, her head pounded; yet she persisted, with fingers stiff from cold and desperation, until the skirt ripped up the front.

Able to kick her feet at last, she surfaced. Brine filled her mouth and throat, gagging her. Stubbornly she pressed on, slicing her arms into the water with the rhythmic strokes of a crawl and trying to ignore the weight of the dragging skirt.

A wave lifted her, seeming to carry her toward the distant brig, but the next crashed over her head, pressing her down. She came up gasping and coughing. Her shoulders ached; her arms and legs were numb with cold and exertion.

It seemed she was destined to perish a mere day's journey from her goal, that she would never see that vast country Aubrey and Barrett Gray had described to her.

Barrett.

She could see him so clearly that she thought for a moment he was there with her, in the cold waters of the Atlantic Ocean. His dark hair was plastered to his head, his green eyes were holding hers compellingly. He was calling to her, encouraging her.

She felt herself responding to his voice as though it had come from the real Barrett, the flesh-and-blood man. Perseverance she hadn't known she possessed infused her with renewed strength. She *would* make it! She would see the United States of America.

Strong hands grabbed her shoulders, turned her around onto her back. Powerful arms locked around her chest, and a voice, an American voice she knew so well, told her to be still.

Georgie blinked, but she could not see him now. Saw only the sky—ominously black. The water was black, too. No more fiery orange glow.

The *Rutledge Pride* was gone.

But the voice, Barrett's voice, was still there. It was real. The brig was the *Boston Belle*. Barrett's brig! He had come to help her.

There were more voices, the creak of oars. Hands, countless hands holding her arms, her shoulders, her waist, lifted her out of the water, laid her on solid planks.

But water was still in her eyes. She couldn't see properly.

The planks swayed. Gentle fingers wiped the water from her eyes. More moisture formed. She was crying, silly peagoose that she was!

Framed in the soft glow of a lantern, she saw Barrett kneeling beside her and looking down at her with an expression of wonder on his face. And she saw something else in his eyes, something she couldn't define.

She smiled at him.

"Georgie!" he uttered in dumbfounded accents. "Well, I'll be—"

He shook his head as though trying to clear it of confusing thoughts, spraying her with droplets of salty water in the process. The shaking must have helped. His usual, brisk self once again, he lifted her head and upper body off the hard planks, wrapped a blanket around her, barked orders to a seaman holding the lantern she had noticed earlier, and pulled her into the shelter of his arms; all seemingly at the same time.

Georgie saw now that she was in the stern of a small boat manned by six oarsmen plying their sweeps with vigor. In the prow of the boat sat Marvin, and Mr. Selwyn with Daniel in his lap.

Thank God they were safe! Her conscience smote her, for she hadn't spared them a thought, even after she'd been pulled from the water. She pushed against Barrett, wanting to go to Daniel.

"Later," said Barrett as though he'd read her intentions. "Unless you want to capsize this nutshell, you'd best stay here with me."

His arms tightened around her in a protective manner, and she let herself relax against him. But her mind, awakened by the sight of her three shipmates, could not relax as urgent questions demanded satisfaction.

"What about the two boats from the *Rutledge Pride*?" she asked. "The crew, my maid—"

"I didn't see any boats. They didn't let them down on starboard, did they?"

She shook her head. "On larboard."

"Then, I imagine, the sloop picked them up."

Barrett's chin came to rest on top of her head. It felt good, comforting. "If only I knew why they fired on us," she murmured. "Is she a French privateer?"

She felt his muscles grow taut, sensed his reluctance to answer her. When he spoke, she could barely make out the words.

"Nay. She's an American craft. A sloop-of-war."

"It must have been a mistake," Georgie muttered when, some time later, the *Boston Belle* lay within hailing distance of the sloop.

Clad in one of Barrett's shirts and a pair of duck trousers borrowed from a blushing youngster, she stood on the quarterdeck of the *Boston Belle*, her eyes on the approaching boarding party.

"A mistake," she repeated. She glanced at Mr. Selwyn, sitting on a stack of coiled rope with the open log book on his lap.

"We'll know soon." Mr. Selwyn, having completed his entry, closed Captain Morwell's book. He looked at it, then, wiping one damp corner with the sleeve of his borrowed shirt, returned it to its oilcloth wrappings.

His slow, deliberate movements seemed to Georgie like a farewell to Captain Morwell, a farewell she had said earlier with a prayer when the *Boston Belle* passed over the spot where the *Rutledge Pride* had gone down.

She shivered, and instantly an arm went around her shoulders, pulling her against a broad chest.

Barrett. He never intruded, but he was there, offering warmth and understanding when she needed it. Grateful, she burrowed closer to his solid strength, her eyes once again on the approaching boat.

The decks of the *Boston Belle* and the sloop were lit with lanterns, which spread their glow on the choppy waters between them. In the rowboat she could see the dark coat and white trousers of an officer, saber at his side. She counted eight men with cutlasses behind him, and when the sailors from the *Boston Belle* threw down lines to allow the marines to board, she could no longer ignore the tight lump of fear in the pit of her stomach.

But she was a Rutledge, not given to showing her weaknesses. Resolutely, she stepped away from Barrett, leaving the shelter he offered. Shoulders straight, head held high, Georgie watched the officer come over the side and approach Mr. Donovan, the captain of the *Boston Belle*.

"Lieutenant Samuel Orwig, United States sloop-of-war *Sandown*, out of Portland." He saluted smartly. "Come to retrieve the rest of the seamen from the British frigate. We got the two boats. Saw you pick up survivors on starboard of the frigate."

Thank God! thought Georgiana. The crew was safe! And Rose!

Captain Donovan acknowledged the salute, identifying himself and his ship. "We picked up two seamen, a child, seriously injured, and a young lady," he said calmly. "What do you want with them?"

At the mention of a child and a young lady, the lieutenant's eyes flickered uncertainly. He was young, gangly, and obviously unsure of his position. His hand flew to the hilt of his sword. He assumed a belligerent stance, but before he could speak, Barrett stepped forward.

"Come now, Lieutenant," he said in a deceptively soft voice. "You sank a British yacht and boarded an American brig; surely you cannot cavil at answering the captain's perfectly logical question."

Like an angry bull, the lieutenant turned on Barrett. "And who the hell are you?"

"Barrett Gray, supercargo of the *Boston Belle*. Finding that I share the dubious honor of being your compatriot, I demand to know why you sank that yacht."

"She was a British frigate!" the lieutenant shot back.

Unable to stay quiet any longer, Georgie rounded on the officer. "Frigate! Yacht! What difference does it make? You had no right to fire on us! Do you know that you killed my brother's captain? I'll see that you're hung for murder! *Sir!*" she added with awful emphasis.

The lieutenant's eyes raked over her, widened as he

noticed the undeniably female shape in the seaman's outfit. "Ma'am," he said, again reduced to a state of uncertainty. "You're English. Your frigate, uh, your yacht was English. I regret to inform you that our countries have been at war since the eighteenth instanter."

Into the silence that followed the lieutenant's words, Barrett's softly spoken expletive fell like an exclamation mark. But there had been no surprise in Barrett's voice, only acknowledgement. Or, possibly, Georgie thought, resignation.

"I must ask you to come with me, ma'am," the lieutenant said. "I am taking you prisoner."

"The devil you are!" Barrett's arm encircled Georgie, pulling her close. "Lady Georgiana is my fiancée. She goes with me!"

Seven

Georgie gasped. She darted a glance at Lieutenant Orwig. His jaw had dropped, as though suspended from his long naval sideburns, and was kept from sinking lower by the stiffness of his high stand-up collar alone.

And he might well stare! If it was a new fashion for gentlemen to seize a bride-to-be by proclamation, well, then, Georgie thought indignantly, it was a practice that didn't recommend itself to her. Not one whit! Even if Barrett Gray didn't mean a word of his staunch pronouncement!

She shook off Barrett's hand. Measuring him with a haughty stare, she said, "You go too far, Mr. Gray! I'm very well able to—"

"I know, my love," he interrupted quickly. "But you must admit that, had we conducted our race in curricles and your carriage had lost a wheel, or one of your horses had gone lame, I would have been the acknowledged winner.''

"What's all this?" Lieutenant Orwig sputtered angrily. "I don't understand a word of what you're saying, Gray. What's a race got to do with anything?''

"Why, everything, Lieutenant." Barrett took a firm hold on Georgie's hand. Giving it a significant squeeze, he said to the officer, "If it hadn't been for the wager, this lady would have been wed to me and sailing with me on the *Boston Belle*. And you, Lieutenant, would never have encountered a British yacht and mistaken it for a frigate.''

Again the lieutenant's hand flew to his saber. "Sir!" he said through his teeth. "If you think you can make sport—"

"Now, now, gentlemen!" Captain Donovan, accepting Barrett's sudden acquisition of a fiancée without a blink, stepped between the two men.

"Must keep in mind that Lady Georgiana is British, Lieutenant," he said. "They like nothing better than a wager.''

Lieutenant Orwig's eyes narrowed. "And are you telling me that this, uh, lady"—his eyes roamed over Georgiana's trouser-clad legs—"entered into a wager, with herself as the prize?''

He turned to Barrett with a smirk. "Well, Mr. Gray? She obviously doesn't think you've won. I heard her protest, loud and clear!"

Georgiana glared at Barrett. Try to get out of this one, my clever friend! But the look she encountered in return was stern, willing her to cooperate, and she recalled with a jolt of shock the alternative to filling the shoes of Barrett Gray's fiancée.

Raising her chin, she favored the young officer with a haughty Rutledge stare. After all, she consoled herself, it would only be for a little while. Only until she was safe with her Aunt Letty.

"It wasn't like that at all, Lieutenant," she said crisply. "You see, we had a slight difference of opinion, Mr. Gray and I.''

"Yes," said Barrett. "An argument as to who should be

the one with the say-so in our union. Lady Georgiana''—he favored her with a bow—''most regrettably, is governed by a very strong will, not to say outright stubbornness. So we made a wager. If I in the brig could make it across ahead of the yacht, *I* would wear the breeches in our marriage.''

Georgie couldn't help but interject, ''It appears we're both wearing them at present.''

Guffaws erupted among Captain Donovan's crew. Lieutenant Orwig's eight men tightened their grips on their cutlasses and advanced a few noisy steps, but it seemed to Georgie that it was done to cover the sound of suppressed snickers rather than in menace.

''And I do not at all agree that I've lost the race by default,'' she continued while trying to look as mulish as Barrett had made her out to be. ''Had we raced in curricles, and one of your friends had felled a tree to block my path, Barrett, it would have most certainly been ruled a foul. And you would have been disqualified!''

Clouds of wrath had been gathering on the young officer's brow during this exchange. ''I must insist that the young lady accompany me to Portland, Mr. Gray. You have my word, however, that she will be treated with respect and consideration. She will have my cabin, and the young female we picked up in one of the boats may act as your fiancée's companion.''

''Rose *is* my companion,'' said Georgie indignantly. ''She doesn't have to act it.''

Barrett's clasp on her hand tightened. ''In that case, Lieutenant, you will have to accept the escort of the *Boston Belle*,'' he said coldly. ''And I'll see to it that you're held responsible for the delay in delivery of dispatches from our ambassador in London to President Madison and the Congress.''

Lieutenant Orwig looked baffled. ''Damn you!'' He spun a quarter turn and started to pace the deck.

Georgie fixed her eyes on the saber at his side as it slapped against his leg with every furious step he took. The rising wind keened in the rigging, timber creaked, breakers smashed into the brig's side, and yet she sensed a sudden stillness, a breathless hush, hanging over the ship. When the officer spoke again, the sound of his voice made her start.

"Very well, Mr. Gray," Lieutenant Orwig said grudgingly. "I shall place Lady Georgiana in your custody."

It was the morning of the last day of June when the *Boston Belle* made fast to her moorings at the Long Wharf in Boston harbor; a dismal morning, overcast and wet, with clouds so low they chased around the bobbing mastheads of the merchant vessels lying at anchor in their berths. In the gray light the warehouses on the Long Wharf, that strip of land jutting like a pointed finger into the sea, looked squalid and dirty; the dock workers in their sodden garb, mean and surly.

Unmindful of the fine mist floating in the air, Georgiana leaned against the bulwarks of the *Boston Belle*. It seemed a fitting day for her arrival in the United States, a fitting frame for her jumbled thoughts and her mercurial changes of mood.

She thought about the *Rutledge Pride*, who should have cast her anchor in Boston harbor this day; she remembered Captain Morwell, who had always before been at hand to see her ashore; she thought about the yacht's crew. And her heart was heavy.

Although Lieutenant Orwig had relented so far as to permit Rose to join her mistress, had even allowed little Daniel to remain aboard the merchant brig, he had been adamant about Mr. Selwyn, Marvin, and the other seamen from the *Rutledge Pride*. They were his prisoners aboard the sloop-of-war.

Barrett had promised, though, to exert himself on their behalf, she tried to reassure herself. He would ask for their release when he delivered his dispatches in Washington.

She turned her head a little to look to the west, where the city of Boston was waiting for her. But, no matter how hard she stared into the distance, only a gray, huddled mass of houses and shadowy outlines of numerous tall spires were visible in the mist.

Georgie planted her elbows atop the rail. Leaning rather

precariously over the side, she could see Barrett standing at the top of some planks that had been laid down to bridge the murky, lapping water between the *Boston Belle*'s lower deck and the wharf. The brig's crew and men sent from Caleb Morris's warehouses scuttled back and forth, emptying the cargo holds. Goods from the Lancashire cotton mills, farm implements, casks of nails all disappeared in huge sheds opposite the brig's moorings.

A smile tugged at the corners of her mouth when she deciphered "Birmingham steel" on one of the crates. Her gaze slid to Barrett's dark head. Did he, too, remember their argument on the balcony of the House of Commons?

As though he had felt her eyes on him, he looked up, grinning. "More than enough blades to shave two generations!" he called out.

"What about mousetraps?"

She saw his shoulders shake with laughter. "None! We'll have to breed cats!" he retorted before returning to his task of checking bills of lading against the crates and casks as they were carried past him.

For a while longer she watched him. His hair was wet and untidy, mussed by wind and his fingers raking through it now and again. He had removed his coat and rolled up the sleeves of his shirt, a mode of dressing he seemed to prefer on shipboard. No wonder, then, his arms were as tanned as his face! Muscles rippled under the clinging shirt, and she remembered the ease with which he had pulled her from the churning waters of the Atlantic.

So much to be grateful for! And yet—

And yet she could not help but feel a spark of resentment every once in a while when she remembered his brazen announcement of their engagement. It was childish to feel that way, especially since the charade would be over in a very few hours. But to be claimed twice—without so much as by your leave, without once having received a proposal of marriage! It was enough to depress the most insensitive of females!

More than that, however, Georgie resented having been placed in Barrett's custody. When questioned by her, a smug expression—odiously smug, she had pointed out to him—had crossed his face. He had explained that his custodianship would last for the duration of her stay in America. He would not, he said, under any circumstances, relinquish it to Lyman Bainbridge, her aunt's husband!

As her thoughts reached this infuriating point, Georgie noticed that Barrett had been joined by a dapper gentleman, clad in a very elegant suit of checkered cloth, who clasped him in a hearty embrace. She had the impression—fleetingly, since the two men disappeared from her view almost immediately—that she had seen the stranger before. She was still puzzling over this when she heard footsteps on the deck behind her.

She turned, her eyes widening as Barrett and the stranger came closer. It was perfectly clear to her now why the older gentleman looked so familiar. His hair might be white, his face seamed, innumerable laugh lines crinkling the corners of his bright green eyes, but there before her stood an older, more dignified version of Barrett. She needed no introduction to recognize Edward Gray, the ''man-about-town,'' as Robert had described his uncle.

''My dear, I am enchanted.'' With courtly grace, Edward Gray swept off his hat and bowed over Georgiana's hand.

She dipped a curtsy. ''As am I, sir. I did not dream I would have the pleasure of meeting you, for Barrett told me that you do not care to leave your home. Serendip, I believe you call it?''

''Alas, my dear! These sad times require sacrifice. There was the President asking my advice on a trifling matter; so I travel to Washington! From there, it was but logical to proceed to Boston to see if this graceless son of mine had returned. And,'' he added warmly, ''I am happy to say he did not keep me waiting above two days.''

''I am grateful Barrett sailed when he did. He saved my life.''

''Nonsense, Georgie,'' Barrett said briskly. ''I could have spared myself the wetting, for you were doing an excellent job saving yourself. I'd be much obliged, however, if you'd remove yourself from the deck now. Wouldn't wish to bring our combined efforts to naught, would you?''

''You may have custody of me, Barrett, but I shan't allow you to dictate my every step!''

''I daresay.'' A flicker of amusement leaped into his eyes. ''You'd rather contract pneumonia in this drizzle, I presume.''

It was only then that Georgiana realized how damply her gown clung to her body. Blushing, she drew Rose's shawl more tightly around her shoulders as though the lacy square could hide the deficiencies of a dinner gown fashioned of sheerest apricot muslin. Quite unsuitable for morning wear, but it was the least ostentatious of the garments Mr. Selwyn had rescued from her cabin, and she was determined not to appear before her aunt in pantaloons and an oversize man's shirt.

''I shall be glad to leave the deck, Barrett. If I may also leave this ship and go to my aunt!''

Her belligerent tone earned her one of Barrett's smiles, the superior, knowing kind of smile she had received when she had asked him for how long she was supposed to be in his custody.

''Had enough of my company already, Georgiana? And here we've been betrothed for less than thirty-six hours. I don't know how I can bear up under a crushing blow such as that.''

Georgie saw laughter dance in his eyes, and it crossed her mind that in due time Barrett, too, would show those endearing crinkles that gave the older Gray such infinite charm.

''Barrett apparently told you a little of what happened at sea,'' she said to Edward Gray.

''My dear Lady Georgiana, Barrett told me nothing. He merely requested that I convey you to the Bainbridge residence.'' Edward Gray regarded her rather quizzically. ''You find me all agog to learn more about this betrothal, my dear.''

''Oh.'' Georgie looked at him helplessly. ''I thought you knew. Barrett shouldn't have mentioned it if he hadn't explained the circumstances yet.''

"I can see that Barrett will have to do quite a bit of explaining, and I promise you that until he has done so, I shall not ask you a single question that will make you uncomfortable. Only, I implore you, let us at once remove from this excessively wet deck!"

She turned obligingly and started to walk toward the companionway leading to the main cabin, but Mr. Gray said, "No, not below, my dear. Let us go to my carriage."

"Allow me to fetch my maid, Mr. Gray. It won't take but a moment. And Daniel!" She raised her eyes to Barrett. "It must be time to dress his burns, but I can do it at my aunt's house."

Barrett cocked one dark brow. "Surely it would be best if you first saw your aunt alone? I daresay she'll be a trifle surprised to find you on her doorstep."

"I daresay." Georgie was hit by a new thought. What if her Aunt Letty didn't welcome the niece who had so unexpectedly arrived from England? What if she were embarrassed by Georgie's sudden appearance?

As though he had read her doubts, Barrett clasped her upper arm, propelling her toward the ladder leading to the lower deck. "Your aunt will be thrilled to see you. She positively doted on your brother. And I will bring Rose and Daniel to Summer Street," he said, preceding her onto the wobbly contraption.

"Mind your step now, Georgie. Raise your gown a little higher! Dammit woman, will you do as you're told! You won't put me to the blush by showing me your ankles, you know."

"I have no doubt of it!" she snapped.

She heard something suspiciously like a chuckle, followed by encouragement delivered in a solemn if slightly unsteady voice. "There you go! That's much better, isn't it? Don't worry, Georgie. I'll catch you if you fall."

As Barrett accompanied his words with physical assistance, guiding her feet to the next rung, once even clasping her around the legs when the toe of her slipper caught in her skirt, Georgie did not at all perceive his aid as beneficial. The damp muslin of her gown was so thin as to be nonexistent, and since Mr. Selwyn had not thought of stockings when he tossed some of Georgie's belongings into the oilskin wrap, it seemed to her that Barrett's strong, warm fingers left scorch marks on her bare legs and ankles.

"I might manage a bit easier if you would give me more room," she said sharply. "I'm not quite a novice on a ladder, you know!"

"I don't doubt it," he said in what seemed to her a mocking imitation of her earlier words.

He let go of her ankle, jumped the last two or three feet to the deck below, and stood there, arms akimbo, grinning up at her. "Young ladies always have experience with ladders. They're bound to, what with climbing up into haylofts, or escaping from their rooms when locked in by a strict guardian."

She threw him a scathing look. "Your mind has the elegance of a pigpen, sir!"

"That's the dandy, Lady Georgiana," Mr. Gray called from above. He swung himself nimbly onto the ladder and proceeded downward. "Give him back his own! He's long been in need of a set-down."

Her face burned, for she had forgotten Edward Gray's presence. She descended the last two steps rather recklessly and, misjudging the distance, landed on the lower deck with a bone-jarring thud. Instantly, Barrett reached out to steady her. A stab of pain made her wince when his hand closed around her elbow where hot tar had splattered her on the *Rutledge Pride*.

"What is it? Did you hurt yourself, Georgie?" Barrett asked with concern.

"It's nothing. A tender spot on my arm, that's all. Pray let me go."

Barrett pulled up the shawl, disclosing an angry-looking red welt, the size of a shilling piece, just above the elbow joint. "You burned yourself!" His fingers trailed gently around the outer edges of the burn mark, soothing the puckered skin. "You little fool," he said softly. "You should have shown me. I would have dressed it for you."

"It's all right, I tell you." Snatching her arm from his

loose grasp, she moved toward the planks leading onto the wharf. His closeness, and more so his tenderness, were unsettling. His gentle touch brought to mind her dream of a knight on a white charger. It made her feel all soft inside.

Maudlin! Intolerable! Surely that dream had died at Almack's! Barrett Gray was the overbearing and autocratic man who had told her that she must remain in his custody for as long as she stayed in America.

Having thus disposed of any inclination to soften toward one Barrett Gray, Georgiana could accept with composure the arm proffered by Mr. Edward Gray.

"Shall we, my dear?" Edward said and, with great care, handed her across the swaying planks to steady ground. "I believe it is raining a little harder, and I did not think to bring an umbrella. Pray accept my apologies, Lady Georgiana."

"I shan't melt, Mr. Gray," she assured him, then broke into a peal of laughter when her first steps on terra firma proved rather unsteady. "I shall need your arm more than an umbrella, sir. My legs are still trying to compensate for the ship's movement, and I fear I'm walking with a most shocking swagger."

"You walk delightfully, my dear."

Mr. Gray guided her across the slippery cobbles toward the carriage he had left near one of the warehouses. Halfway there, he halted and looked back at the *Boston Belle*. He raised a hand in farewell. "I shall see you at Caleb's house in an hour or two, Barrett!"

Georgie fought the temptation to look back. She was glad to be able to escape from Mr. Barrett Gray, she told herself. In fact, she'd be much happier if she never had to see him again! And it was quite by chance, through an unfortunate twist of her head, that she caught a last glimpse of his tall figure as she settled herself on the plush seat of his father's luxurious coach!

Even as Georgie denied any deliberateness on her part to capture that last sight of Barrett, a heaviness settled in her breast and tears pricked her eyes. Illogically, she felt deserted.

Scolding herself for being such a silly watering pot, she

tried to concentrate on Mr. Gray's polite small talk. He told her that the wide street leading off the Long Wharf was called State Street—King Street before the revolution—and pointed out picturesque taverns and inns as the coach rattled away from the waterfront. All in all, it was a pleasant aspect, reminding Georgie of the market towns she had visited in England. Compared to bustling London, Boston seemed tranquil, almost sleepy.

True to his word, Edward Gray asked her no awkward questions. Georgiana could not but admire his fortitude, for the kind old gentleman must have been thrown into quite a pother by Barrett's sudden betrothal to an unknown Englishwoman.

After some deliberation, she herself broached the subject and explained the circumstances of her arrival on the *Boston Belle*. "Rest assured, sir," she concluded, "there will be no further need for me to pose as Barrett's fiancée."

To her surprise, she saw a twinkle in Edward Gray's eyes, and he said very gallantly, "I think I would enjoy having you for my daughter." Then, seeing her confusion, he pointed to a brick building. "That's Town Hall. The Old State House as some still call it. And now we don't have far to go."

Georgiana clasped the strap set into the carriage panels as they turned sharply left. For a while there was silence between them, leaving her free to speculate on the reception she might be accorded at Lyman Bainbridge's house. When she left England, Georgie had not once considered the possibility that she might be an encumbrance to the Bainbridges. They had been pleased to have Aubrey stay with them, had shown him off to their friends, and had given him letters of introduction when he had decided to travel. But circumstances had changed. An English relative might be considered an embarrassment now.

Quickly she changed her train of thought. "I fear I shall be rousing my aunt from her sleep," she said. "It cannot be much later than nine of the clock."

"No, no, my dear. Letty stands in too much awe of old Mother Bainbridge to remain abed past eight."

"Mother Bainbridge? My uncle's mother? I remember distinctly that my brother, who visited here two years ago, told me Mrs. Bainbridge resides with her daughter in Richmond. He spent several weeks there."

"Yes, indeed. But Lyman was called to Washington, and Mother Bainbridge instantly packed her trunks. To chaperon Letty, you see."

"Chaperon my aunt?" Georgie said incredulously.

Mr. Gray chuckled. "Believe me, my dear! Letty was ready to sink when her mother-in-law's cortege turned into the carriage drive. Bit of a tartar, the old lady. But you'll see for yourself, my dear, for here we are!"

Georgie's eyes flew to the carriage window. She saw a high, wrought-iron fence with spiked, gilded tops and a brick gatepost surmounted by an eagle atop a gilt globe. Then the coach rumbled into a paved courtyard, presenting her with a view of a large wood-framed manor house with a gabled roof.

The carriage had barely rolled to a halt when a servant came hurrying from the house, opened the door, and let down the steps. Taking a deep, fortifying breath, Georgie alighted. She felt Edward Gray's hand beneath her elbow and started toward the welcoming sight of the wide-open front door.

Warm colors greeted her in the spacious entrance hall: the cream and brown tones of walls and wooden flooring; red, orange, and buttercup yellow hooked rugs; a strip of royal blue drugget covering the stairs that swept upward, then branched in two graceful curves.

Georgie's eyes widened as they reached the top of the left branch. A lady, a vision in pale blue, came floating down the stairs, saying in a light and very English voice, "My dear Edward, don't tell me it was all a hoax! Was it not the *Boston Belle* that had docked?"

"It was indeed. And look what a wonderful surprise Barrett brought you from London, my dear!"

The vision halted, her slippered foot poised above the last step. She tilted her head a little and blinked, then gave a most unladylike squeal and darted toward Georgiana with her arms outflung.

"You must be Georgie!" she cried. "Oh, I would have known you anywhere!"

Georgie was enveloped in a fragrant embrace, then held at arm's length to be studied by a pair of wide blue eyes—Grandmama Rutledge's eyes as Georgie remembered them from the portrait in the Long Gallery at Wolversham Court.

"And you must be my Aunt Letty," Georgie said with a smile. "But how could you recognize me? Even Aubrey, as well as he knew me, would have been hard-pressed to give a good description. Brothers are not very observant."

"So true! They're apt to say things like, 'She's a very good sort,' or 'You'll like Georgie. Game as a pebble, and never shies at a fence.'" Letty giggled like a young girl, and indeed, thought Georgie, her aunt looked absurdly youthful with her trim, shapely figure, her fresh complexion, and her blond hair untouched by gray. Yet she must be approaching her fiftieth birthday.

"Aubrey carried your miniature," Letty explained. "I was intrigued with the stories he told of you, and so, before he left, he gave it to me."

"Then you don't mind my coming? I was afraid—"

"Mind?" cried Letty. "It's the most delightful surprise I've had this age! It's—But what am I thinking of? Forgive me, my dear! I don't seem to know whether I'm on my head or on my heels. Georgie, Edward, pray come into the parlor."

"I shall leave you two lovely ladies to get acquainted," said Edward Gray. "But if you'll permit, dear Letty, I shall do myself the honor of calling tomorrow."

"We'll be delighted, won't we, Georgie?" Without waiting for an answer, Letty turned to Edward Gray. "Do bring Caleb and Hester. And, of course, dear Barrett! *Au revoir*, my friend, and thank you so very much for bringing Georgie to me. The dear child couldn't have come at a better time!"

"Mother Bainbridge?" said Edward Gray with a significant lift of his brow.

"She's so . . . difficult!" A shadow passed across Letty's features. Then she smiled again. "But I shan't complain anymore. I have Georgie now to keep me from moping."

When Edward Gray's chuckles had been cut off by the closing of the front door, Letty wrapped her arm around Georgie's waist. "Oh, my dear," she said, smiling mistily. "How I've looked forward to this. If only Aubrey could have—"

"Yes," Georgie said, "but if you don't mind, I'd rather not think of what might have been. If I do, I'm afraid I'll burst into tears."

Letty nodded understandingly. "So embarrassing to a Rutledge! We never like to wear our heart on our sleeve. But you mustn't feel bad about it, dear. No doubt you're tired. And your gown is damp. Let us go up to my room. You can change into one of my robes until your luggage arrives, and then I want to hear all about your trip."

With a rueful smile curving her mouth, Georgiana followed her aunt up the stairs. "Yes, Aunt Letty. I'm afraid you'll have to hear about my journey. There are a great many things I must explain."

"Gracious! How ominous you sound." Letty swept into a vast bedchamber furnished in white, gold, and pale jade green. Flinging wide the doors of her wardrobe, she pulled out a half dozen silk robes. "The pink?"

She tilted her head, her eyes darting from Georgiana's face to the garments in her arms. "No. It'll have to be the ivory robe. In fact, you may keep it. Against your dark brown hair the ivory looks ravishing while it looked like a shroud on me."

"Oh, Aunt Letty!" Torn between tears and laughter, Georgie stripped off her gown. "I accept gratefully. In fact, a robe is not the only garment I require. You see, I have almost no luggage!"

Letty blinked. "No luggage? Here, let me tie the robe, child. If you have no trunks with you, it can only mean that you have run away from Wolversham Court. Or—"

Letty caught her breath as memories of long ago flashed through her mind. The spring of 1783. She had been in Paris with her parents, had attended a ball at Versailles. Lyman had asked her to dance. Lyman Bainbridge, a young American diplomat who had come to Paris with Mr. Franklin to negotiate a peace treaty between England and America.

Letty remembered her mother's tears after the ball, her father's wrath that an American had dared touch his daughter's hand. She remembered secret meetings with dear Lyman, and then . . .

"You eloped!" cried Letty. "Oh, Georgie, how romantic! You eloped with Barrett Gray!"

Eight

Georgiana's heart gave a strange little flutter. "No!" she said rather sharply. "That is the most absurd notion, Aunt Letty!"

Letty's face fell. "It is? But it's exactly what Lyman and I did, and I arrived here with no more than two gowns to my name. It was very awkward, I assure you!"

She sat down on the daybed at the foot of her canopied four-poster. "Come, Georgie," she said coaxingly. "Sit with me and tell me why it is so absurd. Barrett is very handsome and, I think, just the kind of husband to suit you."

Georgiana opened her eyes wide. "How can you say so?" She took a seat beside her aunt, drew up her bare feet, and tucked them under the silken material of her robe. "How could he possibly suit me, Aunt Letty?"

"Barrett Gray is the most chivalrous person I know. You'd look for that quality in a man, I think."

Georgie remembered how Barrett had tried to shelter her from the gruesome sight of murder in the House of Commons, how he had knocked down Sir Perceval Hargrave.

"He's a knave!" she said, recalling that her unfortunate meeting with Sir Perceval in Hyde Park had been made public knowledge.

"Barrett is charming!"

"Boorish!" insisted Georgie, thinking of ladders and haylofts.

"He has a well-informed mind and a keen wit."

"He's opinionated."

Letty sat bolt upright. "I know what it is! You and Barrett have had a tiff! Oh, my poor dear! You're tired and cross, and here I am, keeping you with my chatter when you must be pining for an hour's rest."

"I never pine!" Georgie said indignantly. "Listen, Aunt Letty. Matters are not what they seem. I was sent away, you see, banished from Wolversham Court because I landed myself quite shockingly in the briars."

"Ah! It's that starchy one Aubrey told me about. That stuffy William, who's the cause of your feeling blue-deviled."

"William is not stuffy!"

"He must be," Letty said placidly. "He's my brother's child."

"So am I. And so was Aubrey."

"That's different." Letty dismissed Georgie's observation with a wave of her slender hand. She rose, gracefully shaking out the folds of her gown. "I tell you what we shall do, my dear. You will stay here and take a little nap, and I'll see that a room is prepared for you."

Picking up a soft rug, she tucked it tenderly around Georgiana's legs. "You'll feel much more the thing when you've rested," she said cheerfully. "Whatever troubles you now, will only seem half as bad, and after you've told me all about it, see if I don't find a solution to the other half!"

"You will?" Georgiana regarded her aunt with a fascinated eye and, faced with the sad discovery that she was too chicken-hearted to insist on explaining all to her bubbling relative, agreed to the scheme.

At the door, Letty turned to Georgiana once more. "I suppose," she said, a doubtful note creeping into her voice, "I had best let Mother Bainbridge know that we have company. She has eighty years in her dish, if not more, and there are times when she is rather—"

When Letty stumbled to a halt, Georgie arched one shapely brow. "Difficult?"

"Crabby!" Letty colored and darted a glance, half apologetic, half mischievous, at her niece. "I daresay elderly ladies are rather like nurslings when their routine is disrupted. It makes them feel lost and insecure. So, if Mother Bainbridge should speak to you snappishly, promise me to pay her no heed. She's really a very plucky old lady, and I admire her very much."

On these words, Letty hastily left the chamber. Georgie's lips twitched, but as she stretched into a more comfortable position, all desire to smile fled abruptly. She must yet give her aunt the particulars of her disgrace in London and tell her about the untenable position in which Lieutenant Orwig had unwittingly placed her. If Letty hadn't shaken her with that absurd notion—elopement with Barrett Gray of all things!—Georgiana would have discharged that duty and, in consequence, enjoyed her hour of solitude.

As it was, Georgie's peace of mind was quite cut up. She lay thinking about her family in England, about the odious Sir Perceval, who had caused her disgrace, and most of all she thought about Barrett Gray. He had intrigued her in London. He had fascinated her, made her feel special, and the news of his imminent departure had caused a sharp pang of regret.

And now he was her custodian! Her make-believe fiancé! But the latter position he must relinquish. Immediately!

She must have fallen asleep after all, for, when next she became aware of her surroundings, a timid sun was filtering through the white lace curtains at the windows, infusing the milky jade of walls and draperies with a translucence that rippled and eddied like a clear sea. For an instant, Letty's luxurious bedchamber turned into an aquatic mermaid's bower.

Her pulse racing, Georgiana cast the soft woollen rug off her legs and sat up. *Peagoose!* She scolded herself. *There's not the slightest similarity between this enchanting room and the waters of the Atlantic Ocean!*

One of the windows was open. The lace curtains billowed, allowing a stream of warm, rather moist air into the chamber. Georgie smelled roses and honeysuckle, lavender and jasmine. She might be in her own room at Wolversham Court! She padded barefoot to the window. Kneeling on the floor, she rested her elbows on the ledge and peeked into the garden below.

With a gasp of delight she recognized flagged, curving walks, flower beds seemingly planted at random but resulting in a profusion of rioting colors. And beyond, an English yew hedge, shaped and clipped to make a living wall complete with turrets and archways! It was a copy of the Wolversham Court garden on a smaller scale.

Georgie leaned farther out the window to inspect a kidney-shaped terrace directly below her and missed the soft knock on her door. It was her aunt's voice that finally caught her attention.

"Do you like it, Georgie dear?" cried Letty, stepping into the bedchamber. "When dear Lyman told me I could change anything I liked to make this my home, the garden was for years and years the only thing I worked on. But how I do rattle on! That's not at all what I came to tell you."

A male voice just outside the door spoke up in agreement. "Indeed! I was afraid you had forgotten all about me."

"Barrett!" Georgie rose as he entered, and took an impetuous step toward him.

His powerful frame, his dark hair and sunburned complexion formed a bold contrast to the delicate colors and dainty frills of the bedchamber. Sublimely unaware of transgression, he smiled at Letty's indignant protest and took Georgie's outstretched hands, holding them in a warm clasp.

"Did you bring Rose and Daniel?" Georgiana asked breathlessly.

"I did."

His eyes caressed her face, her hair, reminding Georgiana sharply of that time before Sir Charles's dinner when Barrett had looked at her with such warmth. And afterward, when they had sat in the tiny garden, Barrett had shared with her his sorrow and sadness over the death of his brother.

What she wanted, Georgiana realized, was a return to that closeness, that sharing of minds. It was different from the bond of affection that tied her to her brothers. More tenuous. Infinitely more exciting.

"For shame, Barrett! Go and wait in my sitting room!" Her voice an indignant squeal, Letty fluttered her hands as though she wanted to shoo him out the door. "If you have no sense of propriety, at least consider Georgie's sensibilities. She's en dishabille!"

"And very charmingly so," he murmured, a wicked gleam in his eyes as they traveled over the clinging silk of her robe.

Georgie withdrew her fingers from his clasp. Strangely enough, she felt no embarrassment. "You must excuse me now," she said, facing him with a wide, clear gaze. "If Aunt Letty will permit me to borrow one of her gowns, I'll join you very shortly."

"Oh, very well!" Barrett threw his hands up as though acknowledging defeat. "Though why I must be dismissed from my lady's chamber is more than I can say."

Letty gave him a little shove. "Out!" she commanded, but the look she directed at him was that of an indulgent mother for her precocious child. "England has not done you an iota of good. You're more outrageous than ever, you rogue! And never mind that you and Georgie are betrothed! Just leave now."

Georgie's heart skipped a beat. "But we are *not*, Aunt Letty," she said without taking her eyes off Barrett's face. He met her questioning look and countered it with a slight rise of his dark brows.

"If Barrett told you that, he was only teasing you, Aunt

Letty. It was all a hum, you see." Georgiana paused, offering him a chance to put an end to the charade.

He did not avail himself of the opportunity, only smiled at her in what she termed a wolfish manner.

With a toss of her head, Georgiana said rather more forcefully, " 'Twas naught but a Banbury story, Aunt Letty! He said it so I wouldn't be taken a prisoner of war."

Letty, however, had not been paying attention to her niece. Her head cocked toward the open door, she was listening to a faint tapping sound on the floor above.

"Oh, never mind, Georgie," she murmured. "We'll discuss it later." She darted into the corridor but returned just as quickly. Tugging at Barrett's arm, she said in a fierce whisper, "Hurry! To the sitting room! That's Mother Bainbridge's cane on the stairs!"

Georgiana blinked at the door that had closed softly, stealthily, behind her aunt and Barrett. She heard the tapping of the cane grow louder, heard it pass the bedroom, then dim. Mother Bainbridge. Gone to join Aunt Letty and Barrett?

Flying to Letty's huge wardrobe, Georgie pulled out the first gown that came to hand. The fit wasn't bad, except— Ruefully Georgie studied the hem of her borrowed gown in the mirror fastened to the inside of the wardrobe door. The flounce stopped a good two inches short of her ankles. No tugging or twitching of the cambric folds could alter the fact that Letty Bainbridge was shorter than her niece.

A few moments later, Georgie was downstairs, flitting from room to room, searching for Letty and Barrett. A rosy-cheeked girl in mobcap and striped sacking apron halted her mopping efforts below an open window where a puddle of water had stained the polished floorboards of the parlor. She regarded Georgie curiously. "Can I help you, ma'am?"

"I'd be grateful if you would," said Georgie. "I'm looking for the sitting room, you see. And although I'm sure it must be in a very logical and perfectly obvious location, I fear I cannot find it!"

"Gracious, ma'am!" exclaimed the girl. "What a turn you gave me. Don't you speak just like our Lady Letty!"

"You call her Lady Letty! But Americans do not have titles!" The girl rose, wiping her hands on her apron. "To us, the mistress will always be Lady Letty, as she was before she married Mr. Bainbridge." She curtsied. "I'm Ida, ma'am. And the sitting room is on the second floor. You take the right arm of the stairway, ma'am."

"Thank you, Ida!" Georgie sped away, reminding herself that in America the parterre was the first floor, and the first floor was the second floor. Without a further check she found the sitting room, for, through the open door, she heard Barrett's voice, smooth and persuasive.

"It's up to you now, Lady Letty, to make Georgie see the wisdom of my decision."

Someone gave a dry cackle of laughter, and her aunt said, "Pray remember to call me Mrs. Bainbridge, Barrett. When I married Lyman I gave up my title, an excellent bargain—" Letty, seated beside a diminutive, white-haired lady on a brocaded chaise longue, broke off as Georgiana entered.

"Oh, there you are, my dear!" she cried. "And what a tale Barrett has been telling us! How shocking! And how wonderfully romantic that it should have been he who came to your rescue!"

Barrett rose. Encountering his limpid gaze and curiously innocent expression, Georgie was instantly put on the alert. Before she could challenge him, however, the older lady— she must be Mother Bainbridge in those voluminous skirts of a bygone age!—spoke up.

"Romantic fiddlesticks!" She gave a derisive snort, emphasized by a sharp tap of her ebony cane. "In my day," she said, fixing keen, dark eyes on Barrett, "any man worth his salt would have delivered his answer to that popinjay lieutenant with the sword!"

"I could hardly call the man out," Barrett said mildly. "After all he was only doing his duty."

With unhurried movements, he placed a chair for Georgiana so that she might face the two older ladies. "This, as you must have guessed, Mother Bainbridge, is the redoubtable Lady Georgiana Rutledge, who has the uncanny knack of arriving places when shots are fired. Pistol shots or cannon shots. You'll like her prodigiously, I'm sure.''

"Hmm.'' Mother Bainbridge directed her unblinking stare at Georgiana. "Sit down, gal!'' she said testily. "Don't like to crane my neck. Have enough aches and pains to contend with, without adding a crick. Besides, if you sit down, you can hide those scandalous ankles of yours!''

"Charming,'' murmured Barrett, moving his chair closer to Georgiana's.

Mother Bainbridge drew herself up. "It's downright indecent! Just look at the flimsy gowns these two gals are wearing.'' A sweeping gesture with her hand, gnarled and clawed by rheumatism, encompassed both Georgiana and her aunt. "Not enough fabric for a handkerchief!''

"And a good thing it is, too,'' said Letty with spirit. "What with the trade embargo and all that political nonsense, we ladies would never get a new gown if we required the twelve or sixteen yards of silk that make up one of your dresses, ma'am. Not to mention the monstrous amount of lace on your cap!''

Mother Bainbridge patted her elegant cap of lavender lace with complacence. "Fetching, ain't it? You're a jealous cat, Letty. But never mind my gowns. It's that child's gowns I'm concerned about. Can't have her look like Haymarket ware. Sally Otis and Mrs. Parkman would have a fit of the vapors if they saw her showing so much leg.''

Georgie kept a straight face only with great difficulty, and, she gathered from the twitch at the corner of his mouth, so did Barrett. When she caught him in a fair imitation of a Bond Street beau, ogling her ankles through an imaginary quizzing glass, she was almost undone.

"Wretch!'' she said with feeling, then, recalling what she had overheard earlier, demanded, "Tell me of the decision you in your great wisdom have made! I have the most frightful premonition that I shan't like it.''

"I know you won't.'' Barrett smiled with great cordiality. "Just let me move my chair a little before I give you the verdict. I have no desire to get my ears boxed by you.''

"If the gal has any sense at all," said Mother Bainbridge, who, despite her great age, had very sharp hearing, "she'll make certain you can't wriggle out of your promise. You're not a bad catch, Barrett, even if you are a rogue."

Georgie's mouth was dry. She looked steadily at Barrett. "The, uh, engagement still exists? Why?"

"Would you believe me if I said it is for the best?"

Georgie tried to read his thoughts, but his lids hooded his eyes and she had the impression that he was looking at her with speculation and a certain amount of reserve. She heard her aunt explain that Lieutenant Orwig was not unknown in Boston, that in fact he was a frequent attendee at the cotillion balls given at some meeting house, but Georgie could think only, *If we must pose as a betrothed couple, we'll never be able to recapture that closeness we felt in London. I'll be stiff with him, and he, no doubt, will be autocratic.*

"No," she said. "I feel certain that having to continue the charade is the worst fate that could befall us."

His mouth, his jaw were rigid as though hewn in granite. "Would you be so kind as to elaborate?" he said quietly.

Mother Bainbridge's cane thumped against the floor. "Help me up, Letty! These two had best settle the matter themselves."

"Yes, indeed!" Letty rose with alacrity.

As though, thought Georgie, she feared to come under a crossfire of insults—or pistol shots! *Barrett must have painted my character in a most unflattering light!*

She said nothing, however, and watched with outward calm and inner trepidation while Letty helped Mother Bainbridge smooth the layers of her stiff lilac silk gown, then assisted her from the sitting room.

"Shall I order refreshments?" Letty said from the door.

"Thank you. A cup of tea would be most welcome, Aunt Letty."

"Tea? Oh, dear!" Letty cast a distraught look at her niece. "If only I had known! But then, how could I possibly foresee that you'd be coming to visit? You see, my dear, when that silly embargo started in April or whenever it was, we had to smuggle our tea and other things via Canada. And then, when Congress declared war, I—now why *did* I throw away the tea?" she muttered. "Lyman explained it all to me, but I daresay I wasn't attending properly, and all I know is that we don't have any tea."

"Perhaps," suggested Barrett, "your husband said that to ignore a capricious political embargo was one thing; but to use smuggled goods during times of war is insupportable?"

"That's exactly what Lyman said!" Letty looked pleased to have the point cleared up. "And it's probably just as well," she said. "A glass of wine will suit you much better than a cup of tea. And Georgie, too, I daresay!"

"How on earth did you know what Lyman Bainbridge said?" whispered Georgiana while the tapping of Mother Bainbridge's cane and Letty's chatter receded in the corridor.

"My father and Caleb Morris told me much the same thing. It's still doubtful, you see, that we can sell the goods I brought on the *Boston Belle*. But that, my dear Lady Georgiana, is not the topic we're supposed to be discussing."

"No, it isn't, is it?" she said, trying not to let resentment color her voice. "Undoubtedly, though, we'd be less likely to come to cuffs if we stuck to some innocuous topic such as trade embargoes."

"On the contrary. I well remember a quite heated discussion on that same subject. But never mind."

Barrett took a seat on the chaise longue so that now he was facing Georgiana. There was not a trace of his earlier merriment in his eyes. She thought he looked apologetic but dismissed the notion as absurd. He had obviously planned this, had already persuaded Letty and Mother Bainbridge to accept the betrothal. If anything, that would make him look smug!

"You know I wouldn't force your hand, Georgie," said Barrett.

"Then why didn't you ask me whether or not I want to continue with this detestable charade?"

"I take it you would have agreed?" he said dryly.

"No, I wouldn't!"

Georgie glared at him as he sat with his long legs crossed

negligently and one arm draped along the back of the chaise longue; but he remained infuriatingly calm, only raised one dark brow. "Well?"

Her resentment flared. "How can you be so odiously placid? So smug? As though you had done me a favor!"

"I believe I have, Georgiana. And if you would take but a moment to consider, you'd realize that this is the only way."

Georgie stiffened. She looked at him suspiciously. "What do you mean?"

"Think of your aunt, Georgie." Barrett leaned forward. His expression was serious, his eyes compelling. "You wouldn't wish to worry her, would you?"

"Of course not!"

He scooted to the very edge of the chaise longue. His knees touched hers. His face was so close that his breath fanned her cheeks.

"Then don't be so damned stubborn! Absurdly, Letty has taken the notion into her head that she might embarrass her husband, a good friend of President Madison. You heard about the tea! It was quite unnecessary to throw away whatever amount she had in the house, I assure you. You must see that she'll feel much more comfortable if she can introduce her English niece as my betrothed."

Once more, resentment flared in Georgie. What ruthless, scoundrelly methods he employed! He made her feel an absolute monster of selfishness for having suggested that they need not pretend any longer!

"I don't need you to remind me of my duty to Aunt Letty," she said stiffly. "By all means, let's be betrothed."

She waited for the gleam of triumph that must surely spring to his eyes, a twisted smile of satisfaction, but he merely sat back again, relaxing against the upholstery of the chaise longue.

"I can only surmise," he said dispassionately, "that your reluctance to agree to a continued betrothal stems from an excess of scruples on your part, or from an insurmountable distaste of my person. Somehow—"

Barrett paused as he recrossed his legs and adjusted the fit of his pantaloons across his knee, then continued blandly, "Somehow I prefer to believe it is the former."

His studied indifference affected Georgiana more forcefully than a reproach. "You know very well it's not the latter!"

She checked herself, startled by her own vehemence, and directed a cautious peek at Barrett. He did not appear to find anything unusual in her protest.

"It is just—It makes it rather impossible to be at ease with you," Georgie blurted out.

"You need not fear I'd take undue advantage of the situation."

"What would you call undue, Barrett?"

He seemed utterly absorbed in the contemplation of his shiny boots. "Forcing you to submit to unwanted embraces?"

"Bah! I'm not afraid of that."

"Then what are you afraid of, Georgie?"

She had his full attention. Too much of it to suit her. It was Georgiana now, who studied the tips of his boots, for she could not meet his challenging gaze. How could she explain what she felt when she did not quite understand it herself? She only knew she wished she could turn the time back to some point *before* Almack's.

"Did you mention my encounter with Sir Perceval in the park to anyone?" she asked, looking up in time to see a flash of anger in his eyes.

"Of course not," he said curtly.

Georgie's spirits rose. She felt inordinately relieved, considering that it should not matter to her *who* had spread the tale. "I didn't want to believe it," she murmured, partly to herself, partly in apology to Barrett. "I suppose it was Sir Percy himself or some gossip, whose presence I failed to notice."

"Not surprising under the circumstances," Barrett said dryly. "I did notice some ladies in a barouche some distance away, just before I knocked your other fiancé down. I didn't think they were close enough to recognize you though."

Georgiana started to protest that Sir Percy had never been her fiancé, but the words remained unuttered. It was best not to stir matters up too much, she decided. So she only said, "I daresay they gazed through a spy glass. They often do, those spiteful tabbies."

Barrett looked at her intently, a frown creasing his forehead. "Is that why you became engaged to Sir Perceval? Someone reported you to your guardian, and the earl decided you must marry the bounder?"

In vain Georgiana searched her mind for a reply that would come close to the truth and yet leave Barrett with the impression that she was betrothed to the baronet.

"Is that what happened, Georgie? You see, when I saw you waltzing, and then, above all, when I read the announcement, I believed—"

Georgie interrupted. "Oh, I understand completely, Barrett! You believed I was playing fast and loose with Sir Percy, one moment driving him mad with desire by flinging myself into his arms, then portraying outraged virtue when you caught me *in flagrante delicto*."

"What else was I to think when I saw you that same night, nestled in his arms once again!"

"Of all the stupid things, if this doesn't beat all! How was I to know the cad would dare speak to me, let alone ask me to dance after what he'd done that morning!"

"You might have told him nay."

Speechless, she glared at him. How easy for him to suggest she should have refused to dance! He had not been there to see that toad groveling at her feet, attracting everyone's attention. If Barrett hadn't been so late, he could have planted Sir Percy another facer, saving her from that dreadful waltz!

Barrett had been watching her closely. "Ah," he said softly, drawing his own conclusion from the various expressions flitting across her face. "You don't like him."

"No," she said truthfully.

"Yet you are pledged to marry him."

Georgie returned his probing look defiantly. Her lips remained sealed. She would not lie!

"Then what the devil are you doing here in Boston?" Barrett said explosively.

"Visiting my aunt."

Barrett gave a shout of laughter. "You ran away! Why, you're not even wearing his ring! Who'd have believed it? The intrepid Lady Georgiana suffering from pre-nuptial jitters!"

Georgie gasped. "You're beastly! Odious! And I hope our betrothal will prove most tedious! I hope it'll be a veritable millstone around your neck!"

"I am sorry, Georgie." Barrett discarded his negligent pose. He leaned forward, clasping her hands in his. "How unchivalrous of me to laugh when I should rather feel sorry for you."

She looked at him suspiciously. "Well," she said after a brief contemplation of his words. "I daresay you were not very far off the mark. In any case, your laughter shouldn't surprise me. As I already pointed out to my poor, misguided aunt, you're far from charming and chivalrous!"

"Yes," he said, drawing both her hands to his mouth and brushing kisses across her knuckles and fingertips. "She would praise me! Lady Letty always had a soft spot for me."

"Mrs. Bainbridge," Georgie corrected breathlessly. His touch set her skin atingle. Bolts of fire shot from her fingers up her arms, making her feel warm all over. She tried to pull away, but Barrett held fast.

"In a moment, Georgie. Let us first complete all the formalities of a betrothal."

Suddenly Barrett was down on one knee before her. He let go of her hands, cupped her face instead, and pressed his mouth against hers.

His lips on hers were like flames touching parchment, igniting feelings and sensations that flared from imperceptible spark to soaring blaze. Georgie's arms locked around his neck, drawing him closer. The clean smell of his skin and his shaving soap made her senses reel as no rose or honeysuckle blossom could. The taste of him was headier than her first sip of champagne.

She did not want the kiss to end; yet she stiffened, frightened by the intensity of those alien feelings roiling within her. Instantly Barrett pulled back. Her face felt naked, exposed, when he removed his hands, and a wave of disappointment washed through her body. Wanting to draw him close again, she tightened her arms around his neck, but Barrett reached up, unlocked her twined fingers, and deftly guided her hands into her lap.

As though he felt a need for physical separation, Barrett rose to his feet. Looking down at her from his great height, he seemed formidable, unapproachable. His voice, when he spoke, was deeper than she had ever heard it.

"A stolen kiss," he murmured, his expression inscrutable. "But then, you might say it is a fiancé's prerogative."

Nine

Georgiana gave a start. Her face stung as though she had been slapped. A fiancé's prerogative! Of course, he had warned her that they must complete all the "formalities"!

"And very pleasant it was, Barrett," she said. "We must try it again some time."

"You tempt me, Georgie, but I very much fear that we'd be playing with fire."

Georgie tilted her head and gave him a sidelong glance. "Should we, Barrett?" she said, and couldn't help but wonder whether he, too, had felt as though he were consumed by flames. "I daresay you know. You must have vast experience in the art of dalliance. I assure you, though, I shan't mind getting burned."

"Georgie!"

Barrett reached out as though he would have pulled her to him, but a slight sound from the door caused him to drop his arms again.

"Yes, Ida?" he said to the girl who stood, saucer-eyed and with her mouth forming a big, silent Oh!, just outside the sitting room.

Georgie swiveled in her chair. Just how long had Ida been there? "My wretched tongue!" she said. "It appears I had a witness when I tossed my cap over the windmill."

"Oh, no, my lady! I never saw no windmill hereabouts, I promise you! But all the same, Mr. Barrett should have closed the door if he was of a mind to hug and kiss his lady." Ida broke into a beaming smile and dropped a curtsy that threatened to overset the two glasses of wine she carried on a salver, before advancing with a bouncy step.

It had been the sound of glass jiggling against the heavy silver tray that had alerted him and, Barrett thought with a twinge of conscience, prevented him from cautioning Georgiana just how dangerous their little ploy could prove. But, perhaps, she knew. Tossed her cap over the windmill . . . ? She had, indeed, been reckless when she responded to his kiss with ardor. A less scrupulous man than he might easily—

"Mr. Barrett—" Ida's voice, high with excitement and not to be ignored, broke into his troubled thoughts. "May I be the first to offer you congratulations? And you, Lady Georgiana, I wish you all the happiness in the world!"

Ida dropped another curtsy, and Barrett swiftly removed the glasses from the tilting tray. "Yes," he murmured. "We'll drink to that."

Ida offered to spread the news of their betrothal and departed, announcing gleefully that "Salters will turn as green as a freshly shelled pea that she wasn't the first to hear of it!"

Georgie directed a look of puzzlement at Barrett.

"Salters is your aunt's personal maid. From England," he said, handing her a glass of wine. "In the Bainbridge household, war between England and America has never ceased since Salters made her grand entrance, ah, below stairs. Isn't that what you call it?"

"Then I'm amazed Ida showed so much enthusiasm at our 'betrothal.' Wouldn't she resent it? And what about your friends? Won't they look on you as a traitor?"

"A traitor?" The corners of his mouth curled in a mocking smile. "My dear Lady Georgiana, I'll have my work cut out staving off the young sprigs who'd like nothing better than to persuade you to jilt me."

Her breath caught. A drop of wine lodged in her windpipe, making her cough. Barrett thumped her on the back and suggested that she take another sip of wine. She shook her head and set the glass aside only to take it up again and down its contents.

Barrett watched her, his eyes narrowed with speculation. "Now what the deuce did I say to make you go off like that? After a season in London you cannot be totally unaware of your attractions. Neither should a mention of prospective admirers drive you to resort to the tipple."

Georgie blushed. She hadn't told Barrett that William had placed a retraction of Sir Percy's announcement in the papers; she couldn't very well confess that by now the London *ton* had branded her a jilt.

"I'm English!" she said. "No young man would look at me twice. Our countries are at war!"

"England and France have been at war for two decades," Barrett said quietly. "Not every Englishman supports his government."

Georgiana sat quite still, turning his words over in her mind. "You're saying there are Americans who do not want to fight England?" she asked finally. "That my aunt will not be cut by her friends for harboring an English niece? That I shall not be ostracized by the majority of Bostonians?"

"You must take us for a set of bumpkins. No one, no matter what his or her conviction, would be so ungracious as to ostracize you."

"No?" She gave him a saucy look. "What about the young ladies? I daresay they'll be ready to scratch my eyes out."

"I take that as a compliment. Thank you," Barrett said, bowing. He finished his wine. "I must go, Georgiana. I've only seen my father for a few moments, and there's much to be discussed."

"How selfish of me to detain you. Pray convey my

apologies to your father. I know he must be longing to hear about your voyage." Georgie rose, holding out her hand to him. "I do hope that eventually you'll be able to sell the cargo you took on in Bristol."

Barrett's thoughts dwelled for a moment on King George's Army Gold Medal bestowed on his brother for his service to England. To carry the medal to his father had been his reason for the long trip across the Atlantic; otherwise he would have sailed straight home from St. Croix when he learned of Franklin's death. The cargo loaded in Bristol had been a mere incidental.

"If I know my father and Caleb Morris, they'll give the lot to the army."

"Plows and hoes? Cotton goods from Lancashire? What if they turn out to be aprons and gowns?"

"If that is the case, I'll leave it to greater minds than mine to sort out the ensuing confusion."

Barrett raised her hand to his lips. He saw her eyes darken, a delicate glow flush her cheeks. He felt the tremble of her fingers when his mouth brushed across her knuckles. Straightening, he released her hand and started toward the door.

Tenderness filled him. She was so transparent, so innocent in her reactions to a physical touch! He didn't want to leave. He wanted to stay and make her forget Sir Perceval Hargrave.

A less scrupulous man, he thought again, bitterly, would do just that.

Georgiana, following him, said hesitantly, "Will I see you tomorrow, Barrett?"

"I'll be leaving at the crack of dawn. Must take Jon Russell's dispatches to Washington."

Barrett slowed, struck by a sudden thought. "If you wish to send a message to your brother, I'll find a way to get it to England. Have your letter ready tonight and leave it with Letty's majordomo. He'll be up when I go even if you're not."

Georgiana's smile was worth a king's ransom. "Thank

you, Barrett! Will you— Do you think you'll be able to help the crew of the *Rutledge Pride*?''

"I promise you I'll do my best. I'll suggest our government negotiate the release of American sailors in return for your brother's crew."

They came to a halt at the top of the stairs. Barrett looked at her with such warmth that Georgiana felt quite certain they had once again reached the closeness, the sharing of minds that had attracted her to Barrett in London.

Abruptly, Barrett turned and bounded down the steps.

Georgie moved forward as though to follow, but checked herself and watched his tall, powerful figure draw farther and farther away.

In the entrance hall, he looked up briefly. "Keep out of mischief, Georgie—if you can! Letty, I'm certain, will see to your entertainment. And Mother Bainbridge, I hope, will take the place of your formidable sister Lady Charlotte."

The hand she had raised in farewell dropped to her side. Her brows drew together in a scowl. "Be sure to send Lieutenant Orwig to keep an eye on me as well, else you'll find yourself in trouble for deserting your duties as my custodian!"

A lopsided grin curved his mouth. "I'll miss you, sweet torment," he said. "*Au revoir.*"

The front door closed behind Barrett, the snap of the latch startlingly loud in the quiet house. Georgie stood motionless. *Sweet torment.* What did he mean?

She blushed hotly, remembering their kiss. It had held both sweetness and torment for her. But Barrett? He had called it a stolen kiss, such as he might snatch with impunity from serving wench and lady alike.

Georgie turned away from the stairs. She'd give Barrett another opportunity to steal a kiss, and she would stay aloof to judge his response! The only problem was that she had no notion when she would see him again. Aubrey had recounted tales of journeys that had taken him several weeks to accomplish, but those had been to St. Louis, to New Orleans, and to Quebec in Canada. Surely Washington was closer!

* * *

For the next few days Georgiana was kept too busy to feel Barrett's absence. Young Daniel, whose arms and shoulders had been horribly scalded by the contents of a cauldron when the cannonball hit near the galley of the *Rutledge Pride*, was inclined to be fretful and obstreperous. He required patient nursing, which was shared by Georgiana, Rose, and Ida.

Georgie visited the shoemaker, milliner shops, haberdasheries, and other intriguing stores at the Boylston Market. She spent hours with Letty's dressmaker, and it was there, in Mrs. Prescott's elegant showroom, that she saw a length of peach-colored silk pinned to a mannequin. Silk, the same shade as the gown she had worn at Almack's. On impulse, Georgie purchased the material and drew a sketch for Mrs. Prescott of the ball gown designed by Madame Bertin in London.

When Georgie was not kept busy with caring for Daniel and the replenishing of her wardrobe, Letty immediately disposed of idle moments by introducing Georgie to some of her friends. Georgie met Caleb Morris and Hester, his very charming daughter.

And, of course, there was Barrett's father. Edward Gray appeared to derive great enjoyment from his visits with Georgie, asking her about his brother and nephew and about her own family. More often than not Mother Bainbridge, dressed to the nines in stiff brocades or colorful silks, would join them and recount gossip about the follies and foibles of the London *ton* as she had known it more than sixty years ago.

And then there were the nights. Long, lonely hours when Georgie's mind was at liberty to wander, when, inevitably, her thoughts would turn to Barrett and to their last meeting.

Sweet torment. When would he return?

On that first morning after his departure, Georgie had made it a point to become acquainted with Appleby, Letty's butler or, as he preferred to be known, majordomo. Appleby had confirmed that Barrett had departed for Washington with the break of dawn, carrying her letter to William with him. Upon questioning, Appleby had further disclosed that the distance from Boston to Washington was approximately 450 miles, and that Mr. Barrett, an indefatigable traveler, could easily make the journey in three days.

Even if Barrett spent only one day in Washington, she could not look for him again in under a week! Seven long nights to think about him! Probably more. Foolishly, Georgiana started counting the hours until his return.

In the quiet of the nights, she wondered if he would snatch another kiss, his arms sliding around her waist, drawing her close, his warm mouth once more kindling those disturbing flames in her body.

I shan't mind getting burned, she had assured him. She has spoken promptly, instinctively, in an attempt to convince both Barrett and herself that she did not require his warning about playing with fire. She was well up to snuff, knew exactly what she was about! She had, after all, had occasion to observe for one whole month how ladies of the *ton* conducted their flirtations!

Never before had Georgie wanted to be held and kissed. Now she did, and it was not surprising that delicious fantasies kept her awake.

She came to regard their supposed betrothal with secret delight, thinking mischievously that under cover of respectability she and Barrett could carry on a shockingly improper flirtation, and not even Charlotte—were she to hear of it—would raise a brow. After all, Charlotte had more than once propounded on her view that a betrothed couple must be granted a reasonable amount of privacy and time to get to know one another.

Sweet torment.

Two words, filled with depth and meaning. For Georgiana, the sweetness held more importance. She wanted to taste anew the sweetness of Barrett's kiss. She willfully ignored the inherent pain, the knowledge that it all must end.

With tumultuous thoughts such as those to keep her awake half the night, it was not surprising that country-bred Georgie slept later than she was accustomed to at Wolversham Court. Rose literally had to drag her from her bed to ensure that Georgie was dressed in time for morning callers or shopping expeditions at eleven o'clock.

On her fourth morning, however, Georgie was awakened at seven-thirty when Rose noisily opened drapes and casements, and bustled purposefully about the chamber in the preparation of Georgie's morning toilette.

Supporting herself on one elbow, Georgie pried open a heavy eyelid to peek at her maid. "Rose!" she muttered groggily. "What the dickens are you doing? I've only just gone to sleep!"

"Why, it's the Fourth of July, Lady Georgie," Rose said cheerfully. "And Mrs. Bainbridge said it was high time ye learned to be a proper Bostonian."

Georgie sank back into the soft pillows. "Go away, Rose. My aunt would never say anything so silly."

"Not Lady Letty! It's old Mrs. Bainbridge, who wants to see ye at the breakfast table. At eight sharp, Lady Georgie!"

After mulling this over in her sluggish brain, Georgie sat up, rubbing her eyes with as much vigor as she could muster. "Independence Day! But the celebrations don't start until— Oh, never mind. Now that I'm awake I may as well get up."

"Daniel, too, has been askin' for ye, Lady Georgie. He wants his bandages off."

"I don't suppose it'll do any harm as long as he's confined to his room. I'll see Daniel after breakfast and take them off myself."

Georgie yawned, slid out of bed, and stretched vigorously. "Thank goodness my aunt has plenty of coffee!"

"I do miss me cuppa tea," Rose said mournfully.

Due to her maid's efficient ministrations, Georgiana entered the breakfast parlor on the first floor with two minutes to spare. She had shared luncheons and dinners with the two ladies of the house and was, therefore, not surprised to see Mother Bainbridge regally ensconced at the head of the table; but to see her decked out from head to toe in unrelieved black came as no little shock.

Halting in her tracks, Georgie rubbed her eyes once again to make quite certain she had not dreamed the stiff black taffeta of Mother Bainbridge's gown, the austere turban, and the hair brooch on the black lace collar. When the awesome sight of deep mourning did not give way to shimmering brocade or carmine silk, she slipped into her chair on Mother Bainbridge's left, opposite her aunt, who was this morning charmingly attired in a gown of deep rose jaconet. Surely, if the family had suffered a bereavement, Letty would wear mourning?

Georgiana tried to catch her aunt's eye, but Letty studiously kept her gaze on the contents of a wide bowl Appleby had set before her. Moments later, the majordomo solemnly placed a steaming bowl before Georgie. Her nose twitched suspiciously, her eyes widened.

Porridge!

"Appleby," she said. "Take it away!"

Letty put a hand to her mouth. To cover shock? Laughter? Georgie could not be certain until she encountered her aunt's dancing eyes. Appleby stood rigidly to attention, his face set in carefully expressionless lines.

It was Mother Bainbridge who broke the silence. She glared at Georgie from beneath knitted brows. "When you sit down to break your fast with a Bostonian," she said testily, "you will eat Boston fare."

"It's porridge. I don't like it."

"It's oatmeal," countered Mother Bainbridge. "There is no question of liking or disliking it. One eats the stuff and is done with it."

Georgie looked down at her porridge, then at her aunt. "Did Aubrey eat it?" she asked faintly.

A blush rose in Letty's powdered cheeks. "He, ah—" She encountered Georgie's incredulous look, hastily tore her eyes away, and kept them riveted to her coffee cup. "He did, didn't he, Mother Bainbridge?" she said.

The old lady took up her napkin and dabbed at her mouth. "He did when he stayed with me in Richmond," she said firmly. "When Bainbridge and I moved here in '59, we became Bostonians. And a Bostonian I shall be 'til the day I die, whether I live in Richmond or here."

Georgiana picked up her spoon and started to eat.

"You're a good gal," said Mother Bainbridge after watching her for a moment. She added, her voice softened with approval, "Fit to live in Boston—or at Serendip."

Georgie gave her a sharp look, but Appleby's presence prevented her from uttering a reminder that her betrothal was only make-believe. Instead, she asked, "Why are you wearing black, Mother Bainbridge?"

"I always wear mourning on Independence Day! My cane, Appleby!" With the majordomo's tender assistance, the old lady got to her feet. "Come with me, gal!" she barked. "It's time you and I had a talk."

When they reached the elegant suite of rooms on the third floor that had been the dowager Mrs. Bainbridge's apartment since her son's marriage to Lady Letitia Rutledge, Ida was just stepping out of the sitting room. Holding the door wide, the maid curtsied. "I've done everything you asked, Mrs. Bainbridge. Will you be wanting more hot water later on?"

"I'll ring if I do. Run along now, gal. No doubt you're wanted in the kitchen. And tell Cook the oatmeal was lumpy!

"Their picnic!" she said to Georgie. "That's all they can think of today. You'll see! Not a bite of nuncheon will they serve us, but they'll be off now for the Town Meeting at Faneuil Hall, then to South Church for the oration, and then off to cavort along the river and on the Common."

"What a lovely room!" exclaimed Georgie, entering behind Mother Bainbridge. Striped damask in mellow gold and green tones covered the walls, and velvet curtains of matching green draped the two tall windows, which opened, as Georgie knew from her own chamber, onto a narrow balcony running the full length of the back of the house. Her feet sank into soft Persian carpets as she followed Mother Bainbridge to a low table surrounded by chairs with needlepoint covers in a delicate floral design.

"Part of the original furnishing. Stuff Bainbridge and I brought with us from England."

The old lady sat down and, after waving Georgie into a

chair, busied herself with the pots and canisters set out on a large silver tray.

"Tea!" Georgie leaned forward, sniffing the aromatic steam that rose from the silver teapot when Mother Bainbridge poured hot water into it. "But I daresay"—she sighed wistfully—"it's only my imagination. Aunt Letty said—"

"Letty is a silly widgeon." Mother Bainbridge gave a snort. "There's as much tea in Boston now as there was before the war! Other imported wares, too. Didn't you notice how full the silk warehouses are? If our merchants abided by the embargo and the anti-trade laws Congress issued with the onset of war, they'd all end up in the poorhouse. And if the merchants are in the poorhouse, the bankers will follow, and then who'd pay for weapons and uniforms?"

She poured the tea, frowned, and muttered, "Oh, well! It'll be stronger with the second cup."

"If the merchants are still trading," said Georgie, accepting her cup with an absentminded air, "then some of the ships I saw in the harbor must be going overseas."

"Of course they are. Now, listen to me, Georgiana. Today will mark your entry into Boston society. You'll meet *everyone*."

Georgie smiled. "You sound like my half sister Charlotte. She, too, was on edge when I was about to be introduced to the *ton*. Don't worry, I shan't disgrace myself—or my aunt. I wonder where those ships are going, then, if they're not merely engaged in coastal trade?"

"What ships? Oh, I see. They're going to Canada, naturally. Some to the East Indies, others to the Netherlands or Spain." Mother Bainbridge dismissed the ships with a wave of her beringed hand. Pointing an arthritic index finger at Georgie, she said, "Tonight, at Caleb's dinner, I want you to behave like a girl in love, a girl who can hardly await her fiancé's return!"

Vessels sailing to the Netherlands, thought Georgie. *It's but a hop across the Channel. . . .*

"Forget that your betrothal is pretense," commanded Mother Bainbridge. "Else you'll give the game away to the young ladies who planned to snatch him up for themselves. When Barrett walks in—''

''What?'' said Georgie, her attention caught by Barrett's name. ''Tonight? Barrett could not possibly return tonight! Appleby said it would take three days' travel each way.''

''Appleby is a sapskull! Knowing Barrett, I say he drove day and night, delivered his dispatches, and will be back here tonight. I'll eat my turban, yes, *and* my mourning gown if he doesn't squire you to the fireworks!''

Georgie's heart beat faster. She smiled and said teasingly, ''Then what would you wear next Fourth of July?''

The old lady gave the voluminous folds of the black taffeta gown an impatient twitch. ''I can afford to buy another.''

Her eyes took on a distant, blank look, as though she were seeing back into the past. ''I daresay it seems foolish to you,'' she said. ''Especially since I'm proud to call myself a Bostonian. It's difficult to change, though. My husband and I came here, subjects of George III. Bainbridge fell at Yorktown in the service of His Majesty, and as long as the king is alive my loyalty will be to him. Besides, it's expected of me now that I drape myself in black on Independence Day.''

''The king is sick,'' Georgiana reminded her softly. ''He's locked up at Windsor Castle.''

''I know. And as soon as his son ascends to the throne, I'll become an American. In the meantime—'' Mother Bainbridge drew herself up. Her eyes softened as they settled on Georgie. ''In the meantime I shall see what I can do for Barrett's beautiful English lady.''

''Barrett hopes you'll keep me out of mischief,'' said Georgie.

''He does, does he? I daresay I can do that, too—if not in quite the manner he expects.''

Georgiana blinked as a horrid suspicion invaded her mind. ''Surely—surely, Mother Bainbridge, you won't ask me to wear black as well!''

''Don't be ridiculous, gal!'' snapped the old lady. ''We'd have a riot on our hands! What we must do is draw attention to you in such a manner that politics will be the last thought in anyone's head.''

"How?''

"I've changed my mind about the flimsy gowns you and Letty wear. Georgiana, I saw your London frocks when your maid took them into the yard for an airing, and I had a devilishly clever notion. I want you to. . . .''

"Shameless!''

"Brazen!''

The whispers hit Georgie like pebbles thrown at her back. She was relieved when coffee and liqueurs were cleared away and Caleb Morris's servants brought the ladies' wraps from the cloak room. Gratefully she slung the wide, gauzy scarf around her shoulders. It did not cover her skirt as a cloak would have done, but at least she could screen her bosom from hot male glances and female dagger looks.

She had done exactly as Mother Bainbridge had bidden her and had worn her most elegant dinner gown: the diaphanous white muslin with the gold border in Greek key design that had last graced Sir Charles Gray's dinner party in Curzon Street. The night she and Barrett had not engaged in a single bout of verbal fencing!

Georgie had smiled when she donned it, thinking that fate must have lent a hand when Mr. Selwyn grabbed a few of her gowns and carried them off the *Rutledge Pride*. There had been a water stain on the skirt, but Rose had been able to remove it.

Alas, the square neckline, which had seemed quite modest in London, plunged deeper than the décolletages shown by the Boston ladies. The tiny off-the-shoulder sleeves looked like chemise straps when seen next to the puffed half sleeves worn by Hester Morris and her friends. And the skirt of her gown, cut by the master cutter at London's finest modiste to flow and cling with the wearer's every movement, caused a gasp of outrage among Caleb Morris's female guests. It was scandalous! Indecent! It didn't have an underskirt but only a filmy, flesh-colored petticoat.

Yet Barrett hadn't been shocked! He admired the gown in London!

Even Daniel, when Georgie had peeked in on him before leaving for Caleb Morris's house, had voiced unstinting admiration. "Cor, Lady Georgie!" he had mumbled. "Don't you look a picture! I wish I was growed up. I'd take you to the dinner myself!"

Murmuring excuses, Georgie slipped around a cluster of chattering women. *They* appeared to be in no great hurry to drive out to the Common where sheep and cows had been temporarily banished in favor of music and fireworks for the celebration of Independence Day; it was otherwise with Georgie. Wanting only to disappear inside Letty's carriage and praying that the illuminations on the Common would be feeble, she flitted past Caleb Morris and Edward Gray, engaged in a low-voiced conference in the entrance hall.

They smiled at her, and Edward Gray said, "You look beautiful, Georgiana. I only wish Barrett were here to tell you so."

A wave of gratitude made her eyes sting. Impulsively she stepped up to him and kissed him on the cheek. "Thank you," she whispered. "That means more to me than Barrett's compliments could have."

Outside, the courtyard was bright with the glow of lanterns, but beyond the fence Summer Street stretched obscure and shadowy, its only source of lighting a faint half-moon. Boston, Georgie had learned, had fewer streetlights than London.

One by one, carriages started to roll into the yard to stop before the great double doors and take on their passengers. With relief Georgie recognized the first carriage as that of her Aunt Letty, and prepared to climb inside.

Behind her, she heard the unmistakable tap of a cane and Mother Bainbridge's voice, high and irritable as a child's. "What do you think you're doing, gal? The carriage is for me. I want to go home!"

Georgie turned. Mother Bainbridge, tiny and frail beside Hester Morris's sturdy young frame, swayed on her feet despite Hester's supporting hand under her elbow. Georgie took the old lady's other arm. "I'll take you home, Mother Bainbridge. A nice cup of tea and bed is what you need."

"Rubbish!" Mother Bainbridge slowly, painfully, negotiated the steps into the carriage. With a visible effort she forced her back into its usual, poker-straight posture as she sank onto the plush seat. "I'm not tired! I just don't want to join the revelry on the Common! Besides," she added in slightly mellower tones, "Salters is at home. She knows exactly what to do for me."

Then, so low that only Georgiana heard her, Mother Bainbridge said, "You see, I was right. You did cause a stir with your gown."

"The wrong kind of stir, Mother Bainbridge!" whispered Georgie.

"Well, there you're wrong, gal! It's better they should hate you for being flamboyant and beautiful than have them dig into you for being English. And make no mistake about it! Some of the tabbies would do just that—even if their husbands fought tooth and nail *not* to have war declared."

The coachman closed the door, climbed onto his box, and cracked his whip over the horses' heads. Georgie's wistful gaze followed the carriage down the semicircular drive to a second gate, until it rolled into Summer Street to take its lone passenger to the Bainbridge residence, six houses farther up the road. Georgie still thought the old lady had made a grave error in judgment.

"Would you care to join me in my barouche, Lady Georgiana?" A smile hovered uncertainly on Hester's soft lips, as though she were afraid she had been too forward in addressing the noble visitor from England.

"I should like it above all things," said Georgie politely, realizing at the same moment that she had sentenced herself to a long wait beneath the revealing lanterns in the courtyard. As her father's hostess, Hester would naturally drive off last.

"Thank you!" cried Hester. Shrugging off her shyness as one would a bothersome cloak, she demanded eagerly, "Tell me about your sea voyage. Please, Lady Georgiana? When your yacht was sunk, and how Barrett saved you from the perils of the ocean! Oh, isn't it just too romantic for words?"

Bubbles of laughter pushed past Georgie's irritation. She put up a gallant struggle, then gave up. Chuckling, she said, "Oh, undoubtedly! There I was, wetter and more bedraggled than a drowned kitten; yet Barrett nobly refrained from tossing me back into the water. And just think of the romantic picture I presented to Lieutenant Orwig, in trousers and one of Barrett's shirts!"

"Yes, indeed," breathed Hester. "What a tale to tell your children and grandchildren! I wish it had been me."

Georgie was light-headed suddenly, almost dizzy, imagining herself and Barrett old, with green-eyed, dark-haired grandchildren at their knees. Some would have her brown eyes; Barrett would want it so.

"Barrett must love you to distraction," she heard Hester say. "He didn't want to go to Washington. He asked Uncle Edward to go in his stead, but Uncle Edward said he couldn't go until next week. Barrett was crushed. He said he didn't like to let you out of his sight. It must be heavenly to be loved so much. Is it, Lady Georgiana?"

More likely he doesn't trust me out of his sight, Georgie thought ruefully. She wanted to reach out and tousle Hester's shiny blond curls as she would have done to the children at the Wolversham village school. To be so young and filled with romantic dreams! As she herself had been in London— dreaming of her knight.

"Call me Georgie, you absurd child," she said, a smile robbing her words of possible offense.

The last two carriages drew up. Caleb Morris joined Edward Gray and Letty in the chaise, leaving the open barouche for Hester and her friends. Georgie found herself seated beside Wilfred Mannering, a freckled, pale-haired youth who had throughout the evening formed one of the knot of admirers surrounding Hester Morris. Mr. Harrison Steene—a loathsome rival, if Georgie correctly interpreted Mr. Mannering's angry looks—had won the place of honor beside the beaming Hester.

Slowly the barouche followed the rumbling coaches snaking toward the Common. Georgie resigned herself to a chill drive, for the night air struck her as most unpleasant once they had started to move, and to a sulky silence from her companion. She was, therefore, agreeably surprised when Mr. Mannering turned to her and started to ask about London. For his display of good manners Georgie rewarded him with a brilliant smile and such descriptions of the gentlemen's clubs, of Manton's Shooting Gallery, and Gentleman Jackson's Boxing Saloon as she had gleaned from her brothers.

Her regard for Mr. Mannering rose when he suggested that the air might be chilly and that she would be more comfortable with a rug to cover her legs. He bent, clumsily, for he lost his balance, knocking his head against her knees.

"So sorry! Beg your pardon, Lady Georgiana," he stammered.

Yet, somehow, Georgie thought, he did not sound at all as though he was sorry.

He extracted the rug from under the seat and with shaking hands draped it around her. His fingers brushed Georgie's thighs. She stiffened, but as she drew breath to deliver a blistering set-down, the hands were removed and Mr. Mannering leaned back against the squabs.

Berating herself for measuring the clumsy youth with a yardstick of Sir Perceval's making, Georgie relaxed and started to recount some of the more daring feats performed by young English bloods and Corinthians about whom Mr. Mannering had professed a curiosity.

"Hunting the squirrel is a favorite pastime," she said, a smile tugging at the corners of her mouth. Even Aubrey had not been able to withstand the challenge of this irresponsible sport!

"When I was a boy," said Wilfred Mannering with the air of one who counted himself well past that age, "I used to go after squirrels myself. With a slingshot."

Trying to keep her voice steady, Georgie explained, "In England, young men 'hunt the squirrel' by racing their curricles along a highway or turnpike, and every carriage they meet they will pass as close as possible without locking wheels or scraping the—''

She broke off, for Mr. Mannering's hand was back. Under cover of the rug, he started to fondle her thigh.

''Sir!'' Georgie jerked away, squeezing against the side of the carriage.

On the seat opposite, Hester was giggling at something Mr. Steene had whispered in her ear, and paid no attention to Georgiana or Wilfred Mannering. Georgie compressed her lips in annoyance. Why the dickens must she ride with some ill-mannered young sprig who was feeling his oats, and a moonstruck couple of halflings?

It should be Barrett sitting beside her in the carriage! Her so-called fiancé should be her escort!

Mr. Mannering's fingers were busy again, tugging the skirt of her gown upward. She couldn't see the youthful lecher very clearly, but she noted the flash of teeth revealed in a wide grin.

Georgie's hand curled into a fist. With a precision taught her by such notable pugilists as Aubrey and Blakeney, she drove it at a point just below the gleaming teeth.

Ten

Mr. Mannering's shout of pained surprise covered Georgie's own cry elicited by smarting knuckles. She sat stiffly in her corner, shaken and furious but prepared to dole out more of the same medicine.

Wilfred Mannering scooted into the opposite corner, leaving a space between them that would have been wide enough for the Prince Regent's ample form.

Hester and Mr. Steene sat up like startled rabbits, silent

and watchful, but apparently too ill at ease to demand an explanation for the contretemps. Not a word was exchanged. The carriage wheels grinding against the cobbles and the metallic tap of the horses' shoes rang unnaturally loud, but louder still was the rasping sound of Mr. Mannering's breathing.

It seemed like hours, although, Georgie reasoned, it could have been no more than a few minutes before the barouche pulled up behind the other carriages, and the coachman jumped down from his perch to assist them to alight. If he had heard the commotion, he did not betray his awareness by so much as the flicker of an eyebrow.

Georgie placed her hand on his outstretched arm, grateful that she need not accept Mr. Mannering's aid, and jumped lightly down. Glancing about, she saw that the carriages had pulled up in an avenue bordered by majestic elms. This must be The Mall which runs the length of the Common, she thought.

It was brighter here, for lamps had been strung among the trees, and in the jostling, bustling crowd streaming toward the open area behind the trees she saw several men carrying lanterns. Laughter, greetings, and the shrill cries of children surrounded her, and above the din she could hear the blare of horns mingled with the blood-quickening roll of drums.

Independence Day. A celebration of severance of all ties to England.

Georgie pulled her shawl closer around her shoulders. She noticed Hester standing beside her, looking at her with concern and a plea in her wide eyes.

"Please, Lady Georgie! If Wilfred misbehaved, must you tell Papa? You see—" Hester broke off, then said in a rush, "I am sorry, Lady Georgie! Very sorry, indeed."

Georgie smiled reassuringly. "Don't fret. He did nothing that I couldn't take care of. But how exciting this is, Hester!" She gestured at the crowds and the colorful lamps. "Do you do this every year?"

"Yes. But it's the first time Papa allowed me to come at night, and I don't want anything to happen that might give

''Barrett.''

Barrett saw her pale face through a haze of exhaustion. He had spent four days and three nights in a jolting carriage, bouncing over some of the worst roads it had been his misfortune to travel. Grueling days and nights, broken only by an interview with President Madison and Secretary of State James Monroe.

Memories of Georgie had haunted and driven him. Georgie flinging her arms around his neck and kissing him with an ardor that more than made up for her inexperience; Georgie standing at the top of the stairs and looking as though she wanted to call him back.

Unconsciously his grip on her arms tightened.

''You're hurting me, Barrett.''

Her words slowly penetrated his sluggish mind. His hands fell to his sides. ''What the devil are you doing out here alone?'' His voice was hoarse and stiff with fatigue and so low that he couldn't be certain she had heard him.

When she didn't reply, only stared at him as though he had struck her, Barrett repeated, enunciating every word with exaggerated care, ''What the devil are you doing out here? Alone?''

Color flooded her face. ''And what the deuce are *you* doing here when you might have come to the dinner?'' she countered.

There was irritation in the look she gave him, and her nose, that delightful Rutledge nose, assumed a distinctly haughty tilt. Devil a bit! She should be grateful to him!

''Did your nanny not teach you to be polite, Lady Georgiana?'' His tongue stumbled over her name. He wanted to stress his anger with a mocking bow but did not dare for fear of toppling over. His knees were still shaking from the effort of staying upright when she had run into him.

''If you cannot hail me as your rescuer,'' he said stiffly, ''at least you should greet me in a manner befitting a newly 'betrothed' woman.''

''There was nothing in *your* manner to remind me, *Mr. Gray*! And if you plan to manhandle and scold me each time we meet, then I'd just as soon end the charade right now!''

Barrett shook his head. As though that would clear the fog of exhaustion! *Dammit, if only I could think clearly!* But his brain idled, useless, like a windmill on a still day. He knew only that somewhere along the way he had erred. Georgie didn't believe he had a right to be annoyed, to question her. And now she wished to end their betrothal. Make-believe betrothal!

"The deuce you will!" he said roughly. "Must I remind you again, Lady Georgiana, that your precious self is not the only reason we are playing this game?"

"Are you on the go, Barrett?" She tilted her head and looked at him suspiciously. "Whenever Aubrey was bosky, he reacted as slowly as you do and spoke in just such a stilted manner."

He scowled. "I am not."

"Then what ails you, Barrett? You lay eyes on me for the first time after four days, and you scowl! My arms will show bruises for several days, and you wonder why I don't greet you with pleasure?"

"I beg your pardon," he said stiffly. "Will you tell me what happened?"

Around them was talking, laughter, singing. They stood facing each other. Motionless. Silent.

Georgie was still looking up at him. There was sufficient illumination to see her face, but he caught clear glimpses of her expression only when revelers carrying lanterns walked past. In the brief flare of light she looked vulnerable. Lost.

From the Beacon Hill side of the Common, where earlier music had filled the air, came the sound of clapping and cheering. The fireworks were about to begin.

With a jolt Barrett remembered why he had rushed his journey to Washington. "Come," he said, moving more swiftly now, taking her hand. "Let's go find your aunt."

After a brief resistance, she came with him willingly enough. Barrett couldn't help but feel relieved that he need not insist. She shouldn't be alone on this night; this was an American celebration, alien to her, excluding her. She should be with family—with him.

He guided her across the uneven ground, purpose lending

strength and sureness to his step, and his hand firmly closed around hers. "You're wearing a ring," he said abruptly. "And no gloves."

"One glove," she corrected. "I soiled the other one and threw it away. Planted some slimy toad a facer. Cut his lip." Wistfully, she added, "I wish I had drawn his cork as well."

So that was it. That was why she was running. Barrett was totally clearheaded now. His blood coursed swiftly. His fists itched to fulfill her wish.

"I'm glad you didn't, Georgie. A nosebleed is not a pretty sight. You'd have fainted."

"I don't, you know. I get beastly sick, but I don't faint."

"Who was it?"

Barrett sensed her hesitation. He thought she wouldn't answer, but after a moment she said, "One of Hester's lovesick puppies. I daresay he was carried away by some vague notion of making her jealous. He had to watch her coo and flirt with Harrison Steene, you see."

Not Harry Steene, then. Well, that left only about a dozen others.

Georgie tugged at his hand, pulling him sharply to the left to avoid a muddy-looking patch in the uneven grass. "Someone might have explained to the planners of this celebration," she murmured, "that it is not sufficient merely to remove *the cows*. There'll be some unhappy valets in Boston come morning, and angry mothers when they see their offspring's shoes."

Barrett, struggling to regain his still precarious balance after her strong tug, came to a halt. He stared at her for a moment, then burst into a shout of laughter.

Georgie peeked at him from beneath knitted brows. "You must be disguised or at least partway over."

"If I'm drunk, it's your presence that clouds my brain. You're wearing lilies of the valley again."

"A tiny shop in Market Square has the most delightful perfumes. I went there with Aunt Letty."

She would have moved on, but Barrett slipped his arm around her waist, turning her a little. "The fireworks," he said, pointing to a bright flare in the distance. "See if they don't compare favorably with those at Vauxhall Gardens."

Standing within the shelter of his arm, Georgie kept her eyes on the bursts of color opening like flowers against the dark sky, tiny petals dropping earthward. The fabric of his coat rubbed against her cheek. Not scratching exactly; mayhap the way a man's face would feel in the morning before he had shaved. Through the material she felt his body's heat, warming, relaxing.

This, she thought, was the way she had imagined their reunion! Anger and resentment at his reception of her, at his high-handed manner, were forgotten as she nestled closer, catching a faint smell of cigar smoke and the musky scent of sweat.

With a stab of conscience she remembered her charge that he might have come to Caleb Morris's dinner. Obviously, Barrett could not have. He must have arrived from Washington so late that he had driven straight to the Common when, in all probability, he wished nothing more than to soak in a tub and go to bed.

He must have driven like a madman. *For my sake?*

Georgie quickly banished the thought. She wanted to savor the moment, not distort it. Life in America—in Boston—was, indeed, every bit as wonderful and exciting as Aubrey had drawn it for her. And more so!

Faster and faster, bursting colors of the Chinese rockets shot upward, turning the sky into a tapestry of shooting stars. Then, as though someone had drawn a curtain, there was nothing but darkness.

Georgie expelled her breath on a sigh. "I feel like a child that's eaten a sugarplum. Sated and with the sweetness still lingering in my mouth, yet disappointed that there is no more."

"Let's hope you'll be spared the bellyache that invariably followed the sugarplums I ate."

"I imagine you were a greedy little boy and ate too many."

They started walking toward The Mall. Barrett made no move to withdraw his arm from her waist, and Georgie was content to have it so. It was most improper; but it was dark, Charlotte was the breadth of an ocean away, and Georgie didn't give a straw for anyone who might see them.

And besides, Mother Bainbridge was right! If she didn't start acting like a girl in love, all of Boston would suspect before long that the betrothal was nothing but a sham.

"Georgie! Thank God!" Bosom heaving, shining curls tumbling en masse from the ribbon that had confined them to the top of her head, Hester Morris rushed toward them. Following more slowly were Mr. Steene and Mr. Mannering.

When the two young men came close, Georgie saw that Wilfred Mannering wore a smirk as wide as his face, rendered hideous by his swollen lower lip and the dark patch of dried blood on his chin. He doffed his hat to her and bowed with an elaboration that in itself was an insult.

"You dropped your glove, my lady," he said, presenting the article with a flourish.

Georgie felt Barrett tense. Before she could say anything, he had taken the glove and was turning it over in his hand until the stained part lay uppermost.

Unhurriedly, Barrett stepped away from her, stuffing the glove into his pocket. He looked at Mr. Mannering. Wilfred turned red; he hunched his shoulders and put up his fists.

As though released from a tightly coiled spring, Barrett flew at the young man, dealing him two neat punches. One to the nose, and one to the chin. Wilfred didn't stand a chance against so much well-aimed rage. After one jab at Barrett's midsection, he went down like a felled tree.

Barrett looked at the young man sprawled at his feet. Exhaustion once again caught up with him, blurring his vision, and in his fuddled mind Wilfred's bloodied face changed into that of Sir Perceval Hargrave.

Shaken, Barrett took a step backward. How he wished it were Sir Percy! He'd force him to get up and fight until he released Georgie from her promise.

But, perhaps, she didn't wish to be freed.

Georgie saw Barrett sway on his feet. Her breath caught in her throat, and she would have rushed to his side had not Hester caught her around the waist and held her fast.

"A mill!" Hester said under her breath. "How exciting!"

But Hester was to be disappointed. Wilfred Mannering stayed where he was, safe in the knowledge that Barrett Gray would never hit a man who was down. And then Letty, and Caleb Morris, and Edward Gray were there, scolding Georgie fondly and making much of her.

Letty hugged her niece. "Oh, what a scare you gave me, you naughty girl! Hester told us you boxed Wilfred's ears. Did he misbehave, love? I'm not surprised. He was odious even when he was no more than knee high."

Edward Gray, after giving Georgie a fatherly pat and a wink, turned to his son. "I suppose," he said, trying to conceal his concern for Barrett, "that you were in dire need of physical exercise after your journey. Did it make you feel better?"

Barrett produced a weak grin. "Much better, sir. May I beg a ride with you, or must I walk? I dismissed my carriage when I arrived here."

"I daresay I can squeeze you in."

Barrett bowed to the ladies. "I've sent a little surprise to your house," he said to Letty. "Let me know if it meets with your approval."

Georgie saw Barrett trying to focus on her. His eyes were red rimmed. He was so tired, she thought, in another moment he'd fall asleep on his feet.

"Get some rest," she said, stepping up to him and holding out her hand. "And thank you, Barrett."

His fingers closed around hers, pulling her closer. No weakness was evident in that grip. He leaned down as though he would have kissed her cheek, but he only said a few words into her ear.

"I hope," he whispered harshly, "Sir Percy knows enough to appreciate my care of his betrothed!"

Sir Percy! Georgiana watched in stunned silence as Barrett walked off, deep in conversation with his father. At the time it had seemed best to leave Barrett in the belief that she was pledged to the baronet, but now her omission to tell the truth was beginning to haunt her.

Subdued, she followed her aunt into the carriage Mother Bainbridge had sent for them. Letty was silent while the coach rattled through the dark, deserted streets. Georgiana, loath to break into her aunt's absorbing thoughts, wondered if Barrett would call on her in the morning and whether he would be warm and friendly as in those golden moments before Hester had burst upon them, before he had knocked down the horrid Wilfred.

"What happened?" Letty asked suddenly. "I mean with Wilfred Mannering."

Georgie's face burned with embarrassment, but in the dark seclusion of the carriage it was not so difficult after all to talk to her aunt about Mr. Mannering's lecherous habits.

"I daresay it was my gown," Georgie concluded. "I shan't be able to wear any of my beautiful London frocks if they give men the notion that I am a lightskirt. And Mr. Selwyn saved them at the risk of his own life!"

Letty relapsed into silence, and Georgie stared out the carriage window. Was her aunt also of the opinion that her gown was immodest? Barrett didn't think so! *He didn't hesitate to scold me for being alone on the Common or to remind me of Sir Percy. If he objected to my gown he would have said so!*

She noticed lights ahead, and as they drew closer, she recognized Caleb Morris's semicircular drive with its distinctive border of barberry hedging. The front door of the Morrises' house was closed, but she could see Hester's barouche being driven to the stables behind the house.

"Almost home, Aunt Letty," she said, wishing she had caught just one more glimpse of Barrett. Or did he have his own rooms in town?

"What?" said Letty. "Oh, so we are. I've been thinking about your gowns, Georgie."

"Well, I have, too," said Georgie. "And I have come to the conclusion that it is pure envy that made the ladies stare, and Wilfred—"

"Wilfred is an uncouth oaf," Letty said firmly. "You must wear your beautiful gowns as often as possible, and tomorrow we'll see Mrs. Prescott again. We'll have her alter your new dresses. They are far too demure, I realize now."

Georgie stared at the dim outline of her aunt's face under a wide-brimmed hat. Letty's dictum was so contrary to what

Georgie expected that she could not believe she had heard right.

"You are a Rutledge," said Letty. "A Rutledge never bows to anyone's opinion. Those ladies and gentlemen who might censure you for wearing a transparent gown must be made to realize that they are behind the times. That they are stodgy and bourgeois."

Letty reached for the leather strap set into the interior paneling of the coach and held on while they turned into the gate. "Very soon every young lady in Boston will copy you. They know London takes its fashions from Paris, and they wouldn't want to be thought dowdy or lacking in dash."

A spark of mischief lit in Georgie's eyes. "If the young ladies copy my example too faithfully, the gentlemen will soon set their own fashion: a split lower lip."

"Don't be absurd, child!" Letty allowed the coachman to hand her from the carriage before adding, "Our young men know how to behave as well as any London buck."

"The exception being the odious Wilfred."

"He's a cad. And that," Letty said philosophically, "is a weakness of character, which has to do with family and upbringing. Not with nationality."

Arm in arm, the two ladies entered the foyer where they were greeted by a beaming Appleby. "The master has returned, my lady."

Letty's cheeks glowed pink. She flung off her cape, tossing it onto a chair, and tore off her gloves. "Appleby," she said, trying to sound severe, "if I've told you once, I've told you a dozen times to call me Mrs. Bainbridge."

"Yes, my lady."

"Well?" Letty demanded. "Where is he? In the study?"

"I'm here, my love."

Georgie's gaze was drawn to the stairs by that booming voice. Her eyes widened at the sight of her uncle by marriage, descending in a leisurely fashion to catch his wife in a bear hug that wreaked havoc with the wide-brimmed silk confection on Letty's head.

Lyman Bainbridge was as tall as Barrett, possibly an inch

or so taller, but he was built along more powerful lines. In fact, Aubrey's description of him had sadly understated Lyman's size. Letty's husband was a mammoth.

An amiable mammoth, Georgie thought when Lyman came toward her, smiling and with his hand outstretched. "And this must be my little niece!"

His voice echoed warmth and goodwill. It filled the huge entrance hall, and Georgie felt as though she had been heartily embraced.

"Welcome, Georgiana." Her hand was swallowed by his large one. "May your visit be a happy one."

Letty, having disposed of her troublesome hat, fluttered to her husband's side. "It's not a visit, Lyman! Georgie is betrothed to Barrett."

"Not really," Georgie said hastily. "You see, sir—"

"Uncle Lyman, if you please," he interrupted her. "And there's no need to say more, Georgiana. Barrett was so kind—or should I say cruel?—as to offer me a seat in his carriage when he left Washington. Believe me, I am well acquainted with your situation. He fully explained why you are betrothed to him."

"You came with Barrett! Then *you* are his little surprise!" cried Letty.

Little, indeed! Georgie smiled. She could not help but be grateful to Barrett. She had not looked forward to her first interview with Lyman Bainbridge, the man who supported the government's war efforts so faithfully that he had asked his wife to do without tea since it was an imported article.

"Then you won't mind if my visit turns out longer than any of us might have expected?" she said.

There was kindness in the look Lyman gave her, and understanding. "The longer the better," he said. "Letty has always regretted that we have no children. She'll enjoy mothering you."

"Oh, indeed!" cried Letty. "I wish you wouldn't harp on the nature of your betrothal, Georgie. If you married Barrett, you could take a house in Boston, or you could live at Serendip, which I adore! I'd visit you so often you'd soon wish me to Jericho."

"But I couldn't!" said Georgie, horrified.

"Why not? Aubrey planned to bring you, to make your home here."

"Aunt Letty, don't you see? Barrett is not my brother. I simply cannot take advantage of his chivalry just so I can stay in America! It would be the most infamous piece of treachery."

"Fiddle-faddle!" said Letty.

Her husband chuckled. "Just so, my love. But there's nothing we can do except wait and see. For all we know, Georgiana may be wishing herself back at Wolversham Court."

Georgie started to nod in agreement but couldn't complete the motion when she realized, shockingly, that it wasn't true. She missed her brothers, worried about Blakeney fighting in the Peninsula. She missed Wolversham Court. What she wouldn't give to be in the country! She missed her mare Stardust and the exhilarating gallops on the downs.

But she had no desire to leave America!

She frowned at the tips of her dusty satin slippers peeking from beneath the hem of her gown. A dilemma, indeed, to be wishing to remain when common sense dictated to flee Boston as fast as possible.

"Come, dear heart," she heard Lyman say to his wife. "I can see you're tired. And if you're not, *I* am. Barrett was so restless, he never slept. Kept me from sleep as well with his ceaseless talk of Georgie. I'm afraid Barrett will turn into a dead bore if he doesn't watch out."

"Very promising," said Letty, giggling.

Georgie looked up, burning to know what Barrett had had to say about her, but Lyman was already steering Letty toward the stairs. Over his shoulder, he smiled at her.

"Good night, Georgie. Don't let it worry you, child. If for some reason your stay becomes intolerable, tell your Uncle Lyman. I'll find a way to get you home."

There were still ships sailing to the Netherlands, remembered Georgie as she followed her aunt and uncle upstairs to seek the privacy of her own chamber. *From the Netherlands I can easily go to England.*

She meant to form a plan, meant to figure out a way to strike up an acquaintance with one of the merchants still plying their overseas trade despite the government embargo. If she were to leave Boston before this silly war came to an end, she must do it without involving her aunt and uncle. . . . She ought to speak to Barrett about it. . . .

Barrett, she thought drowsily as she slipped beneath the covers. Barrett, who made it so frightfully hard for a lady to enjoy a flirtation. . . .

"Lady Georgie, wake up!"

Startled, Georgie sat up in bed. Surely it couldn't be morning yet. But there was Rose, stamping around the room, slamming drawers, and muttering wrathfully, "That imp of satan! That wretched little boy!"

"Are you speaking of Daniel?" Georgie said, incredulous. As Rose approached the four-poster bed, she realized that her maid was not only angry but also torn by anxiety. "What has happened, Rose?"

"Daniel has run off! And I don't know how long he's been gone, Lady Georgie!" cried Rose, distressed. "Neither Ida nor I thought to look in on him when we came back from the fireworks."

Neither had she, Georgie thought guiltily. She jumped out of bed. "He's as weak as a kitten, Rose. His legs wouldn't carry him farther than the garden. Has it been searched?"

"Yes, Lady Georgie. And the stables. And the orchard, but we cannot find him!"

Eleven

Georgie had never dressed faster, did not even bother to put up her hair. When she entered the kitchen wing at the north side of the house, she found her aunt's servants assembled there, including Salters, Letty's gaunt, cheerless abigail.

"No doubt the lad saw his duty," Salters was saying in the clipped, over-refined accents of a British upper servant. "No doubt he's even now on his way to England"—she flicked a look of disdain at the male servants—"to take up arms against England's brazen enemy."

Georgie must have made some small sound of distress, for the abigail spun in a swirl of black bombazine. "My lady!" she gasped. "I had no notion—" She broke off, dropping into a belated curtsy, and saying stiffly, "This is no fitting place for you, my lady. Pray come away at once."

Ignoring the abigail's attempt to usher her from the kitchen, Georgie asked, "Why would Daniel try to get to England, Salters? All of us have done our best to soothe his fears when he asked about the sinking of my brother's yacht."

"Not all of us, Lady Georgiana!" Ida looked straight at Salters, saying, "There's some as I could name who did their best to scare the poor little mite."

"Aye," said Appleby. "And I think it's about time the master heard of this." He turned on his heel and marched from the room, leaving an ominous silence behind him.

It was not long before he returned to summon Salters and Ida to Lyman Bainbridge's study. Georgie followed, determined to speak to her uncle as soon as he had finished interrogating the maids.

Keeping an eye on the closed door, she started pacing up and down in front of the study. Why had she not realized that Salters was fretting the boy? Why Daniel not confided in her? Every day Georgie had spent time with him, reading to Daniel or playing card games and board games to help him over the tedium of his convalescence. Why had he not spoken up?

Where was he? He didn't know Boston, and even though four years under the tutelage of Captain Morwell and Mr. Selwyn had improved his speech, there was still a trace of cockney in his voice, especially when he was excited or frightened. He must be frightened now. Someone might take offense at his accent, might hurt him. Oh, why the dickens had she not noticed that Daniel was contemplating flight?

Reproaches and questions chased each other in Georgie's head in a dizzying circle. She began to realize that although she had spent time with Daniel and with her aunt, although she had gone through the motions of taking an interest in everything, her involvement had only been superficial.

She had made herself believe that she was thinking of Barrett Gray only at night, when she was alone; but subconsciously her preoccupation with Barrett, with her reaction to his kiss, and with the sham betrothal had continued. In effect, she had been blind to what was happening around her.

Well, Barrett was back, and he had shown her that dalliance was far from his mind. Why, he might be a stern Quaker father, the way he had spoken to her!

Georgiana spun when she reached the stairs and retraced her steps to the study door. Would they never get finished in there? She must know if her uncle intended to send out a search party. If not—

She halted in her tracks, a set, stubborn look on her face. If Lyman Bainbridge would do nothing, then she would search for Daniel herself! The boy was *her* responsibility.

And Barrett must help! He might refuse to flirt, but he could not refuse to look for a lost child!

The door finally opened. However, it was only Letty and Ida who stepped out. Ida scurried off, and Letty turned away, tears streaming down her face, to hurry toward the sitting room.

"Aunt Letty!" Georgie easily caught up with her aunt. "What happened? Has Daniel been found? Is he hurt?"

"Oh, my dear!" wailed Letty. "How awful! I never suspected how much Salters hates America. Can you believe it? She told that poor little boy that our soldiers are massacring English families up in Canada, and that it is his duty to go home and enlist! If only I had known! I'd have sent her back years ago."

"Yes, but what about Daniel?" Georgie pushed open the

sitting room door and guided her overwrought aunt to the nearest chair. "Has Uncle Lyman had news of Daniel?"

"No, but he will. Lyman is very good at that sort of thing. Very efficient." Letty gave a doleful sniff. Her eyes were red rimmed, and her lashes clung together in wet little clusters. "Believe me, Georgie, I would not have had this happen for the world!"

"It's not your fault," Georgie replied mechanically. *No, not Auntie's fault but mine! Not only have I failed Daniel, but I've also made Aunt Letty unhappy. I must do something!*

The sound of a pitiful sob firmed Georgiana's resolve. "Please dry your tears, Aunt Letty. I want to go and check outside the gates and all along Summer Street, but how can I leave you when you're about to flood this pretty room?" Georgie said with an attempt at lightness.

Letty dabbed at her eyes and nose. "Please don't go! Lyman will send out men—" She broke off, her face brightening as footsteps approached in the corridor. "That must be Lyman now!"

Her eyes on the door, Georgie shook her head. The steps were too swift for Lyman. It could only be—

"It's Barrett! He'll want to help. I know he will!"

Georgie was out of her chair and rushing toward the door when Barrett entered. She came to an abrupt stop, for close on his heels trudged an exhausted boy, who hung his head and glowered at her in a mixture of pride, defiance, and shame.

Her knees went weak with relief. Daniel. Thank God!

Georgiana wanted to crush him to her breast, to hug and to scold him, but she knew better than to follow her impulse. Daniel would regard it as coddling, and it would sit ill with his twelve-year-old dignity. Instead, she ruffled the boy's tousled blond hair, and over his head her eyes smiled at Barrett, thank you.

Letty knew no such restraint. Once again her tears spilled over. Arms flung wide to receive the little sinner, she came tripping toward the shrinking boy.

"Ah, Lady Letty!" Barrett stepped smoothly into her

waiting arms. "Is this your reward for my surprise last night? It's exactly the kind of greeting I like."

Letty gave a watery chuckle. "Barrett, you rogue! 'Twasn't meant for you." But she hugged him anyway.

"In that case," he said, grinning, "you had best go to Lyman and complain about my outrageous behavior. And while you have his ear, you might drop him a hint that our truant has returned."

"Oh." Letty looked doubtful. "Shouldn't I put the poor child to bed first? He must be—"

"Certainly not!" Georgie said crisply. "Daniel is a young man. He's in no need of a nanny, and he knows he must first answer the questions I shall put to him. Then, unless I sentence him to a diet of bread and water and *porridge*, he may take himself off to the kitchen."

While Daniel's face had brightened during Georgie's speech, Letty's eyes had grown round with distress. "Georgie, how can you—"

Again, Barrett stepped into the breach. "Yes, indeed," he broke in smoothly, leading Letty out into the corridor. "Cruel, cold-hearted words from such a charming young lady, but I have no doubt that Mrs. Appleby has her own notions about the requirements of naughty, troublesome boys."

Banishing the smile elicited by Barrett's words, Georgiana turned to Daniel. She took in his ripped shirt, the muddy nankeen breeches, the filthy bandages covering his arms and hands, and closed her eyes in silent prayer that the dirt had not penetrated to the still raw burns.

"Lady Georgie?" Daniel took a hesitant step toward her. "I'm sorry, Lady Georgie."

"And so you should be," said Barrett, coming back into the sitting room. "You acted in an irresponsible manner, quite unbefitting a young man your age."

"Aye, sir."

Georgie motioned the boy to the chaise longue. "If you don't get a fever from this escapade, it's more than you deserve, Daniel! But at least you had the sense to cover your burns again."

"It hurt too much otherwise."

"Admirably commonsense," Barrett muttered dryly, then added, with a quizzical look at Georgiana, "There's one other who might benefit from a dollop of common sense."

Georgie's face flamed. Barrett might have waited until the boy had gone before reminding her of their awkward meeting the night before! "I must apologize for seeming to ignore you, Barrett," she said with cool dignity. "I was, ah, taken by surprise when you came in. You see, I was just about to send for you."

He bowed, a hand over his heart. "I'm honored. I did not dare hope you'd forgive me so soon."

"To ask you to help look for Daniel," she said repressively. Now was not the time to discuss their own affairs! "Did you know that he was lost? Where did you find him?"

"I am snubbed," Barrett had the audacity to murmur. "Lady Georgie, I most humbly beg your pardon for my behavior last night. Pray take into consideration that I was dead on my feet. Alas, I did not know what I was doing."

"You showed considerable prowess for a dead man," she countered. "That was quite a punch you dealt Mr. Mannering." Then, noting Daniel's confused glances darting back and forth between her and Barrett, she asked again, "How did you find the boy?"

"I was out on a small matter of business this morning, and when I returned I quite literally stumbled over him. He was huddled in the recess of a pedestrian gate at the corner of Summer and Marlborough Streets."

"But that's quite close! Why didn't you come home, Daniel?"

"I was gone farther," the boy confessed gruffly. "But then I got scared when they turned on me, and I came back."

"Who turned on you, Daniel?" asked Barrett.

"Them big boys, when I asked 'em for directions to the 'arbor. Harbor," Daniel corrected himself hastily. "And then, when I was back in this street, all them carriages came rolling along, and I hid."

"That must have been after the fireworks," said Barrett. "I daresay you fell asleep while you were waiting."

The boy nodded sheepishly.

Georgie seated herself beside Daniel. "Why? Why did you do it?"

"I'm an Englishman, Lady Georgie." Daniel spoke slowly, as though reciting words learned by heart. "It's treason to consort with the enemy."

"Salters!" exclaimed Georgie with disgust. "Daniel, don't you have more sense than to listen to a bitter old woman?"

Daniel looked rebellious and would have argued, but Barrett, taking up a wide-legged stance before the boy, silenced him with a frown.

"In case you have forgotten, young man, let me repeat what I told you aboard the *Boston Belle*. First of all"—for emphasis, Barrett started to tick off the various points on his fingers—"Lieutenant Orwig did not set you free; he placed you in my custody along with Lady Georgie and Rose. Second, Lady Georgie had to give her word that none of you would try to escape or engage in any activity harmful to the United States of America. Third, you gave me *your* word not to do anything cork-brained."

Georgie hadn't known that Barrett had spoken "man-to-man" with Daniel. She gave him a look of surprise, but Daniel, latching on to the last reminder, cried out defiantly.

"Ye weren't here, sir! And when Salters said that a British ship of the line was sighted just outside the bay, I knew I couldn't keep me word. And I couldn't hang around neither, waitin' for ye to come back, an' give ye fair warnin'!"

"Daniel," said Georgie, refraining nobly from asking the boy whether he had intended to swim out to the supposed ship of the line. "You once told me that you were saving the money Lord Wolversham pays you to buy a commission in the navy."

"Aye. I wants to be an officer, not just a seaman."

Georgie nodded. "Like Lieutenant Robert Gray."

Daniel's eyes lit up in admiration for the naval officer,

who had often sailed with Lord Blakeney and had told rousing tales of naval battles against the French. Then he frowned.

What for did Lady Georgie want to drag his hero into this? Daniel wondered suspiciously. Warily, he replied, "Aye. Like him."

"Then you must know that to an officer and a gentleman his parole is inviolable."

Daniel blanched. He looked at Barrett with a horrified expression on his thin little face. "I vi—I broke me parole, sir. I ought to be shot."

"Hmm." Barrett put a hand to his chin, stroking it as though he were lost in grave reflection, but Georgiana was not misled. She had caught the suspicious twitch at the corner of his mouth.

"Daniel!" Barrett said sternly.

The boy rose and bowed. "Aye, sir."

"Since I discovered you not very far from here, and you didn't try to evade me, I doubt I'd find a judge willing to order your execution. I sentence you to three days' house arrest, and I'll have your promise that next time you *will* wait to talk it over with me first."

"I promise, sir!"

"Then go and have some breakfast and put yourself to bed."

"Aye, sir!"

"But not before you have Ida or Rose take that filthy bandage off," Georgie called after the boy, who was already halfway to the door.

She looked up at Barrett when Daniel had gone, and it seemed as though the spacious chamber was shrinking. Barrett had not moved, but he was so close all of a sudden. Too close.

"Daniel is much stronger than I suspected," she said, her voice thin and breathless. "But weaker than he will admit to himself. Thank you for bringing him home."

"It was no hardship, Georgie. I had planned to call on you in any case."

"To apologize?"

"And to give you something."

"Oh." She was too preoccupied to wonder what it was that he wished to give her; all she could think of was her responsibility to Daniel and Rose, and the distress she had unwittingly caused her aunt.

If only Barrett wouldn't stand so close and look at her with that half smile, half question in his eyes!

Georgiana rose from the chaise longue and started to wander aimlessly through the room, her mind in turmoil. Once she had been established in her aunt's house, the war had seemed remote. There were no military reviews, no uniforms at social gatherings, and, with the exception of a few merchants grumbling about the disastrous effect of trade restrictions on their businesses, no one regarded the war as a topic for discussion.

But there was no denying it: America was at war with England.

During her visits with Edward Gray and Mother Bainbridge, Georgie had learned that Edward as well as Caleb Morris knew no animosity toward England or the English but felt in honor bound to give their loyalty to their adopted country.

Barrett must feel the same way.

As must Letty and Lyman. Georgiana and her charges, Daniel and Rose, could be naught but an embarrassment to them.

"What is it, Georgie?"

She heard Barrett's voice as though from a far distance. He was still standing near the chaise longue where she and Daniel had sat, separated from her by the width of the sitting room. Mere physical distance. It was nothing compared to the wide chasm Georgiana saw gaping between them.

She stopped in her perambulations to stand at one of the windows. With her back turned toward Barrett, she said tonelessly, "I must return to England. Please, Barrett, will you arrange passage on one of the merchant vessels?"

There was a long silence, time enough to count the rosebushes in the garden three times over. Time enough to wish he'd come and take her in his arms. Georgie clasped the window frame, her knuckles white with strain, for, above all, she wanted to turn around and look at Barrett.

"It's not possible, Georgie," he said finally.

She spun to face him then. He had not moved, was still standing by the chaise longue. His face had a closed, guarded look; she could not read his thoughts.

"Yes, it is possible!" she protested. She ached all over from the effort it took to appear calm and collected. She had made her decision to leave. Why didn't he respect that? Why must he look for obstacles?

"Ships are leaving daily to trade in the Far East and in Europe, Barrett. I can go to Holland, take the packet across to Dover, and—"

"No."

"Why, Barrett? If you don't wish to associate with the merchants who are breaking the embargo, *I* could speak with them. Surely it wouldn't be thought odd."

A muscle twitched in his cheek. She thought he might smile, but instead his jaw tightened into even harsher lines. When he spoke, the drawl she found so delightful had disappeared. His voice was clipped and emotionless.

"Ours is a close-knit society, Georgiana. I 'associate' with those merchants daily. It is quite another thing to ask one of them for a favor."

"Why?"

"You may remember that I have just spoken to President Madison and Secretary of State Monroe. There is a political group—merchants and ship owners among others—who will do *anything* to stop this war. I do not want you to fall into their hands."

"Why?"

"Why? My God, Georgiana!" Emotion was back in his voice. His eyes blazed at her. "They'd want you to take information to England! They'd use you as a messenger for their seditionist plans!"

She caught her breath in sudden anger. "Only if I agreed, Barrett! But I'll be a messenger for no one! I am my own woman, under obligation to no one, and making my own decisions!"

Barrett started to move around the chaise longue. "It would be too dangerous to cross the Atlantic, Georgie. There'll be British navy patrols, and I can't in all conscience let you go and be shot at a second time. This time by your own countrymen."

"Then let it be on *my* conscience. I'll take the risk. And a small risk it is! England will barely have learned about the declaration of war, and I doubt our navy would attack a merchant vessel."

Georgie watched him as he came closer, a determined glint in his eyes, and a grim, tight expression firmly engraved on his face. He came to a halt mere inches from her.

"I repeat. I cannot let you go, Georgie."

"Cannot or will not?"

She sensed a stillness in him, a watchfulness. "Does it make a difference to you?" he asked.

There was a flutter in her stomach. She was breathing too fast. Barrett was looking at her at though he placed great importance on her reply when all she had wanted to find out was whether it was fear for her safety or pure and simple mule-headedness that drove him to say no.

If Barrett had another reason for asking, she wasn't certain she wanted to hear it. Her mind was in a muddle. Nothing was working out in quite the way it should! She ought to feel anger at Barrett's arbitrary refusal to let her sail on one of the merchant vessels, but she could detect none.

In her heart she knew she did not want to leave.

"Does it, Georgie? Does it make a difference?" Barrett repeated.

"No!" She put out her hand as though to ward him off.

Barrett captured it, drawing her closer until he felt her body's warmth through the cloth of his coat. He looked into her eyes, seeing apprehension in their velvety brown depths. So his feelings made no difference to her, did they? Now that she had proven her independence to that cad Hargrave, she'd return to England and marry him?

Hell and the devil confound it! She'd be throwing herself

away! Hargrave was a bounder. A wastrel. A lecher. If Georgie didn't know it, he, Barrett Gray, would teach her the difference between a black-hearted, useless fop and a man! Then, when she was wiser, he would—

Barrett's thumb brushed over Mother Bainbridge's ring. "You may return the emerald," he said harshly. "I have been remiss, but since this is my first try at a betrothal, I expect I may be forgiven."

His every word stung like the lash of a whip. Georgiana felt a tremor that started deep within her and spread until she was shaking all over.

Holding her captive with one hand, Barrett dug in his coat pocket with the other. He pulled out a small box, turning it so she could read the name of a leading Boston jeweler stamped on the lid.

Her eyes widened. He had bought a ring! To taunt her?

"Oh, I'll forgive you," she said. "It will be the lady in your second or third attempt, who might find it a mite harder to accept this pledge. A secondhand token!"

She tried to pull away. "No, really, Barrett! Mother Bainbridge's ring will do very well for the duration of our . . ." Flustered, she let her voice trail as she remembered that there was no set limit to their charade.

"And have it recognized by one of Mother Bainbridge's bosom bows?" He twisted the emerald off her finger, pocketing it. "You must allow me *some* regard for my dignity, Georgie!"

He finally released her hand. Giving him a sidelong glance, Georgie sank into a curtsy. "I beg your pardon, sir. I assumed—stupidly, I realize now—that the ring would be accepted as my own."

"Not by me! Even had I not recognized the emerald, I would have known it wasn't yours. After all, we spent two days in close proximity aboard the *Boston Belle*. You wore no ring then, and neither did you wear one after my father brought you here."

"Indeed! How foolish of me."

Barrett thrust the tiny box at her. "Open it, Georgiana!"

Still she hesitated. Had she been asked, she would have

been unable to explain her reluctance to accept his ring. After all, it shouldn't matter; it was only pretense, as had been the kiss.

She saw Barrett's dark brows rise until they touched the shock of black hair falling onto his forehead. "I was told all women find jewelry, and especially rings, irresistible," he said impatiently. "Yet here you are looking as though I were offering you a toad."

Georgie snatched up the box and started to pry at the snug-fitting lid. "Had you attempted to hold a toad on your open palm, it would have been gone before you could say croak. Oh!" Speechless, she stared at the ring nestled in blue velvet.

Barrett took box and lid, setting them aside. He recaptured her hand, and his touch as he slipped his ring over her finger set every nerve in her body atingle. Playing with fire! A game more dangerous than she had anticipated.

He turned her so that the light from the window reflected in the stones. A cluster of five large diamonds ignited into brilliant, ice blue sparks. A circle of sapphires, ringed by smaller diamonds, surrounded the central cluster like flower petals.

Georgie stood, transfixed by the sight of the betrothal ring adorning her hand. The stones seemed to mock and taunt: What are you thinking, Georgiana Rutledge? We can never be real to you!

"Well?" Barrett demanded. "How do you like it?"

She raised her eyes to his face, taking in every detail—his deeply tanned skin, lean cheeks, square chin; his eyes that had reminded her of young birch leaves on their first meeting; and his mouth that could look so harsh and yet had caressed her lips with tenderness and warmth. Once.

"Beautiful," she said, breathlessly aware that she was referring to more than a mere ring. Then, afraid that her thoughts might be mirrored in her eyes, she looked down at her hand again.

"How on earth did you get it at this hour of the morning, Barrett? And on a Sunday, too!"

"My wicked trade connections." Barrett spoke lightly

enough, but the look he gave her was sharp. He added, "I also brought you your glove, Georgie."

The change in subject was too abrupt. Her mind refused to jump from a betrothal ring to a glove. "My what? Oh, no!"

Revulsion shook her when Barrett offered her the long white silk glove she had worn the night before, and she took a hasty step backward.

"Take it. It's clean," he assured her.

Georgie picked it up with two fingers, holding it at arm's length. "So it is," she said, looking at the glove from all angles. "Still, I daresay I shan't wear it again."

She crossed to one of the spoon-backed Queen Anne chairs, which looked rather too elegant near the fireplace of rough-hewn granite, the hard gray stone used in many of Boston's fine homes.

If he scolds me again for running across the Common, I shall box his ears! Does he believe I encouraged the odious Wilfred in his outrageous behavior?

Flinging the glove onto a nearby table, Georgie sat down, worried that Barrett might not consider a punch sufficient punishment for Wilfred Mannering.

Do Americans duel? Georgie wondered.

Although the bloodstain had been removed from the glove, her fingers felt sullied. She gripped a fold of material in the skirt of her gown and wiped her hand.

Barrett had followed her to the fireplace. "For a blood-thirsty lady who wanted to draw Wilfred's cork, you're very fastidious. Dare I hope you're satisfied with my performance last night? True, I was not in very good shape, but I did make his claret flow."

Claret? she thought. What was he talking about? *We were speaking of his ring, and then of that awful glove.* She realized that Barrett must have made a reference to his fight with Wilfred Mannering.

"Oh! You bloodied his nose," she said. "Then I'm glad I wasn't close enough to see. Poor Aunt Letty would have had to introduce me—green in the face and shaking like a blancmange—to my Uncle Lyman."

"Yes. It might have been a trifle awkward." Barrett sat down on the leather-clad arm of a wing chair, facing her. "Just what happened with Wilfred, Georgie?"

Color flooded her cheeks. "I daresay you think—"

"I think nothing of the kind," he interrupted. "I do not repeat my mistakes."

"Oh. You were annoyed, though."

"Do you wonder, Georgie? Has it not occurred to you that it should have been your actual fiancé who avenged you, and not the pretender?"

She looked at him bleakly. "Yes," she murmured. "Yes, of course. I daresay it's a bore having to act my champion."

"Boredom is the least of my worries," he said dryly. "My concern is that I shall be prematurely worn out from all the heroic deeds I'm called upon to perform on your behalf. Couldn't you at least try not to fall into quite so many scrapes?"

To her confused mind the question was an accusation. She hadn't meant to involve Barrett in her scrapes, and neither had she expected him to extricate her. Yet he always did, and she knew intuitively that he always would be at her side if she needed help, no matter what the cost to him.

It was her lie regarding Sir Perceval Hargrave, however, that most pricked Georgiana's conscience. No longer did she excuse it as mere suppression of fact. If Barrett knew that she had lied, he would feel insulted. Or, worse, he would be hurt, knowing that she had not trusted him.

Resolve stiffened her spine. Meeting Barrett's challenging look squarely, Georgie said, "I am sorry to have been such a trial to you, Barrett. I'm afraid, though, you don't know the worst yet."

"Good heavens! I was gone four *days*, not weeks. Surely not time enough for more havoc?"

"Please, Barrett! Hush!" Georgie perched on the edge of her chair, her hands clutching the carved frame of the seat. "I am in no mood to jest. You see, I—"

"Here you are, my dears!" Letty danced into the sitting room, oblivious to the crackling silence her sudden entry had caused. "I have *such* a surprise for you! Lyman—"

She whirled, laughing up at her large husband, who entered the room in his leisurely fashion. "Come, dearest. Let's tell them our surprise."

Georgie could have wept with frustration. There would be no stopping her aunt, and neither could she excuse herself and drag Barrett into some other chamber. Aunt Letty— providence or nemesis? Georgie was aware of a feeling of defeat as she listened to her aunt's plan to hold a reception and ball in her and Barrett's honor.

"Our friends will expect it," said Letty. "After all, they don't know that you are only playing at being betrothed, and they'll wish to congratulate Barrett."

Georgie started to protest. She got no further than, "But, Aunt Letty!" before Lyman interrupted her calmly.

"Letty is right, my dear. Barrett and his father are well known and liked in Boston. Barrett is one of our closest friends. We cannot seem to be ignoring his betrothal to our niece."

As though it were a physical contact, Georgie felt Barrett's gaze on her face. "The time is not right yet to cry off," he said. "I daresay it seems like an eternity to you, Georgie, but you've not been in Boston a week."

Georgiana stared into her lap. When she had insisted that William insert a notice of retraction in the London papers, her family had pointed out that she would carry the stigma of "jilt." She had accepted that and had not spared a thought for Sir Perceval. Here in Boston, the second party to her "betrothal" was very much on her mind. Barrett, she realized, would suffer as well when the time came to cry off. He would be branded a "jilted groom."

Georgiana raised her chin. It was up to her to make certain that Barrett at least would emerge from this "betrothal" with his reputation intact. He was harsh and overbearing at times, but it had been chivalry that led him to offer his protection.

"A ball would be lovely," she said. "When is it going to be, Aunt Letty?"

She listened with apparent interest to Letty's explanation that the ball must, unfortunately, be a rather hurried affair. It must beheld on the following Saturday, since both Lyman and Edward Gray planned to leave town on Monday, the thirteenth of July. Lyman to return to Washington, and Edward Gray to travel back to Serendip.

Georgie nodded absently, promising to help with the invitations. And while Letty, marvelously recovered from her upset over Daniel and Salters, discussed particulars of the ball and asked Barrett whom he wished her to invite to the preceding dinner, Georgie thought about the moment her aunt would leave and Barrett would hear that there was no betrothal to Sir Percy.

Mother Bainbridge hobbled into the sitting room just as Georgie tried to assure herself that Barrett would *not* accuse her of mistrusting him. She was not very successful, and it was therefore with a measure of reserve that she responded to Mother Bainbridge's demands to be told of their plans now that Barrett had returned from Washington.

The old lady graciously approved the ball, accepted her emerald from Barrett, and inspected Georgie's new ring, saying, "You had better see to it you didn't waste your money on those diamonds, Barrett!"

"No waste," Barrett replied firmly. "It's my best investment yet."

He shot a look at Georgie that she found impossible to interpret. It roused her pique with its challenge and set her pulse racing with its promise.

When Barrett followed up with an invitation to take her for a drive along the Charles River, Georgie accepted with alacrity. Not that she was looking forward to having to confess to a lie—but she knew the longer the confrontation with Barrett was postponed the harder it would be to maintain her courage.

Inwardly she shook like a blancmange, but, thank heavens, there was no outward sign of her cowardice! Her hand was quite steady, she noted with pride when Barrett helped her into his open carriage.

He, too, seemed eager to be gone, for he shouted to the groom to "let 'em go" even before he had taken his seat beside her. He snatched up the reins, gave the horses the office to, go, then—it seemed they had barely started to roll—reined in again.

"Devil a bit!" he muttered. "What execrable timing!"

It was only then that Georgie noticed Hester Morris in the courtyard. The young girl stood quite close to the carriage, a frivolous parasol tilted at a useless angle behind her head and an expression of bitter disappointment on her face.

"Oh," she said, a pleading look in her wide blue eyes. "You're going for a drive."

Twelve

They had all three gone for that drive. Georgie, wedged between Barrett and Hester, had been stiff and tongue-tied for the better part of the outing. Barrett's ring on her finger and his muscular, leather-clad thigh pressing against her had served as constant reminders of her cowardly, disloyal surrender to his decree and a lie as yet to be confessed.

Her silence had hardly mattered, she thought as she sat in front of her dressing table mirror that night. Throughout the drive, Hester had chattered like a magpie and Barrett had teased the young girl about her many beaux, leaving Georgie free to let her mind roam. A mind confused by feelings and emotions she did not recognize.

It was very disturbing, for it was not at all like her *not* to know how she felt or what she wanted!

While they had stopped at the Charles River Bridge and watched the draw near the center open to allow passage for a convoy of barges, Georgie had recalled the night on Lady Sparling's lantern-lit terrace in Kensington. She had just told Fenella that she had no use for the cowardly fribbles and padded weaklings of the *ton*—very certain how she felt about *them!*—when Charlotte had come out to introduce her to more of those fops.

And Georgie had seen Barrett!

Tall, broad-shouldered, his skin bronzed by the wind and sun of St. Croix. An American. A merchant who shipped rum. A man a world removed from her own. Or so it had seemed at the time.

Georgie's hairbrush slipped from her idle fingers, startling her with the clatter of ivory against hard wood. She picked it up, putting it to use with firm, purposeful strokes. She was to attend a *converzatione* at the Otises' in Beacon Street, and Aunt Letty might come in at any moment to check on her dawdling niece.

Rose, of course, would have put up Georgie's hair in no time at all; but Rose was with Daniel, and rather than accept the reluctant services of the sniffling, red-eyed Salters, Georgie had decided to do without a maid. Catching the long, chestnut brown tresses in one hand, she twisted them into a soft coil at the base of her neck and skewered them in place with pearl-tipped pins.

Not the highest stickler would be able to accuse her of immodesty this evening. Georgie had chosen a gown of deep blue gauze with long, fitted sleeves and a neckline that came up to the base of her throat. The color might be thought extravagant for an unmarried young lady; but, she thought, the demure cut of the gown more than made up for that bit of flamboyance.

And Barrett—surely Barrett would appreciate the gown.

A large blue and white Lowestoft punch bowl was habitually set out on the half landing of the lofty, spiral stairway in the Otis mansion—refreshment for those of Harry Otis's guests who found the climb to the upper floor thirsty business.

Drawn by the irresistible aroma of rum, Edward Gray and Caleb Morris had stopped, effectively blocking the stairway to Barrett and Hester, who had ascended behind them.

"West India Muses," Caleb Morris said appreciatively, sniffing the contents of the bowl.

Edward Gray reached for a cup. "I hope Sally Otis didn't spare the sugar this time."

"Or got carried away with the lemon juice," muttered Caleb. "Hester, you don't want to appear too eager to join your beaux. They're too swell-headed already. Come and serve us."

"Must I, Papa?" Hester shrank against the baluster. "It's such sticky stuff! What if I spoil my gown?"

"I'll serve." Manfully, Barrett took up the ladle and started to pour punch into the cups held out to him by his father and Caleb.

He heard a door open below and Hester's excited cry, "Oh, there are the Bainbridges! Good evening, Lady Letty! Georgie, hurry and you can go in with me!"

With a silent promise that he'd prevent Hester's teaming up with Georgie, Barrett looked down into the entrance hall. A manservant had taken Letty's fur stole and stood waiting while Lyman helped Georgie out of her cloak. Georgie turned and raised her face to the half landing as the silken wrap slid off her shoulders.

Barrett caught his breath. A cloud of midnight blue froth that flowed like a veil against a low-cut, sleeveless underdress of some silver material teased with glimpses of bare arms and the creamy swell of bosom.

Damn her impudence! Did she think to taunt him after showing him so clearly that she wanted to return to England?

"Barrett! Watch what you're about, son!"

His father's warning reached him at the same time as a splash of punch soaked through the silk of his elegant knee breeches; but neither the cry nor the spill could draw his gaze from Georgiana.

Barrett tossed the ladle back into the bowl and stepped to the edge of the landing to watch Georgie's ascent. He saw her smile, the curve of her mouth tantalizing, stoking his anger. He knew himself mocked by the glow in her dark eyes, and his resolve to make her forget Sir Percy strengthened. He had warned her about playing with fire, hadn't he?

"My betrothed!" He took her outstretched hand in his, helping her up the last step.

"Barrett—" Georgie moved aside to allow Letty and Lyman to pass, then turned back to him.

Before she could speak, Barrett brushed his mouth against her ear, across the softness of her cheek until he found her lips. He lingered, tasting their sweetness as they melted under his touch. He drew back. The others, he noticed, had ascended to the second floor.

"How docile we are," he murmured. "You surprise me, Georgie. No reminders that we are playing a game? No stiffness or reluctance?"

"If you're referring to the carriage ride this morning—" She sounded breathless, flustered. "Oh, Barrett, I was hoping you'd be here!"

He raised a brow. "It is not conceit, then, that makes me think you donned this gorgeous confection for me?" His bold gaze raked her slim form from head to toe. "Perhaps you're thinking of changing my mind about your passage to England?"

For an instant she looked hurt, but then she pointed her nose high, assuming the familiar Rutledge look.

"I just might, now that you've put me in mind of it. Didn't you tell me you could captain a ship, Barrett?"

"Aye."

"Then," she said with a glittering smile, "I could charter one of Mr. Morris's ships and hire you as my captain."

"Aye."

She blinked, dispelling the air of haughtiness she had assumed. "I could? You'd take me back?"

"There'd be only one problem, my love. Mind, I'm not saying we wouldn't reach England in one piece, because we might—by judicious switching of flags, depending on whether we sighted an American or a British craft. It's your fiancé's reception of you that might be a stumbling block. I doubt he'd be pleased to accept you after you spent the better part of a month in my cabin."

"To the devil with Sir Percy!"

"My sentiments exactly," Barrett said smoothly. "But what of your brother, the earl? He, too, might consider you compromised."

"Yes, he would!" Georgie said angrily. "He'd make you marry me! And besides, I was never betrothed to Sir Percy at all!"

"What?" Barrett's hand shot out, closing tightly around her wrist.

"Are you two planning to spend the whole evening on the landing?" Hester called imperiously from the second floor.

"Certainly not!" Tearing herself from Barrett's grip, Georgie marched purposefully up the stairs.

Barrett frowned at her back as he ascended the spiraling steps behind her. *What game is she playing now, the minx? I saw the damned announcement! Bold and clear.*

He moved swiftly to claim his place beside Georgiana. "I'd have a word with you, ma'am."

She kept walking, sparing him neither a glance nor a word. They approached the salon from whence issued a babel of voices, laughter, and the clink of glasses. The opportunity to question her was lost. Sally Otis was waiting in the door to welcome Georgiana and introduce her to a cluster of young people.

Georgie was glad of the reprieve. Barrett, she was certain, was in a stew to question her, mayhap to box her ears; but he'd have to wait until the morrow. She might let him invite her for another drive—without Hester this time!

Georgie recognized Eliza Quincy, also a Summer Street resident, among the young people surrounding her and made no demur when Eliza propelled her through a set of double doors into an adjoining oval-shaped room.

"We've been dying to speak with you," said Eliza. "We're all friends of Aubrey."

"Let's sit in the bay." The young man who made the suggestion did not wait for anyone's consent but started to rearrange chairs to accommodate the half dozen young ladies who had followed Eliza. The gentlemen—among whom, Georgie was grateful to note, Wilfred Mannering was conspicuously absent—preferred to sprawl on the soft carpets.

Barrett sat down in front of Georgie. Reclining with one elbow propped onto the rug, his muscular legs stretched out before him and crossed at the ankles, he twirled the stem of a wineglass between his long, tanned fingers. He appeared utterly absorbed in the contemplation of his ruby wine—or in keeping the base of his glass atop a small stain Georgie noticed on his oyster-colored silk breeches.

She was aware of dark, frowning looks directed at her from beneath his thick black lashes and welcomed the excuse to turn away from Barrett when a young man, whom Mrs. Otis had introduced as Samuel Tremaine, addressed her.

"It was a blow to all of us, Lady Georgiana, when your aunt told us of Aubrey's death."

"You must be 'Paadner' Tremaine," she said impulsively. "That's a name Aubrey mentioned often, but he never spoke of a Samuel."

The young man grinned sheepishly. "That's me all right. 'Paadner' Tremaine." He took a gulp of his wine, then said, "It was a joke, you see. I used to tease him about his pronunciation. Aubrey and I were all set up to go into a partnership just as soon as—" He saw Georgie's face and broke off, blushing to the roots of his slick blond hair. "Sorry, ma'am. Didn't mean to cause you distress."

Trying to ignore the pain his words had evoked, Georgie completed his statement. "You were planning to form a partnership once Napoleon is beaten. Yes, I know. Aubrey intended to bring me to America as well. As it turned out, I came alone. I was curious about this country that Aubrey wanted to make his home . . . and mine."

Georgie was very much aware of Barrett's eyes fixed unwaveringly on her face. Defiantly she met his look. *Yes, you may well stare! It wasn't only to escape Sir Percy that I came to Boston!*

"But, perhaps," she heard a soft voice to her left, "it was all for the best that Aubrey fell at *Fuentes de Oñoro*?"

Georgie recoiled. Unable to believe her ears, she faced Regina Powell, a petite brunette, whom Aubrey had described as a "moonling, believing herself a romantic soul and spouting drivel until you want to shake her."

"Daddy says," continued Regina, sitting ramrod straight

and with her hands folded demurely in her lap, "that England will have to draw troops from Spain to fight us. It might have been Aubrey, were he alive now. I think we should be glad—for his sake—that he doesn't have to turn against us."

Regina's placid face started to blur before Georgie's eyes. She tried to focus on the curve of the bay window behind Regina, but the mullioned panes spun dizzily. *Blakeney was in Spain!*

"I've never heard such rubbish in my life!" Barrett said bitingly. "Lord, Regina, you must be totally out of your head to think such rot, let alone say it!"

Other voices rang out in protest of Regina's words, but it was Barrett's that cut through the painful confusion in Georgie's mind. The crazy whirl before her eyes stopped.

She turned to Barrett. He was closer than before, sitting directly at her feet and holding out his hand to her. She gripped it, feeling strength flow from him to her. He studied her anxiously for a moment, then addressed Regina again.

"Mayhap you'd care to offer your opinion to my father, Regina? No doubt he'd be gratified to hear that Franklin is better off dead. Or have you forgotten that my brother lost his life during the storming of *Ciudad Rodrigo*? Fighting with his English comrades?"

In the tense silence that followed Barrett's words, Georgie heard the hiss of a sharply drawn breath. She saw Barrett look at her with concern and an apology in his eyes, and realized that it had been her own breath, caught painfully in her throat.

Barrett, too, had lost his brother in the fight against Napoleon!

And while Eliza Quincy gallantly created a diversion with a reminder of Lady Letty's upcoming ball, and Hester aimed a swift, sharp pinch at Regina's plump thigh when that young lady tried to harp back to her own subject, Georgie looked at Barrett and wished that he had confided to her the circumstances of Franklin's death.

"Lady Georgiana?" Harrison Steene, Hester's beau, cleared his throat in embarrassment when not only Georgie but half the assembled young people turned to him. "Ah," he stammered. "Some neighbors of ours are traveling in Europe, Germany and Austria mostly, and they wrote about this, ah, this waltz. I wonder, have you heard of it?"

"What's a waltz?" said Hester, round-eyed.

"It's a dance," replied Georgie.

"A very new and scandalous dance." Barrett held out his glass to a manservant circulating with a bottle of Madeira. "I doubt it'll be acceptable to Bostonians or Philadelphians."

"It's not really new," protested Georgie. "The Viennese have enjoyed it for over three decades."

"But in what way is it scandalous?" Hester demanded to know.

Georgie darted a glance at Barrett. "It's only scandalous in the minds of *some*!"

There was a glint in his eyes when he retorted, "The waltz can give a man quite the wrong notion about a lady."

Hester complained, "I don't understand a word!"

"It's like this, Hester." Still looking at Georgiana, Barrett rose, setting his glass on a table. He bowed, holding out his hand. "Lady Georgie, may I have the honor?"

"With pleasure, sir." Placing her hand in his, Georgie got to her feet.

"You hold your partner"—Barrett drew her into the curve of his arm until she stood so close that his breath stirred tendrils of hair escaping from her chignon—"like so, and you dance thus entwined for the entire duration of the waltz."

"Oh!" breathed Hester. "How very improper."

"Some ladies enjoy it," said Barrett, the wicked gleam in his eyes burning Georgie's face.

"Some men," she countered, "take advantage and ask for a waltz when they know a lady cannot refuse!"

His dark head came closer. "Why," he murmured into her ear, "did you let me go on believing in your betrothal to Sir Percy?"

"Because you were so odious and overbearing," she whispered. "You laughed at me!"

"But later—"

"This, Mr. Gray," Georgie said loudly, "is not at all the correct form to dance the waltz. Allow me to point out that the distance between a waltzing couple should be at least twelve inches!"

"Will you ask the musicians to play a waltz on Saturday, Barrett?" asked Hester.

Barrett's hand dropped from Georgie's waist. He turned with a wry grin. "I doubt they'd know how, honey."

"What a shame!" Hester's words and sigh echoed Georgie's sentiments exactly.

Shortly afterward, Mrs. Otis invited her guests into the dining parlor where a supper of scalloped oysters, cold meats, fruit, and more Madeira wine had been set out.

Letty darted away from her husband's side and joined Georgie and Barrett at the sideboard long enough to whisper, "Now didn't I warn you it would be a dead bore? Who wants to talk all night about literature and religion? Even politics is a taboo subject nowadays! And scandal! Fashion! Oh, dear me, no! Never mention those!"

"Well!" said Georgie when her aunt had flitted back to Lyman. "I certainly could not tell in our little gathering that some topics are off limits!"

She reached for her wineglass, which she had set down while she served herself with strawberries and slices of chilled melon. Someone jostled her arm from behind, spilling the wine on the cloth-covered mahogany sideboard and splashing a few drops onto Barrett's coat.

"Dash it, Georgie!" he muttered. "First my best silk breeches, now my coat! I like my drink *inside* me, I'll have you know."

"I beg your pardon." She looked at him in surprise. "I was not aware, however, that I had spilled on you earlier."

Responding to the caustic request of another hungry guest, Barrett moved on, helping himself to a spoonful of halibut in aspic. "Well, you did. The sight of you in that delectable confection so bowled me over that the punch I was pouring for my father ended up on my breeches."

Her eyes brimmed with laughter. "I daresay you'll demand satisfaction. Must I name my seconds, sir?"

"No seconds! We'll meet alone. I'll take you for a drive at sunrise."

From her balcony, Georgie watched the sun come up, a pale golden haze creeping along the sculpted hedge at the back of the garden and lending sparkle to the morning dew. She tiptoed from her room, past her aunt and uncle's chamber, guiltily conscious that she had told no one of her assignation with Barrett.

Hunching her shoulders as though to shrug off her troublesome conscience, Georgie moved stealthily down the stairs. Were she still living with Charlotte, she wouldn't have felt the *slightest* pang!

When she turned the curve of the stairway, she saw the foyer and the front door. It stood open, and there, on the stoop, was Appleby in conversation with Barrett! So much for a secret assignation!

"Good morning, Appleby!" She greeted the majordomo with a wide smile. "If I'm not back in time for Daniel's lessons, you may send him into the garden with his books."

Only then did she look at Barrett. He was bare-headed, and his black hair glistened with reddish brown lights in the sun. A corduroy riding coat fit snugly to his broad shoulders, and his long, muscular legs were encased in pantaloons and short boots. A man, not a fop!

She caught a look of pleasure in his eyes when they met hers, and instantly her pulse started racing; but when he handed her into the box seat of his carriage, she also noted wariness in his expression and a measure of reserve.

He swung himself up beside her and skillfully guided the horses through the narrow gate into Summer Street. "We'll drive up Beacon Hill," he said, keeping his eyes on the nodding heads of the bays. "It was too dark to see the top last night when you drove out to the Otises, and I think you'll find the sight interesting."

"The—cutting down of the hill?" Georgie swallowed. She had prepared herself for an inquisition about Sir Percy and had stored away a question or two about Franklin that she wanted to ask. But, apparently, this was to be another sight-seeing tour!

Stiffly she sat beside him and stared at the homes they passed. After a moment's reflection, however, her disappointment gave way to a surge of relief. She'd rather not talk about Sir Percy in any case! If only she had thought before she blurted out the truth to Barrett!

The carriage swayed as they turned into Common Street and shortly afterward into Park Street. She felt Barrett's eyes on her, for the first time since he handed her up into the seat of the carriage.

"*If* you have no objection," he said as though not a considerable number of minutes but mere seconds had passed since he had proposed the drive up Beacon Hill.

She gave him a sidelong look and felt her stiffness melt. Her mouth softened, responding to his infectious grin. "None at all, Barrett."

"Excellent." He slipped an arm around her waist, drawing her against him. "There's something I want to show you on Beacon Hill."

As he told her some of the history of the hill, his voice wove a magic circle around Georgie. She saw and heard only Barrett; other carriages, riders, and bustling pedestrians might not have existed for all that Georgie was aware of their presence.

The carriage turned again, the horses slowing as the incline of Beacon Hill grew steeper. Work crews were digging and cutting away at the top of the hill, wagons and carts on their way to dump loads of rock and dirt in the Mill Pond trundled past them; but Georgie scarcely noticed. She had eyes for Barrett alone.

Georgie heard his words telling her of the old beacon that used to keep watch atop the hill, of a Doric column that had borne the golden eagle now residing in the New State House; but it was the timbre of his voice she really listened to.

Barrett guided the carriage into Walnut Street. He reined in when they came abreast a large building site, beautifully terraced and timbered with elm, walnut, and chestnut trees.

"This is mine," he said, the sweep of his hand encompassing the plot of land. "Someday I shall build a home here."

He tightened his arm around her waist and turned to look at her. "I saw the notice of your betrothal to Sir Percy. So what's all this about never having been betrothed at all?"

"It—it was a mistake. William had it retracted the following day."

"Why did you not tell me sooner, Georgie?"

The green of his irises was brighter than she had ever seen it. She sat spellbound, unable to tear her gaze away. She wanted to lie but couldn't.

"It seemed . . . safer."

"Ah! But last night? You deemed it safe to tell me then?"

Her nails bit into the palms of her hands. "It was thoughtless of me. I'm sorry, Barrett! I realized too late—"

"Realized what too late, Georgie?"

"If I had not told you," she said in a rush, "you could have used my betrothal to Sir Percy as an excuse to end our charade!"

The brightness left his eyes. Once again he was aloof. "And you believe I would have used that excuse?" he said coldly. "Would have let you face the scandal alone?"

"What else could we have done?"

His mouth curled. "You might keep my ring! Hold me to my word!"

"I would not serve you with such a dastardly trick!"

"But you'd have me waste my money! Give Mother Bainbridge the satisfaction of saying 'I told you so!'"

"You said it was an investment!"

"Yes, I did, didn't I?" The harsh planes of his face relaxed. "That knowledge must serve to keep the dismals away. For now."

He gathered the reins, giving the horses the office to go. "I'm beginning to think better of your notion to send you back to England in one of Caleb's ships. I'll talk it over with him and my father. But first we must face our 'betrothal ball.'"

"Yes," said Georgie in a hollow voice. "We mustn't disappoint Aunt Letty, must we?"

Georgie shook out her cramped fingers after inscribing the last place card for the dinner that was to precede the ball that night. Leaning against the caned back of her chair, she drew a deep breath of air scented by roses, lavender, and jasmine blooming around the terrace.

Beyond, in the miniature replica of the Wolversham Court garden, the flower beds looked nude. Every bloom worth cutting had fallen victim to the gardener's shears earlier that morning and was awaiting Georgie's nimble fingers in the coolness of the stillroom.

More work. Thank goodness!

Georgie wiped her pen and closed the inkwell. An abundance of work, she thought with gratitude, was the only weapon against thinking and useless speculation. When she had returned from her drive with Barrett, Letty had pounced on her with stacks of invitations to be addressed. It had taken all of Monday and Tuesday to write them. The rest of the week, Georgie had run innumerable errands for her aunt, had supervised the cleaning of chandeliers, and lent a hand when it was time to wash the crystal goblets and Letty's best china.

Exhausted, she had crawled into bed each night and fallen asleep before her head touched the pillow. Every morning she had risen an hour early so as not to neglect Daniel's lessons.

Again Georgie's gaze drifted across the denuded flower beds. Only a few hours left until the "betrothal" ball. She must hurry with the floral arrangements if she wished to have a moment to collect her thoughts before she must face Barrett.

His words on Beacon Hill echoed in her mind: "You might keep my ring! Hold me to my word!" How angrily he had spoken! And then he had admitted that he was thinking of sending her to England after all.

Gathering her writing tools and the stack of place cards, she went into the house. It was cool and quiet; all activity now was concentrated in the kitchen wing where Mrs. Appleby and the cook reigned supreme.

Georgie had just stepped into the foyer when the front door burst open and Daniel hurled into the house, a few steps ahead of Letty. After the three days' house arrest imposed by Barrett, the boy had appointed himself Letty's page, snatching at every opportunity to get outside.

"Oh, Lady Georgie!" he shouted, skidding to a halt a hair's breath before he would have cannoned into her. "I saw this man while I was waitin' for Lady Letty outside the milliner's!"

"A man? How exciting. Was he on stilts, dear?" said Georgie, frowning at the writing materials in her hands. "Aunt Letty, would you please—Oh, you have your arms full!"

"Gloves and the sheerest silk stockings you ever saw," Letty said cheerfully. "I wish you had been with me, Georgie. The Misses Stillwell have just received a new shipment of lace collars."

"Lady Georgie!" Daniel tugged at her skirt.

"Just a moment, please, Daniel. Aunt Letty, can you squeeze these"—she pointed her chin at the place cards and the inkwell—"into a pocket or under your arm? I must get the flowers done, else the ballroom will be bare tonight."

"I'll take 'em, Lady Georgie," Daniel said eagerly. "My hands don't hardly hurt anymore. Please let me take 'em!"

"Thank you, Daniel. Lady Letty will show you where to put everything." Georgie gave the boy's hair a quick ruffling, then hurried down the hall to the stillroom beneath the kitchens.

"But I haven't told you about the man, Lady Georgie! He was askin' about you!"

"Tomorrow, Daniel! You can tell me all about it tomorrow before your lessons." Firmly Georgie closed the cellar door behind her. Only three hours to do what looked like a million blooms and sprigs of fern and evergreen. She really should have started sooner!

At five o'clock, when the half dozen footmen hired for the night by Mrs. Appleby had carried the last vase and a score of flower-filled baskets to the first floor where the two adjoining salons had been converted into a ballroom, Georgie dragged herself wearily to her bedchamber.

When Rose peeked in a short while later, she found her mistress fast asleep on the counterpane, one knee drawn up and a hand curled around the laces of the still tied slipper.

Shaking her head and muttering darkly about the foolishness of young ladies, Rose went down to the kitchen to prepare personally a tray of food that would be irresistible to Lady Georgie, who had shown a distressing tendency lately to peck at her meals or skip them altogether.

Alas, Rose's efforts were wasted. She carried the delicacies upstairs shortly after six, but Lady Georgie would only drink a cup of tea prepared from Mother Bainbridge's hoard. She started to nibble at a biscuit, then set it back on the plate.

"I think I have a headache coming on, Rose. Perhaps I need a cordial."

"A cordial? You?" Rose gave a snort. "What ye need is a good smack, if you'll pardon me saying so. Or else," she added sagely, "a good gallop across the downs—or wherever they do ride here in Boston."

A ride! Georgie thought with longing. But Uncle Lyman only kept carriage horses.

"Anyways," Rose continued briskly, "if ye don't want to eat, we best get ye ready for the ball. Lady Letty's expectin' the dinner guests to arrive at seven-thirty."

Georgie went through the routine of bathing and dressing with a sad lack of enthusiasm. Even her ball gown, copied painstakingly by Letty's dressmaker from the sketch Georgie had drawn, failed to lift her spirits. She stared at the clinging, peach-colored silk, the exact shade of the gown fashioned by Madame Bertin for her visit to Almack's, and wondered why on earth she had ever believed that she and Barrett could recapture those golden moments of friendship before Sir Perceval Hargrave had spoiled everything.

When Rose, shortly after seven o'clock, finally declared herself satisfied with her mistress's appearance, Georgie remained seated at her dressing table.

"If ye don't come down on time, Lady Georgie, people will think ye don't want to celebrate yer betrothal!" warned Rose, opening the door. "And Mr. Barrett being such a fine, upstanding man!"

Mother Bainbridge's voice, high and querulous, preceded her into Georgie's chamber. "I'll see that your mistress gets down with time to spare. You run along now, gal!"

Before leaving, Rose shot Georgie a look that showed her outrage at being thus dismissed and satisfaction that the matter of Lady Georgie's timely appearance downstairs rested now on a tongue more cutting than her maid's.'

"What's the matter, gal?" Mother Bainbridge's dark eyes scrutinized Georgie keenly. "If you're feeling blue-deviled, the best medicine is to go into company. Not hide away in your room!"

"I have some thinking to do, Mother Bainbridge." Georgie helped the old lady into one of the easy chairs by the window before resuming her seat on the stool. "I can best think in privacy."

Mother Bainbridge gave a sharp cackle of laughter. "Meaning, I take it, that I should go to the devil."

"You know better than that, Mother Bainbridge. Besides" —Georgie darted a mischievous look at the old lady—"I daresay he'd send you straight back."

"You can bet your last groat he would! In my day, we were not taught to be mealymouthed, namby-pamby misses with die-away airs, dropping in a swoon if a man so much as breathed a swear word. Dammit! We used 'em ourselves. To out-ride, out-swear, and out-gamble any man, that was our goal."

Mother Bainbridge plucked at the folds of her elaborate, full-skirted dinner gown. "Times have changed, though," she muttered. "And I with them, I suppose. Came to have a talk with you, and don't seem able to find the right words."

"Are you going to scold me for accepting Barrett's ring?" Georgie asked. "I shan't keep it, you know."

"You disappoint me, gal, if you believe that's what I meant when I told Barrett to make certain he hadn't wasted his money."

Georgie absently traced the carvings on the back of her hairbrush. "No," she said slowly. "I don't think that's what you meant."

"Then? What's the stumbling block, Georgiana? Why aren't you making a push to attach Barrett permanently? You're in love with him, aren't you?"

Georgie caught her breath sharply. She felt as though Mother Bainbridge had poked her in the midriff with the ebony handle of her cane.

In love with Barrett?

Her face started to burn, then her whole body, as though she were standing too close to the fire after being chilled by a day's hunting. She rose shakily to her feet and went to the open door that led onto the balcony. Cool night air gently fanned her heated body but did nothing to diminish the glow in her veins.

In love!

Her blood sang in her ears; her pulse raced. She should have known it when he kissed her . . . when he slipped his ring on her finger and the stones seemed to mock her . . . when his every touch, his every look, his very presence, made her heart beat faster. She should have known!

It came as a shock to hear it from Mother Bainbridge before she herself had recognized it. As Charlotte only looked at the surface eligibility of a suitor, so Georgie had refused to examine her feelings for Barrett. Instead of admitting her growing love, she had chosen to believe it was a flirtation she wanted.

"Georgiana!" Mother Bainbridge rapped her cane against the wooden arm of the chair and said sharply, "I want to see your face, gal, not your back!"

Georgie pressed her palms against her burning cheeks and took several deep breaths before turning. Keen, dark eyes bored into her, no doubt taking in the flush she could not suppress, and her shaking hands.

Mother Bainbridge nodded, unwittingly confirming Georgie's fears regarding her traitorous face and hands. "Aye," the old lady said in softened tones. "There you are, then.

"But why the deuce"—one gnarled finger pointed

accusingly at Georgie—"are you still saying you'll return his ring? Why won't you marry him?"

"Because I don't know whether Barrett loves me." Georgie pulled her stool closer to Mother Bainbridge and sat down. "If he loved me—"

"If, if, if!" the old lady said impatiently. "Find out! For heaven's sake, gal, I thought you had pluck! Ha! A butterfly shows more spunk than you!"

A spark lit in Georgie's eyes. No one had ever accused her of lack of courage.

Squaring her shoulders, Georgie said firmly, "I'll find out."

"Knew you'd not shy at a fence." Mother Bainbridge nodded contentedly. "That brother of yours, Aubrey, bragged more than once what an intrepid horsewoman you are."

"Aubrey also used to say I have more bottom than sense," Georgie admitted.

"Rubbish! It never hurt anyone to show pluck. And now that you know what you want, go after it!"

"Yes, indeed." Georgie smoothed the folds of her peach-colored silk gown. "Let's go down, Mother Bainbridge!"

The old lady hesitated. After a moment, she reached for her cane, saying gruffly, "Bainbridge and I were promised to each other when we were still in the cradle. Nothing unusual in my day, of course, and on the whole we rubbed along very well. But—"

"But?" Georgie prompted as she helped Mother Bainbridge to her feet.

"But having watched Lyman and Letty for more than a quarter century, I know that Bainbridge and I were cheated out of something precious. Love."

Georgie stood motionless. *Cheated out of love!*

No! That should not happen to her. Not if she could help it!

Thirteen

They sat down forty to dinner, a very elegant, formal affair. Immediately after the six-course meal Georgie took her place in the receiving line, with Lyman and Letty to her left and Barrett and Edward Gray on her right.

One hundred fifty of the two hundred invited to the "betrothal ball" had sent their acceptance. Slowly, the two large salons began to fill. And still so many more hands to shake, thought Georgie as she smiled at a Cambridge professor and his wife, and greeted several selectmen accompanied by their families.

"I'm afraid I shan't be able to hold my champagne glass when the times comes," she whispered to Barrett. "My fingers are numb!"

"Worse! I shan't be able to kiss you after the toast. My mouth is stiff from this infernal smiling."

Georgie darted a glance at him as he bowed over the hand of one Mrs. Warren. There was nothing wrong with his mouth, she thought, watching it curve most beguilingly.

In the far salon, the violinists were tuning their instruments. Soon the young people gathered inside would be dancing while she and Barrett must stand near the doors for who knew how long!

A fresh burst of arrivals kept Georgie occupied for some moments, then, during a lull, she heard the lilting tune of a Virginia reel. She'd give much to be on the dance floor with Barrett. There wouldn't be any waltzing, of course, but a Virginia reel was nothing to be sneezed at. Hester had shown her the steps, and Georgie had no doubt that she'd enjoy herself.

Barrett nudged her arm and looked pointedly at her tapping foot. "Shall we excuse ourselves?"

"Certainly not!" Guiltily, Georgie stilled the offender. "We cannot desert our posts."

Letty had overheard. "There's no reason for you to miss the fun," she said. "Edward and Lyman will stay with me to greet any stragglers. So run along, children!"

Georgiana needed no further urging. With her hand nestled in the crook of Barrett's arm, she floated in the direction of the arched aperture leading into the far salon, where all furniture had been removed to accommodate the string quartet and as many dancers as the four walls would hold.

"You look charming, Georgie." Barrett's deep voice was a caress. "I've wanted to tell you so all during dinner, but what with Mrs. Bulfinch on my left and 'Paadner' Tremaine on your right continually interrupting, I've had no chance to say *anything* to you."

"Thank you, Barrett." Georgie walked more slowly. Much as she wanted to dance with him, his words were too promising to be ignored.

"When you came down," he said, matching his pace to hers and further delaying their arrival on the dance floor by suddenly steering her in the opposite direction, "I had a sense of being transported back in time. Surely this is the gown you wore at Almack's?"

"So you did notice my gown!"

"Can I help it?" Barrett came to a halt, facing her. "*I* am no slowtop, Georgie," he said, giving her a hard look, then added under his breath, "Although I may very well turn out a fool."

"Why the emphasis, Barrett?" she asked, ignoring the latter part of his speech. "Are you implying that I am a slowtop?"

The chatter and laughter around her appeared to swell in volume while Barrett took his time with an answer. She had, indeed, been a slowtop, Georgie acknowledged. But surely only *she* knew that!

"Time will tell," Barrett said finally.

She could have stomped her foot. This conversation was leading nowhere!

Georgie saw Mother Bainbridge, nodding vigorous encouragement at her from a thronelike chair in front of the flower-decked fireplace, from which vantage point the old lady could observe the goings-on in both salons. Georgie smiled and waved, thinking ruefully that a prod with the cane would be more effective encouragement than a nod. She was determined to pay attention to every word uttered by Barrett, to listen to the nuances of his voice, and to understand even those words he left unspoken.

But, dash it! It was difficult!

"Well," said Georgie, resuming the slow circuit around the salon. "You're wrong about my gown, Barrett. It is *not* the one I wore at Almack's. That gown lies at the bottom of the ocean."

He studied her face, then, once more the peach-colored confection. "A good imitation. Do I detect purpose behind this seeming irrelevance?"

"Yes."

Her reply, stark, uncompromising, hung between them. Vainly, Georgie searched for the right words to explain her impulsive decision to have the gown copied when she had seen the silk tacked to a mannequin in Mrs. Prescott's establishment.

"Well?" Barrett prompted.

"I hoped to remind you of London. I hoped—" Georgie broke off. Snatching a glass from the tray of a passing footman, she took a sip of wine, forcing it down her suddenly dry throat.

"Dash it, Barrett! Must you be so obtuse?"

His brows rose. "Obtuse? My dear, I *am* reminded of London. Most forcefully so. But what is that to the point?"

"Barrett!" Embarrassment and exasperation warred in her breast and, she feared, in her voice as well. "Surely you won't deny that there was a certain rapport between us before that stupid misunderstanding at Almack's?''

"I won't deny it."

Her mouth tightened at his maddening calm. "Well, then," she said, her fierce look daring him to laugh at her. "Pretend that we are at Almack's! Pretend you came in *before* that insufferable baronet asked me to dance!"

"I am sorry. I cannot do that, Georgie. For one thing, there's no waltzing here."

Barrett turned away from her, but not before she had seen a tiny, suspicious twitch at the corner of his mouth. He *was* laughing! And now he made a great ado of nodding to acquaintances, who showed very little interest in him. In fact, Georgie noted, everyone they passed studiously avoided looking their way. Their contretemps had not gone unnoticed.

And it had all been for naught! She had swallowed her pride, had shown the pluck and backbone of a Rutledge; yet nothing had been gained.

Georgie raised her glass to her lips, draining it to the dregs. She wouldn't give up. Not yet.

"But most importantly," Barrett said so softly that she almost missed the words. "I cannot pretend, because what I feel for you now is far different from what I felt then."

She stopped and looked at him, her eyes wide and questioning. He was not laughing now. His arm slid around her waist. "In England," he said huskily, "I was taken by the debutante who would not simper or flirt with every available bachelor. I was intrigued by her frankness and her disdain for the empty talk and posturing of the *ton*."

"And now?" Georgie's voice was but a breath.

"Now," he said, drawing her so close that the buttons of his waistcoat pressed through the thin silk of her gown. "Now—"

He paused. His eyes clouded as though he had been struck by a sudden, painful thought.

"What are you thinking, Barrett?" Unmindful of the glass in her hand, Georgie reached up to clasp his shoulders.

"Are you going to kiss her, Barrett?" someone asked in scandalized tones. Hester Morris.

Georgie gave a guilty start, and removed her hands from Barrett's sleeves. Disappointment at the interruption settled in her stomach like a leaden weight.

Barrett remained unruffled. "Will you go away, Hester?" he said quite pleasantly.

"Don't be silly!" Hester replied pertly. "I don't have to go away. I was invited! Besides, it's not time for you two to kiss yet!"

Hester's words recalled Georgie to her surroundings. Their slow circling of the salon had taken them near the receiving line. Barrett had his back to the door, but Georgie could see Edward Gray smile at them. Blushing, she pulled away from Barrett, only to be instantly drawn close again by strong hands that refused to let go of her waist.

Edward Gray's smile turned into a veritable grin, but Georgie was no longer focusing on him. Past Barrett's father, she saw Wilfred Mannering approaching her aunt.

Georgie scowled. The odious Wilfred had *not* received an invitation. She was certain of it; after all, it had been she who addressed the gilt-edged cards. Determined to give the brash young man a set-down and to send him off with a flea in his ear, Georgie tried to wriggle out of Barrett's embrace.

"Oh, no, you don't!" Barrett said firmly while keeping a tight clasp on her. "It may be premature according to Hester's reckoning, but I know that there are times when a stolen kiss can be most satisfying. And this, I think, is such a time."

Georgie gasped. It was not that she had objections to being reminded of that earlier stolen kiss, or that Barrett wished to steal another one. *No, not at all!* she thought, standing stiff and as responsive as a gatepost as Barrett's mouth covered hers. It was seeing another man behind Wilfred Mannering. A chestnut-haired dandy, whom she had believed at the other side of the Atlantic Ocean!

Sir Perceval Hargrave!

The wineglass slipped from her fingers, shattered into tiny sparkling fragments on the polished floor.

"Broken glass!" wailed Hester. "That's seven years' bad

luck! You ought to have waited with the kiss until *after* the announcement, Barrett!''

"It takes a mirror, Hester. Not a broken glass,'' muttered Barrett. With a puzzled, probing look at Georgie, he moved slightly away from her. "What is it, love?''

"A nightmare.''

He turned his head to follow her gaze, and tensed. His grip on her tightened. "Damn!'' he burst out. "How the devil did *he* get here?''

And then Sir Perceval Hargrave's voice, very self-assured and very English, penetrated the buzz of conversation of those near the door.

"A thousand apologies for bursting in uninvited,'' Sir Percy said to Letty. "But I know you'll forgive a man nigh out of his mind with love and concern. My fiancée—''

He broke off. Apparently overcome by emotion, he dabbed at his forehead with the lace-edged square of linen he carried in his left hand. In his right hand he held a folded newspaper.

"I was given to understand,'' Sir Percy went on, his voice carrying to the far corners of the salon, "that my betrothed Lady Georgiana Rutledge resides with you?''

Into the sudden hush—even the violinists had conspired and stopped their fiddling—exploded Georgiana's indignant "No!''

"Oh, dear!'' whispered Hester.

Georgie saw Letty and Lyman, their startled faces turning from her to Sir Percy and back to her in bewilderment. She saw Edward Gray's troubled frown. But most clearly of all, she saw Sir Percy's smile as he came toward her. A sly smile. Insinuating and triumphant.

"Georgiana!'' he cried, spreading open the newspaper. The London *Gazette*. "Your brother relented. He published the announcement. My dear, we may be married without delay!''

"You, sir, are a liar!'' she said loudly, clearly.

Georgie encountered no resistance when she pulled away from Barrett's clasp. It surprised her, but she was too intent on ridding herself of the baronet to wonder about Barrett's desertion. She took a step toward Sir Percy, her hands clenched. They ached to deal the baronet some of the hits Aubrey and Blakeney had taught her.

Sir Percy's light blue eyes darted to Barrett. Once. Then they quickly returned to Georgie to crawl with obnoxious intimacy over her silk-draped body.

"Ah!" he sighed. "Peach silk. How it does take one back!"

"With a difference!" There was menace in Barrett's voice. He was suddenly very close again to Georgie.

Alarmed, Sir Percy retreated a step. A ripple of excitement stirred those of the guests near enough to see Barrett's anger.

"Barrett, don't, I beg you!" cried Letty.

Nothing, however, could save Sir Percy from Barrett's punishing right as it shot out to connect precisely with the tip of Sir Percy's chin.

"Well done, Barrett!" Georgie clapped as the baronet toppled in a manner reminiscent of the *Rutledge Pride*'s mast when it pitched onto the deck. "I cannot help wishing, though," she added wistfully, "that you had knocked him down at Almack's."

"My apologies, Lady Letty," Barrett murmured absently. He darted a look at Letty's guests. They stood as though posing for a *tableau*, their faces frozen variously in expressions of outrage or of admiration.

Barrett gave Georgie a crooked grin. "You've done it this time! Bostonians do not often meet a young lady of your violent nature."

"*My* nature!" she said indignantly.

"But, somehow," he continued smoothly, "your wish doesn't surprise me one bit. And had I known your brother would respond with a betrothal announcement, no matter how quickly retracted, I *would* have planted Sir Percy a facer at Almack's!"

Georgie blinked. "But William didn't! It was Sir Percy who inserted the notice. We never knew about it until we read the *Gazette*."

"You don't say," drawled Barrett, watching through

narrowed eyes as Sir Percy struggled to his feet. "What a rattlesnake!"

"I demand satisfaction, Gray!" Sir Percy rubbed his jaw where a dark bruise was already beginning to show.

"And you shall have it, Hargrave!"

Again Barrett's fist shot out. "Payment for the 'betrothal notice'!"

"Bravo!" Mother Bainbridge's shout and the enthusiastic raps of her cane as Sir Percy went down a second time roused the assembled company from their stupor.

A buzz of excited voices filled the salon as those who had observed all imparted their superior knowledge to the unfortunates who had missed the first, most exciting part of the encounter: Lady Georgie was betrothed not only to Barrett Gray but to the Englishman as well!

Sir Percy prudently stayed down until Barrett had turned away. His face distorted with rage, the baronet sent a hate-filled look after Barrett and Georgie, who strolled off, stopping now and again to exchange a few words with friends along the way, just as though nothing untoward had happened.

"You may have won this hand, Gray!" Sir Percy muttered through his aching teeth. "But I haven't conceded the game."

"What's to be done?" asked Lyman Bainbridge.

He ran the fingers of both hands through his thick, graying hair as he strode up and down in front of the fireplace in his wife's sitting room. Georgie had just rendered a full accounting of Sir Percy's treachery, and Lyman—not unlike William, Georgie thought—was worrying about scandal.

"Stop fidgeting, Lyman!" Mother Bainbridge directed a fierce look at her son, then, for good measure, included Edward Gray, Letty, Georgie, and Barrett in that glance. "If either one of you had shown some gumption and rid us of our company an hour or two earlier, we could have made a decision by now and retired to our couches!"

I shan't be able to close my eyes as long as Sir Percy is in Boston, thought Georgie.

She nestled deeper into the wing chair, her gaze on Barrett, who stood with his shoulders propped against the rough granite of the mantel. He did not seem aware of anything but the tips of his black evening shoes, and what he saw there could not have been gratifying, for he frowned most ferociously.

"I shall cut Sir Percy," said Georgie, determinedly directing her thoughts away from Barrett. She looked at her aunt and Mother Bainbridge on the brocaded chaise longue. "It is the only way to deal with a toad."

"Yes, indeed," said Letty. "And there's absolutely nothing I'd enjoy more. Only, I daresay, it'll prove very tiresome."

Mother Bainbridge nodded in confirmation. "A cursed nuisance, that's what it'll be! The bounder seems to be acquainted with the Mannerings. Came with Wilfred, didn't he?"

"Wilfred introduced him to me," said Letty. "And why he'd do a stupid thing like that is beyond me. Why, Wilfred wasn't even invited!"

"That's water under the bridge," Mother Bainbridge said impatiently "But I'll wager a monkey that the Mannerings will take that dandy about. What a coup for them! They'll dine out on it for months, and we'll run into them and that Sir What's-his-name wherever we go."

"Edward!" Lyman Bainbridge stopped in his tracks to direct a look not unlike one of his mother's piercing stares at Edward Gray seated in a second wing chair on Georgie's right. "What about that notion you once mentioned to me? I mean having Barrett take Georgiana home in one of Caleb's ships?"

"No!" Georgie sat bolt upright. "I shan't beat a cowardly retreat! You cannot possibly ask it of me! You may ship Sir Percy home but not—"

"Calm yourself, my dear," Edward Gray reached out to pat her arm. Some of her indignation melted under his fatherly touch, and when he added, "We are on your side, child. We shall make no decision that you do not fully endorse," she relaxed sufficiently to slump back against the upholstery of her chair.

She slanted a look at Barrett, but he was still contemplating the tips of his shoes. Her barely regained composure wobbled. If only Hester hadn't interrupted! Georgie was certain that Barrett had been about to say he loved her. Well—almost certain. She would not fool herself and deny that Barrett had hesitated even before Hester arrived.

"I apologize, Georgiana." Again Lyman worried his thick mane. The look he gave Georgie was kind but also filled with concern. "It's so deuced difficult to decide what will be best for you. This is the twelfth, no, the thirteenth of July. They may or may not know in England that we have declared war. But they will know sooner or later, and then—"

"There's no need to badger the gal!" Mother Bainbridge prodded the tip of her cane into her son's shoe. "Do sit down, Lyman! You, too, Barrett!"

Although Lyman complied and reluctantly pulled up a chair, Barrett ignored the old lady's command. He switched his intent gaze from his shoes to Georgie's face.

"You are determined, then, to stay in Boston?" Barrett asked.

"Absolutely." Georgie met and held his probing look. "You'll have to tie and gag me to get me aboard a homebound ship," she said fiercely. "I refuse to turn tail and run from Sir Percy. I will fight!"

"I'll help you, dearest Georgie!" cried Letty. "Together, we'll make Sir Percy's life so miserable that he'll wish he had never come here!"

"Rutledges to the core," said Mother Bainbridge, and gave a dry cackle of laughter.

Georgie smiled back at the old lady. She had heard the note of pride in Mother Bainbridge's voice and recognized approval, disguised as it was under a gruff tone.

"In that case," Barrett said firmly, "you had best marry me as soon as possible, Georgie."

She threw him a startled look. Barrett *did* love her! But, dash it! He might have waited for a private moment to declare himself!

"As my wife," Barrett went on smoothly, "you will have

no need to fight anyone. It shall be my pleasure to dispose of Sir Percy, and Wilfred Mannering if necessary.''

"And you accused *me* of having a violent nature,'' murmured Georgie. She looked at him expectantly. Surely the words of love would be forthcoming now!

"It's all settled then.'' Barrett pushed away from the mantel and stepped toward her with his hands outstretched. "We'll marry at Serendip,'' he said. "Pack a few things, Georgie. I want you to leave with my father tomorrow morning.''

As Barrett took her hand and helped her to her feet, the awful truth dawned on Georgie. No avowal of love! This was just another act of chivalry!

She snatched her hands from his clasp, hiding them behind her back. "Nothing is settled, Barrett! Nothing at all! And I shan't marry you either!''

Barrett looked as though he wanted to shake her, but before he could put his intention into practice, Edward Gray spoke up.

"You're wise not to rush into marriage, Georgie. As Lyman started to point out, life may get very complicated for those of us with English ties once England sends her troops to our shores. You do not need an American husband to add to your conflict.''

"Oh!'' Georgie turned to Edward Gray in quick sympathy. "How difficult it will be for you! I am sorry.''

Edward shook his head. "You're thinking, no doubt, of Franklin's death while in service to the crown. But Franklin was an idealist, Georgie. Had our government seen fit to join England in the fight against Napoleon, Franklin would have fought with an American division. As it was, he had no recourse but to add his mite to England's struggle.''

Georgie nodded. "You were speaking of our living relatives. Of my brothers, especially Blakeney, who has joined Wellington's troops. Of your brother and your nephew Robert, a British naval officer.''

She pondered for a moment, then said, "I understand, Mr. Gray, but it really makes no difference where I live, does it? As long as our two countries are at loggerheads, you, I, and many others will suffer heartache and will be torn by conflict.''

Edward Gray rose. Enveloping Georgie in a warm embrace, he murmured against her ear, "I'd be proud to call you daughter."

Aloud he said, "I think it's time we all got some rest."

"Yes, indeed, Edward." Letty smiled at him warmly. "I am convinced that a good rest will drive half the problems away, and what's left we can ignore."

"Father." Barrett gripped the older man's arm. "I beg you, take Georgiana with you to Serendip."

"No!" Georgie protested. "I'll stay right here!"

Edward nodded reassuringly at her. To Barrett he said, "I'm afraid I cannot do that, son. Even if Georgie were willing. I have decided to stop in Washington for a day or two before driving on to Serendip. Lyman has kindly offered me the couch in his study, and a boarding house is no place for your betrothed."

"Pray reconsider, Father." Barrett was pale, the set of his jaw rigid. "I don't trust Sir Percy. He is utterly without scruples, and I fear he may try to do Georgie harm."

"How ridiculous!" stormed Georgie. "All Sir Percy can do is stir up the old London scandal—that I was seen 'trysting' with him in the park. And if he believes he can force my hand with that, he will find himself very much mistaken!"

For the first time since she had repulsed him, Barrett looked at Georgie. "You have no notion what treachery such a blackguard as he is capable of."

"And you don't know how resourceful I am at evading such a cad!"

"Are you, Georgie? It appears your resourcefulness was not of much help to you in London."

More shaken than she cared to admit by the grimness of Barrett's expression, but unwilling to admit that he might be correct, Georgie took refuge in bluster.

"That is hardly fair, Barrett, and I for one shan't listen!" Spinning on her heel, she marched to the door. "And it seems to me," she flung at him over her shoulder, "that *your* handiness will make up for any lack of skill in self-defense I might have!"

"Georgie, stop!" Barrett strode after her, but the sitting

room door slamming in his face brought him to an abrupt halt.

"Leave it be for now, son. Give me your arm to Caleb's house so I may get out of this evening toggery."

Barrett hesitated only briefly. It was going on five o'clock in the morning, and his father, he noted, looked tired. "Very well," he said. "Let us go."

When they stepped out into the night and started walking along the drive in the Bainbridge courtyard, Edward said, "I was right, you know."

"Right? I beg to differ, Father. No doubt you'll laugh at me, but I suspect—dammit, I *know*!—that Hargrave has not given up. There's no saying what the man will do. Gad, I wish I could convince you to take Georgie to Serendip!"

"I do not at all deny that Sir Perceval will try to force Georgie's hand," Edward replied calmly. "You will have to take good care of her, son. But that's not what I meant when I said I was right."

"Watch your step here. The ground's uneven," Barrett warned when they passed through the gate into unlit Summer Street. "What *did* you mean?"

"Had I allowed you to go after Georgie while both of you are in a huff, you might have found yourself 'unbetrothed.' And without the handle 'fiancé' you would have no right to protect her."

Barrett walked on in silence, and after a moment Edward said diffidently, "May I suggest, though, that you refrain from further bouts of fisticuffs at formal gatherings? Those feats of pugilism cannot help but embarrass your hostess, son."

"I can safely promise you that any further hostile meeting with Hargrave will take place with four witnesses only. On the Common. At dawn."

Edward made no reply.

Barrett's foot hit some small object lying in the road. The sudden clank of metal against stone as it bounced once or twice broke the mounting tension in him. He squeezed his father's arm. "You're right," he said, opening the pedestrian gate into Caleb Morris's yard. "I have acted and spoken like a hotheaded fool incapable of rational thought. And yet," he added in a puzzled voice as his mind inevitably returned to Georgie, "I don't know why she should have flown up into the boughs when I said we'd marry."

"You don't, eh?"

"Earlier tonight, Georgie gave me reason to believe she cares for me."

In the light of the lanterns Caleb had left burning, Barrett saw his father's wide grin.

"Of course she cares," said Edward. "And I'm asking myself when will *you* acknowledge your feelings for her?"

Barrett did not respond immediately. He had no doubts at all about his feelings for Georgie. He might not be able to say exactly when he had started loving her, but love her he did. In fact, it seemed as though he had loved her always.

"The trouble is, Father, that at the crucial moment, when I want to declare myself, I am plagued by my conscience. It tells me it's not right to marry her now. It's not right to bind her to the country that's fighting her homeland."

"I see. That, of course, explains why your offer of marriage sounded as though it were made against your better judgment," said Edward, entering the house.

He picked up one of the candles on the hall table and started upstairs. "If you care to hear a word of advice from an old man, Barrett, think about Georgie's words regarding heartache and conflict. It seems to me," Edward said pensively, "that any decision about marriage should be hers as much as yours."

Fourteen

In the days following Lady Letty's ball, Boston society was divided into two camps. There were those—close friends of the Bainbridges, the Grays, and the Morrises—who staunchly maintained that Lady Georgie had been the victim of a vicious prank. Yet those Bostonians, who stared through her as though she did not exist, who snickered behind her back, or, worse, said openly that she had made maygame of Barrett Gray, were distressingly in the majority.

Worse than that, Barrett had erected a barrier of aloofness between them that Georgie found impossible to breach. He did not shirk his duty as her "betrothed" and faithfully accompanied her and Letty to diverse entertainments, but he was preoccupied, as though a problem weightier than Sir Percy's presence in Boston were nagging him.

By now, Georgie had had time to regret her angry outburst after Barrett's offer of marriage. Georgie's sentiments had not changed. To become his wife because he felt in honor bound to give her the protection of his name was unthinkable! She should not, however, have lost temper and reason. She should have refused him politely and with dignity. Georgie considered an apology but dismissed it, fearing Barrett would take it as an invitation to renew his ill-conceived proposal.

By and by, they learned that Sir Perceval Hargrave had arrived from Liverpool on an American merchant brig. The *Venture* had been held by English custom officials, and the baronet made no secret of having "earned" his passage and a sizable fee by pretending to charter the American brig for a voyage, supposedly to India.

Immediately upon arrival in Boston, the day before the ball, Sir Percy had started his search for Georgie. Daniel, when Wilfred and the baronet were pointed out to him, confirmed that Sir Percy was the man he had overheard asking about Lady Georgiana Rutledge and that Wilfred Mannering was the one questioned by the Englishman.

"Out and out blackguards, both of them," Mother Bainbridge had grumbled. It was only one of many sobriquets she bestowed on the two men, only one of many occasions that she sharpened her tongue at Sir Percy's and Wilfred's expense in the following weeks.

"Oh, for heaven's sake!" cried Letty when Mother Bainbridge again muttered darkly about scoundrels, ne'er-do-wells, and profligates while they were driving to Faneuil Hall to attend one of the cotillion balls held there. "Let's forget about them for one night at least!"

"Don't sit so close, Letty!" Mother Bainbridge said huffily. "You're crushing my gown."

"These carriage seats are not meant for two to sit abreast. Especially when one of us wears skirts made up of yards and yards of fabric!"

An indignant sniff was Mother Bainbridge's only reply to Letty's impertinence. When she spoke again, the old lady reverted to her former subject of Sir Perceval and Wilfred Mannering. "We're bound to run into them tonight. Wilfred Mannering always attends the cotillion balls."

"But that's no reason for us to stay away," cried Letty. "You're not thinking of turning back, are you, Mother Bainbridge?"

Georgie had paid little or no attention to her elders' bickering. She sat wedged between Barrett and Mother Bainbridge's voluminous fur cape and muff without which the old lady never ventured from home. Barrett's closeness and his silence had proven very distracting, but Letty's anxious query finally caught Georgie's ear.

"Of course we're not turning back," she said. "Why should we?"

"Weren't you listening, gal? I just said that we're bound to meet that scoundrel Hargrave at Faneuil Hall!"

"I've met him at various functions, Mother Bainbridge."

"He did not dare do anything," Letty corroborated, "aside from throwing languishing glances at Georgie. And Barrett never leaves her side. So what *could* Sir Percy do?"

"He could put his name down beside Georgie's in the master of ceremonies dance book," snapped Mother Bainbridge. "She'd have to stand up with him then!"

"Gracious," said Georgie. "Boston cotillion balls sound as stuffy as the assemblies in Bath. Shall I be blackballed if I refuse to dance with Sir Percy?"

Georgie darted a look to her left where Barrett sat with his arms crossed over his chest and apparently oblivious to the three women. She couldn't see his face in the dark interior of the carriage, but, she guessed, it would show nothing but disinterest in the ongoing dispute.

"Well," she said, a note of defiance coloring her voice, "I shan't mind being blackballed. It all sounds a bore to me. I wish you had a country estate, Aunt Letty."

Barrett turned to Georgie with the first sign of animation since he had entered the carriage in Summer Street. "Just say the word! I'll take you out to Serendip. We have a mare—Franklin used to ride her—a beautiful chestnut mare. She could be sister to your Stardust. I know you'd enjoy riding her!"

"Oh, how I wish I could!"

Regret, sharp as a knife, sliced through Georgie. She had not allowed herself to think about her refusal to go to Serendip, the place she had longed to see above all others. And she wouldn't now. First she must defeat Sir Percy!

If only leaving town wouldn't smack of flight!

Once again, Barrett seemed to read her mind. "Forget about appearing a coward," he said. "Think of yourself and what *you* want to do."

She hesitated. "Give me time to consider. Please, Barrett?"

"Three days, no more."

"A week."

"Done!" Barrett clasped her hand and shook it. She could hear a smile in his voice when he said, "I feared you'd ask for three weeks."

And you're very certain that I'll accept the invitation! But then, Georgie admitted to herself, *so am I.*

The cotillion ball might not turn out a bore after all, she thought when Barrett handed her from the carriage in Market Square. Faneuil Hall was brightly lit for the festivity, the sound of violins drifted through an upper window, and, more to the point, Barrett had at last shaken off the mood of distraction that had held him aloof during the past weeks!

"Surely you're not going to take your furs inside?" Letty

asked when Mother Bainbridge instructed the coachman to hand her the muff.

"But of course I am! The place is a demmed barn since they enlarged it. Vast and drafty!"

Georgie looked at the old lady and her furs, and felt her own body temperature mount. "I pray there may be a draft! The stronger the better!"

Plying her fan with vigor, she mounted the stairs to the meeting rooms above the shops on the ground floor of Faneuil Hall. As July drew to a close, the days and nights had turned hot and sultry. There was a stillness in the air that presaged a storm, but so far no such welcome break in the weather had occurred.

When she and her party entered the vast meeting room used for the cotillion balls, Georgie sensed another kind of stillness. It lasted only a few seconds, only until her friends had seen her and rushed over to welcome her, but the sudden hush in the room, the unabashedly curious stares directed at her, were nevertheless daunting. She was grateful for the fleeting touch of Barrett's hand on her arm, and his bracing smile as he introduced Monsieur Roulôt, a dapper little Frenchman who was the master of ceremonies and otherwise earned a living as dancing instructor.

Letty and Mother Bainbridge made their way to chairs set out for chaperons, while Georgie chatted with Eliza Quincy and Hester and indicated to Monsieur Roulôt in which of the dances she wished to participate.

When the formalities had been taken care of, Hester drew Georgie aside. "Wilfred is here," she said, a look of concern on her face. "And that baronet."

"And no doubt Sir Percy is hard at work besmirching my name," retorted Georgie. She had not missed the whispers and comments flying through the meeting room: "Jilt." "Shameless!" "Aristocratic hussy!"

Georgie raised her chin. "Well, it makes no odds to me."

Wondering if Barrett intended to stand up with her for the first dance she turned to look for him, but he was still writing in the dance book.

"What the—" Young Mr. Tremaine, standing at Barrett's elbow, exclaimed in annoyance. "See here, Barrett! You can't claim all Lady Georgie's dances! What about me?"

"You may have a dance." Barrett returned the pen to the master of ceremonies. Slapping "Paadner" Tremaine on the shoulder, he grinned and said, "You only have to ask, old man. *Me*."

"Barrett, how *could* you!" Georgie took an impetuous step toward him. She hoped she sounded indignant and severe, not an easy feat when one was secretly delighted. "I believe it is the lady's prerogative to choose her partner."

"Very well. Whom do you choose for this minuet, my lady?"

"Mr. Tremaine," she replied promptly.

"Just as I thought," Barrett said dryly. "But I shall reserve the Virginia reel and the cotillions!"

"And I should like—" stammered a young naval lieutenant. Coloring, he bowed before Georgie.

Her eyes widened. "Lieutenant Orwig," she murmured. "This is quite a surprise."

The officer tugged at the black cravat showing above the gold braid of his lapels. Taking a deep breath, he said in a rush, "I'd be honored if you'll stand up with me for the pavane, Lady Georgiana."

Georgie raised a quizzing brow. "Are you sure, Lieutenant, you wish to be seen dancing with an Englishwoman?"

"Yes, ma'am." Another tidal wave of color flooded the boyish face framed by sideburns that dipped down to his jaw. "I figure I owe you an apology."

Georgie nodded. "I shall see you later, Lieutenant."

As she walked off with "Paadner" Tremaine, Georgie thought of Captain Morwell. No apology, however sincere, would bring him back to life. And the crew . . . perhaps the lieutenant knew where the men were imprisoned. She could ask, couldn't she?

Several couples made a point of leaving the dance floor when she and Mr. Tremaine took their positions for the minuet. Georgie pretended not to notice, but when Sir Perceval Hargrave with Regina Powell on his arm maneuvered himself and his partner into one of the wide gaps left next to her and Mr. Tremaine, she could not suppress a gasp of annoyance.

"Best to take no notice, Lady Georgiana," said "Paadner" Tremaine gravely.

Excellent advice! And had Mr. Tremaine not become preoccupied with the steps of the minuet, concentrating on his feet instead of distracting his partner, Georgie might have been able to ignore Sir Percy nearby. As it was, she could not help but notice the baronet. He kept Regina in giggles and blushes with a constant flow of small talk. Sir Percy's eyes, however, never left Georgiana.

She was very much aware of that burning gaze following her every move. It made her skin crawl. Occasionally, she could overhear Sir Percy's words to Regina: "You're delightful, Miss Powell . . . I say, who is that clodhopper Lady Georgiana is . . . cold and utterly cruel! Toyed with my affection! . . . adore your nose, Miss Powell . . . so charming . . . must make one more attempt to offer Lady Georgiana the protection of my name . . . a matter of honor."

Tried beyond endurance, Georgie cast Sir Percy a smoldering look. How dare he speak about her to that empty-headed chit! Regina was pretty—and without two thoughts in her head. She'd prattle to anyone who'd listen, and although Letty now knew what had transpired in London, the spreading of Sir Percy's version must nevertheless be felt as an embarrassment.

As though he read Georgiana's angry thoughts, Sir Percy smiled. He bent his head closer to Regina and whispered something. Regina's step faltered. She blushed crimson, her startled gaze flying to Georgie.

"Oh!" cried Regina, just as the music ceased. "Is she quite without shame?"

Several heads turned in Regina's direction. "Eh, what's that?" said "Paadner" Tremaine, finally looking up from his feet.

The young lady only blushed more furiously. Spinning on her heel, she ran toward the chaperons to cast herself in her mother's arms.

A frown creased Georgie's brow as she watched Regina's precipitate flight. And when Mrs. Powell, after listening to her near hysterical daughter for a few moments, flung a cloak around Regina's shoulders and bundled her out of the room, any pleasure Georgie might have expected from the ball slipped out the door with the Powell ladies.

There was no doubt in Georgiana's mind but that Sir Percy had bragged to Regina about that meeting in Hyde Park, making it seem as though it had been by assignation. Perhaps he had gone so far as to say that Georgie had flung herself into his arms!

Georgiana was so angry, she could have throttled Sir Percy with her own hands! But he, coward that he was, sped away to find protection with Wilfred Mannering and his friends.

She was still burning with resentment when "Paadner" Tremaine returned her to Barrett's side. Barrett searched her face keenly. "What was that all about? Did the cad proposition our sweet Regina?"

"I wish he did! At least," Georgie amended, "I wish he'd try to fix his interest with her. That would get him out of my hair."

"Would you like to leave?"

She drew herself up, her eyes blazing, but before she could tell him what she thought of such a cowardly suggestion, Barrett said, "For heaven's sake, don't fly into a pelter! I was only thinking of your health, you know. It can't be good for you to swallow so much spleen."

His words so exactly described how she felt that she gave a gasp, half outrage, half laughter. "Or," she countered after a shrewd look at him, "for you either."

"No," drawled Barrett, looking across the room at Sir Perceval. "It's not good for me either."

Georgie shivered. There had been something in the tone of his voice. . . .

She laid her hand on his arm. "You won't fight him again, will you, Barrett?"

"Fisticuffs?" His mouth curled in a smile that Georgie

did not find at all reassuring. "Don't fret," he said. "I told my father I wouldn't."

With that Georgie had to be content, for several of Aubrey's friends whom she had met at the Otises' *conversazione*, joined her and Barrett to talk or persuade Barrett to give up one of his dances.

Neither Sir Percy nor Wilfred Mannering asked Georgie directly to stand up with them. The rotation of partners required in some of the dances, however, made direct contact unavoidable. Wilfred was content to give Georgie sly glances and smirks. Not so Sir Percy.

"I must see you," the baronet hissed as he linked arms with her in a contredanse. "I've called half a dozen times, and each time that insolent butler of your aunt's said you were 'not at home.' My patience is running out, I warn you!"

Georgie warmed with gratitude and affection for her aunt, who must have tipped off Appleby. Smiling, she passed on to the next gentleman, and the next, until she met up with her original partner Barrett.

"I wish," he said savagely, "the waltz were known here! What good did it do that I made certain Hargrave would not claim your hand when each dance still offers him opportunity to annoy you!"

"He did not, Barrett. On the contrary, it is he who is extremely peeved."

Barrett's look of displeasure deepened, but he said no more. His hard, narrowed eyes sought out Sir Percy and remained fixed on the baronet, a situation that did not escape Georgie's attention. She made every effort to appear unconcerned. She laughed and chatted, whirled around the dance floor, or stood sipping punch and exchanging views on fashions with Hester, Eliza, and their lady friends.

Yet her unease mounted. Something was about to happen. She could sense it. Tension charged the air around her, and whenever Sir Percy encountered Barrett's watchful gaze, a look of hatred distorted the baronet's features. The animosity between the two men was so blatant that a most horrible thought took hold of Georgie's mind, and would not let go. She prayed they would not pass within speaking distance. If one were to hurl a challenge at the other—

Sir Percy, like all young gentlemen of the *ton*, had practiced fencing and shooting at Manton's Gallery since he had outgrown shortcoats. But Barrett— Were American young men instructed in such arts?

When the cotillion, the last dance before the refreshment break forced Georgie once again to pair up with Sir Percy for a measure, the baronet squeezed her fingers painfully.

"Not long now, my proud beauty," he said with a leer. "You'll beg me on your knees to marry you! How I look forward to that moment!"

Only strong resolve kept Georgie's smile in place. Much as she longed to wipe the insidious grin off his face, she would *not* hit him. She must bear the hot, crawling gaze of his glittering eyes, if only to convince Barrett that nothing was amiss. If only to show those who watched her and Sir Percy with avid curiosity and speculation that Lady Georgiana Rutledge could not be stared out of countenance!

When the cotillion ended, however, Georgie had no glance to spare for the favor Barrett pressed into her hand, nor could she trust herself to make a calm reply when he asked if she wished to take supper with Letty and Mother Bainbridge. She was at the end of her tether. She could pretend no more.

The chaperons had left their seats to search out their charges and herd them into the adjoining supper room; only Letty and Mother Bainbridge still sat in the corner farthest removed from the musicians. Neither one looked happy or eager to take refreshments.

"If you don't mind, Aunt Letty," Georgie said after one glance at her aunt's pale face, "I'd as soon go home as stand in line for supper."

"Oh, yes!" Letty snatched up her wrap. She was out of her chair so fast and helping Mother Bainbridge to rise, nothing remained for Barrett to do but murmur that he'd be off to fetch the carriage to the door.

When he had left to go downstairs, Georgie was once

again aware of a hush in the large room, of eyes resting on her with curiosity or even with open condemnation. Letty's face, so pale a moment earlier, turned pink. She took Mother Bainbridge's arm.

"Come," she said, her usually soft voice loud and harsh. "Before I tell these gossips what I think of them!"

"Scandalmongers!" Mother Bainbridge said succinctly. Frail shoulders thrown back, the old lady started across the room on Letty's arm.

Georgie followed slowly. She had done right to make a clean breast of all that had transpired in London between her and Sir Percy. At least the lurid tale Sir Percy was spreading came as no surprise to Letty and Mother Bainbridge; and yet, the scandalous gossip still had the power to hurt them!

She saw Lieutenant Orwig trailing behind a long line of refreshment-seeking young people. "Aunt Letty! There's something I must do before I leave. You and Mother Bainbridge go on. I shan't be but a moment."

As Georgie moved away, Mother Bainbridge called after her, "I left my muff. Be so kind and fetch it, Georgiana!"

Georgie raised a hand in acknowledgment as she hurried to catch the naval officer before he entered the supper room. "Lieutenant Orwig! May I have a word with you?"

He stopped, turning his head, then strode to meet her. "Lady Georgiana. You're leaving?" he said, glancing at the lacy shawl she had thrown around her shoulders.

"My aunt is not well. I am sorry that I shan't be able to stay for the pavane."

"I understand," he said gravely.

He, too, had apparently heard the gossip. Else he felt slighted that she wouldn't honor her promise to dance with him, but there was nothing she could do about it. "Lieutenant," she said. "Can you tell me where my crew is detained?"

"They were still in Portland when I set sail a week ago, Lady Georgiana. I know, however, the commander was expecting orders from Washington to move them."

"Move them where?" she asked eagerly.

"I am sorry," Lieutenant Orwig said stiffly. "I have no information on that." He bowed, offering his arm. "May I escort you to your aunt?"

"Paadner" Tremaine appeared at Georgie's side and gripped her elbow before she had a chance to reply. "I'll escort the lady, Lieutenant."

Georgie felt breathless, so speedily did Mr. Tremaine propel her across the stuffy room. "I must fetch Mother Bainbridge's muff!" she gasped. "She left it. Probably beneath her chair."

"All right." Veering in the direction of the chaperons' chairs, Mr. Tremaine's step slowed. "Damn! There's Mannering. Pluck up, Lady Georgie. Looks like he's going to speak to you."

And, indeed, as Georgie snatched the huge fur muff, which Mother Bainbridge had stuffed behind the chair and forgotten in the rush of leaving, Wilfred Mannering stepped up to her, saying, "My mother's compliments, Lady Georgiana. She'd be honored if you'd call on her tomorrow. Say eleven o'clock?"

"Not if Sir Percy will be there!" Clutching the muff to her breast, Georgie glowered at Wilfred. "I understand he's a guest in your house, Mr. Mannering?"

"Ah, well—"

"Sorry, Mannering," interrupted "Paadner" Tremaine. "Lady Georgie is promised to call on *my* mother tomorrow morning." And with these words, he whisked Georgiana away.

"Thank you, Mr. Tremaine." Georgie smiled at the young man who had been Aubrey's closest friend in Boston. "But it really was not necessary to fib for me. I'm quite capable of snubbing the odious Wilfred, you know."

"No fib exactly, Lady Georgie," he said, holding open the door to the stairway for her. "My mother did ask me to invite you. She doesn't go about much. She's an invalid. Would be pleased to see you."

"Georgie!" Barrett came bounding up the steps, the worried look on his face changing to relief when he saw that she was not alone. "Why the devil didn't you come down with Letty?"

Georgie raised a brow. "I went to fetch Mother Bainbridge's muff." Holding out her hand, she turned to Mr. Tremaine. "I shall be delighted to call on your mother. Would eleven o'clock suit?"

From the corner of her eye, she saw Wilfred Mannering standing in the open door of the meeting room and quite unashamedly eavesdropping. Georgie turned up her nose at him and, barely waiting for "Paadner" Tremaine's assurance that eleven o'clock would indeed suit, left Faneuil Hall with her head held high and a smile fixed on her face. The smile disappeared as soon as she had climbed into Letty's carriage. Without a word she handed the muff to Mother Bainbridge.

"When can we leave for Serendip?" she asked as Barrett dropped into the seat beside her.

"As soon as you can be packed. Georgie"—even in the darkness of the carriage, she could feel Barrett's eyes bore into her—"I saw Mannering behind you. Did he annoy you? Did you speak to him?"

"I gave him a set-down," she retorted. In a softened tone she added, "Barrett, there's no need for you to guard my every step. I'm very well able to look after myself."

"'Twas foolish of you to stay behind! You should have come down with your aunt."

"I was promised to Lieutenant Orwig for the pavane. The least I could do was explain why I wouldn't be there to dance with him. And besides, I wished to ask him about William's crew. Orders from Washington are pending, Barrett, for their transfer!" Her voice rose excitedly. "What do you think that means? Will they be freed?"

"Perhaps," Barrett said guardedly. "We'll have to wait and see, won't we? Now, about our journey to Serendip..."

After some arguing, it was decided that Georgie would go ahead and visit "Paadner" Tremaine's mother as promised and that the following day, Wednesday, Georgie, Barrett, Rose, and Daniel would set out for Virginia.

It was not until they reached Summer Street and Mother

Bainbridge requested, nay, commanded Barrett to accompany her to her private sitting room, that Georgie started to wonder about the unusually quiet demeanor the old lady had shown during the ride home. A question put to her aunt elicited only a blush, and with the mumbled excuse of an excruciating headache Letty dove into the sanctuary of her own chamber.

Intending fully to waylay Barrett when he left Mother Bainbridge's apartment and to learn from him what had caused the old lady's unusual reticence and Letty's "headache," Georgie paced the floor of her bedroom. It seemed highly improbable that a spreading of the Hyde Park incident should have caused such reaction in the two ladies.

After an hour of restless prowling and opening her door to listen for some slight sound from the other end of the corridor, Georgie realized that despite her vigilance she must have missed Barrett's departure. Her unease mounted. Something was horribly wrong! She *knew* it!

"Georgiana is Hargrave's wife in all but name! That's what Regina told her mother."

Barrett shot out of his chair. *"What?"*

As the implication of Mother Bainbridge's words penetrated Barrett's mind, his eyes narrowed to green slits of fury. He clenched his jaw, biting down an expletive that would shock even a lady of Mother Bainbridge's caliber.

"What are you going to do, Barrett?" With a shaking hand, the old lady poured cognac into glasses set out on the tea table before her.

"Need you ask?" Snatching up one of the glasses, Barrett downed the contents in a gulp. The corners of his mouth curled sardonically. "In your own words, dear Mother Bainbridge, any man worth his salt can have one possible answer only."

Raising her glass to him, Mother Bainbridge nodded. "The sword, or the pistol. God bless, my boy."

"I'll leave via the balcony." Already Barrett had flung aside the draperies and was pushing the casement wide. The ghost of a smile flitted across his harsh features. "Pure cowardice," he said. "I cannot help but fear that Georgie has changed her mind about leaving and will try to intercept me. But if I want to catch up to Hargrave, I mustn't tarry and argue with her."

"Hurry then!" Mother Bainbridge prodded him across the windowsill and watched him straddle the balcony rail. " 'Twould be best if you could settle the matter immediately."

One leg still draped across the rail and one foot planted firmly on the first of the narrow iron steps leading to the balcony below, Barrett froze into immobility.

"Damn!" he muttered under his breath. He met Mother Bainbridge's curious stare. "I cannot force Hargrave to meet me this morning! He's a foreigner. Honor demands I give him a day at least to settle his affairs."

"Wednesday, then. There'll be plenty of time before you and Georgie leave for Serendip. Only problem will be to keep it from the gal for a whole day!"

"Don't leave her alone with Letty or with Hester. I don't want Georgie to hear this new rumor, and they might let something slip." Barrett swung his leg across the rail and started downward. "Take her to the Athaeneum and to the Historical Society! Anything to keep her occupied!"

Daniel darted a frowning look at his preceptress. A long time ago, he had stopped reading aloud, yet she had not prompted him to continue. Lady Georgie just kept staring across the terrace as though the garden were of much more interest to her than her pupil.

Fumbling in the pockets of his nankeen breeches, Daniel drew forth a slingshot and a handful of smooth pebbles. Taking aim, he flung one of the pebbles at the head of a full-blown rose ten or twelve paces distant from the glass-topped table where he and Lady Georgie were sitting.

It drew no response from Lady Georgie. Not even a reprimand!

"Lady Georgie!" he shouted. "What does it mean if ye're someone's wife in all but name?"

She blinked. "Daniel! How often have I told you that it is not polite to shout?"

"Ye weren't payin' attention," Daniel grumbled. "What does it mean, Lady Georgie?"

"You're right, Daniel. I was *not* paying you the attention I should." She smiled in the way Daniel liked: her mouth all sweet and curving, and her brown eyes dancing. "I daresay it's the weather. So hot and still. Now, tell me again which word you don't understand."

"I understand all the words, Lady Georgie. It's what they mean that has me all apuzzle! Ida came back from the market this mornin', and she said as you're married to that Sir Perceval in all but name."

He saw Lady Georgie grow pale. Her smile and the dancing lights in her eyes died. She swayed as though she'd topple off the chair in a dead swoon.

"I thought ye hated the cove, Lady Georgie! Are ye married to him? What's 'in all but name' mean?"

Lady Georgie, it seemed, had not heard him. With shaking fingers she flipped open the watch pinned to her bosom. She drew a deep breath.

"Daniel," she said—and even her voice was shaking! "Today we will stop a little early. It is nearly ten o'clock, and I am promised to visit the mother of one of Mr. Aubrey's good friends. Remember now what I told you! Pack all your books and clothes so that we may leave tomorrow morning bright and early."

She ruffled his hair, as she always did at the end of his lessons, but Daniel could not help feeling that her heart was not in it. When she got up and went into the house, he crept after her, wondering what was ailing his beloved Lady Georgie.

As soon as she knew herself out of the boy's sight, Georgiana hastened her step. "Appleby!" she called when she saw the majordomo standing in the open front door. "I shall need the carriage now. I have decided to visit Mrs. Tremaine an hour early."

Appleby turned, a folded note in his hand. "Fancy that, Lady Georgiana," he said, handing her the missive. "Mr. Tremaine just sent his carriage for you."

Skimming the note, she said, "Yes, it says his mother is expecting her physician at eleven-thirty."

Georgie hesitated only a moment. When Daniel had so innocently repeated Ida's words about her and Sir Percy, her first sane thought—after the initial wish to run the baronet through with a sharp, pointed sword—had been to call on Sir Percy at the Mannerings' home and demand an explanation and a public apology. She had planned to take care of that *before* her visit to Mrs. Tremaine, but if that were not possible, it could wait until eleven-thirty.

"Very well, Appleby. Be so good as to send Lady Letty's carriage to fetch me in an hour. There is one other call I must make this morning."

Handing the majordomo "Paadner" Tremaine's note, she stepped past him and out into the courtyard where a sturdy young groom in plain tan livery assisted her into the waiting coach. The door shut on her, the groom swung himself up beside the coachman, and the vehicle started rolling toward the gate.

Appleby was about to close the front door when he saw a boy in nankeen breeches and a white cotton shirt dart around the back of the house and across the courtyard. He hoisted himself onto the precarious perch at the rear of the carriage, just before it swung around the gatepost into Summer Street.

"Young varmint!" muttered Appleby. "Just you wait 'til Mr. Barrett takes you in hand at Serendip!"

Fifteen

Inside the carriage, Georgie had felt the slight, jarring dip at the rear of the well-sprung vehicle but thought no more about it than that the groom had taken rather long in mounting his perch. She was more concerned about the fact that the carriage turned right toward Marlborough Street rather than left to Arch Street, which would have been the fastest route to the Tremaine residence in the fashionable Tontine Crescent.

But why should she have supposed that America was spared incompetent servants or ignorant coachmen? Georgie gave a mental shrug. She'd use the time to formulate annihilating remarks she would throw at Sir Perceval.

With such phrases in mind as "deceiving wretch," "scaly fortune hunter," "money-grabbing commoner," and "puffed-up old muckworm," she paid little heed to landmarks until the carriage slowed to a mere crawl, and she saw the Old State House looming ahead at the corner of State Street.

"Gracious!" she muttered. "At this pace and on this roundabout route I shan't arrive at the Tremaines' before it's time to leave."

She rose to open the communications window and give the coachman a piece of her mind, but even as she reached for the catch on the sliding panel, the carriage door on her right swung open.

Sir Perceval Hargrave jumped inside.

Instinctively, Georgie threw herself against the opposite door. She rattled the handle. In vain.

Sir Percy's soft laughter rang odiously in her ears before it was drowned in the crack of the coachman's whip and a wild clatter of hooves. A jerk as the team broke into breakneck speed knocked her onto the seat.

"Get out!" She sat up straight. Never had she looked more haughty as when she turned her icy glare on the baronet who had dropped into the seat beside her, his long legs stretched out before him, his hands stuffed into the pockets of his elegant coat.

Never had she felt more frightened.

"I advise you not to try my patience too far, Lady Georgiana," Sir Percy said with a sneer. "Before the day is out, you'll be my wife. You have no choice in the matter.

However, the way I treat my bride on her wedding night is determined by you and your behavior alone.''

He sounded so sure of himself, for a moment she actually believed her fate sealed. She thought of the vile rumor Daniel had parroted, and bile rose in her throat.

The carriage rattled and swayed, but still the coachman cracked his whip, forcing the horses to give their utmost. Where was he taking her?

"You'll never get away with this! I'll see you hanged for abduction!''

"Once the marriage is consummated—''

Her eyes flashed daggers at him. "Never!''

Sir Percy's laughter rang out again, raising goose bumps on her skin. "Spoken like a true heroine, my dear Lady Georgiana. I daresay you'd rather kill yourself,'' he taunted. "But never fear! Your courage won't be put to the test. I'll see to that.''

"You're mistaken, Sir Percy. I shall kill *you*.''

She clutched the strap set into the paneling of the coach to avoid being flung against him by a sudden turn and, feigning an indifference she was far from feeling, turned her back on him and stared out the window.

They were barreling along on State Street. And State Street, Georgie knew, led directly onto the Long Wharf.

Her palms grew moist. Letting go of the leather strap, she surreptitiously wiped her hands on the skirt of her gown. She need hold on no longer. There would be no sudden turns to throw her against Sir Percy. As surely as though he had told her, she knew he was taking her to the ship he had chartered in Liverpool.

Frantically, she searched for a way of escape. The door nearest her did not open. She could make a dash for the far door, but even if she did not trip over his outstretched legs, she'd certainly break her neck if she flung herself from the speeding carriage.

She must—temporarily—admit defeat.

Must gain time. Time to be missed in Summer Street. Time for Barrett to find her. Barrett had always come to her rescue. He would not fail her now—if only she could gain time!

With a show of reluctance, which was not at all difficult to achieve; and with grudging respect, which, on the contrary, was extremely trying, Georgie addressed Sir Percy. "If it's a rich wife you need, why not court a young Boston lady? Miss Powell was taken with your charm, I believe."

She met his suspicious stare without a blink, and after a moment his frown relaxed to an expression of smugness. "That she was, Lady Georgiana. But I've no desire to live in this primitive country. I want an English heiress."

"There are others in England, more wealthy than I."

She had touched on a raw spot. "Aye!" he said bitterly, with a furious look at her. "But I was encouraged to dangle after *you*, my lady! I was one step ahead of the debt collector when you skipped out of the country. There was no time to court another; so I followed you. And if I want to return, it must be with a wealthy bride unless I wish to take up residence in debtor's prison."

Georgie kept her gaze fixed on her hands so she wouldn't betray the contempt she felt for men of his ilk. Improvident wastrels! Cheats!

She looked at Barrett's ring on her finger, a sight that was infinitely reassuring. Drawing a deep breath, she asked, "How on earth did you get Mr. Tremaine's coachman to cooperate with you?"

"I didn't attempt anything so foolish. He is Wilfred's coachman." Sir Percy grinned. "All we had to do was, ah, borrow one of the Tremaine liveries and compose a note from your friend 'Paadner.'"

"A clever plan."

"Not as good as my original scheme." His voice, his look were accusing. "If you hadn't refused to visit Mrs. Mannering, there would have been no need for this cloak-and-dagger race across town."

"I daresay you've also found a parson who'll marry us," she said in what she hoped was the right mixture of fear and curiosity. "You may have forgotten, Sir Percy, but I'm under age and require a guardian's permission."

"I have forgotten nothing, Lady Georgiana. But the captain of the *Venture* will not ask your age, and your brother, when we reach England, will hardly wish to have our marriage annulled. Why, you might be with child by then!"

Her hands clenched in her lap. "You've taken everything into account."

"Except that infernal little page of yours! It was very foolish of you to drag the boy along, and he can count himself lucky," Sir Percy said viciously, "if he hasn't tumbled off and broken his neck on the blasted street! Gad! You'd think they might have acquired the craft of proper paving by now!"

Georgie stared at him in horror. Daniel! It was he who jumped onto the rear of the carriage, not the groom!

Good intentions forgotten, she rounded on the baronet. "Make them slow down!" she cried, pummeling his chest with her fists. "Immediately!"

Sir Percy shot up, caught her wrists in a steely grip, forcing them behind her back. "Lady Tenderheart!" he said with a sneer. "You almost convince me that the boy might be of use after all. A tool to bring you to submission."

"Fiend!" Georgie kicked, but only succeeded in stubbing her toe on the leather of his boot.

Sir Percy laughed. "Shrew," he said softly, watching her with glittering eyes.

When she did not retaliate, a look of disappointment crossed his face. With a jerk, he pulled her close. "My dear Lady Georgiana. You will have to learn to please me."

Georgie recoiled from the heavy reek of alcohol on his breath, but there was no escape from him in the confines of the carriage. His mouth curved in a cold, ugly smile as he slowly bore her arms upward behind her back. He smiled and waited—waited until the thrusts of pain in her shoulders and a particularly nasty bump in the road drove her against his chest. Then he fell upon her, his mouth devouring hers with greedy lust.

Georgie forced herself to sit still. She knew instinctively that the less resistance she offered, the sooner he'd be tired of the game. In any case, her arms and hands were numb, useless.

With an exclamation of disgust, Sir Percy shoved Georgie into the corner of the seat. "You're all alike, you fine ladies! As exciting as jellyfish!"

She paid him no heed. Staring at the long warehouses flashing by, and the hulks of ships, she cried, "We've arrived on the wharf! *Now* will you stop and see if Daniel is all right?"

"Damn the boy! We shan't stop until—" He broke off in mid-sentence. His eyes bulged as he listened to the warning sounds of splintering wood.

"The wheel!" he shouted. "Stop, you fool!"

Even as he was yelling his command to the coachman, Georgie heard a noisome crack. The carriage listed at a sharp angle to the right. She was thrown against the baronet, who, less fortunate than she, crashed into the door frame.

For a few paces the carriage lumbered on, one axle dragging with a protesting screech on the cobbles, the horses screaming, plunging with a great clatter of hooves. Before Sir Percy had recovered from his stun or the coach had come to a complete halt, Georgie scrambled to the door and thrust it open.

"Daniel!"

Feet first, she slid from the tilting vehicle. She dashed around to the rear of the coach. The groom's perch was empty, but several yards back she saw what looked like a bundle of rags lying on the cobbles.

"Daniel!" Georgie picked up her skirts and started running. Within seconds, her gown clung damply to her skin and drops of perspiration beaded her forehead; but it wasn't the oppressive heat alone that made her break out in a sweat. Was that Daniel's white shirt? His nankeen breeches?

As she came closer, she recognized that it was naught but a heap of rags after all; yet she did not slow her pace.

She heard the distant rumble of thunder. Close by, she heard the pounding of booted feet. Several pairs. Sir Percy's shout, "Don't let her get away! Dammit! Stop her!"

Concentrating on the slow, rhythmic breathing Aubrey

had taught her, Georgie forged ahead. Never turning. Never breaking her stride.

The pounding boots came closer. She heard the rasping breath of her pursuer directly behind her. Something hit the base of her skull. Pain exploded in her head.

A scream rose in her throat, spilled from her mouth, but she heard no sound. She felt herself falling, but did not see the ground rising to meet her.

She was lying on something soft. Soft and rocking. Georgiana wanted to look where she was, but her eyelids were too heavy. Her head and neck hurt like the dickens.

Memory returned with painful clarity. The wild drive through town. The accident on Long Wharf. Running away from Sir Percy. The blow to her head.

Forcing her eyes open, Georgie sat up. The rocking motion increased, and for a moment the stabs of pain in her head were so sharp that she saw nothing at all. Nausea shook her. With gritted teeth, she waited for the pain and sickness to recede.

The first sight that greeted her when she was able to focus was Sir Perceval Hargrave's visage, smiling, triumphant. A new wave of nausea washed over her.

"How exceedingly stupid you are," he said. He came a step closer, studying her face carefully. "I never meant for you to get hurt, but that oafish groom couldn't know that, could he? So he knocked you down when you kept running."

"May I have some water?"

He frowned but turned and went to fetch the water from a bottle atop the washstand. While his back was turned, Georgie looked about her. Table and chair bolted to the flooring; the cot on which she sat affixed to the ceiling with ropes; and a grimy porthole in one of the walls.

She was in a cabin aboard a ship.

A moving ship. She remembered well the rolling of a ship at sea, recognized the creak of timber when sailing under full canvas.

"Here you are." Sir Percy handed her a glass. "Drink it

slowly. Wouldn't want you to cast up your accounts. This is our wedding day. Remember?''

Georgie heard the distant rumble of thunder. She had heard it earlier, on the wharf. Were they still near Boston, then?

"This is your ship, the *Venture*?" she asked. "How long since she cast off?"

"Not long enough for me." Sir Percy stalked to the door. Opening it, he shouted, "Captain Webster! Bring your Bible. Time for the nuptials!"

"No need to make such racket!" Captain Webster, a wiry man of middle age dressed in a faded blue coat and duck trousers, squeezed past Sir Percy into the tiny cabin. "Are ye ready, lady?"

"No, Captain Webster." Georgie slipped off the cot. For a moment she held on to one of the ropes, steadying herself. Then she confronted the master of the *Venture*. "I shall never agree to marry Sir Perceval."

"Eh! What's this?" The captain's weathered face took on a worried look. He stabbed a grimy forefinger at the baronet. "Ye said she had swooned, and that's why ye had her carried aboard! I tell ye, sir, I won't marry none that's not willing!"

"Of course she's willing!" Sir Percy said irritably. "She's my fiancée."

"I am not!" Georgie took two wobbly steps toward the washstand.

Sir Percy shot her a baleful look but did not stop her as she poured more water. He spoke to the captain in low, urgent tones, which she could not make out.

The master of the *Venture* shrugged. "If that be the case," he said gruffly, "what's the hurry, Sir Percy? If ye can't change her mind in the month we'll be at sea, maybe it's not worth marrying her at all."

Georgie set her empty glass down. Her heaving stomach had finally settled, and only a dull ache at the base of her neck reminded her of the knock she had received.

"Captain Webster! I've been brought aboard against my

will. Take me back to Boston," she demanded. "I'll make it worth your while."

"Eh now, miss. Kidnapping be a serious charge! And hearing as y'are as English as Sir Percy here, I'm of a mind to believe he's taking ye home. In any case, Sir Perceval is the one as sets the course. Unless he orders me to return to Boston—"

"I order you to leave us!" Sir Percy said through clenched teeth.

With a shrug, Captain Webster stamped from the cabin and slammed the door shut behind him. Silence, thick and threatening, engulfed Georgie. Sir Percy's grin sent a shiver down her spine.

"Very well, Lady Georgiana." His voice was silky. Two strides brought him to her side. "I tried to do it the honorable way, but since you prefer to taste the delights of love before the knot is tied, so be it!"

"Honorable! You wouldn't recognize an honorable deed if it slapped you in the face!"

His fingers bit into her upper arms, pinned them to her sides. His glittering eyes, his mouth distorted by rage, came ever closer. Memory of the kisses he had forced on her on previous occasions made Georgiana's blood boil. She leaned her head back as far as her stiff neck allowed, then brought it forward with all her might.

The pain as her already smarting head made contact was excruciating. Stars danced before her eyes. As from a far distance she heard Sir Percy's yelp of pain. The cruel grip on her arms loosened, then let go altogether. Swearing and groaning under his breath, the baronet was fully occupied dabbing his nose and lower face with a handkerchief.

Cautiously, Georgie took a step backward. To reach the door, she had to pass Sir Percy. She darted another look at him, and gasped. Under her fascinated stare, the snowy cloth turned crimson.

Georgie's stomach heaved. She made a dash for the door, but he caught her easily, imprisoning her with one arm.

"You'll pay for this, my lady!" The threat was no less menacing for being muffled by a blood-spotted handkerchief.

"Let me go!" she gasped. "Must get up on deck! Vilely ill!"

He dropped the cloth. His hand went to her throat. "No more tricks!" he said huskily, first squeezing, then stroking her throat and neck until she started to shake.

"Sir Percy!" she choked out. "I'm ill!"

"You'll feel better soon, I promise you," he crooned, tightening the viselike grip of his arm around her waist. His voice changed to razor sharpness. "But first I'll make damned certain you won't leave this cabin until I'm ready to let you go. *After* I've bedded you!"

His fingers trailed along the high neckline of her gown. Suddenly, with one vicious tug, he tore the lace and the muslin down to the riband below her breasts.

Georgie screamed.

"Go ahead and struggle!" Sir Percy's eyes roamed over her exposed flesh. "The more you fight the more I'll enjoy taking you."

"Beast!" she gasped. "Lecher! Muckworm!"

Nausea forgotten, she kicked and punched at him in blind fury until his grip around her waist slackened. He swore, tried to grip her shoulders. She tore away, clutching her bodice, just as the cabin door burst open.

Georgie whirled, her eyes wide with fear lest Captain Webster had decided he must come to the aid of his principal. But it was not Captain Webster who stepped into the cabin.

It was Barrett, whose shoulders filled the doorway. Barrett, whose glance covered her with warmth and whose presence made her heart beat faster. He gathered her in his arms, rocking her like a child.

"It's all right, my love," he whispered. "You're safe now."

Safe, her heart echoed.

Sir Percy's laughter, harsh and brittle, filled the cabin. "Edifying words, Gray!" he said jeeringly. "But you shouldn't make promises you can't keep."

Barrett gave no sign of having heard the baronet's words. After a moment, he shrugged out of his coat, guided

Georgie's arms into the sleeves, then buttoned it for her. The warmth of his body clinging to the material was most comforting.

"Go with Lieutenant Orwig," he said, his voice holding an unmistakable note of command. Firmly he pushed her toward the door where the naval lieutenant stood with his sword drawn. "Sir Percy and I have unfinished business to attend before I join you on deck."

"There will be no more punching, Gray!" said the baronet. "We shall settle the matter, but we'll settle like gentlemen."

"You're no gentleman, Hargrave," Barrett said contemptuously. "You're a cad!"

"I'll make you eat your words!" Sir Percy strode to a sea chest standing beneath the porthole. Flinging up the lid, he withdrew a rapier.

"No!" shouted Georgie. She would have rushed to Barrett's side, but Lieutenant Orwig quickly stepped in front of her.

"I'd be honored if you'll accept my sword, Mr. Gray," said the young naval officer.

"Thank you, Lieutenant." Without taking his eyes off Sir Percy, Barrett accepted the foil. He bowed. "On deck, I believe, Sir Percy?"

No! The agonized cry never left Georgie's mouth. The duel was inevitable. The set of Barrett's jaw, determined, implacable, told her that nothing would sway him from his course. She'd only distract him were she to voice her fears.

Silently, they filed out of the tiny cabin and up the companionway to the main deck. The sun that had beaten down so mercilessly earlier, was blanketed by a leaden haze. It was still hot and humid, but a wind had sprung up, blowing strongly from the south. Thunder rumbled. Forks of lightning flashed against banks of dark clouds.

Georgie saw Captain Webster and his crew lined up against the bulwarks on starboard. A handful of Lieutenant Orwig's marines stood to attention at larboard.

Barrett rolled up his shirtsleeves, then, while Sir Percy struggled with his tight coat, drew Georgie into his arms once again.

"I love you," he whispered against her ear. "No matter what happens, I shall always love you."

Tears pricked her eyes, her mouth trembled as he covered it with his. How she had longed to hear those words! Sweet torment to hear them now!

Frightened, she pushed the thought aside. Nothing would happen to Barrett. Nothing must happen!

Slowly Barrett released her. "Courage, my love!"

He beckoned to Lieutenant Orwig. When the officer stood beside them, Barrett took Georgie's hand and placed it in the officer's. "You know what to do, Lieutenant."

"I'll guard her with my life."

Lieutenant Orwig pulled her toward his men, away from Barrett. Numbly, Georgie followed his lead. Her throat was raw from tears that must be swallowed, must not be allowed to roll down her face. A large, painful knot formed in her chest.

She heard Barrett's *"En garde!"* and whirled to see Barrett and Sir Percy engage. The baronet fenced with vicious force and agility. Barrett's parries came dangerously late. Georgie tensed. Sir Percy's blade flashed here and there and everywhere, and more than once it looked as though the point must surely drive straight through Barrett's heart.

Her nails cut into the palms of her hands as she saw her fear confirmed. Fear that her love did not know the art of fencing very well. Compared to Sir Percy's quicksilver steps and thrusts, Barrett's movements were slow, hesitant.

It was only when she heard the baronet's rasping breath over the clash of steel, when she saw the cambric of his shirt cling to his back and even to his arms that she recognized the deliberate economy of movement, the precision of Barrett's style.

After an especially wild thrust by Sir Percy, Barrett jumped back. Dropping the point of his sword, he shouted, "Dry your forehead and your hands, Hargrave!"

"Afraid you'll slip on my sweat?" Sir Percy's laughter mocked Barrett, but the baronet nevertheless accepted the cloth Captain Webster handed him and wiped his face and hands.

Without warning, Sir Percy leaped to attack with renewed vigor. Georgie gasped when Barrett's parry was late. He deflected the thrust, but the point of Sir Percy's blade still cut through Barrett's sleeve, nicking his left arm.

Georgie pressed her fists to her mouth lest a sound escape and break Barrett's concentration. He was quicker now, more forceful. He had changed tactics after Sir Percy's dastardly attack. It was Barrett now, who was on the offensive, and Sir Percy was hard driven to keep up his guard.

Suddenly, after a brilliant, quicksilver feint, Barrett's foil pierced Sir Percy's right shoulder. Barrett withdrew as the baronet's rapier clattered onto the deck.

For a moment, the two men stood facing each other. Barrett, his arm extended, poised to deliver the fatal thrust; Sir Percy, his eyes glittering with rage and hatred, ready to receive it.

In a gesture of contempt, Barrett dropped his point.

"If he paid you well," he said to Captain Webster, "you had best take him to England without delay."

Barrett turned his back on his defeated opponent, and Georgie released her pent-up breath in a great whoosh of relief. She wanted to run to Barrett, but her knees had turned to jelly. All she could do was stand and watch him with love and pride shining from her eyes as he wiped the sword with his handkerchief.

She felt as though she were coming alive again after what seemed an eon spent in torpor. She noticed the gusting wind ruffling Barrett's dark hair, the thunder and lightning that was now directly overhead. She heard the marines and Captain Webster's crew cheer.

Barrett started toward Lieutenant Orwig with the hilt of the sword extended to the officer.

From the corner of her eye, Georgie saw Sir Percy pick up his rapier with his left hand. She saw his fingers curl around the hilt.

"Barrett!"

Her scream rent the air, even before Sir Percy leaped to close the distance to Barrett's exposed back. Barrett spun.

A sudden squall drove a wall of rain across the deck, and for an instant both Barrett and Sir Percy were hidden from Georgie's view. Then she saw Barrett. Struggling to rise from the streaming deck. Sir Percy ready to thrust.

She started to run, heard Lieutenant Orwig's shout, "Out of the way, Lady Georgiana! Dammit!"

Barrett, crouched on one knee, raised his sword, deflecting the thrust aimed at his heart. As a bolt of lightning split the sky, his own blade flashed. Drove into Sir Percy's chest.

Sir Percy staggered backward, then crashed onto the deck. Blood pulsed from the wound in his chest, was washed away by the rain, and welled anew.

Georgie dropped to her knees beside Barrett. He caught her in his arms, nestled her face against his wet shirt. But she had already seen the blood. Too much blood for one day. She fainted.

When Georgie regained consciousness, she found herself slung like a sack of grain across a wide shoulder, her face bouncing upside down against a muscular shirt-clad back. Alarmed, she raised her head and opened her eyes. Then wished she hadn't. Directly beneath her, she saw choppy water and black boots moving down a bit of swinging rope ladder.

"Hold still!" The voice was gruff, tight, but to her it sounded like music. It was Barrett's voice.

She closed her eyes again and kept herself motionless, even when she was dumped—with unnecessary force, she thought indignantly—onto some hard, wooden planks that rocked violently. A longboat, she told herself, and squeezed her eyes more tightly. If he thought she was still unconscious, Barrett would carry her again, and even if it was like a sack of meal, she'd rather be in his arms than anywhere else.

"So you *never* faint?"

Her eyes flew open. "Must you gloat, Barrett?"

"No." Gently he wiped a strand of wet hair from her face. "If I promise to hold you once we are aboard

Lieutenant Orwig's sloop, will you climb the rope to the *Sandown* by yourself?" he asked softly.

Georgie's face flamed. "How do you always know what I'm thinking? It is really quite disgusting!" she complained.

"I wish I did know. *Always*, I mean. Unfortunately I can only read some of your thoughts. Those that are most important to me remain your secret—until you tell me."

She was still puzzling his words when she climbed aboard the United States sloop-of-war *Sandown*. Once she was safely on deck, she had no time for further thought. Daniel swooped down upon her, demanding to know if she was hurt and assuring her, all in the same breath, that he would have come for her himself had Mr. Barrett been less selfish!

"Daniel!" Georgie cried. "Sir Percy told me you had climbed on the back of the coach. I was afraid you had fallen off!"

"That one!" Daniel said with disgust. "He's a bad one, he is! And him an Englishman!"

The boy shot a covert look at Barrett, who was still in his bad graces for refusing to let him come aboard the *Venture*. Curiosity overcame grudge. "What happened, sir?" he asked. "Is he dead?"

"Yes. Sir Percy is dead."

Georgie started to shiver. Whether from mention of Sir Percy's death or from the effects of wind and rain she could not tell. Barrett wrapped both his arms around her, and instantly her trembling stopped.

Lieutenant Orwig brought blankets and offered the shelter of his cabin, but Barrett said, "No point in wetting your cabin, my friend. Just get us ashore."

"Are we very close?" asked Georgie, snuggling against Barrett as he flung one of the blankets across both of them.

"Less than an hour out. You never quite left the bay."

"Look over yonder, Lady Georgie!" Daniel pointed west. "You can see the beacon atop Fort Hill. They lit it early on account of the weather."

The three of them huddled in the lee of a large pivot gun while the *Sandown* flew toward Boston and Daniel recounted his part in what he termed "a bang-up adventure!"

"When that Sir Percy got in the coach, I thought at first ye planned to run away with him. On account of him being an Englishman," Daniel explained sheepishly.

"I still don't see how you could have hung on and then got off without breaking your neck," said Georgie.

"Well, it was hard," he admitted modestly. "Even though my hands are good as new. But I heard ye yell at that Sir Percy and I saw that we was headin' straight for the waterfront. And I *knew* ye wouldn't take off without Rose and me! So I hung on like a leech to a gouty leg!"

Georgie shuddered but made no comment. Barrett's mouth brushed across her ear. "My intrepid Lady Georgie," he whispered. "It's a truly heroic battle you fight against this particular weakness. And sometimes," he added, smiling wickedly, "against your second one."

She stiffened, opened her mouth in protest, fully intending to deny the existence of a second weakness, but in the end subsided meekly. The light touch of Barrett's finger against her lips as he gently traced their curve, the kisses he trailed from her ear to her temple, along her cheek, proved him right. She had a second weakness, after all. One she found much harder to fight than the first one.

But no longer did she need to deny her attraction to Barrett! He loved her. He had told her so.

"Ye aren't listenin', Lady Georgie!" complained Daniel. "This is the most exciting part."

Exciting, indeed! echoed Georgie's mind. She tore her gaze away from the challenging green eyes so close to her and looked at Daniel.

"Tell me," she invited.

"Well, when I saw that the carriage was headed straight for the Long Wharf, I knew I must fetch Mr. Barrett. So, when we overtook a wagon from the duck factory, I jumped."

"Daniel!" Georgie sat up in horror. "You jumped from one moving vehicle to another?"

"Don't ye see, Lady Georgie? All those piles of canvas on the wagon was bound to be softer than the cobbles!"

"I said it before," Barrett murmured, his breath stirring

tendrils of hair against her temple. "The boy has admirable common sense."

"And by then Mr. Barrett and Mr. Tremaine was already lookin' for ye, and so I found him very soon—"

"I found *you*," Barrett corrected, "trotting along State Street with a pack of panting dogs at your heels."

Daniel grinned. "Anyways, Mr. Barrett sent Mr. Tremaine to the Mannerings' in case I was wrong about Sir Percy takin' you to his ship. And Mr. Barrett an' I went hell for leather down to where the *Sandown* was anchored, and then we got Lieutenant Orwig to chase the *Venture*. I only wish the marines had used their cutlasses when—"

The creak of a windlass and the rattle of chains interrupted Daniel's tale. He jumped up. "We're back!" he shouted, rushing off to find a vantage point where he could observe the berthing of the *Sandown*.

Barrett, too, rose. Holding out his hand to Georgie, he pulled her up and into his arms. "Welcome back to Boston."

Sixteen

"Paadner" Tremaine was waiting for them with a closed carriage. "Lady Georgiana!" he shouted when she was barely within hearing distance. He was smiling from ear to ear and waving. If he didn't have to hold his horses, she thought, he might have come running the way Daniel had aboard the *Sandown*.

"By Jove!" he exclaimed when she was close enough to shake his hand. "You're a sight for sore eyes, Lady Georgiana! And don't you worry about a thing here in town. I did my share in your rescue. The Mannerings will do anything in their power to clear your name."

"That's better than I hoped to hear," said Barrett. "What did you do? Threaten to skin their precious Wilfred?"

Mr. Tremaine grinned. "I would have, had I thought of it. As it is, a look at the forged note gave Wilfred the devil of a scare. Sir Percy had Wilfred write it, and fool that he is, Wilfred didn't consider it would make him an accomplice in Lady Georgiana's abduction. So, just tell the Mannerings what you want them to do."

Barrett helped Georgie into the coach. "You may have that pleasure, Tremaine. I'll brief you as soon as we've taken Georgie home. But do me a favor, will you? Invite that young rattlepate"—he indicated Daniel—"up on the box with you."

With a squeal of delight, the boy scrambled up onto the high perch. Tremaine watched him with some misgiving, then directed a knowing grin at Georgie and Barrett inside the coach. "Looks to me like our Lady Letty will have to throw open her doors very soon for a second ball, eh? A wedding ball!"

Georgie smiled to herself and drew closer to Barrett. He reached out, taking her hand in his. "Let's get going, Tremaine," he said, caressing the palm of her hand with his thumb. "There is an urgent matter I would discuss with Lady Georgie."

Mr. Tremaine had been about to close the door, but now he tore it wide. "Urgent matter! How the devil could it slip my mind?" he exclaimed, fumbling in an inside pocket of his coat. "A messenger from Serendip arrived shortly after you left the Morrises' house the morning. Gave this"—he withdrew a sealed letter and handed it to Barrett—"this note to Caleb, since you weren't there. Caleb instantly set out in hot-footed pursuit of you, and if I hadn't met him and calmed him down, he'd still be chasing all over town."

"Barrett! Your father—Oh, I hope your father hasn't fallen ill!" said Georgie, her voice catching.

But Barrett seemed in no hurry to open the missive. "I was expecting this, Georgie," he said. "Though not quite so soon. I only hope the content is what I looked for."

He nodded to "Paadner" Tremaine. "Thank you. Do you know if my father's messenger is at Caleb's house still?"

Tremaine shook his head. "Had to turn back posthaste. Something about fetching a letter from President Madison to your father, I believe."

Shortly, the carriage started on its way to Summer Street. Barrett was absently tapping the letter against his knee as though still undecided whether to open it. After watching him for a moment, Georgie asked abruptly, "What will happen to Sir Percy?"

The tapping ceased. Breaking the seal and unfolding the sheet of vellum, Barrett murmured, "Captain Webster will give him a burial at sea."

Georgie saw Barrett's mouth tighten, heard a sound as though he were suppressing a groan. "What is it?" she said, alarmed. "Something happened to your father after all?"

"No." The one syllable had definitely been a groan.

"Your arm!" She moved away from him. "I am sorry, Barrett! I've been leaning against your hurt arm! And you even carried me! Let me see that cut."

With an effort, Barrett pulled himself together. " 'Twas the merest scratch, I promise you, Georgie. It hardly bled, and Lieutenant Orwig washed it before we left the *Venture*. Do you think I would have held you had there been the slightest possibility of upsetting you with a deep wound?"

She scrutinized him anxiously. Except for rusty stains along the rip in his sleeve and a long, angry-looking scratch, his arm *was* all right.

Her eyes flew to his face. "Then it must be that I am no longer welcome at Serendip!"

Instantly, Barrett clasped both her hands. "No. Of course not, Georgie."

But neither the tone of his voice nor his grave look held the power to convince her. Hurt and disappointment washed over Georgie, leaving her drained and tired. A tear splashed onto their linked hands. Horrified, she stared at the wet drop.

Drawing herself up, Georgie said, "Bah! My brother

Lewis would call me a cursed watering pot. And rightly so! After all, we can go to Serendip some other time. Can't we?'' she said, speaking quite belligerently to cover her upset.

"I'm making a sad mull of this, Georgie."

Before she could guess his intent, Barrett had pulled her onto his lap and proceeded to kiss a lingering teardrop off her eyelashes. His way of dealing with a "watering pot" was so much more satisfactory than the means employed by either of her brothers that Georgie made no great effort to hold back any further moisture.

After a bit, when she realized that Barrett's caresses did not depend on tears alone, she asked, "What are you making a mull of?"

With his fingers buried in her tumbling hair, he said, dangerously close to her mouth, "Your crew has been released into my father's custody. They are on their way to Serendip."

"Barrett!" She sat up, looking at him with suspicion. "You knew, didn't you? You knew it when I asked you about the pending transfer."

"I hoped it would be so, but until I received this message I could not be certain. When I saw President Madison, I laid several proposals before him. He listened to all, committed himself to none."

"Thank you, Barrett," she said huskily. "I knew you would get them freed."

She flung her arms around his shoulders, hugging him. Then, with great daring, Georgie raised her face, closing her eyes and puckering her mouth in an invitation of his kiss.

When nothing happened, she whispered, "Shy, Mr. Gray?"

The ardor of his response was all that she could desire. Not so its length. Barrett released her far too soon for her liking. Georgie sat up with great dignity. "I daresay you think it forward in me to permit ardent kisses when you have not yet formally proposed?"

"Georgie!" Barrett crushed her against his chest as

though he were afraid she'd try to escape. "You are free to leave as well."

"As though I'd want to!" His shirt was still a little damp under her cheek. She felt his heart, beating strong and fast. She smiled, remembering his avowal of love aboard the *Venture*, and a glow of happiness spread through her. "It is expected of you now," she murmured. "A formal proposal. Else you shouldn't have promised to love me always."

Barrett gritted his teeth against the pain that tore at his heart. How could he give her the second part of his father's brief message? How could he possibly tell her that a ship lay at anchor in the hidden cove near Serendip? A ship, waiting to take her and her crew back to England.

"Barrett, I love you."

The words, uttered in a soft, husky voice, brought his head up sharply. He met Georgie's gaze, so full of her love, so confident that he would respond with a proposal of marriage.

"And I love you!" he assured her fiercely.

"Then what are you waiting for, Mr. Gray?" she said with a primness of voice belied by the look she gave him. The look of a woman awakened to love and passion. "Or are you set on punishing me for being such a . . . what was it you called me? A slowtop?"

"You cannot deny that for a London debutante, who, after all, is supposed to be quite up to snuff, you were agonizingly slow to recognize your feelings."

"Hmm." Through the carriage window, Georgie saw the familiar houses of Summer Street. In a very few moments they'd pull into the courtyard, and their tête-à-tête would be at an end. She nestled her cheek against the curve of his shoulder, content to savor his closeness.

Early in the morning they'd be leaving for Serendip. They'd have ten, perhaps twelve, glorious days to explore their love, to tell each other when they first recognized that life without the other was meaningless. And at Serendip, Barrett would formally propose.

A tender smile curved her mouth. Barrett, it seemed, was as much a romantic as young Hester. Of course he would not propose in a rattling carriage! He would want everything to be just right. And what could be more romantic than a proposal of marriage on a moon-bathed night under the whispering pines of Serendip?

Wednesday morning dawned bright and clear. The Bainbridge traveling chaise and a second carriage piled high with trunks and bandboxes stood in the courtyard. Letty fluttered from one coachman to the other with last-minute, and often contradictory, instructions. Inside the chaise, Rose opened the food hamper for a third time to make quite certain that the wineglasses had not slipped from their wrappings. And seated on the box of the traveling chaise, Daniel drove the coachman to the brink of turning in his resignation then and there with incessant questions and assurances that he, Daniel, could very easily handle a four-in-hand.

"Tare an' 'ounds!" Leaning heavily on her cane, Mother Bainbridge peered down the drive. "I've never known Barrett to be late. Why the deuce must he start a bad habit today of all days?"

Georgie, pacing restlessly, spun with a swirl of skirts. "He's not late! We're early."

"And whose fault is that?" Mother Bainbridge bent her piercing stare on Georgie. "You've been like a cat on a hot bake stone since Barrett brought you home yesterday. Are you certain," she demanded worriedly, "that ne'er-do-well Sir Percy is not behind your fretting?"

"How could that be, Mother Bainbridge? I assure you, Sir Percy is dead!" Georgie gave the old lady an affectionate hug. "Can you keep a secret?" she whispered. "Barrett will propose at Serendip!"

"What! And nary a word yesterday? You knew how anxious I've been to get matters settled between you!"

"Listen!" Georgie turned to the gate in time to watch Barrett astride a magnificent black horse trot into the yard. On a long rein he was leading a dappled mare.

"Compliments of Miss Quincy," he said, dismounting

when he reached Georgie. "Eliza thought you might be more comfortable if you could ride part of the way."

Their eyes locked, and for an instant it was as though they were alone in the courtyard. She saw only Barrett, his love and warmth as he embraced her with his glance; but she also noted his tension, the harsh lines of weariness that even his smile could not erase. She heard the pounding of her own heart, heard Barrett's breathing, fast and shallow; and she knew a moment of unease.

"Rose!" she called, turning abruptly. "Did you pack all my riding habits?"

"All but the red one ye wanted to return." Poking her head out the chaise, Rose said worriedly, "Surely you don't want me to *un*pack 'em, Lady Georgie?"

"I've changed my mind," said Georgie, hurrying off. "I shan't return the red habit after all."

"I'll help you dress." Ida, who had patiently waited on the stoop beside Appleby and his plump wife to see the travelers off, followed Georgie upstairs.

"Well, Barrett!" said Mother Bainbridge. "You certainly took your time before you made up your mind to propose to the gal. So it's to be at Serendip, is it?"

Letty had joined them. "Propose?" she said, her eyes sparkling.

Barrett's hands on the horses' reins clenched until his knuckles turned white. "A British frigate lies at anchor near Serendip," he said, his tone brusque. "Commanded by my cousin Robert Gray. Robert will carry Georgie, her crew, and a dispatch from President Madison to England."

There was a moment's stunned silence. Then Letty gave a cry. "Are you telling us that Georgie shan't be returning to Boston?"

"Yes, Lady Letty. And I beg you to hide your distress from her."

"You haven't told her, eh?" Mother Bainbridge gave him a dark look. "Why, Barrett? Dammit! You were willing to marry her after the ball!"

"Georgie loves you, I'm sure of it," murmured Letty in stricken tones.

"And I love her! More than my life!" Again Barrett was racked by pain at the thought of parting from Georgie. Again, as during the interminable hours of the past night, anger at the cruel hand of fate stabbed his breast.

"How could I marry her now, knowing that her safe passage to England is assured? Even Sir Percy is a threat no more! Don't you see? I *must* let her go. No man of honor would—"

"Honor!" Mother Bainbridge gave a derisive snort. "You're a demmed fool, Barrett Gray!"

"Indeed, Barrett!" Letty cried in distress. "Why should your honor demand that you break Georgie's heart? Why does a man's view of honor always differ from a woman's?"

Barrett looked helplessly at the two ladies. Why was it that females could not understand the demands of honor?

"Georgie's welfare must always be my primary concern. Mother Bainbridge! Your husband sent you to Niagara during the revolution—against your wishes. He knew you'd be safe there!"

"You compare this silly war to the revolution?"

"The fighting will not indefinitely be confined to Canadian soil, Mother Bainbridge. It is inevitable that England will send her troops into our towns."

The two women exchanged glances, defeat mirrored in their faces. "We'll guard our tongues when we say goodbye," Mother Bainbridge conceded gruffly. "For Georgiana's sake."

"Thank you."

Briefly, the old lady's eyes softened with compassion. "I daresay the hell you'll live through until she sails will be punishment enough for your foolishness!"

Mother Bainbridge's words pursued Barrett like a curse. Day and night while they traveled south, the words echoed in his mind. Day and night, they proved all too true. He felt tortured, alternately accusing himself of cowardice for not telling Georgie the truth, then fighting selfish desire that wanted to keep her with him, no matter what the cost.

Barrett hid his feelings well, but now and again Georgie could not help but notice a certain brittleness in his demeanor. It was impatience, she told herself. Impatience to reach Serendip.

Soon they would be there. Soon Barrett would propose to her.

They spent their last night at a small roadside inn a few miles west of Windsor. The dining room, when the landlord showed them to their table for a late supper, was smoke filled and crowded with men who were obviously holding a meeting.

Barrett threw a frowning glance at the noisy, gesticulating men. "If there's no private dining room available, we'll take supper upstairs," he said to the host.

Georgie resisted Barrett's attempt to steer her out of the oak-paneled room. "Please let's stay. It's so quaint and comfortable, and the ruckus doesn't bother me one whit."

"Thank you, miss." The host nodded at her approvingly as she sank down on the leather-covered settle and leaned back against a cushion sewn of the same bright calico cloth that covered the table. " 'Twould have been a downright pother to be carryin' food and drink to your chambers, and all the while the committee here ahollerin' for more punch and ale."

A stout serving maid bustled in and set before them succulent ham, green beans, and a deep orange vegetable which, Georgie learned, was sweet potato.

"Don't look like no taters I've ever seen," muttered Rose. She took a small bite and wrinkled her nose, but Daniel and Georgie fell to it with a will, enjoying every buttery bite.

At the other end of the room, where six or eight tables had been pushed together, the committee meeting grew noisier. Georgie heard shouts for more militia, and angry denials. "Why should the South and the West bear the brunt of the war burden?" a redheaded giant roared furiously. "We've already sent as many of our militia into Canada as we dare. I say it's Massachusetts's turn! And Pennsylvania's!"

"Aye!" a graybeard shouted. "Got to keep some of our men close to home. Have to have someone to defend our women and children when those damned murdering redcoats turn up here!''

A wizened old man clambered stiffly onto his chair and surveyed the unruly group. He waited for a moment of relative quiet, then said, ''During the revolution, I strung up more redcoats than you can count on your combined hands and feet. Just let some damned Britisher enter the state of Virginny, and I guarantee he'll be a dead Britisher!''

Georgie pushed away her plate. When she had first arrived in Boston, she had expected and mentally steeled herself against hate-filled talk. She had heard none, and now was totally unprepared.

''Daniel is half-asleep,'' said Barrett. ''Shall we retire, Georgie?''

Her eyes flew to his face. She saw his concern, his compassion, and knew that he had also heard the old man's words. He held out his hand to help her rise; he did not let go until they reached the door of her chamber.

The following morning, their last day of travel, Georgie started out in a somber mood. But on horseback she had never remained subdued for long, no matter what was troubling her, and as the long, smooth strides of her dappled mare carried her farther and farther east, her spirits buoyed.

The ground was soft and fertile. Drained marshes, Barrett explained as they rode beside fields of corn, wheat, rye, and oats. Georgie saw houses here and there, two- or three-storied mansions built of wood and painted white, with a covered porch running the full length of the house. Not at all like Sussex, where most farmhouses were small and only the occasional manor added grandeur to the scenery, where the fields were smaller and divided by hedges or even brick walls.

They kept going east, and the vista changed. The ground became marshier. She saw the first cypress trees, draped with Spanish moss, and then again stretches of the ever-present pine. And she could smell the sea.

The sun was dipping low when Barrett reined in his stallion. The rough lane still stretched before them, but Georgie saw the knoll covered in pine trees at the end of the road, saw a glimmer of white through the trees atop the knoll.

"Serendip," she breathed.

"Aye," said Barrett. He pointed to a moss-covered stone marker. "You have just crossed onto my father's land." He had to stop, take a deep breath to steady his voice, before adding, "Welcome, Georgie. May your stay be a happy one."

The two carriages rumbled past, but Georgie and Barrett sat motionless. The horses started to nibble at a few blades of green while their riders stared at the wooded knoll, then at each other.

"It will be," said Georgie, her eyes sparkling. "I know it will be a happy stay."

Gathering the reins, she spurred her mare and rode off toward Serendip.

Barrett followed more slowly, his eyes on the slender figure in the crimson habit. How proud the tilt of her head, the set of her shoulders! His chest tightened. He felt as though his heart were torn from his flesh. And it was. Day after day, it had torn a little bit more. And when she sailed, she would carry his heart with her.

He arrived in the yard where Georgie had already been welcomed by his father, had greeted the first mate Mr. Selwyn and the beaming crew of the *Rutledge Pride*. She turned to him as he gave his horse into the care of a groom. Her wide brown eyes held a look of tenderness, and her mouth was curved in a soft smile.

"Serendip is beautiful, Barrett. It's just how you described it to me. Please take me inside."

He clasped her hand, and the warmth of her skin shot bolts of fire from his fingertips to his shoulders. He watched her face as they approached his home, saw her delight in the graceful structure that rose three stories, vying for supremacy of height with the tall pines surrounding it. The setting sun stained the whitewashed wood frame, and some of that rose glow was reflected on her face.

Georgie stumbled. Instantly his arms went around her. He scooped her up, carrying her to the top of the wide steps, across the porticoed veranda, and into the house.

He set her down in the tiled hall, and when she looked at him, murmuring a thank you, he noted the gleam in her eyes. A gleam of mischief mixed with satisfaction.

"You did that on purpose, Georgie."

She raised a brow. "Are you reproaching me, Barrett? You don't sound very convincing."

"I know." He shot her a rueful look. "I enjoyed it too much."

"Come, Barrett." Edward Gray touched his son's shoulder. "I daresay you'd like a mint julep and then a bath before dinner."

While Rose and Daniel were bustled upstairs by Edward's housekeeper, Georgie took her host's proffered arm and allowed him to lead her into the drawing room. "Shall I have a mint julep?"

"I advise against it, my dear," Edward said with a smile. "I've ordered champagne for you."

But Georgie no longer paid him any attention. She stood transfixed at the sight of a blond young man in familiar naval uniform lounging against the fireplace.

"Georgie!" he shouted, pushing away from the mantel. "Barrett! By Jove, it's good to see you."

"Robert!" With a cry of delight, Georgie flew into his arms. "I can't believe it, Robert. What a surprise!"

He raised a brow. "Pardon me, Georgie. My presence can hardly come as a surprise to you. After all, you are to be my passenger, aren't you?"

Seventeen

The floor seemed to sway beneath her feet. She hardly heard Robert's adjunct, "And, of course, your brother's crew."

Georgie shook her head. She wanted to shout that there had been a mistake, but not a word left her mouth. She saw Barrett's face, and her dream of happiness burst like a bubble around her, leaving her cold and naked.

Barrett came toward her. She whipped around, unable to face him, not wanting to see again what she had read in his eyes. Her own hurt was too stark and new.

Edward Gray touched her arm. He handed her a glass and closed her fingers around it. "Drink, child," he ordered.

Georgie obeyed, but it was as though someone other than she were performing the ritual of swallowing. She did not taste what she drank, did not feel the liquid roll down her throat.

"Why, Mr. Gray? Why do you want me to leave? It is you, who arranged this, is it not?"

As though dealing with a child, Edward guided her to an armchair and pressed her into the upholstery.

"It's not what I want you to do, child. It's what I feel I ought to urge you to do."

He pulled up a second chair and sat down close to her. "But you'll forgive a selfish old man if he doesn't, won't you, Georgie? You see, I want you very much for a daughter-in-law. I told you so the day we met."

A wan smile flitted across her face as Georgie nodded.

"But there's no denying that Robert would be an ideal escort," said Edward. "Ah, and there he is. Georgie, forgive me for leaving you to that rapscallion nephew of mine while I have a word with Barrett."

Robert flung himself into the chair vacated by his uncle. His eyes, which Georgie had seen filled only with laughter and mischief, looked grave. "Gad, what a mess this is! Uncle Edward told me that Congress here declared war on June eighteenth. Dash it, Georgie! On the sixteenth, formal motion for repeal of the Orders in Council was made in Parliament, and a week later repeal was *fact*!"

Georgie's head jerked up. She frowned at Robert. "I wasn't thinking clearly. Your announcement that I'm to sail with you..." Her voice trailed off, then she said sharply,

''What the dickens *are* you doing here, Robert? When I left London you were expecting orders for Gibraltar!''

''I took command of my new frigate and at the same time received orders to proceed to Nova Scotia with stores and replacements. I sailed into a storm, and when it had finally blown itself out, we had one cracked mast, canvas that was mostly in tatters, and I found myself so much off course that I decided to search for Barrett's cove and lick my wounds.''

''You were lucky,'' said Mr. Selwyn, joining them, ''that you weren't sighted by an American gunboat.''

Robert's mouth tightened. ''We were, in fact, chased into the cove by a navy cutter. Six men and one small gun! But, dammit, we didn't know there was a blasted war on! And we were so weak from lack of food and water—everything spoiled in the storm!—that one man alone could have taken us prisoner.''

''Then you are a prisoner of war?'' Georgie looked at him intently. ''You are not at liberty to sail?''

Robert shook his head. ''I must sail. You see, that young whippersnapper who commanded the cutter was all set on burning my ship and carting me and my crew off to some stinking prison. Only then Uncle Edward arrived on the scene. A child, I believe, playing in the cove, had run to him, telling him that the English had come to attack!''

''Did your uncle know you?'' asked Georgie. ''Had you ever met?''

''No, but I look enough like my father in his young days that he couldn't doubt my word. Got to admit,'' Robert said with admiration, ''he's quite a man, my Uncle Edward. Didn't blink an eye when I told him who I am. He took the whippersnapper from the cutter aside. Don't know what Uncle Edward said to him, but the long and short of it is that he granted me safety of my ship and crew as long as I gave my word not to proceed to Canada but to deliver a dispatch from President Madison to Lord Liverpool.''

''You gave your word, of course,'' said Georgie.

''I had no choice.'' Robert's blue eyes narrowed with resentment. ''I hated having to give my word to that young

American firebrand, but the Admiralty wouldn't thank me if I put my pride before the safety of ship and crew.''

Georgie absently twirled the stem of her glass. "Is there really going to be a message from President Madison?"

"Uncle Edward received it two days ago. We'll sail tomorrow with nightfall.''

Georgie's heart started to race as the impact of Robert's words hit her. Tomorrow night! So soon!

She looked to the open window where Barrett stood in conversation with his father. Her vision blurred. A painful lump in her chest made breathing difficult.

Cheated out of love!

Was it Barrett who robbed them of their happiness? Or was it circumstance? And what did it matter!

Georgie became aware of the familiar stiffening of her spine and the tightening of her jaw. "Pardon me," she murmured, setting down her glass, and rising. "I must speak with Barrett.''

Robert gripped her wrist, detaining her as she passed his chair. She met his questioning gaze with a clear, bold look of her own.

He nodded. "Aye," he said slowly. "That's the way it's been between the two of you since the moment you met.''

Georgie disengaged her arm. "I will see you tomorrow, Robert. Good night, Mr. Selwyn.''

She walked to the center of the spacious chamber and stopped, looking at Barrett. Across the room their eyes met. A quick word to his father, a bow, and he closed the distance between them with his long stride.

Standing alone before the softly billowing lace curtains, Edward smiled. He raised his glass to Georgie in a silent toast.

"Where can we speak in private?" she asked as she laid her hand on Barrett's arm. It was stiff, the muscles beneath the cloth of his coat hard with tension.

"In the library.''

Barrett led her across the hall and ushered her into a room dimly lit by a branch of candles atop a low, round table. Two armchairs were drawn close to the table; the rest of the apartment lay hidden in darkness. Only the musty smell of old parchment and rice paper, the more pungent odor of leather betrayed the presence of books.

Georgie refused a chair but stood in the soft pool of light near the table. Her throat was dry, her tongue too large and awkward for speech. She sensed rather than saw Barrett's eyes on her, for his height kept his face in shadows.

It was he who broke the crackling silence with two words, tossed at her in a low, tight voice. "Tomorrow night."

"Why, Barrett?" Suddenly she knew no hesitation. She did not have to search for words. "You said you love me. Have you changed your mind?"

"Georgie, don't!" He put out his hands as though to ward her off. "You'll only make the parting more painful."

"Are you a coward, then? And a liar?"

His arms shot out, his fingers gripping her shoulders. "By God, Georgie! Would you *make* me a coward, a dishonorable weakling, a selfish brute? If you can live with that, I'll marry you now. This very instant!"

His mouth claimed hers, harshly, punishing her. She held still, knowing his anger could not last.

But when his kiss gentled, when he weakened her with murmured endearments, and his hands slid to her back, caressing her, wooing her, she pushed him away.

"Is it dishonorable to love me?" she demanded.

"It is dishonorable to disregard your safety, to ignore the British frigate that can carry you to your family!"

"Do you, then, hold our love so cheap that you can toss it away, simply forget it, for the sake of your honor?"

Barrett flinched. She ached to throw her arms around his neck and hold him close; but she stepped away from him, moving backward until the chair pressed against her calves.

"Nothing," he said tightly, "can stop my love for you, Georgie. But I cannot, must not, ask you to marry me now. After the war—"

She cut him off with an impatient gesture of her hand. "Oh! You'd marry me after the war, would you? And what will you say to our children when they ask where we were during the war? Will you tell them their mother ran off to England—a dishonorable coward?''

She heard his sharply drawn breath. He came closer, and when he reached the table he stopped, standing in the full light of the candles. The green fire in his eyes was like a magnet, drawing her. She moved without being aware of it until she was caught against his chest. Then awareness was pure delight.

''Shameless!'' he said huskily. ''Brazen! To throw my unborn children in my face!''

''It stopped your arguments. Or did it?''

''Yes, Georgie. But are you sure? Quite—''

He could not go on, for Georgie did the only sensible thing to stop a man from talking and raising further objections: she flung her arms around his neck and, raising herself on tiptoes, made certain his mouth was engaged in more rewarding occupation.

Hands entwined, they stood in the hidden cove beneath the cypress trees and watched the frigate ship slip away into the night. Her sails were furled; two longboats manned by Robert's men and the crew of the *Rutledge Pride* towed her into deeper waters. At the stern of the frigate, Daniel jumped up and down, waving his arms at Georgie and Barrett. He made no sound and before long, boy and ship were swallowed by the darkness.

Slowly Barrett turned to Georgie. ''Regrets?'' he asked, wiping a tear off her cheek.

''Oh, no! How can you ask?'' She burrowed her face against his chest. Her voice was muffled when she spoke again. ''It's just that I'll miss him. I'll have no one to teach.''

''If that's all!'' Barrett clasped her around the waist and swung her up into the air. ''Have you forgotten about *our* children? Were they but an excuse to entrap me?''

Georgie blushed. ''And you called *me* shameless! Set me down, Barrett. I want to walk along the beach.''

''In a moment, love. First I want you to agree to something.''

"What?" she asked, frowning suspiciously.

"That we'll go to Boston and build that house in Walnut Street."

"You're afraid that here in the South I'll meet people like that old man at the inn. Barrett, you mustn't try to protect me from every small adversity!"

He shook his head but insisted, "Please agree, Georgie!"

She smiled down at him. "Rose will like living in Boston. I suspect she has a sweetheart there."

"Rose?" Swinging her in a circle, he demanded, "Say that *you* will like it!"

"Put me down! Barrett, you're making me dizzy!"

He laughed, swinging her faster still, until she cried for mercy. "I'll like it tremendously," she assured him. "But my head spins."

Barrett set her down gently, catching her in a breathless hug. "A fine pair we are! My head's been spinning since last night, and I daresay it won't stop until we're both old and gray."

"Not even then," she promised.

Regency Romances

__PHILADELPHIA FOLLY
by Nancy Richards-Akers
(D34-893, $2.95, U.S.A.) (D34-894, $3.95, Canada)

A beautiful and titled British aristocrat with a penchant for social pranks finds romance and adventure in Philadelphia.

__TEMPORARY WIFE
by Samantha Holder
(D34-994, $3.95, U.S.A.) (D34-995, $3.95, Canada)

A wealthy and independent-minded young lady and a young lord engage in a marriage of convenience, until it becomes a tangled affair of the heart.

__GENTLEMAN'S TRADE
by Holly Newman
(D34-913, $2.95, U.S.A.) (D34-914, $3.95, Canada)

A sparkling story featuring a New Orleans belle caught up in a contest of wills with a dashing English nobleman.

 **Warner Books P.O. Box 690
New York, NY 10019**

Please send me the books I have checked. I enclose a check or money order (not cash), plus 95¢ per order and 95¢ per copy to cover postage and handling.* (Allow 4-6 weeks for delivery.)

___Please send me your free mail order catalog. (If ordering only the catalog, include a large self-addressed, stamped envelope.)

Name _____

Address _____

City _____ State _____ Zip _____

*New York and California residents add applicable sales tax.   329